THE LONG WALK HOME

www.rbooks.co.uk

THE LONG WALK HOME

Valerie Wood

BANTAM PRESS

LONDON · TORONTO · SYDNEY · AUCKLAND · JOHANNESBURG

TRANSWORLD PUBLISHERS
61–63 Uxbridge Road, London W5 5SA
A Random House Group Company
www.rbooks.co.uk

First published in Great Britain
in 2008 by Bantam Press
an imprint of Transworld Publishers

A CIP catalogue record for this book
is available from the British Library.

ISBN 9780593060216

Addresses for Random House Group Ltd companies outside the UK
can be found at: www.randomhouse.co.uk
The Random House Group Ltd Reg. No. 954009

The Random House Group Limited supports The Forest Stewardship
Council (FSC), the leading international forest certification organization.
All our titles that are printed on Greenpeace-approved FSC-certified
paper carry the FSC logo. Our paper procurement policy can be found at
www.rbooks.co.uk/environment

Typeset in 11½/14pt New Baskerville by
Kestrel Data, Exeter, Devon.
Printed in the UK by
CPI Mackays, Chatham, ME5 8TD.

2 4 6 8 10 9 7 5 3 1

Mixed Sources
Product group from well-managed
forests and other controlled sources
www.fsc.org Cert no. TT-COC-2139
© 1996 Forest Stewardship Council

For Chris Buckle

ACKNOWLEDGEMENTS

The author is pleased to acknowledge the useful background information that she has gleaned from the following two books: John Hollingshead, *Ragged London in 1861*, Dent, Everyman Classic 1986, and Edward Gillett and Kenneth A. MacMahon, *A History of Hull*, Hull University Press 1989.

CHAPTER ONE

Hull 1852

He ran; swift as the estuary tide, spry as the breeze which rocked the barges and lashed the cracking canvas sails; full gallop like a gypsy horse escaped from its harness and bidding for glorious freedom.

One rabbit slipped from his pocket to be caught up by other grasping hands, but its mate was clutched even tighter, the blood-matted fur sticky on his fingers.

Voices shouting; the butcher waving his arms. 'Stop him! Stop thief!' A crony, 'Go on, Mikey,' giving away his name.

A woman stopped to watch, her fingers clutched to her mouth, a tenseness in her stance urging him on. A man took a tentative step towards him and then thought better of it.

But still he was caught. The tall gentleman in black coat and top hat put out his arms and Mikey ran straight into them. From beneath the man's armpit, which smelt faintly of sweat and spice, he looked at the young girl who had prevented his escape. If it hadn't been for her he would have swerved and got away, but she was standing so close to the man that he could not have done so without knocking her over.

They stared at each other, she from sea-blue eyes, he from dark brown. Mikey gave a sudden grin as he thought of how he might look from her standpoint, with only his face showing beneath the man's armpit; but she tossed her fair head in a haughty gesture, turned up her nose and darted out the tip of her pink tongue.

A constable came rushing up, his baton swinging, followed by the butcher brandishing a cleaver. 'What's all this then?' the officer asked no one in particular but expecting an answer from someone.

Mikey wriggled. 'I'm choking,' he gasped. 'Let me out.'

'I'd say you will choke, my lad.' The gentleman eased his grasp on Mikey's neck. 'One day you'll swing from a rope if you don't mend your ways.'

Mikey saw the girl grow pale and put her hand over her mouth. He shook his head to reassure her. No, he wouldn't.

'Pinched two rabbits from outside my shop, Mr Kendall,' the butcher complained. 'How am I expected to make a living when these young ruffians are forever stealing?'

'Not me, mister.' Mikey shook himself like a young dog when the gentleman released him into the constable's firm grip. 'I've never pinched owt from you afore.'

'Haven't been caught, more like,' the butcher retaliated. 'I've seen you about looking for mischief.'

'Well, 'evidence is here.' The constable pointed to the rabbit. 'I'll have to confiscate it,' he told the butcher. 'It's proof of theft.'

The butcher put his hands on his hips, the cleaver glinting dangerously. 'That'll be 'last I'll see of it, then. Some copper'll have a nice rabbit pie. I might as well give it to 'lad!'

The gentleman broke in. 'He has to be taught a lesson.' He wagged a finger at Mikey. 'He must learn that he can't get away with such misdemeanours. Society would break down if we allowed it.'

The girl pressed her lips together and from wide blue eyes stared anxiously at Mikey, but said nothing.

The butcher turned away. 'Tek it then, and him as well.' He glared at Mikey. 'And if I should see you within a mile o' my shop' – he waved the cleaver – 'you'll be sorry.'

'I am sorry!' Mikey said hastily. 'It's just that my ma—'

'Come on!' The constable reached into his pocket and

brought out a pair of handcuffs. 'No excuses. We've heard 'em all before. Your ma's dying, your da's done a runner and you've nowt to eat in 'house!'

I don't think she's dying; at least I hope not. But she is poorly, Mikey thought, glancing over his shoulder at the girl as he was led away. She too turned her head as the man put his hand on her shoulder and ushered her across the road. She looked frightened, he thought, and winked at her to reassure her.

His da! No, he hadn't done a runner. He'd gone to sea and the ship never came back. Lost somewhere in the fishing grounds in search of cod. That had been nearly four years ago, when Mikey was ten, and his mother had struggled ever since to work and feed her family. Mikey was the eldest of her four children; after him came his brothers Ben and Tom, and his sister Rose. He was old enough to work if only he could get a job. But not at sea. His mother refused to let him go. 'I've lost one man,' she'd told Mikey. 'I'm not going to lose another.'

'You'll spend 'night here,' the charge clerk sitting on a tall stool in the Blanket Row police station told him. 'Then in 'morning you'll be up before 'bench.'

'My ma'll worry about me,' Mikey said. 'She's not well. She'll expect me home.'

The clerk shook his head. 'You should've thought of that afore. Name?'

'Quinn. Mikey.'

'Michael Quinn.' The clerk began to write, his pen scratching in the ledger.

'Not Michael,' Mikey said hastily. How many times did he have to tell people that? 'It's Mikey.'

The clerk gazed at him from over his wire-rimmed spectacles. 'Irish, are you?'

'No. Hull. Born and bred. My grandda was Irish. My father's father.'

His father had told him the tale many times. Mikey's grandfather had settled in Hull, married a Hull girl and had three children. He had lived there for fifteen years, never out of work, until one day the authorities swooped, rounded up all the Irish migrants and sent them home to an uncertain future. His wife and children had escaped the net as they had been born and raised in the town, but Mikey's grandmother, bowed down by the shame and the poverty, died in the town's workhouse, leaving her children to fend for themselves.

Mikey's father had vowed that his own children would never suffer as he had done. He was a sober man who saved his earnings as a trawlerman, not wasting them on drink as many of his fellow fishermen did, yet the sea had taken him, leaving his wife and children in the kind of poverty his own mother had suffered.

'Can I get a message to my ma?' Mikey pleaded. 'She won't know where I am.'

'How old are you?' the clerk asked.

'Thirteen, sir.'

'Did anybody see you being brought in? Any of your pals? If they did they'll tell her.' He frowned at Mikey. 'She'll know you're in bother, I'll be bound.'

Mikey shook his head. 'She won't. I allus look after 'little 'uns while she's at work.'

The constable, who had been listening idly, grunted. 'I thought you just said she was sick. Now you're saying she's going to work.'

'Yeh! She has to work even when she's sick.' Mikey stared uncomprehendingly at his accuser. If his ma didn't work then they didn't eat. That's why he'd pinched the rabbits. He'd thought that if he could bring home some supper she could take the night off from her work at the cotton mill where she cleaned the thick dry dust off the machinery and the floors: dust that clung to her throat and chest and had given her the cough which kept her awake at night.

'Well, there's nowt I can do about it.' The clerk continued to write. 'Where do you live?'

'Back of Whitefriargate, sir. Winter's Alley.'

'Mm. Well, you'll not catch me going down there after dark

otherwise I might have offered. Besides, it's not my job to run errands for prisoners.'

'Am I a prisoner?' Mikey was shocked. He'd get a walloping from his ma. She would no doubt have cooked the rabbit if he hadn't been caught but she would be horrified to know he was branded a prisoner.

The clerk put down his pen. His fingers were ink-stained. 'Don't you realize that you might be locked up for a long time? You've been caught stealing somebody else's property. If 'magistrate wants to make an example of you he might lock you up for a month. He could even transport you to Australia.' He looked sternly at a quaking Mikey. 'If you keep up this life you might even be hanged! What would your ma do then?'

Mikey blinked. He felt like crying, but he wouldn't. He wouldn't let anybody see how scared he was. He bit hard on his lip. 'She'd be upset,' he said in a small quivery voice. 'And she'd be right mad at me.'

'Well, all you can hope for is that 'butcher will drop 'charges. You'd better tek him,' the clerk told the constable. 'Put him in cell number two. Somebody'll keep an eye on him in there.'

He was given a shove in the back which propelled him into a small barred cell. There was no place to sit, no bed or chair, just a metal pail in the corner and a narrow window set too high for him to see out. He slid down on to the floor and bit on a broken fingernail as he considered his position. Stealing the rabbits had been sheer impulse. He'd seen them hanging outside the shop. The butcher had had his back to him as he served a customer and Mikey had jumped to grab them. The hook attaching the rabbits to the wall had fallen to the ground with a clang, alerting the shopkeeper to the theft.

Don't suppose he knows what it's like to be hungry, he thought. I'm hungry now and I'll miss my supper. Breakfast had been gruel, dinner a slice of bread and dripping, and he'd had nothing since.

He got up and called through the barred door. 'Is anybody there? Hello. Hello!'

A constable strolled towards him. 'What's this racket? What do you want?'

'Can I have a drink o' water?'

The officer scowled at him. 'What do you think this is? You'll get a sup o' water later and if you're lucky a slice o' bread.' He turned away and ambled back the way he had come.

Mikey slid back into his corner and hunched into himself. It was cold in here, colder even than outside. He put his hand on the wall and felt the damp. What can I do? What'll I say in 'morning when I go before 'magistrate? I'll have to plead guilty, I expect.

He heard voices out in the corridor which led to the front office. He could hear a girl's voice. Did they keep women in here as well? This wasn't the proper prison. The proper prison where prisoners were sent to serve their time was in Kingston Street near the Humber bank. There was a treadmill there, so he'd heard, and a yard for breaking stones which were used for road building.

'Somebody to see you,' the clerk called through the door. Now that he was out from behind his desk and off his stool, he was revealed as a small fat man with an agitated scurrying walk. 'Don't take long,' he said, as Mikey peered through the bars. 'You're not supposed to have visitors.'

Mikey stood on tiptoe. 'Bridget! What you doing here?'

'I saw 'em catch you. I ran to tell your ma.'

Bridget was his sister Rose's friend, though at fifteen she was older than both Mikey and Rose.

'What did she say? Was she mad at me?'

'Aye, she was. She said you had to plead guilty and say you were very sorry and you'd never do such a thing again. She sent you this.' Bridget thrust a slice of bread, wrapped in brown paper, through the bars. 'There's nowt on it,' she said. 'No dripping or owt.'

'Oh, thanks, Bridget. You're a pal!' He bit hungrily into the bread, not noticing the disdainful curl of her mouth.

'Sure I am,' she said. 'Who else would come here, begging to see you?'

14

Mikey lifted his head and saw the flash of Bridget's green eyes. She was very sharp, prone to temper and harsh words. Mikey's mother said it was because of her Irish mother. But Bridget was also full of charm and gaiety when she had a mind to be.

'Nobody I can think of,' Mikey answered, his mouth full of bread. He would owe her now; there would be a payback time. 'Will you tell Ma that I've to stop here tonight and go before 'magistrate in 'morning?'

She nodded. 'I told your ma that I don't think they'll hang you, not for a pair o' rabbits. But how would you feel if they sent you to Australia?'

'I shan't have a choice, shall I?' Mikey fingered his neck and wondered if hanging hurt. What if the rope wasn't tight enough and you were left dangling, half alive, half dead?

'I heard about somebody going to Australia but they died on 'ship afore it got there.' Bridget put her hand on her hip and would have continued but for a shout from the constable telling her to clear off home.

Mikey was glad to see her depart. He felt worse now than before she had come, and how did she know about somebody dying on the way to Australia? Who had come back to tell? 'She's mekking it up,' he muttered. 'She's allus telling tales about summat.'

He spent a cold uncomfortable night on the floor, although he was given a thin blanket and a slice of dry bread and a cup of water. He barely slept, and when he did drop off his sleep was punctuated with nightmarish dreams of hangings and pitching ships on heavy seas.

As dawn was creeping through the narrow window, the door of his cell was abruptly opened and a man flung inside. Mikey sat up and put his hands to his head, bemused for a few seconds as to where he was and where were his brothers who shared his bed.

He gazed at the intruding stranger, who had landed in the opposite corner of the cell and was glaring, bleary-eyed and hostile, at him. 'Who are you?' the man grunted. 'Nivver seen you afore.'

'Quinn,' Mikey muttered. He didn't like the look of the newcomer at all. He had an angular face, a long nose and wild black hair. He looked aggressive and seemed the worse for drink.

'Quinn? What sort o' name is that?'

Mikey shrugged. 'Dunno. It's mine. Onny one I've got.'

'Onny one you've got! Haven't you got another?' The man continued to glare, menacingly, Mikey thought.

'Mikey,' he said. 'That's my first name.'

'Hm!' His cellmate considered, his eyes keen. 'I'll call you Quinn.' He leaned across the floor and grabbed Mikey by the wrist. 'You can call me Tully.'

CHAPTER TWO

Tully! Mikey shrank back against the wall. He'd heard of Tully. It was a name to be feared. Robber. Murderer. Embezzler. Every crime that was not resolved was attributed to Tully. Mothers of disobedient children threatened that they'd send for Tully if they didn't behave, but as far as Mikey knew no one had ever set eyes on him. He was a threatening shadow of a bogeyman, and now he was sharing Mikey's cell.

He leaned towards Mikey, still holding him by the wrist. 'Got any poppy?' he whispered.

Mikey shook his head. 'Got no money either,' he said in a hoarse voice.

Tully let go of his wrist in an impatient gesture. 'Damned peazans. Good for nowt.' He sniffed and wiped his nose on the back of his hand. 'What you in for?'

'Stealing rabbits from 'butcher.'

'A pair?'

Mikey nodded. 'I dropped one. Somebody else picked it up.'

'Careless,' Tully growled. 'The trick is to keep tight hold of 'em by their necks. Which butcher?'

Mikey described the shop in the Market Place. 'Don't know his name.'

'Smith, I'll bet. He'll not drop 'charges.'

Mikey stared at him, then licked his lips. 'Will I be hanged?'

17

Tully gave a harsh laugh. 'This your first time?'

When Mikey nodded, he said, 'No. But you'll get sent down; mebbe a month. You'll not like it. Nobody does first off.' He yawned, a great gawping yawn showing blackened teeth. 'But you get used to it. I even know some folk who break 'law deliberate like, just to come inside for a bit.'

He lay down on his side, facing Mikey. 'Wake me up in time for breakfast. Tell 'warder I'll have a nice slice o' bacon wi' my bread, and a hot cup o' tea.' He closed his eyes, then opened one of them. 'I'll buy your bread off you if you don't fancy it. Not everybody does when mice have been dancing over it.'

Mikey was familiar with mice. Their room at home was infested with them. The mice were as hungry as the family was. 'I'll want it,' he muttered.

He didn't sleep any more but watched the daylight creeping round the cell and listened to Tully's snoring. The man had rolled over on to his back and with his head back and his mouth open, his whistles and snorts might have woken the dead.

Wonder what he's in for? Dare I ask him? Suppose he takes offence if I do? He could beat me up and no one would know. They could find me throttled when they bring our bread and water. He kept an anxious eye on his cellmate, too wary to relax his guard.

Tully woke with a start when the constable rattled the door. He was instantly alert, though his eyes were half closed as he peered at Mikey; then he put his finger to his mouth.

'This lad's sick,' he muttered to the officer. 'Kept me awake wi' his belly-aching. You'd better fetch him some more bread afore he passes out on you. It'll not do if he collapses in 'dock. You'll get 'blame.'

'Not me, Tully. I've onny just come on duty.' The constable gave a wry grin. 'You tried that on last time you were in.'

'Oh! Is it you, Benton?' Tully pretended he couldn't see and screwed his eyes up at the warder. 'Well, how 'andsome you've become. I didn't recognize you. What happened to that warty nose and bloodshot eye?' He rubbed his eyes with his knuckles. 'Oh, yes! Sorry, my mistake. They're still there.'

Benton shoved a metal tray containing two cups of water and two slices of bread towards Mikey. 'Don't get mixed up wi' him,' he warned as if Mikey had had a choice in the matter. 'He'll lead you into worse trouble than you're in now.'

Tully grabbed a cup and took the thicker slice of bread. 'Shove off, Benton. We don't want 'likes o' you in here wi' us. Lets 'tone of 'place down.'

Mikey wanted to laugh, feeling a sneaky admiration for Tully's bravado. How dare he insult a police officer in that way? Wasn't he scared of what the man might say when he came up before the magistrate?

'Listen.' Tully took a gulp of water and dropped his voice when the warder had left. 'When you go up afore 'bench, plead guilty and mitigating circumstances. Can you remember that?'

'Don't know.' Mikey wasn't even sure he could say it, and he certainly didn't know what it meant. 'My ma said I had to plead guilty.'

'Wise woman, your ma.' Tully chewed on the dry bread. 'What about your da?'

'Dead. Lost at sea.'

'There you are then! Tell 'em you're 'chief breadwinner; your ma is sick and so on. Give 'em a sob story.'

Mikey nodded. 'I was going to.'

'Oh!' Tully seemed peeved. 'Don't need my advice, then. Got it all planned.'

'Oh, no.' Mikey didn't want to upset him. 'I'd be grateful for any advice. It's just that my ma sent a message and said I had to plead guilty.'

Tully continued chewing and gazed thoughtfully at Mikey. Then he glanced at the slice of uneaten bread in Mikey's hand. 'Don't you want that?'

Mikey suddenly felt sick. 'No.' He handed the bread to Tully. 'You can have it if you like.'

'For free?' Tully grabbed it. 'You're a green lad, Quinn.

19

Don't ever give owt away. There's a price for everything.' He bit into Mikey's breakfast and chewed, his eyes constantly on him. 'If we get sent to 'same place, I'll look out for you. Just mention my name and you'll be all right. Just say you're a pal o' Tully's and you'll gain respect.' He nodded his dark un-kempt head. 'Don't forget, now.'

Mikey was taken into the court room at ten o'clock. He'd rinsed his hands and face in a bowl of cold water and patted down his unruly hair. He was shaking with nerves and disbelief that he was in this situation. He had friends and acquaintances who regularly stole food or small items that they could sell, and he had heard of some notorious people of the district who had stolen pocket books, gloves, and once a gold-topped walking cane that had been laid down for a moment whilst the rightful owner contemplated a purchase.

Mikey had thought these stories mildly amusing and considered that the loss of such possessions was solely due to carelessness. If he had been the owner of similar items he would have held on tight to them so that no thief could ever steal them. Now, however, amusement had been replaced by fright as he stood trembling and handcuffed in the dock.

He answered to his name and the charge was read out. 'There is a witness to this incident, I understand,' the magis-trate, Mr Zachariah Pearson, commented. 'Is Mr Kendall in court?'

Mr Kendall was in court and Mikey saw the man who had stopped his headlong flight take the stand.

'You saw what happened, Mr Kendall?' the magistrate asked. 'I believe you were able to apprehend the accused?'

'Indeed I was.' Kendall lifted his sharp nose and gazed at Mikey. 'And if I hadn't done so, there might well have been a more serious charge.'

'What do you mean by that?' Mr Pearson enquired. 'Was the defendant intent on other misdoings?'

'I believe that in attempting to make his escape, he would have stopped at nothing, nor let anyone stand in his way,' Kendall answered. 'My young daughter was in his path and he was heading straight towards her; had I not seized him he might well have caused her serious injury.'

No. No, I wouldn't, Mikey thought. I had seen her. That's why I didn't swerve.

'In my opinion,' Kendall continued, 'he is a dangerous young criminal.'

'Yes, possibly.' The magistrate pondered. 'But this is his first appearance and we cannot, as you well know, Mr Kendall, charge someone with what they might or might not have done had the circumstances been otherwise.' He took a deep breath. 'So the charge stands at stealing a pair of rabbits from Mr Smith the butcher. Has Mr Smith had trouble from Quinn previously?'

'He says he's seen him hanging about, sir,' the arresting constable said. 'But he's never caught him stealing before.'

'Not *caught* him,' Mr Pearson queried. 'Does that mean he has seen him stealing?'

'No, I don't think so, sir. It's just a manner of speech.'

'What have you to say for yourself, Quinn?' The magistrate turned and frowned at Mikey. 'Do you plead guilty to the charge?'

'Yes, I do, sir.' Mikey spoke in a low voice. 'And I'm very sorry. I'd offer to pay 'butcher back but I've no money. I've been trying for work but haven't been able to get any. My ma's not well and we've no money for food. I saw 'rabbits hanging outside 'shop and was tempted.' He licked his dry lips. 'I just fancied some rabbit stew.'

'Well, I dare say,' Mr Pearson said. 'But just because we fancy something doesn't mean we can help ourselves to it. Especially if that something belongs to someone else. There are rules and there are laws, and without those rules and laws society would break down and there would be lawlessness throughout the whole of the country. Do you understand me, Quinn?'

'Yes, sir.' Mikey hung his head, trying to look as meek and sorry as he felt. The magistrate seemed fairly understanding, he thought. Perhaps he would let him off with a caution to be on his best behaviour in future.

'However,' the justice continued, 'I am mindful that this is your first offence and understand that, very foolishly, you thought you were helping your mother by bringing home some ill-gained supper. I hope that if you are given a short sharp lesson you might not be tempted into such misdemeanours again.' He shuffled through some papers, tapped them on the desk and then took off his spectacles. 'I therefore sentence you to one month in prison.'

A cry rang out from the public gallery. Mikey knew it was his mother even before she started to call his name. 'No! Mikey! No! Please, sir, no!'

Mikey was led away by two police constables. One of them was Benton, who gave him a shove when they were going down the steps to the cells. 'That'll larn you, my lad. When you've broken up a ton o' stones you'll not want to come back here again.'

'No, I won't.' Mikey could hardly stop the tears from falling. What would his ma do without him? Who would watch out for his brothers and his sister? He had always been the reliable one, the one his mother could depend upon.

'And don't get mixed up wi' Tully,' Benton continued. 'He'll have you doing jobs for him, running errands and so on. He'll promise you 'world and a quick way of getting rich.' He opened a cell door, took a key from his pocket and unfastened Mikey's handcuffs. 'Go on,' he said roughly. 'Get in there and wait.'

'Is this where I do my time?' Mikey grasped the bars.

The two constables laughed. 'You should be so lucky,' Benton said. 'This is a holding cell. Somebody'll come and fetch you and take you to Kingston Street. You'll serve your time there.'

Mikey nodded. He'd cry when they'd gone, but not before. He wouldn't let them see how frightened he was, or how he was missing his mother. I want to go home, he thought desperately.

Bridget was allowed in to see him. 'Your ma wouldn't come,' she said, peering through the barred door. 'She said she couldn't bear to see you locked up. I said I'd come instead and tell her how you were bearing up.'

'Are you enjoying this?' Mikey muttered. She seemed very perky. 'A bit of excitement for you, is it?'

'Well there's thanks!' Bridget retaliated. 'I had to coax 'constable to let me in.'

'How did you do that?'

She tossed her head. 'Never you mind. I just did. Anyway, your ma said was there owt you wanted? I told her they wouldn't keep you in here. You'll probably go to Kingston Street in 'morning, so if there's owt you want I'll have to fetch it in today.'

Mikey pondered that Bridget was very well informed. Did she wheedle that information from the warder too?

'No, there's nowt. Ma hasn't got any money so there's no use in asking.' He sighed. 'If there was a bit o' pie I wouldn't mind, but I don't suppose there is. I expect there'll be some more bread and water later on.' He was hungry now, and wished that he hadn't given his bread to Tully.

'I'll tell you what,' she whispered. 'I know 'baker's delivery lad.' She winked. 'I'll see if he's got owt spare in his basket.'

'What? How do you mean?'

Bridget gave an exasperated sigh. 'Never mind. I'll try to get back later.' She started to walk away, but then turned back. She stood on tiptoe and pressed her face to the bars. 'Come here,' she said.

Mikey did as she bade and put his face to the bars, expecting her to murmur something into his ear that she didn't want the hovering constable to hear.

'Give us a kiss then,' she said softly. 'If I'm going to fetch you some dinner, it's 'least you can offer.'

Mikey frowned. Why would she want a kiss? She wasn't his mother. He was startled when Bridget took his face in her hands and kissed him full on the mouth, even running her tongue over his lips. He pulled back. It wasn't that it was unpleasant; just unexpected.

23

'That your first time of kissing a girl, Mikey?' She gave a mocking smile. 'Did you like it?'

'Erm. Yes.' Did he? He wasn't sure. It certainly made him feel very strange. A sort of tingling in his body which then ran down his legs. But if that was what was required to obtain some food, then it was no hardship.

Bridget gave him another wink and ran her tongue over her lips; then, with a shrug and a swirl of her torn skirt, she left.

How strange, he thought. Is that what girls do? He couldn't imagine his sister asking for kisses, and, he mused, he hoped that she didn't. His mother would not be pleased. But Bridget . . . well, it seemed that she was a law unto herself, and he wondered how it was that he was in prison whilst others, such as the baker's boy, giving away his master's bread, and Bridget, receiving it, were not.

CHAPTER THREE

'Here.' The warder on duty clanged open the cell door. 'Present for you.' He handed Mikey a moist paper bag stained with gravy. 'Nice lass you've got. Lucky devil!'

'She's not my lass,' Mikey said. 'She's my sister's friend.' He took the offering and sniffed. Meat pie! However had Bridget managed that? He was starving hungry in spite of the slice of bread they'd brought him at midday.

'Better get it eaten,' the officer said. 'It'll be 'last good food you'll get for a month. You'll be moved at about half past two. Doubt you'll get meat pie brought in at Kingston Street.'

Mikey bit into the pie. It was still warm and running with gravy. 'Won't I be allowed visitors?' he asked, his mouth full of pastry.

'Depends who's on duty and what 'visitors are offering.' He gave a grin. 'Your lass might be able to get in.'

Mikey considered. Bridget had obviously charmed the warders, so perhaps he should pretend that she was his lass if it meant that she could come in to see him and perhaps bring a message from his mother, or even, he pondered, deliver an ill-gotten pie.

He was manacled and taken by handcart across the town to Kingston Street prison, which had been built near the banks of the Humber some thirty years before. It had once been considered to be amongst the best houses of correction in the country, and over the years it had been extended to accommodate the growing prison population. There were separate buildings for men and women, a holding cell where the worst prisoners would languish awaiting their sentence or transference to the County Assizes, cells for debtors, work buildings where some prisoners were put to the treadmill, and a large courtyard where others were set on the back-breaking work of crushing stones.

Mikey was stripped of his clothes and given prison garb of scratchy cotton. It was too big for him, the trousers flapping below his ankles and the sleeves hanging lower than his fingertips. It had been made for an adult man, whereas he was still growing out of childhood into adolescence. Stitched on to the jacket was a number: 3624.

He was marched down a flight of stone steps and past locked doors, and put into a cell where he was left alone for several hours. The bare brick cell had a fixed board to sit or lie on, a metal pail beneath it and a greasy tin bowl for washing. It was cold and very damp.

Mikey sat down on the bench and this time he did cry. He cried for his mother, and he cried for himself and the enormity of the situation in which he found himself.

'I'll never do owt wrong again in my life,' he vowed, sniffling. 'Never. Not even if I'm starving at death's door.'

But although he was frightened and ashamed, he was also resentful. He and his family had not had a proper meal in weeks. His mother received a small allowance from a seamen's society which helped the families of those lost at sea, but it was barely enough to pay the rent on their room, which was in a narrow dark entry and shared a pump and one privy with several other families. What little their mother earned was spent on food, but there was never enough for all of them and there was no work for boys such as Mikey.

'Here you are, three six two four.' The warder handed a bowl of soup through a hatch in the door. 'Get that down you.' He offered Mikey a slice of bread on a tin plate. 'There'll be nowt else till morning.'

Mikey took the bread from the plate and took it and the

26

bowl to the bench, where he sat down and sniffed at the soup. It was pale green and strong-smelling. 'Yuck!' he muttered. 'Yesterday's cabbage. I hate cabbage!'

He ate it nevertheless, his hunger getting the better of his revulsion, but ten minutes after finishing it he was violently sick, vomiting his stomach's contents into the pail, which left him feeling weak and nauseous and still hungry.

Three days he was left alone in his cell and there were times when he felt he had been forgotten; he would hear the sound of boots on the stone floor, the clang of cell doors and an echo of voices, and then silence. The tedium was broken at break-fast and midday by the arrival of a warder with bread and water, and in the evening he was brought a bowl of some kind of thin liquid which went under the name of soup.

On the fourth morning he was told that after finishing his breakfast of gruel and a cup of lukewarm tea he should prepare himself for work. He was given a brush and shovel to sweep out his cell and told to bring out his slop pail for emptying.

It was a relief to know that he wasn't going to spend the whole month in the cell, though he was slightly apprehensive as to what kind of work he would have to do. 'Hope they don't put me on 'treadmill,' he muttered as he swept. 'Seems senseless to me, as well as being painful.' He recalled an old man, local to the Hull streets, who was bent almost double and, rumour had it, could no longer straighten up after enduring years of working the treadmill in prison as a young man.

'Three six two four!' The warder opened the cell door. 'Fetch your pail and don't spill any or you'll have to scrub all of 'corridor.'

Mikey put down his sweeping brush, picked up the pail and followed the warder down the passageway. He was still below ground, but the air was fresher than in his now stinking cell, a draught blowing down from outside. He took a breath as he went up the flight of stairs and stepped at last into the open air.

The warder showed him where to empty his pail and swill it out under the pump. Mikey ducked his head and face under the stream of cold water to refresh himself. He shook his head and hair and took another breath. Right, he thought. What's next?

'Papa?' Eleanor hesitated. Her father did not encourage questions, but on evenings when he was home early from his office and not working late, as he often did, she visited her parents in the drawing room before they went down to the dining room for supper to tell them about her lessons and the happenings of her day. He was the one who instigated the questions, and she answered them. Never, in all her eleven years, could she remember daring to pluck up the courage to ask him anything.

Her days were long. There were lessons every morning from her governess, Miss Wright, who was, she insisted, always right; after the midday meal there was a walk to the pier if the weather was clement, or to a museum if it was not, with either her governess or one of the maids. There had never been anything she wanted to ask or tell her father. He was a remote figure who happened to be married to her mother.

Her mother might come to the schoolroom occasionally and sit on a chair for five minutes and question Miss Wright vaguely on the subject that Eleanor was studying, or tell her about a letter received from her older brother Simon, who was away at a hated boarding school. Then she would drift away, saying she had masses to do before Eleanor's lawyer father returned home for luncheon.

Eleanor never received letters from her brother. Once, when he was very young and had first gone away, he had written to her, but Eleanor wasn't allowed to read the letter. It had been intercepted by her father and confiscated. Eleanor knew in her heart that it had contained a message of misery, for Simon hadn't wanted to go to school. He feared it, and on subsequent visits home told Eleanor how terrible it was; how the masters

28

beat him and the other boys did too. Now, at almost thirteen, he stood up for himself and boasted to her that he gave out similar punishments to younger, newer boys.

Her father raised his eyebrows. 'Do you wish to ask me something, Eleanor?'

Eleanor bit hard on her lip. Her heart was pounding. 'I just – I just wanted to ask—'

'Speak up, child,' her father said impatiently. 'Don't mumble.'

She swallowed, wishing she hadn't begun the conversation. She glanced at her mother for encouragement, but Mrs Kendall was gazing down into her lap and was no help at all. 'I wondered what had happened to that boy. The one who stole the rabbit.' She trembled at her own boldness. If her father hadn't chosen that particular day to take her to his place of work for the very first time, so that she might see for herself how he conducted his affairs and made a living for the family, then she would have known nothing about the incident. But she had witnessed it, and she had not been able to dismiss it from her mind.

Her father drew himself up in his chair, his shoulders even straighter than usual, though he never slouched. 'And what, young lady, is that to do with you?'

'Nothing, Papa; but I wondered if he'd been very hungry and that was why he stole it.' She felt her cheeks growing pink, but she raised her eyes to his.

'Two rabbits, Quinn stole. That was the crime, even though he had only one in his hands when he was so timely caught. The other he probably passed on to an accomplice.' He narrowed his gaze. 'I hope you are not feeling sorry for him?'

She didn't answer, but put her hands behind her back and hung her head.

'He has gone to prison,' he said scathingly. 'The best place for him. But not for long enough, in my opinion. One month is not sufficient time for him to consider the error of his ways. Look at me, girl! You are not to even think about it, do you understand?'

'Edgar, dear,' her mother protested, but uneasily. 'I'm sure she won't. She is merely curious. Isn't that so, Eleanor?'

'Yes, Mama.' Eleanor heard the entreaty in her mother's voice, but was exceedingly glad that her father wasn't able to read her mind, for if he could she would surely get a whipping, just as Simon sometimes did.

Her father ignored her mother's appeal. 'You must take a lesson from it. Breaking the law is a crime and punishment is the only answer. It's a great pity that public whipping and the pillory are no longer sanctioned,' he continued, getting on to his favourite topic. 'That's the answer: sharp deterrents to stop these young criminals from offending again.'

Eleanor was excused and told to return upstairs. Nothing was asked about her day. Supper was always served promptly and her allotted time had been taken up by her father's disquisition on crime. She still had no answer to her most pressing question: why had the boy stolen the rabbits?

She decided she would consult Nanny. Nanny wouldn't shout at her or tell her it was nothing to do with her. Nanny had been her mother's nurse, and had looked after Mrs Kendall when she was young. She was old and white-haired and stricken with rheumatism, but she regularly gave Eleanor a hug when she sensed the girl was feeling sad or lonely. It was the only affection that Eleanor received. Her mother gave her a peck on the cheek every evening, but her father only inclined his head as she dipped her knee in goodnight.

Eleanor hadn't discussed the subject with Nanny before, but she told her now as they sat by the nursery fire and she drank milk and ate bread and butter and Nanny had a glass of stout.

Eleanor was, of course, too big for a nursery now and the old bassinet which had been Simon's and then hers had been removed. When Simon came home he slept in a small room, not much bigger than a cupboard, on a truckle bed which was put away when he returned to school, and the nursery now only contained Eleanor's bed and washstand and chest of drawers. But Nanny kept her squashy old chair by the fire and Eleanor had a cane basket chair drawn up on the other side of the hearth, and here they sat in companionship every evening, although Nanny often fell asleep after finishing her stout whilst her charge read a book for an hour until bedtime.

'So this young feller-me-lad stole some rabbits and got caught,' Nanny mused, and took a sip from her glass. 'And went to prison?'

Eleanor nodded. 'That's what Papa said. He said he had gone for a month and that it wasn't long enough. But I wondered – I wondered why he had stolen them. Do you think, Nanny, that he did it for a lark, or was someone going to cook them for supper?'

Nanny pondered and took another satisfying draught of ale. 'Did he look like a young swell that'd do such a thing for a lark, or a roughneck from the hoi polloi who was down on his uppers?'

'Oh, he wasn't a swell,' Eleanor protested. 'And he had blood on his hands which would have been distasteful to a gentleman.' She considered. 'He had a dirty face and his boots were shabby. Oh, yes, and his breeches were ragged.'

'So what do you think?' Nanny asked softly. 'It would seem to me to be quite obvious.'

'Yes.' Eleanor felt very sad. 'I think that he must have been very hungry to do such a shameful thing. But I'm sorry that he had to stoop so low.'

'Yes, indeed,' Nanny commented sourly. 'The butcher must have been devastated to lose his income, and who knows what happened to the rabbits.'

'Oh, the policeman took the one the boy had. He said it would be used in evidence. But I don't know about the one he dropped; perhaps whoever found it took it back to the butcher.'

'More than likely,' Nanny nodded. 'Yes, could well be so. On the other hand' – she gazed affectionately at Eleanor and wondered who would ever advise her on the way of the world – 'it might have made somebody a good supper.'

Eleanor gazed wide-eyed at her. 'But do you not think it would turn sour in their stomachs with the knowledge of its being stolen?'

Nanny drained her glass. 'No, my dear. I don't. But don't tell your father I said so.'

'You don't think he'll be hanged, do you?' Eleanor asked after a moment's silence. 'Papa told him he might swing from a rope one day.'

'Did he? Well, your papa would know about such things, being in law himself. But I shouldn't worry,' Nanny said kindly. 'They'll not hang him this time, and mebbe after a spell in prison he'll walk a straight line. If he's not starving, that is,' she added, and gave a little grunt as she bent to put more coal on the fire. 'It's incredible what lengths a person will go to if he's got a hunger in his belly.'

Eleanor took another small bite of bread. She had been hungry too, but now her appetite seemed to have vanished. Poor boy, she thought. Yet he hadn't seemed too downcast; rather it had seemed as if he was trying to reassure her when her father had mentioned the hanging and she had given such a start. If I could only see him, she thought, I could warn him of what might become of him if he continues on this downward path. But then I don't suppose he would listen. I'm only a girl and not very wise, and only know about spelling and art and music, and even if I was grown up it would be the same, except that, like Mama, I would know my duty.

CHAPTER FOUR

'I'll do as I like.' Bridget tossed her head and turned her back on her mother.

'That you won't, Bridget Turner. You'll do as I say and you will not stay out half the night like a wanton.' Her mother shook a dish rag at her daughter. 'If your dada finds out—'

'He'll not find out and if he did he wouldn't care. He's drunk in 'alehouse more often than not.' Bridget knew her mother had no answer to that. She had escaped from a merrymaking Irish family only to marry an English drunkard. 'Anyway, I was doing nothing, onny chatting with friends.'

'Until two in a morning! Sweet Mary, what kind of reputation will that get you?'

Bridget shrugged. 'Don't care. Folks can think what they like.'

'Was Rosie Quinn with you?'

Bridget gave a scornful laugh. 'That bairn! Her ma won't let her out of her sight.'

'Quite right too,' her mother responded. 'With a son in prison she must be at her wits' end to keep her other children on the straight and narrow.' She gave a deep sigh. 'Poor woman. What a disgrace. Such shame, and he seeming such a grand lad. I'd never of thought of Mikey Quinn's being a thief.'

'For heaven's sake, Ma! He onny stole a couple o' rabbits. They were hanging there right in front of his nose. If I'd seen 'em I might have done 'same. And I'd have run faster,' she added.

'Don't you dare! Never set foot in this house with stolen goods. Do you hear?' Una Turner raised her voice as she always did when her unruly children ignored what she was saying. 'The Irish get blamed for everything in this town. It's always our fault.'

'I'm not Irish,' Bridget disclaimed. 'Onny half.'

'True! You're your father's daughter all right.' Her mother knew when she was beaten. 'You'll go to the bad just the same as he has.' She threw the dish rag on to the table and put her shawl round her shoulders. 'I'm going out. Somebody in this house has to try for honest work.'

She banged out of the door and Bridget crashed into a chair. Her head was splitting. It wasn't true that she had only been talking with friends last night. She had been talking; but to seamen in a hostelry in the town and with a glass of gin in her hand. Not an inn which her father frequented, for had he seen her he would have sent her off with a humiliating sharp word or a slap. It wasn't only the boys in this family who had felt the lash of his belt.

The seamen had plied her with drink, urging her to have another and then another. She accepted two and then offered to go up to the bar counter to collect a further jug of ale. 'I know 'landlord,' she'd said with a wink. 'He knows me.'

There was much ribald comment on this remark and as she'd leaned over to collect the jug from the table she'd felt a rough hand up her skirt. She'd opened her palm for money for the ale and smiled sweetly at the bleary-eyed seamen who dropped in the coins. She bought the ale and asked the land-lord to top up her gin glass with water, slipping the change into her skirt pocket.

She poured them all a glass of ale, then tossed back her gin and water and, with a little hiccup, swayed towards the door. 'Shan't be long,' she slurred. 'Must just go outside.' She blew them a kiss. 'Don't go away.'

She had run to the next street and into another hostelry,

where she had again met up with a group of seamen. 'Just looking for a friend,' she said, leaning provocatively over them. 'Have you seen her? Fair hair, pretty, dressed in a blue shawl?'

'No, darling, but come and join us until she turns up,' they'd insisted. 'You shouldn't be on your own. It's not safe.' And once again she had felt their wandering hands and escaped with their loose change, but by then she had partaken of a generous accumulation of gin, which this morning was causing her headache.

She stretched and considered having a lie-down on her parents' bed. It was more comfortable than her own pallet, which at night-time she unrolled in front of the fire. Her brothers too had either a pallet or a blanket, whilst their two youngest sisters slept at the bottom of their parents' bed.

Her father hadn't come home last night and she surmised that he was either under a table in one of the inns or bedded down in some woman's room. 'I'll risk it,' she murmured. 'I'll just have ten minutes.'

She dropped off to sleep in minutes and an hour later was rudely awakened when her father crashed in through the door. He didn't notice her, and perched on the edge of the bed to take off his boots, which he threw across the room. He tore off his trousers and fell back on the mattress clad in only his grey shirt. Then he saw her.

'What you doing?' He glared at her. 'Is it Bridget?'

'Yes, Da.' She pulled the blanket up to her chest. 'I didn't feel well so I came to lie down.'

He grabbed hold of her arm. 'Where's your ma?'

'Gone to look for work.' She bit nervously on her lip. Please God, don't let him be violent.

He gave her a smack across the face. 'That's where you should be instead of your ma.' He grabbed her shoulders and shook her. 'Go and look for her. Tell her I want her back here.'

'What if she's in work, Da?' Bridget rose hastily from the bed.

Her father gazed narrowly at her. 'Then you come back; and bring me a jug of ale.'

'Yes, Da.' She had no intention of doing so, or of searching for her mother. Too often had she listened to her cries when she had been forced into the marital bed by a drink-sodden, abusive husband. No, she would wander the streets until she was sure that her father had had time to drop off to sleep, and then she might or might not return home, depending on what else was on offer.

I'll not lead a life like my mother's, she pondered as she went out of the narrow Todd's Entry and headed towards Silver Street, where bankers and silversmiths and their well-to-do customers didn't even notice the poor who lived amongst them. She passed the White Harte Tavern and on impulse turned back and went inside. The landlord eyed her keenly. He didn't like lone women in his inn.

'Give me a neat gin and a slice o' bread and beef.' Bridget handed him some coins. 'Don't worry. I'm not stopping.'

She drank the gin in one gulp and waited whilst he carved the beef and put it on a slice of bread. Then she took it without a word and went outside. She slid round the corner of the building and sat on the step to the side door, and hungrily devoured the food. Easiest money I've ever made, she thought as she chewed. If I had somewhere else to live I could manage on my own. I need enough money for a room but I'm not going to beg for it, nor slave in a factory or mill.

Having finished eating, Bridget got to her feet and wandered aimlessly down towards the Market Place. There was generally something going on there: traders shouting out their wares, preachers telling of kingdom come, soldiers on leave idling away their precious time and eyeing up the girls. Hm, she mused. Soldiers with a coin or two to spare.

She caught sight of Rosie Quinn and her mother in front of her and slowed down so that she didn't have to speak to them. She only cultivated Rosie's friendship because of Mikey. Whiney little Rosie, she thought. As if I'd have her as my friend, a bairn like her! But Mikey! He wasn't like any other lads she knew, and when he was older, say in a year or two, he would look at her with different eyes. They would be good together, she knew. He was nice-looking now in a boyish way, with a humorous gleam in his eyes, but he would become handsome and all the girls in the district would be after him; but he'll be mine.

She continued into the Market Place, walking with a swagger, swinging her hips, her head held high. There was nothing demure about Bridget Turner; she was confident and aware of her own good looks, her dark glossy hair and green eyes, and aware too of the admiring glances cast her way by men old and young, pouting and tossing her head or giving an appealing smile when she thought it was merited.

'Hello, Biddy,' Jamie, a local man with a dubious reputation, called to her, but she ignored him, not even acknowledging him.

I'll not speak to the likes of him, she thought. Dirt, that's what he is. He should be in jail. He uses women to line his own pocket. Well, he'll not use me. I'm above that. I'll give myself to a man when it suits me, not before.

Her plan was to meet a rich older man who would buy her nice clothes, give her flowers, chocolate and perfume and pander to her every whim. They would leave Hull and live somewhere like London in a grand house and have their own smart carriage. She had not yet fathomed out how she would attract such a man, for she knew in her heart that she was shabby and poor, and in spite of her beauty he wouldn't even notice her if she should meet him.

She continued on, stopping for an occasional chat with stallholders who offered her an apple or an orange and asked for nothing in return – or not at the moment anyway, she thought, smiling sweetly as she accepted, thinking that most people did nothing for nothing. She passed the apothecary's shop and pondered that he had a son worth cultivating. Oliver Walker was young and handsome and had good prospects, but she shuddered as she thought of the boredom of being wed to a man in such a dull profession and having to stay in this town, when she longed for excitement and the chance to travel to other places.

'Now then!' A uniformed policeman stood in front of her, barring her way. 'And where are you off to?'

Bridget frowned. Why had he stopped her? She was doing nothing, just wandering about. Then her face cleared. He wasn't a street bobby, though he wore the top hat and white gloves and carried a rattle. He was the prison officer who had let her in to see Mikey.

He grinned at her. 'Didn't recognize me, did you?'

'I'll be honest, I didn't. I didn't know you all dressed up in your best topper and gloves,' she said. 'Quite a dandy, ain't yer?'

He nodded. 'We're supposed to keep toppers on at all times, but my head itches sometimes, wearing it all day.'

She gazed at him. He was an enormous man, rotund and very tall, towering above her. He hadn't asked for much of a favour in return for his. Merely to slip his hand inside her blouse to touch her breast and nipple, and she hadn't minded that.

'Are you on duty at Kingston Street?' she asked innocently. 'That's where Mikey's gone.'

'Aye, I know.' He gazed down at her. 'They've got regular warders in there, not police officers like me, so I can't help get you in.'

'That's a shame,' she pouted, pushing out her bottom lip. 'I thought I'd be able to cheer him up.'

He shook his head. 'Don't even think of it. You'll get him into worse trouble than he's in now.' Surreptitiously he ran his hand over her waist and bottom. 'You could cheer me up, though.'

She gave a little shrug. 'We might both get into trouble if I did,' she said. 'Have you got a wife?'

'No. Who'd want to marry a bobby wi' hours we work, and all for a pittance?'

She raised her eyebrows. 'At least you're in work. Not everybody's so lucky.'

'Meet me later,' he cajoled. 'I get off duty at ten.' He saw her hesitation. 'Don't tell me you're sweet on that young lad? He's onny a bairn.'

She shrugged. 'He's a friend's brother, that's all. He's nowt to me.'

He laughed. 'Just as well. He'll go to the bad.'

'What do you mean?' She tried to appear unconcerned. 'He's all right is Mikey.'

'He might be now,' he said. 'But he'll get in wi' wrong company in Kingston Street prison. For a start he'll be wi' Tully. They shared a cell in Blanket Row and no doubt he'll come across him while he's serving his time.'

'Tully? Who is he? I've heard his name.'

'He's a villain, that's what. And he's allus on 'lookout for young lads to do his dirty work.' Benton shook his head. 'Warn Quinn, if you can. Tell him not to mix wi' Tully or he'll get short shrift and a long rope.' Then he grinned. 'Or a sail across 'ocean.'

'To Australia?' Bridget took a breath. 'But how is it that Tully hasn't gone to Australia, if he's as bad as you say?'

'He did. And then he came back.'

CHAPTER FIVE

''Ere! Quinn.'

Mikey lifted his head slightly at the hissing voice. They were not supposed to speak. Not that he had the breath to talk as he smashed at the stones with the sledgehammer. His hands were raw and his shoulders burned with pain.

'Who is it?' he whispered back, raising the hammer once more. The guard was prowling. Mikey would have to wait until he reached the other end of the yard before he dared to turn round to see who was addressing him.

'Tully!'

Mikey felt even hotter and sweatier than before. He'd heard undertones in prison where Tully's name had been muttered. Why's he calling me? I don't need trouble. I just want to serve my time and get out of here.

'They've not broken you yet, then? Still in one piece, are you?'

'Yes,' he hissed back. 'I'm all right.'

He wasn't really. He was in pain most of the time; he felt as if a red-hot poultice had been applied to his back and shoulders. Breaking stones was a worse job than picking oakum, which had been his first occupation after being taken from his cell. He had been marched to a large room filled with old rope where other prisoners were picking away with their fingers at the rough coir. Most of them were elderly, and he could see that their bent, thin-skinned fingers were cracked and bleeding.

For the first few days he couldn't stop sneezing as the dust from the fibres got up his nose and made his eyes itch. Then, at the end of a week, he was told that he was to be sent outside to break stones.

He had felt quite relieved and had looked forward to being outside rather than in the dust-laden room, but on the first day the rain had poured down and he was soaked to the skin in minutes. When the rain stopped, the heat from his body and the sheer exertion of lifting the hammer and smashing it down on the boulders had dried out his clothes, leaving them stiff and scratchy and very uncomfortable.

'I'll get you off, if you like,' Tully whispered. 'Get you put in 'kitchens.'

Mikey glanced round before answering. 'So how come you're not in there?'

'I shall be,' was the answer. 'But I've got to be seen breaking stones first. Then I'll hurt me leg and won't be able to work.'

Mikey looked at him. Tully gave a crooked grin and a sly wink.

'You've got to know 'system,' Tully said. 'Know what you can get away with. I know some of 'warders, you see, and I can get stuff brought in.'

'What sort o' stuff?' Mikey murmured. 'I'd give owt for a slice o' meat pie.' His mouth watered when he thought of the pie that Bridget had brought for him.

'Don't want much, do you?' Tully muttered as the guard came closer. 'Shut your mouth now. This one's a stickler.'

When the guard drew away once more, Tully moved nearer to Mikey. 'I wasn't talking o' food,' he mouthed. 'I was talking o' poppy. Opium. I get it brought in and sell it. Then I give 'warders a cut of 'profit. They're allus glad of a backhander.'

'But where do 'prisoners get the money from?' As he looked at his fellow labourers, Mikey thought they all had an appearance of poverty and wretchedness, with their thin scraggy faces and whiskery chins. They looked even poorer than he was.

'They'll allus find money for poppy. It's 'onny thing that

keeps 'em alive.' Tully gave a chortle. 'If it doesn't kill 'em off!'

'I don't need it.' Mikey raised the hammer to strike again. 'Never tekken it.'

'What? Never?'

'No,' Mikey said breathlessly. 'My ma'd skin me alive if I did.'

'Mammy's bairn, are you?' Tully sneered. 'Little milksop!'

'Yeh, if you like.' Mikey wasn't bothered about taunts. He'd been offered a chew of opium or a sip of loddy before by some of his pals, but had always refused, knowing full well that his mother would find out and he'd never hear the end of it. Besides, he'd seen others under the influence of the stuff and he preferred to be in command of his senses.

'See that fellow over there?' Tully hissed, nodding towards a muscular man wielding a hammer. 'He buys it off me. Swears by it. Says he can break up twice as many stones because of it.'

Mikey wasn't convinced. 'And does he get his sentence cut in half then?'

Tully frowned. 'No, course he doesn't.'

'So what's 'point? Is he trying to please 'guard?'

'No!' Tully put down his hammer and glared at Mikey. 'Point is he's stronger cos of it.'

'Aye? Well, I shouldn't think he's got a ma who'd mek his life a misery if she found out.'

Tully grunted. 'Like I said. Milksop!'

I'm not, Mikey thought. But my ma would be disappointed in me. *Is* disappointed, I expect, now that I'm in jail. Hope she's managing without me.

He felt downhearted and even a little tearful, and hoped that if any of the other prisoners saw his wet eyes they would think it was because of the physical exertion and not because he was weeping.

A week later he was sent to the kitchens. The work wasn't as arduous as breaking stones, just very boring. He was set on to peel bucketloads of potatoes for soup, and after hours with

42

his hands in cold water he could barely feel his fingers or grip the blunt knife. Never again, he thought. Never again will I do anything wrong and come back to prison.

Being in the kitchens meant that he could help himself to a larger portion of gruel for breakfast and an extra piece of bread, and occasionally he chewed on a piece of raw carrot, though he never ate raw potatoes, his mother's warning ringing in his ears that some of his father's Irish relations had died of potato poisoning during the famine.

'Did Tully get you this job?' one of the prison warders asked him one morning. Mikey was filling a bucket with water from the pump.

'Tully?' Mikey feigned surprise. 'How could he do that?'

The guard surveyed him thoughtfully. 'We all know what Tully can do.'

Mikey shook his head and heaved a breath as he lifted the overflowing bucket. 'I don't. I've onny just met him. Why would he want to do owt for me?'

The officer followed him back to the kitchen. 'He'd have a reason, it's true. If he did get you this soft job, then he'll have summat lined up for you to do for him. When you get out, I mean.'

'Not me,' Mikey insisted. 'He's a criminal, isn't he? I made a mistake. I was hungry,' he added. 'And so were my ma and our bairns.'

'You shouldn't be in here,' the warder said. Mikey started to protest, thinking he meant in the kitchens. 'No, I mean in this lock-up with all 'hardened villains who'll learn you how to thieve. Men like Tully.'

'Where else is there? I wouldn't have wanted to be shipped to Australia.'

'That's coming to an end.' The guard allowed himself a thin smile. 'No. Reform schools for boys. That's what they're building in some parts of the country. Strict regime. Regular birching for young criminals who misbehave. That's what's needed round here. In my opinion,' he added as he moved away. 'Now get on with those spuds and no talking.'

43

Mikey hadn't seen Tully since coming to the kitchens and didn't know whether or not he had been influential in the move. If he had been, then Mikey was grateful to him, for it made his life less hard and he could think of the end of his sentence as only a short time away. When he was breaking stones it had seemed as if he was suffering a lifetime of penance and would never see the end of it.

Three days to go. He could hardly wait. He was thorough in the kitchens, clearing up the spilt water and peelings and washing down the floor assiduously with the mop.

'What 'you up to?' one of the guards asked suspiciously. 'Nobody ever moves 'chairs and tables when they're cleaning.'

Mikey grinned. 'I want you to remember me,' he said. 'Cos I shan't be coming back!'

'Hah.' The officer folded his arms in front of him. 'That's what all you young 'uns say. Then a couple o' weeks away from here and you forget all about how it is; temptation is put in your way and you think nobody'll catch you and afore you know it you're back inside again.' He stared Mikey in the eyes. 'Onny next time is allus longer.'

Mikey dipped the mop into the pail. 'Not me,' he muttered. 'I want to go home.'

At the end of the third day he was let out of the prison gate. He was back in his own clothes again, which oddly felt smaller and shabbier. I must have grown, he thought, gazing down at his shirt cuffs, which now finished halfway up his arms. He shivered. Summer was well over and the smell and chill of autumn overlay the familiar aromas of fish and seed oil which always permeated the town. Usually he didn't notice them, but after a month spent incarcerated within the prison walls they were very obvious.

Hope Ma is all right, he thought. I wonder if Rosie managed to get a job? She'd been trying, though at just twelve she hadn't found many positions available to her, except in the cotton mills and they already had waiting lists of women and girls eager for work.

'Mikey!' A girl's voice called to him. It was Bridget, and she

44

was waving. 'I've been waiting for ages,' she reproached him. 'They said you'd be out at four o'clock and it's nearly five.'

'Why're you here?' he asked. 'There was no need. I'm going straight home.'

She bit on her lip. 'Erm! That's why I've come to meet you. Your ma's not there.'

He stopped walking and faced her. 'What do you mean? Has she got work? I know where 'key is.' It would have been better if his mother had been at home when he arrived, so he could have listened to a long lecture on his wrongdoing and bringing shame on her and got it over with. Now he'd have to wait until later and his guilt would build up even further.

'No.' Bridget seemed furtive and shifted about from one foot to the other. 'None of them are there. Sorry, Mikey.' She stared at him for a second and then dropped her eyes. 'Landlord's tekken 'house back. Somebody else is living in it.'

'What?' He grabbed her arm. 'What do you mean, somebody else is living in it? We weren't far behind wi' rent. Onny a week or two.'

'That was then, Mikey. Afore you went to prison. 'Rent hasn't been paid since then cos your ma couldn't find work.'

His mouth dropped open. 'So where've they gone?' This is my fault, he thought. If I hadn't done what I did I might have found a job, some kind of work to pay the rent.

Bridget lifted her eyes to his and put her hand over the one which was still on her arm. 'Rosie came round to see me. She said would I tell you when you got out.'

He shook her hand off his. 'Tell me what, Bridget? Spit it out. Have they found another room?'

She emitted a deep sigh. 'No. They've gone to 'workhouse, Mikey. Your ma is poorly; they've put her in 'workhouse infirmary and I don't know what'll happen to Rosie and 'lads.'

Mikey gasped. Never! Never to the workhouse! His mother would be appalled. She was so proud. She would never be able to lift her head again. He must get her out. I'll do anything, he vowed. Anything at all.

45

'I must go to her,' he told Bridget. 'I can't let her stay there.'

'I just told you, Mikey. She's sick. There was nowhere else she could go.'

'I'm still going,' he said determinedly. 'I have to see her and tell her I'll get her out of there.'

He left her and ran, leaving her trailing behind him. He ran to his old home in Winter's Alley, just to check in case Bridget had made a mistake, but she was right, someone else was living there. A man, his wife and their six children; three more in number than his own family. He wondered how they would all manage in the one small room.

He turned and ran back into Whitefriargate and towards the workhouse. He knew it well enough, having lived within a stone's throw of it for most of his life. He hammered on the locked gate and shouted.

'What do you want?' a man's voice called back. 'You can't come in till 'morning.'

Mikey put his eye to a crack in the wooden gate. 'My ma's been brought here and my brothers and sister. I want to see them.'

'Well you can't. Come back in 'morning.'

'No. She's sick. My ma, I mean. She's been put in 'infirmary ward.'

'Just a minute. I'll have to fetch somebody.'

Mikey watched the man shuffle away towards the building. He guessed he was one of the paupers. His clothes were in rags and he coughed as he walked.

A few minutes later a woman walked briskly to the gate. 'Yes?' she said. 'I'm in 'middle of supper. What do you want?'

'To see my ma. Please,' he added. 'She was brought in because she's sick. My brothers and sister were brought in as well. Name of Quinn.'

'Quinn? Just a minute.' The bolt on the door rattled as the woman opened it. 'Who are you, then?'

'Mikey Quinn. I've – I've been away. Just got word that my ma's been brought here.'

'Mm,' she said, as if pondering. 'Do you have a father?'

'No.' Mikey stared at her. Why the questions? 'Is she here or not?'

'She is here. In a manner of speaking, that is. But I'm afraid you're too late. Mrs Quinn died this morning.'

CHAPTER SIX

'But – but she can't have! There's been a mistake. Jeannie Quinn.' Mikey grew hot and then cold. She'd got the name wrong. It wasn't his ma. It was somebody else.

'Come in, lad.' The woman wasn't unkind, but she was impatient. 'There's no mistake. Mrs Quinn was brought in a week ago, with her bairns, two boys and a girl. Rose, is it?'

Mikey nodded, dumb. Rosie. What had happened to Rosie?

'Your sister's gone to work at 'cotton mill,' the woman was saying. 'They'll tek pauper bairns from here even when they won't tek other bairns that's waiting for work. They've got priority, you see. But your brothers are here. Do you want to see your ma? Funeral's tomorrow.'

'I – I don't know.' He felt his body growing cold and his legs weak.

'Are you feeling all right? Not going to pass out, are you?'

He knew he was and the woman seemed to know it too, for she ushered him into the building and pushed him towards a wooden chair. 'Sit there for a minute,' she said. 'I'll be back.'

She left him and hurried off down the corridor. He bent over, putting his head towards his knees. This wasn't happening. He felt sick with fright, his forehead beaded with sweat. He got up from the chair and dashed back outside where he retched and retched until his throat gagged.

He staggered back inside and fell on to the chair. There was no one about, though he could hear the clattering of crockery and rattle of pans coming from a room at the end of the corridor. The matron was having her supper, that's what she said, or maybe she meant she was giving the inmates their supper. What about Ben and Tom? Would he be able to see them? Did they know about Ma? He felt numb, as if all emotion, all life, had drained out of him.

He waited for what seemed like hours. A man came and lit a lamp which was standing on a shelf. It stank of old oil. He looked at Mikey but didn't speak and then went away again. The woman came back.

'You can have some supper if you like,' she said. 'I shouldn't really as you're not a resident but I'll mek an exception.'

'I'm not hungry,' he said weakly, 'but can I have a drink o' water, please?'

She nodded and led him into a small room containing a desk and two chairs and a fire in the grate. He went to the fire and put his hands towards the flames. He was shivering, and when he took the cup of water from her his hands shook so much that he spilt some of it down his shirt.

'Your ma said you'd come looking for her,' the matron said. 'She said you were away. Where've you been?'

His mother obviously hadn't said he'd been in prison. She wouldn't have wanted anyone to know. 'Out of town,' he muttered. 'Looking for work.' His ma was an honest, proud woman; he wasn't going to let her down now.

'And did you find it?' Her eyes were piercing as she gazed at him.

He shook his head. 'No.'

'It'll be a pauper's funeral, you realize? Unless you've money to pay for a grave?'

Again Mikey shook his head, and the matron sighed. 'Do you want to see her then, before she goes?'

Mikey considered. Did he? Why had she died? 'What did she die of?' he asked.

'Heart failure brought on by starvation. Doctor said she

49

hadn't eaten in days, weeks even. 'Bairns hadn't either, but they've recovered. They'd been scavenging, apparently.'

And I was grumbling over the prison food, Mikey thought, whilst they didn't have any.

'Your ma probably had consumption as well,' the matron went on. 'She had a cough, anyway, when she was admitted. So that hastened her death.'

Mikey suddenly decided. 'I don't want to see her.' He didn't want to look at her thin and wasted. He would prefer to re-member her lively, her sharp tongue chastising him, her last words shouted out in court as he was sentenced.

'Can I see my brothers? And Rosie?'

'Your sister's not back from work yet, but you can see 'lads. Come wi' me.'

She led him into a large room set with long tables where the children were eating their evening meal. Boys were sitting on benches at one table and girls at another. All were dressed in grey, the boys in knee-length trousers and shirts and the girls in flannel dresses with aprons over them. Their pale faces almost matched the colour of their garments.

'Quinn boys!' the matron bellowed. 'Come here!'

There was a shuffling along one of the benches and Mikey's brothers got up and came to stand in front of the matron, their hands behind their backs and their heads bowed.

'You can look up,' she said. 'Your brother's come to see you.'

They both glanced up at Mikey and then at the matron.

'Go on,' she said. 'You can speak.'

'Can we come wi' you, Mikey?' Tom, at five, was the youngest of the brothers. 'We don't want to stop here, do we, Ben?'

'No, we don't.' Ben, though older than Tom, was the quiet one. 'Our ma's dead,' he whispered. 'We had to go and see her.'

'I know,' Mikey said. I've only been away a month, he thought, yet I feel much older, as if I've been away for years and I've grown up. He looked down at his pasty-faced brothers. 'I've been told about Ma; but you can't come wi' me cos I've nowhere to live. I'll have to find work of some kind otherwise I won't eat.'

'We have bread and a pot o' tea for our supper,' Tom said. 'And suet pudding on a Friday.'

'Well, there you are then,' Mikey said with forced jollity. 'That's more'n I'll be having.'

'Can't you stop wi' us, Mikey?' Ben said. 'Rosie has to go to work.'

Mikey glanced at the matron, who gave a dubious shake of her head. 'No,' he said. 'But as soon as I'm in work, I'll come and fetch you.'

'Off you go, then,' Matron told the boys, 'before anybody eats your supper.'

They both turned their heads to look at Mikey before taking their places at the table again and he saw Ben pressing his lips together as if to stop himself from crying.

'There's nobody older than you who can take responsibility, I suppose?' the matron asked as they walked back down the corridor. 'You said you've no father?'

'No, he died at sea. We're orphans now.'

'Will you come to 'burial?' she asked. 'The boys will be excused their lessons so they can attend.'

'Lessons?' He was surprised. They'd never been to school; his mother never had money for such luxuries.

'Pauper school,' she said. 'But onny for a short time. Soon we'll all be moving to 'new workhouse and 'childre' will be educated there.'

There had been a rumour for years that the workhouse was to be moved to a brand new building on the outskirts of town, but a rumour was all it had been. Now the matron was assuring him that it was about to happen.

'So will you come?' she asked him again. 'To 'funeral?'

'Yes.' He didn't want to, but he had to be there for the sake of the boys and Rosie.

'Nine o'clock sharp,' she said. 'Don't be late or we'll go wi'out you.'

He didn't know what to do or where to go next. He'd been

looking forward to going home; to greeting his ma and promising that he'd never get into trouble again. He longed to hear her scolding him and then, when she relented, giving him a soft cuff round his head. Now he was quite alone.

He wandered across to the Market Place, but most of the traders were packing up to go home. He bent to pick up an apple that had fallen from somebody's cart and put it in his pocket. Then he meandered about looking to see if there was anything else that was fit to eat. A few stray mangy dogs were doing the same.

A man was damping down a brazier. Mikey sniffed. Hot potatoes! He could eat one of those with no effort. It was a long time since his dinner at the prison and he was feeling hungry.

'Got owt left?' he asked the trader.

The man laughed. 'Who are you kidding? I stop here till everything's sold and 'fire's out.'

Mikey nodded vaguely. 'Just wondered, that's all.'

He wandered off again, looking about him, but nothing caught his eye. Everybody had cleared up; no one could afford to leave anything behind. Not a green potato, not even a sprouting carrot. He sat on the church wall to have a think. In the winter, charity workers brought soup kitchens to the Market Place. But poor folk need to eat all through the year, he pondered. Not just in winter.

He thought of what the matron had said about his mother dying from starvation. She must have been feeding all of us and not herself. Come to think of it, he couldn't remember his mother ever sitting down to eat with them; bread, or potato soup, had always gone to the children first. He took the apple from his pocket and bit into it. It was green and sour and made his mouth crease with its sharpness. He threw it across the square and a pigeon flew down to peck at it.

Where can I go for the night? Who would give me a place on their floor? Tomorrow, he thought, after the funeral, he would be able to think straight, decide what to do, try for work. But tonight he just wanted to put his head down and sleep, and try to forget what had happened.

'Mikey!'

He didn't know whether to be glad or sorry to see Bridget again. She always seemed to turn up from nowhere, as if she was constantly on the prowl. He nodded to her as she approached, but didn't speak.

She jumped up beside him. The wall of Holy Trinity Church was a regular meeting place for young people in the town, though few of them ever ventured inside the building. 'Did you find your ma?' she asked. 'My ma said it was a great shame that she had to go, but as I said to her, it's better than living out on 'streets.'

'She's dead,' Mikey muttered. 'Died this morning. I was too late.'

'Oh, Mikey!' She put her arm round his shoulder. 'I'm really sorry. What'll you do now? What about Rosie and 'boys?'

'They're all stopping at 'workhouse, but Rosie's working at 'cotton mill.'

'Rosie working?' Bridget pulled a face. 'Still, I suppose she'll have to do summat to earn a crust.'

'How come you don't have a reg'lar job?' Mikey asked. He felt rather peeved with her; she seemed smug about Rosie's working at the mill. 'You're older than me. How does your ma manage wi'out wages from you?'

'Oh, I do a bit o' this 'n' that,' Bridget said airily. 'I can bring in a bob or two.'

'Doing what?' he said.

She shrugged. 'Just said. This 'n' that. Errands and suchlike.'

'Wish I could,' he said gloomily. 'Don't know how I'm going to live. It was bad enough finding work before I went to prison. I haven't even anywhere to stay tonight.'

'Come to our place,' she said eagerly. 'Da will be out, he allus is, and Ma won't mind. There won't be any supper, though. There's never owt left over.'

'Don't mind about that,' Mikey said, though ideally he wouldn't have chosen to stay at Bridget's place. She made him feel uncomfortable, always coming up close to him, touching his arm or taking hold of his hand, as she was doing now. 'I just want somewhere to sleep. Ma's funeral's tomorrow,' he added.

'Shall I come wi' you?' she offered.

'No. Thanks. I've to look after Rosie and Tom and Ben. We'll be all right on our own.'

He went home with her, and Mrs Turner made him welcome and said how sorry she was about his mother. She'd just heard the news, she told him. 'You'll have to get a job, Mikey; something settled, like a butcher or baker's boy. Pity you can't be apprenticed to a trade, but who's got the money for that? Not poor folk like us, that's for sure.'

'I might go to sea, Mrs Turner,' he said. 'Ma didn't want me to, she said she'd allus worry about me, but now that she's gone . . .' He left the sentence unfinished. There was no one to worry about him now, except his brothers and sister, of course, but they'd have to choose what to do with their own lives when the time came.

'Sure and your mammy will be looking out for you, Mikey,' Mrs Turner said softly. 'Sure she will. Have no worries on that score if that's what you want to do.'

'I don't want to, Mrs Turner,' he explained. 'It just seems 'only option open to me.'

She managed to find him a slice of bread for his supper and a cup of weak tea, and as darkness drew on she gave him a blanket to sleep on. 'There's only the floor I can offer you, Mikey. If Mr Turner comes in, then curl up small and he'll not even notice you. Ten to one he'll be drunk anyway and think you one of his own.'

'You're very kind, thank you,' he managed to say, for he was overcome with the emotion that had been gathering ever since he'd left the workhouse. 'I'll not be a bother.'

He wrapped the blanket round him and lay down on the floor at the side of the fire, near where Bridget had made up her bed.

'G'night, Mikey,' she said softly. 'Sleep well.'

He didn't answer, but pulled the blanket over his head. He

thought he would never sleep well again, never in his life. His thoughts were in turmoil: the loss of his mother, what to do, where to try for work; but in minutes, through sheer exhaustion, he fell fast asleep.

A few glowing embers of the fire stopped the room from being totally dark when he awoke and felt the warmth of one of his brothers curled up next to him. 'Move up, Tom,' he muttered. 'You're pushing me out.'

He felt an arm creeping over him and then a hand touching his face. He shifted away. 'What 'you doing?' he grumbled. 'Tom! Stop it.' Then he took in a sharp breath. It wasn't Tom, or Ben either; he was suddenly aware that whoever it was was wearing very few clothes, for he could feel naked flesh, bare legs and thighs wrapping round him.

He opened his mouth to speak but a hand was put over his lips. 'Shh,' Bridget whispered. 'Don't mek a sound or you'll wake Ma.'

She took her hand away and ran it down his body; she had undone his shirt buttons already and was now trying to unfasten the waistband of his trousers.

'Don't,' he gasped, his senses aroused, his body throbbing. 'If your ma should hear . . .'

She pressed closer to him; he could feel her breasts next to him, her nipples erect. 'You can touch me if you like, Mikey,' she breathed. 'I want you to.'

'No,' he whispered, his voice strained. 'It's not right.'

'It is,' she insisted, her hands wandering over him. 'It's what I want, Mikey.'

A sudden crash came from the bed and Mrs Turner exclaimed, 'Damned brick! It's all right. The brick's fallen out of bed.'

Mikey froze and Bridget held her breath as Mrs Turner threw back her blanket and bent to retrieve the hot brick which she had put in the bed to warm it. As she straightened up she saw Mikey and Bridget together on the floor.

She took a breath and Mikey saw the shock and outrage in her expression. 'Holy Mary! He's taken my daughter in sin!'

CHAPTER SEVEN

'No. No I haven't, Mrs Turner.' Mikey struggled to get out of the blanket to show Mrs Turner that he was still fully dressed. 'It's – it's . . .'

He didn't want to get Bridget into trouble, although she was the one who had come to him.

'I was cold, Ma.' Bridget slipped out of the blanket. 'Mikey was nearer to 'fire. That's all. Nowt happened.' She gave Mikey a glance of disapproval, blaming him, he felt, because nothing did.

'Nothing happened? Nothing happened?' Mrs Turner glared furiously at Mikey. 'If the brick hadn't fallen out of bed, then something might have! Get out of my house, you jailbird! I give you food and shelter and this is how you repay me? Seducing my daughter right in front of my nose! What would your poor mother think?' She crossed herself. 'God rest her soul.'

Mikey hurriedly fastened his shirt buttons and hitched up his trousers. 'I'm sorry,' he stammered. 'It's not how it looks, Mrs Turner. Honest to God it isn't.'

'Honest to God!' She aimed a futile blow at him. 'Don't you take the Lord's name in vain with your lies. Get out!' She turned to Bridget. 'And as for you, you brazen hussy, if your father had been here you'd have felt his belt all right, and you still might if I choose to tell him.'

Bridget clutched the neck of her shift. 'Please don't, Ma!

Please don't tell him. It was a mistake. I was cold. It wasn't Mikey's fault,' she finally conceded.

'You can still get out,' her mother told him. 'I'll have no libertine taking advantage of my daughter. She'll stay pure until she's wed.'

Mikey picked up the blanket. I don't think she will, he thought. Another few minutes and we'd both have been deflowered. Or maybe, he pondered as he headed for the door, just maybe, Bridget had done this before.

He kept on uttering his apologies as he went out and it wasn't until he came to the top of Todd's Entry that he realized he was still clutching Mrs Turner's blanket. He daren't take it back in case she started haranguing him again, and as he hesitated, wondering what to do, he recognized the drunken figure of Bridget's father swaying in his direction.

Mikey started to run. The last thing he wanted was to be in the way of Turner's fists. He was well known for his violence, both towards anyone who disagreed with him or got in his way and to his wife and family. I just hope that Bridget and her mother have settled their differences and got back into bed before he crashes through the door.

He cut through various dark passages and alleyways, past several inns where Turner had probably spent the evening, eventually coming out in Silver Street. He ran along it, looking back several times to make sure he wasn't being followed, and instead of turning right into the Market Place he continued on towards the old church of St Mary's, where his mother sometimes went to pray. There were seats for eight hundred people inside and many of them were free for the poor to attend the services. He knew his mother had worshipped there as he had followed her one Sunday some years ago, shortly after they had been given the news that his father's ship had gone down.

But Mikey wasn't going to pray. He was going to look for shelter beneath the archway which abutted the road. But there was someone there already and as he walked into its shadow he heard a woman's voice in the darkness asking, 'Hello, darling. Lookin' for company?'

'N-no.' His voice broke as sometimes it did when he was startled. 'I'm looking for shelter. I've got nowhere to stop.'

'He's just a kid, Peg,' the voice said, and another one butted in, 'Well, you're on our patch, laddie. You can't stop here.'

To Mikey's horror he started to cry. Great gulps of tears and sobs which poured out of him and wouldn't stop.

'Hey! Hey! Come on,' the first woman said. 'What's up?'

'My ma's dead,' he wept, 'and I've just come out of prison and 'rest of our bairns are in 'workhouse.'

'Phew!' one of the women whistled. 'You've got a skinful o' trouble, haven't you? What you been in prison for? Beating up some old lady?'

'No,' he sobbed. 'I stole a rabbit from 'butcher.'

'For your dinner, was it?'

As his eyes became accustomed to the gloom, he saw that one of the women was young, the other probably the same age as his mother. 'Yeh.' He wiped his eyes and nose on his sleeve, feeling ashamed and humiliated that he had broken down in front of them.

'And you've nowhere to live? No pals who'd give you a bed for 'night?'

He sniffled. 'I did have, onny – onny I was chucked out. They said I couldn't stop cos of summat that happened. Onny it wasn't my fault.'

He heard the women muttering together. 'All right,' the older one said. 'You get bedded down here and we'll move along a bit, but if anybody comes lookin' for us, tell 'em we'll be in a shop doorway further on. Just for tonight, mind. Tomorrow we'll want our place back. Understood?'

'Yes. Thanks.' He knew that he should have said that he would take the doorway, but it would be draughty and less sheltered than here, and he also knew that they wouldn't stay long in the doorway. As soon as they had a customer, they would move along.

Prostitutes, that's what they are, he thought, without

58

prejudice. The sort of women his mother had warned him against when she realized he was growing up. Full of disease they are, she had told him, so keep away. Not that they would want a poverty-stricken lad like you, she had added, and at first he hadn't understood what she meant. Now he did. Ma didn't say that they would be thoughtful, did she, he pondered, huddling against the wall. She didn't say they would be kind. Perhaps she didn't really know any.

There were not many hours left until dawn and he slept only fitfully until then; he was disturbed once by an old tramp who bent over to look at him and then moved on, and then by a mangy dog who sniffed him and lay down beside him. The dog stank and scratched and scratched and Mikey eventually shooed him away.

Horses and trundling carriers' wagons, carts with cages of clucking hens and squawking ducks on their way to the market, woke him and he remembered that today was his mother's funeral. He got to his feet and set off to look for a water pump where he could swill his hands and face. The two women had gone and he wondered where they slept during the day.

He arrived at the workhouse door at seven o'clock and the matron said he was far too early. 'You'll have to sit outside,' she grumbled. 'I'm busy with breakfast. I'll send your kin to you when they've had theirs.'

Mikey licked his lips. I wonder what they're having. 'Will there be owt left?' he said plaintively.

'No,' she said. 'There won't. I have to ration out my supplies. There isn't enough for waifs and strays as well as for 'residents.' Her benevolent manner of yesterday seemed to have disappeared and she was abrupt and offhand. 'Go and sit on 'steps in 'yard till we're ready.'

He sat on the steps to a hayloft with Mrs Turner's blanket round his shoulders and watched the comings and goings of the inmates. Young girls in shawls and heavy boots crossed the yard and went out of the gate; most of them were pale-faced and looked tired and he guessed they were on their way to work at the mills. Rosie wasn't among them and he hoped she had been given the day off to go to their mother's funeral.

After waiting for about an hour, he got up and started pacing about. He was desperately tired and knew that if he sat much longer he would drop asleep. The workhouse gate swung fully open and a horse and cart drove in. On the cart was a wooden coffin, the wood so flimsy that he doubted it would be strong enough to hold a body. He started to shake. Was this for his mother?

He went back to the steps and put his hands over his eyes. He didn't want to see. He just wanted to shut out everything and not believe that this was really happening.

'Mikey!' A soft voice disturbed his seclusion and he opened his fingers to see Rose standing in front of him. 'Mikey,' she said again. 'You've to come now.'

He took his hands away from his face. Rose had been crying; her eyes were red and her cheeks blotchy. She put her hand out to him. 'I'm scared,' she said. 'And Matron said I had to be brave for Tom and Ben's sake.'

He rose and took her hand. 'We both do,' he said. 'They're onny bairns, while you and me . . .'

Rose nodded. 'I'm grown up,' she said in a choked voice, 'and working at 'mill. I get a wage, two and sixpence, but I've to give most of it back to 'workhouse.'

'Where will they tek Ma?' Mikey asked. 'Do you know?'

She gazed up at him. 'There's a paupers' patch at 'General Cemetery. We've got to walk,' she added, 'and it's a long way.'

The four of them walked together behind the cart, which carried two coffins, their mother's and another. There were no other mourners. The matron rode in a hansom cab and Mikey thought that there would have been enough room for them all if she squashed up a bit. But she didn't offer and so they plodded on behind. In fact they enjoyed the walk. The day was sunny and for all of them it was the first time they had been out of town and into the countryside.

Spring Bank was a long and pleasant tree-lined road which culminated in the cemetery, itself laid out like a park with flower beds and shrubs. 'Ma'll like it here,' Rose murmured after the burial, which was in a corner set aside for paupers, away from the mass grave of cholera victims of a few years before. She clutched the hands of the two younger boys. 'It smells nice.'

Mikey agreed. Better by far than the obnoxious smell of blackened earth in the overfull graveyards of St Mary's and Holy Trinity. 'Mebbe you could come here on a Sunday to visit,' he said, as they started their journey back to town. 'If Matron'll let you out.'

Rose was doubtful. 'I don't think Tom and Ben'll be allowed.'

'Mebbe when we move to 'new place they'll let us,' Ben said enthusiastically. 'We're going to walk in procession up Anlaby Road to 'new workhouse and we're going to have new breeches; lads that is. These scratch,' he added. 'They mek my legs sore.'

'Will you come wi' us, Mikey?' Tom asked. 'I'll ask Matron again if you like.'

Mikey looked back into the distance. The road onwards was long and straight and he could see tall trees with their branches waving, and green grass, and far away the rise of low shadowy hills. 'I can't,' he murmured. 'I've to look for work and I might have to go out of town to find it.'

Rose started to cry. 'We might not see you again, Mikey, and if you go away I'll be 'eldest and have to look out for Tom and Ben.'

Mikey considered. If he stayed in Hull he might not find work. Every lad he knew was looking for a job of some kind and he'd never be able to earn enough to keep his brothers and sister. 'They'll be looked after all right, Rosie,' he told her. 'Until they're old enough to work and then they'll be able to fend for themselves. And you'll have a good job at 'cotton mill, I expect.'

Rose shook her head. 'Girls at 'mill said we're kept on eight hours till we're thirteen, when we can work for twelve hours, but after that we're put on short time and can't earn much.'

He was silenced. If that was the way things were, what could he do? Then he said, 'I'll go and try to mek my fortune, Rosie, and I bet that when I come back you'll be forewoman of 'mill or else married wi' a bairn of your own.'

'That means you'll be gone for a long time, Mikey,' Ben said sadly.

Mikey nodded. He felt choked. 'Yes,' he said softly. 'It might.'

CHAPTER EIGHT

Eleanor's day seemed even longer than usual. Miss Wright had a cold so they couldn't go out for a walk, and the maids were too busy to take her, so she had to be content with walking round indoors for exercise.

'I wish you could come out with me, Nanny,' she had said as they ate their lunch of cold chicken. 'It would do you good, you know,' she added seriously. 'Perhaps put some colour into your cheeks.'

Nanny laughed. 'Or I could use some from out of a box like Miss Wright does.'

'Oh! Does she? I hope Papa never notices it.' Eleanor was dismayed; it wasn't that she would be concerned about losing Miss Wright if she should be dismissed for wearing rouge, but the thought of having a new governess who might be even stricter than Miss Wright filled her with fright.

'He won't,' Nanny said. 'Gentlemen rarely notice such things unless it's made very obvious. Now, dear, run along and find something to occupy you. I have a million things to do.'

Including having a nap, Eleanor thought. But what am I going to do until supper time?

She wandered about upstairs, even going along the corridor and up another short flight of uncarpeted stairs into the attic where the maids slept. She wasn't supposed to go up there and she felt quite a thrill because she was doing something forbidden. She peeked into the maids' bedroom; the walls were whitewashed and two narrow, neatly made beds were set close together. A washstand with a bowl and jug was against one wall and a chest with two drawers stood against the other. The floorboards were bare apart from a thin rug by the bed nearer the door.

Much like my room, she thought, except that I have oilcloth on my floor, and I have an oil lamp to light the room and they don't. Only a candle. Oh, but they don't have a fireplace either. How cold it must be in winter.

She slipped downstairs and then down again on to the landing of the first floor. She'd heard the front door slam and wondered if it was her father late home for luncheon. Perhaps he was not returning to his chambers. Sometimes he brought legal papers home and worked on them in his study. He looked after the wills and estates of rich clients.

Eleanor peeked over the balustrade and saw a pale pink patch on the top of her father's head as he went across the hall and into the morning room, where her mother would be waiting for him. She thought he wouldn't be pleased at her seeing his thinning hair, for he always kept it carefully groomed and held in place with some greasy, spicy-smelling ointment.

She gave an anxious sigh. She much preferred it when her father was away from home. The maids tiptoed about when he was in the house, and her mother was tense and distracted, flitting from room to room to make sure that everything was in place and exactly how her husband liked it. He was extremely particular that his living style reflected his successful position. The flowers were changed every day in the drawing room, the curtains must be draped just so – he would twitch at them if they were not – and the furniture was always replaced in the same spot after cleaning; only the finest table linen was used whenever they had guests, though he condescended to second best when he and his wife dined alone.

Mrs Kendall complied with his every whim and had done so since the day they were wed, when he had made it quite clear that this was what she should do if she wanted to please him and so enjoy a happy and successful marriage. She had even provided him with a son and daughter in the proper order.

Eleanor shrank away from the stair rail as the morning room door opened and first her mother and then her father came out. 'I will not discuss the matter before luncheon,' she heard her father say. 'You know that my digestion suffers if I am contradicted over any issue.'

'I did not mean to contradict you, Edgar.' Eleanor had to strain her ears to hear her mother's submissive voice. 'I only meant—'

'No more!' he snapped. 'I said no!'

Eleanor, listening, flushed and then grew cold; she shouldn't have been eavesdropping. Her father would be furious if he found out. But she was curious. What was it that her mother had said or asked that made her father so irritable? Was it something about her? Had she done something wrong? Anxiously, she tried to analyse her morning's activities. Had she unthinkingly done something to displease one or both of her parents?

But I haven't seen Mama this morning or Papa either, so perhaps they were not discussing me. Maybe it was Nanny! She had once heard her father debating what the old lady cost them in food, and it wasn't until her mother had pointed out that she saved them the expense of another servant to look after Eleanor – for Nanny didn't have wages, only her bed and board – that he had reluctantly conceded that on this occasion she was right.

If Nanny should have to leave, then I would run away, Eleanor thought, for I would be quite alone. She sat with her back to the wall as she deliberated. But Mama wouldn't want Nanny to leave. Nanny had always been there as a comfort to Mama as well as to herself, and once, when Eleanor had caught her mother in tears, she had seen that Nanny had had a consoling arm round her. If only Mama and Nanny and I could find a nice little house to live in, and leave Papa here. I'm sure he would be perfectly happy with just the servants to look after him.

She daydreamed for a while and mentally arranged the imaginary little house with a cosy parlour and a kitchen for the cook, for they would have to have a cook, although perhaps they could manage with just one maid to do for them since she, Eleanor, wouldn't mind doing a little dusting now and then to help. And perhaps there might be a little dog or a cat to play with.

'What are you doing, Eleanor?' So engrossed had she been that she hadn't heard the dining room door open or heard her father as he quietly strode upstairs. Now he was standing in front of her.

'Nothing, Papa.' She scrambled to her feet. 'I was – I was memorizing my tables,' she invented. 'Miss Wright is unwell and I thought I would learn them ready for tomorrow – if she is better.' She fell silent and hung her head.

'And why can you not learn them in the schoolroom instead of cluttering up the landing?' He stared down at her. 'This is not the place for lessons.'

Eleanor swallowed. She had run out of excuses. 'I – I thought that if I had a change of view, it might focus my mind better.' Miss Wright had often told her about focusing.

Her father looked down his nose and pursed his lips as if considering her statement, something she imagined he did in court. 'Hm,' he said. 'And did it?'

She was astonished. Her father never asked her opinion. 'Perhaps it did,' she said meekly. 'But I think I'm ready to go back now.'

With a wave of his hand he dismissed her and it took all of her willpower to walk sedately along the landing and up the next flight of stairs to where the schoolroom and nursery were situated, when really she wanted to scoot away out of his forbidding presence as quickly as she could.

She sought out Nanny and confided that she was worried that perhaps she had misbehaved in some way, for her father had seemed cross about something. She was careful in her choice of words, bearing in mind that Nanny, though not exactly a servant, wasn't family either.

66

'What makes you think he was cross with you?' Nanny asked. 'He would surely have had it out with you if that was the case.'

That was true, Eleanor conceded. Her father was never one to hold back over an issue of what he might consider disobedience.

'It's just that I accidentally heard him saying he would not discuss something with Mama, and I thought that perhaps it might have been about me.'

A concerned expression fleetingly crossed Nanny's face, but then she smiled to soften her words as she commented, 'That just goes to show that eavesdroppers never hear anything good! But I think it was probably something else entirely and not to do with you at all. Perhaps it might have been about Master Simon; he'll be home from school very soon. Or perhaps your father has concerns at work. Whatever it was, there's no use worrying your head over it.'

'No,' she replied. 'I'll try not to. Nanny,' she began again. 'Will I have to get married when I'm grown up?'

Nanny took a breath. 'What a lot of questions today. Won't you want to get married and have a husband and a home of your own?'

'I'm not sure,' Eleanor said quietly. 'But I don't know what else there is.'

Nanny frowned. 'Would you rather stay at home and eventually look after your parents in their old age?'

'Oh, no!' Eleanor gazed at the old lady. 'I don't think so. But you didn't, Nanny. You looked after Mama and then Simon and me. You didn't get married, did you?'

'No,' she replied. 'But then nobody asked me. That's why I became a children's nursemaid and later a nanny. I wanted to be with children and there wasn't any other choice. I wasn't clever enough to be a governess or teacher like Miss Wright.'

'I see,' Eleanor said sadly. She cast her mind over her parents' friends and acquaintances and thought that out of all the married men they knew, there wasn't a single one that she would have chosen as a husband to love, honour and obey as would be expected of her.

The next day Miss Wright resumed her duties, though she sniffled a lot and constantly blew her reddened nose.

'Miss Wright,' Eleanor ventured as the morning wore on, 'are you very poor?'

Miss Wright stared at her with watery eyes. 'Certainly not! Whatever gave you that idea?'

'Did no one ask you to marry them?' Eleanor continued. 'Nanny said no one asked her and that's why she became a children's nursemaid. And I wondered whether if perhaps you were poor and yet clever, and that's why you chose to become a governess.'

A frown wrinkled Miss Wright's forehead. 'You ask far too many impertinent questions, young lady. You are in great danger of becoming a busybody.'

'Oh, but I wouldn't tell anyone,' Eleanor assured her. 'It's just that I don't know what I want to do when I'm grown up. I don't know whether to marry somebody if they should ask me or become a teacher like you, because I expect by then I shall be educated enough to do that.'

Miss Wright permitted herself a small smile. 'I think, Miss Eleanor, that you won't have to think about it too much. When the time comes I'm quite sure that your parents will choose somebody suitable for you; and you'll be as happy as they are,' she added ironically.

'Yes.' Eleanor nodded, and sighed. That is what I am afraid of.

Several weeks went by, and from time to time Eleanor heard snatches of her parents' conversation as she entered the drawing room. They always stopped talking abruptly when she went in and she felt that her father perused her, assessing whether or not she had heard what they were saying. But she kept her expression closed as her mother always did, never letting her emotions appear on her face.

Then one evening as she stood in her usual place in front of them, her father without any preamble said, 'Your brother is coming home from school.'

Eleanor looked up at him. Was she supposed to be surprised? Or pleased? He was early, at any rate. It wasn't the end of term yet.

'He has been expelled.' Her father waited as if she should make a comment, but she didn't know what to say. Should she feel guilty? What had he done to be sent home?

'For some weeks now he has been behaving badly, so the school has informed me.' Her father continued to gaze at her. 'They have punished him, as I suggested they should, and given him several chances, but to no avail. He is set on a downward path, I fear.'

'I'm sorry,' she managed to say. 'He doesn't like it there; perhaps that's why.'

Her father frowned; a deep furrow which delved into his forehead. 'I didn't ask for your opinion,' he reprimanded her. 'I am giving you this information so you understand that when he comes home you are not to speak to him. No one must; not your mother, not Nanny or any of the servants, and neither must you. Do you understand?'

'Yes, Papa,' she whispered. Poor Simon, she thought.

'He will be kept in complete isolation for a month. A month in Coventry; we'll see how he likes that.' Her father stretched his neck and drew back his shoulders. 'And then he will be sent away to another school. One that knows how to treat recalcitrant boys. Cold baths, exercise every morning, beating when they misbehave. And,' he added, 'if I should find out that you have been communicating with him in any way – do not think you can slip him a note when I have told you not to speak to him – then you will be punished too. Is that understood?'

Eleanor cast a glance at her mother, who was sitting still as stone, her face so pale and drawn that she looked as if at any moment she might slide out of her chair and fall in a faint to the floor.

'Is that understood?' he thundered. 'Do not look at your mother. Look at me and swear it.'

'Yes, Father,' she whispered. 'I swear it.'

CHAPTER NINE

Mikey spent another night under St Mary's arch. It seemed to be the most sensible thing to do. No point in setting off in search of his fortune on the day of his mother's funeral. He was dead tired and felt wrung out, emotional and guilty too about leaving his young brothers and sister; but what could he do? If he could have found a job which paid enough to cover rent and food, then perhaps they could have all lived together, but that was asking the impossible. It was at least a shilling a week for a room.

Besides, he thought honestly, if I only have myself to think about, then I can do so much more and travel further. He had it in his head that he would go away from Hull and the places he was familiar with. I shall be unencumbered, he thought. Just myself and the high road. I'll try for work chopping wood and so on, but even though those low hills I saw looked inviting, I'm no country boy and I think I'd be best heading for another town.

He didn't know the country, never having been. He didn't know the sea either, only the Humber estuary which carried the salty smell of the sea and where on wild days seagulls came shrieking in over the tops of the churning water.

He huddled against the wall. I could follow 'river's course, as far as it goes, and then cut across to the highways and make my way to . . . to where, he wondered. Where could I go to make my fortune? London? I don't know anybody who's been.

The town clocks struck eight; people were moving about the streets. The theatres and music halls would already be filling up, as would the inns and hostelries. Good luck to them all, he thought sleepily, if they've money to spend. He closed his eyes and saw flower beds and trees and the place where they had put their mother to rest.

'Hey!' A voice woke him from his slumber. 'You've pinched our spot again.'

He rubbed his eyes. The two women he had seen last night were standing over him.

'Sorry,' he mumbled. 'But I was that tired.'

'Have you still not found anywhere else to sleep?' the older one asked him.

'No. I haven't looked,' he confessed. 'I've been to my ma's funeral today. I'm going off tomorrow. I'm going to leave 'district.'

He saw in the gloom that the women looked concerned. 'Going to seek your fortune, are you?' one of them asked.

'I might be,' he muttered. 'Don't see why not.'

'Tell you what,' the younger woman said. 'You can stop wi' us tonight.'

He gazed at them warily. His mother's warnings came into his mind. 'Erm, I can't pay you. I've got no money.'

They both grinned. 'We hear that all 'time; but we believe you. Go on,' the older woman said. 'Go to Leadenhall Square. Second house on 'right. You can't miss it. It's got a broken front door and a cracked upstairs window.'

'H-how will I get in?' he stammered. 'Can I have a key?'

'No.' She laughed. Her teeth were blackened and worn down to short uneven stubs. 'Door's always open. If you see Milly or any of 'other lasses there, tell 'em that Peg and Sissy sent you and that you're stopping 'night.'

He clambered to his feet, hanging on to Mrs Turner's blanket. 'Thanks,' he said. 'If you're sure it's all right?'

They both nodded and waved him away and he knew that they wanted him to leave so they could have their pitch back.

There were no street lights in Leadenhall Square, but most

of the houses had lamplight in the windows. At first he thought
that the second house on the right was derelict. The door was
broken, as Peg had said, but she hadn't said that it was hanging on by one hinge. The upstairs window was cracked, but
so was the one downstairs, and both were covered over with
cardboard. A young woman was sitting on the steps.

'What do you want?' she shouted at him as he approached.
'This your first time?'

'Peg and Sissy told me to come,' he said nervously. 'They
said I could stop here for tonight.'

She got to her feet. 'You what?' She sounded incredulous.
'For free?'

'Yeh. I haven't got any money and nowhere to stop. My ma's
just died.' He couldn't help the tremor in his voice and the
woman – only a girl, really, though older than him – gazed at
him curiously.

'Just for tonight, do you mean? Where will you go then?'

'I don't know. I was in their place – Peg and Sissy's. It was
'second time and they wanted me to move on.'

She sighed. 'So they sent you here! I don't know where you'll
sleep. There're no beds; you'll just have to find a corner somewhere. Better'n being outside, I suppose. Not comfortable on
'street, is it? I should know.'

She led him inside, into a narrow hall and through to a
kitchen. 'You can kip in here if you like. There's onny us comes
in here to mek a cuppa tea or summat. What's your name?'

The floor was bare, but under a rickety table covered in
crockery, bottles and bits of mouldy food was a thin rug. It
might be flea-ridden, he reckoned, but more comfortable
than lying on the cold ground he'd just vacated.

'Mikey,' he answered. 'Can I sleep under 'table?'

'If you like,' she said. 'But don't wake 'bairn.' She nodded
over to the corner of the room. A drawer was placed on two
chairs and in the drawer was a bundle. 'He'll sleep all night if
he's not disturbed.'

'Whose bairn is it?' he asked curiously.

'Mine,' she said belligerently. 'That's why I'm here and not out on 'streets. I look after him and 'house and mek sure no-body else comes in.'

'I see,' he muttered, though he didn't really. The girl looked too young to be the mother of a child. But what do I know? It's all a mystery to me. He thought back to Bridget crawling under his blanket, and the touch of her flesh. He'd been excited by and yet ashamed of the sensation that had come over him. Suppose, just suppose that he'd been undressed and not still in his clothes. He broke into a sweat. Might Bridget have become pregnant?

He was an innocent. His mother had made sure that he was. Don't be thinking unclean thoughts, Mikey, she had said often enough. And keep away from girls. They'll only get you into trouble.

'What's your name?' he asked the girl. 'Are you Milly?'

She nodded. 'Yeh. I came here when I was expecting. Peg and Sissy looked after me.'

'Where's your babby's da? Does he live here?' He was bothered that some man might come in and want to know why there was a strange lad asleep under the table.

Milly laughed. 'I don't know. I don't know where he is or who he is. Don't much care, either. He'd not help me out even if he turned up and claimed 'bairn as his own.'

Mikey stared at her. He remembered his father very well, even though he didn't come home from sea very often. Money was so scarce that he only ever took short leave before going back to a ship again, but Mikey recalled that he was always worried about leaving them all, especially their mother.

Milly sat on a wooden chair and crossed her legs. Mikey averted his eyes; she obviously didn't realize that her legs were showing almost up to her thigh. 'Have you got a lass?' She smiled as she asked it, her mouth turning up at the corners, and he thought how pretty she was, even though she was rather shabby and not very clean.

'A sister,' he said.

'No, I meant a girl friend; somebody you're walking out

with.' She laughed as she spoke. 'Somebody to have a kiss and cuddle with.'

Mikey blushed up to his hair roots. 'No.' He thought of Bridget, who had kissed him through the cell bars. 'No, I haven't.'

She laughed again. 'Still pure and chaste, are you? You do right to come here!' She put her head back and hooted.

Mikey hung his head. Was it a laughing matter? Should he have been with a girl by now? He hadn't felt the need before, although sometimes he had avoided the company of girls like Bridget because of the physical sensations that came over him.

'Sorry.' Milly wiped her eyes. 'It's just that I don't get to meet many wholesome, decent men.' She leaned forward and touched his hand, and he drew it away. 'I didn't mean to laugh at you,' she said soberly. 'It's just that I've been corrupted. I'm sixteen and I've never before met a man or boy who didn't want to tek me to bed.'

'I wouldn't know what to do,' he mumbled.

'Somebody'll teach you,' she said softly. 'Onny don't be in a hurry. There's plenty o' time. How old are you?'

'Thirteen and a half.'

She blew out her cheeks. 'That's how old I was when I went on 'streets. It's different for lads, though, unless they're on 'game as well.'

Mikey drew in a breath. There was a whole world out there of which he knew nothing. 'I'm leaving 'district,' he said hurriedly. 'I'll be gone in 'morning.'

'Don't worry,' she said. 'You can stop here as long as you want. Nobody'll bother you.' She smiled again and her cheeks dimpled. 'And nobody'll proposition you. We onny do it for money, not for pleasure.'

Mikey licked his lips. 'Just suppose.' He wasn't sure how to phrase the question, but guessed that Milly would know the answer. 'I mean – if a lass got under a lad's blanket, would she be doing it to keep warm or cos she wanted – well, summat else?'

She gazed at him. 'How old would this lass be? Is she just a bairn, or older?'

'Older than me. About fifteen, I suppose.' He felt himself growing hot again just at the thought of it.

'Oh, well, in that case, definitely because she wanted summat else.' She grinned at him and he felt himself smiling sheepishly back at her. 'That's what you'd call a proposition, and if she didn't want any money from you,' she added, 'it's definitely because she'd tekken a fancy to you.' She waved a finger at him. 'However! Watch out, cos a lass as bold as that can trick you and tie you down and expect you to set up house wi' her.'

Mikey nodded. That was probably what Bridget wanted. Or at least to get away from home. He contemplated. It wasn't what he wanted. The more he thought about it the more he wanted to leave this town and find adventure. 'Thanks,' he said. 'That's what I thought.'

Milly got up from the chair. 'I'll have to go. I've not earned any money tonight. Keep an eye on 'bairn, will you? I'll just be outside.'

'What if he wakes up?' he said in alarm. 'I might be asleep.'

She waved an airy hand. 'He'll wake you. He meks a racket like 'artillery.' She glanced over towards the makeshift cot. 'He's 'best bairn in 'world,' she said softly. 'And one day he'll mek his ma's fortune.'

Mikey slept like a baby himself. He opened his eyes once and saw the bare feet of the women as they sat round the table, and then he dropped off again. He felt safe and secure huddled into the blanket, and didn't wake until dawn crept in and he blinked as the early sunlight touched his face. He turned over and saw Milly asleep in a chair with her head bent over the child in her arms. One breast was bare as if she had been feeding him, and he thought sadly of his mother, whom he remembered feeding Ben and Tom when they were little.

I'll try to do right, Ma, he offered up on a silent prayer. I'll not do anything to disgrace your name, even though I've already been in prison. But I've a life to lead, and a living to make, and it'll not be easy to keep on 'straight and narrow. I'll try to make something of myself without harming anybody.

Milly stirred. Opening her eyes, she saw Mikey and covered her breast. It seemed a modest thing to do, he thought, considering the kind of work she was in. She gazed at him and he saw defiance.

'Sorry,' he murmured. 'I didn't mean to stare.' He swallowed, half in embarrassment and partly with the need to explain. 'But you look beautiful.'

She gazed at him, and then shook her head. 'What a strange lad you are, Mikey,' she said softly. 'Nobody has ever said that to me before.'

CHAPTER TEN

Mikey stayed with the women for three days. They'd insisted that he did. 'You're still upset about losing your ma,' Sissy told him. 'Stop wi' us for a couple o' days until you feel better. We'll feed you and you can sleep here nice and safe and run errands to pay us back. How does that sound?'

It sounded good to him, for he was very weary and overcome with emotion. He was comfortable with this band of women. Six of them stayed at the house, and others came and went. Some of them he shrank from for they were coarse, with evil manners and voices, and dirty in their habits. But the others, Milly, Peg and Sissy, did attempt to keep clean, pumping brackish water into the kitchen sink and washing their hands and faces. Sometimes they stripped off their outer garments and then he made an excuse to go out. He saw them smile as if they knew why, but they didn't say anything to embarrass him.

On the fourth morning, which was bright and sunny but windy, he decided to leave. He folded up the blanket and put it over his shoulder. 'I'm going,' he said. 'Thank you for letting me stop, but I'd best be on my way.'

'Oh, Mikey,' Milly said. 'We'll miss you, and so will little Walter.'

Mikey stroked the child's cheek. 'I'll miss him too.' He smiled. 'He was just getting to know me. I'll come and see you if I'm this way again.'

'If you mek your fortune you won't want to,' Peg said sagely. 'You'll not want to be seen wi' likes of us.'

'Unless we can help you in any way, Mikey,' Milly said cheekily. 'I'd be happy to oblige.'

He flushed. 'I'll remember that,' he said, and then grinned. 'I might tek you up on 'offer.'

'Do,' she bantered. 'It'll be my pleasure and I'll give you a special rate!'

Whatever would my ma think, he wondered as he left the house and ran down the steps. Would she be mad at me or would she be pleased that they'd looked after me? For that was what they had done. They'd taken him into their care when he was feeling sad and vulnerable. Bridget's mother had taken him in too, but she was quick to blame and not charitable enough to listen or understand.

So which way shall I go? Shall I set off for London or go to York? York is nearer and I could walk there if I can't get a lift. But will there be work? There'll be work in London; sure to be. But how to get there? He rubbed his chin and set off through the town, avoiding any thoroughfares where he might have been seen by neighbours or people who knew him, such as Bridget or her mother, or even his sister Rose.

If I had some money I could catch 'ferry to New Holland and go to London that way. That's 'quickest route unless you're lucky enough to afford 'train, which I'm not.

'Mikey! Mikey!'

He turned as the voice called him. 'Please don't let it be Bridget,' he muttered. 'I'll never get rid of her.' He turned and saw her waving, but it wasn't Bridget calling his name. It was Milly, and she reached him first.

'Mikey! Phew! I thought I'd never catch you.' Milly was breathless. 'Look,' she panted. 'We had a collection for you when we realized that you hadn't any money. Here.' She thrust a fist towards him. 'Two bob and threepence.' She grinned. 'Don't know how far you'll get on that.'

He took the money and impulsively kissed her. 'Thanks. I'll get to London now,' he said eagerly. 'That's what I was planning. Do you think it's enough for 'ferry across 'Humber? I can walk 'rest of way.'

'Walk!' she said incredulously. 'How brave you are, Mikey. Wait till I tell 'other lasses. They'll be that proud!'

'Well,' he said bashfully, 'that's 'intention, anyway!'

'Wait,' she said and fished in her skirt pocket. 'Here. Another penny. No, tek it. I'll mek some more tonight.'

He wavered. It didn't seem right. Ill-gotten gains; money for – money for . . . But she was gone, a quick wave and a garbled excuse that she had to get back to Walter, and he was left holding a handful of coins.

'Mikey.' Bridget came over. 'Who was that?'

'Nobody you know,' he said abruptly.

'Huh! I know that all right.' She was scornful. 'She's a street lass, en't she? I've seen her about on a night.'

Mikey didn't answer, only shrugged.

'What did she give you?'

'Nowt to do wi' you.'

Bridget eyed him suspiciously. 'It's usually 'other way round. Men give them summat. For their services,' she added.

'How do you know?' he retaliated. 'Who told you about such things?'

'I just know,' she said. 'I'm older than you so I know about women like that.'

Mikey turned away. 'Well you don't know everything and like I said, it's nowt to do wi' you. Anyway, I'm off. See you about.'

'Where you going, Mikey? Can I come?' She seemed anxious, yet eager.

'No,' he called over his shoulder. 'I'm going away and I don't know where.' He certainly wasn't going to tell her he was going to London, as she would want to come with him. 'I'm off to look for work.'

'Go on then, see if I care. You won't get far on your own,' she sneered. 'You was allus a mammy's boy. Allus being good!'

'What's wrong wi' that?' he snapped. 'My ma was a good

79

woman. She'd not have turned anybody away if they were in trouble.'

He didn't say 'like your mother did', but that's what he meant and she knew it.

'That was my fault,' she said contritely. 'I didn't mean to get you thrown out of 'house.' She gazed archly at him. 'Ma wants me to stay pure till I'm wed. She thinks I'll be a catch if I am.' Her lips turned down in a cynical gesture. 'As if any man would know!'

He turned to her one more time. 'Some might,' he said. 'They're not all like me. Cheerio, Bridget. Be seeing you.'

He walked away, leaving her looking forlornly after him. No, she thought. They're not all like you, Mikey. But where was he going? He was heading towards the pier. She gave a gasp. I know! He's going to catch 'ferry!

She turned swiftly and ran back home, hoping that her mother wouldn't be in. She flew through the door and gathered up her few belongings, a shawl and an underskirt with a few coppers sewn into the hem. Then she searched for a stub of pencil and a scrap of paper, but finding none she called up the stairs to the woman who lived in the room above.

'Mrs Brown! Mrs Brown!'

When an answering shout told her the woman was in, but too idle to come to the top of the stairs, she yelled up to her, 'Will you tell my ma I'm going away for a bit? Tell her I'll be all right.'

The door upstairs opened and a blowsy middle-aged woman appeared, smoking a pipe. 'Where you going then?'

'Away,' she said. 'I'll be gone for a bit. Going to look for a job.'

'That'll be the day,' the woman grunted. She turned back into her room and shut the door.

'Thanks, you old cow,' Bridget muttered. 'I'll do 'same for you sometime.'

She hurried back across the town and headed for the pier. Mikey could be catching a market boat, she thought, and not necessarily the New Holland ferry. But where's he got 'money

80

from, she wondered. Unless – what did that lass give him? She put something into his hand. Money. It had to be, but why? And where has he been since Ma threw him out?

She watched Mikey go into the ticket office and saw him come out a few minutes later looking down at something clasped in his hand. He's bought a ticket, she thought. He really is going away. How am I going to get on 'ferry? I don't have any money for 'fare.

Bridget had always been resourceful, artful some might have said, in getting her own way. If she was set on something then nothing would deter her, and she was set on Mikey. She checked the timetable on the wall and saw that she had twenty minutes before the boat departed.

She left the pier area and went round the corner of a building, arranged her shawl about her head and sat in the nearest doorway. With her head bent and her shoulders shaking, she began to rock and moan.

'Glory be to God,' she wailed softly. 'What am I to do?'

Several people passed her and glanced down. One or two men seemed about to stop but were urged on by their women-folk, then as she peered from under her shawl she saw a lone man coming her way. He was in his early forties, rather portly, and wearing a dark tailcoat and top hat.

She raised her eyes heavenwards, knowing how appealing they would be. The deepest green with dark-fringed lashes. 'What am I to do?' she moaned. 'Who can I turn to?'

The man stopped. His face was florid, as if he'd been hurrying. 'Something wrong, miss? Are you begging?'

Bridget scrambled to her feet. 'Indeed I'm not, sir,' she said in the sweetest Irish accent, filched from her mother. She wiped her eyes. 'I need to get across the water. I came over yesterday to visit a sick relative and when I came to hand over my ticket to the clerk today it had gone. Lost,' she wailed. 'And I don't know how to get home. My poor mammy will be waiting for me to bring her news of her dead sister.'

'Dead?' He stared at her. 'I thought you said a sick relative?'

81

'Sure I did.' Bridget dropped her voice. 'But my poor auntie passed away not ten minutes after I got there.' She broke into sobs. 'And I've no means of getting home.'

'So, erm, where's home?' His eyes flickered over her face. 'Do you mean you were going on the ferry?'

Haven't I just said, she thought. Are you thick or something? 'Yes,' she hiccuped. 'To New Holland. I can walk 'rest of 'way. But I can't walk on water!' She crossed herself reverently.

'Well.' He hesitated, and glanced round. 'I'm going across myself.'

'Oh, sir.' She reached to clutch his arm. 'If you'd be so kind as to lend me my fare and give me your address, I'd post it back to you tomorrow morning, honest to God.' She was about to cross herself again but then thought better of it. No point in over-egging, she considered. He might not be a believer.

She gazed at him appealingly, and as she saw the doubt disappear from his face she gave him the merest hint of a tender coaxing smile.

'Come on then,' he said, yielding. 'Let's get the tickets. It's nearly sailing time.'

Bridget scurried after him. 'You're so kind. I'm so grateful.'

'Are you?' He turned and gave her a grin. 'How grateful?'

She lowered her eyes. 'I'm not sure what you mean, sir.'

He gave a low laugh. 'I think you do. How badly do you need to cross over into Lincolnshire? I know I'll never see my money again.'

As she gazed up at him now, she saw that he was no gentleman. He was well dressed, but didn't have the air, or the manners either, of a real gentleman. He's probably just a jumped-up clerk in a shipping office, she decided.

'I need to get on that ferry,' she said softly. 'What payment do you need? Sir,' she added.

'That's more like it,' he said. 'I'll let you know once we're on board.'

*   *   *

Mikey leaned over the rail of the paddle steamer and looked down at the choppy water. He breathed in deeply. He was sure he could smell the sea. Couldn't smell the aroma of seed oil or factory waste, anyway. Across the water he could see the low-lying Lincolnshire coastline. A few buildings, one or two chimneys belching out smoke, but otherwise it looked quite empty. Shan't stop there, he thought. I'll need a bit of company. But it's a starting point and I'll ask for the London road.

He felt a surge of excitement in the pit of his stomach at the prospect. I'll come back one day, of course. He turned round and leaned against the rail to look back at the pier head before the ferry departed, and saw Bridget coming across the gangplank in the company of a man.

'Dammit,' he muttered. 'She's followed me.'

He saw her look his way but she didn't acknowledge him and he was puzzled. Who's she with? It's nobody I know, and where did she get 'money for 'ticket? A faint suspicion filled his head when he saw the man put his hand on Bridget's waist and usher her towards the saloon.

I don't want to be responsible for anybody else. She's a girl. I'll have to look after her and how will I find work with her tagging on?

He dug his hands deep into his trouser pockets and jingled the remaining money. She'll be a liability. Then he jumped as the ship's steam whistle blew a warning and the last few passengers came running. The water churned beneath the paddles, throwing up sparkling frothy foam, and he caught his breath in anticipation at the knowledge that he was on his way at last. To where and what? It didn't seem to matter. It was going to be exciting anyway.

'Cheerio, Hull,' he murmured, his throat tight. 'See you again sometime.'

CHAPTER ELEVEN

Bridget had intended to ditch the stranger as soon as she was on board ship but he kept hold of her, ushering her towards the saloon. Except that he didn't enter, but steered her further along the companionway and into a corner, where he pinned her against the bulkhead.

'Now,' he whispered into her ear. 'Stay quite still until we set off.' As he spoke she heard the shriek of the ship's whistle and felt the throb of the paddles as they began to turn. 'Nobody'll take any notice of us,' he went on. 'The crew will be occupied and the passengers finding their seats.'

'Wh-what 'you doing?' she gasped. 'I can't breathe. Move off a bit!'

He smiled. 'And let you escape? Have you forgotten already that you owe me?'

'I said I'll pay you back,' she protested, struggling against him.

'Lift your skirt,' he commanded. 'Come on, there's nobody looking.'

She stared at him. 'Here? Are you mad? Wait till we're off 'ship, why don't you?'

'I'd not see you for dust,' he grinned, and began unbuttoning his trousers.

'Yes, you will. Honest.' She began to panic. This wasn't meant to happen. Bold, flirtatious and saucy as she knew she was, she was still a virgin. 'Somebody'll see us.' What if Mikey should come, and find them? Or the captain? But no one did. The passengers it seemed had settled into the saloon or were leaning over the rails breathing in the salty air.

He roughly pulled up her skirt and pressed himself against her. 'Come on,' he demanded. 'You know what to do.'

'I don't,' she protested. 'You're hurting me.'

He licked his lips and she saw his eyes gleam. 'Don't tell me you haven't done this before? A brazen young madam like you? What are you, just a tease?'

She shook her head and tried to push him away, but it only seemed to make him more excited and he pushed harder and harder into her.

A crewman went by and glanced in their direction. He whistled and muttered, 'Go it, mate,' and walked on. Bridget opened her mouth to shout out but the stranger put his hand over it, stopping her breath.

'Come on,' he urged. 'You're enjoying it, you know you are.' Just as she felt that she was being torn in two, his face became red and he started to grunt and pant. She wanted to scream; she felt as if she was on fire as he plunged deeper and deeper into her, gripping her buttocks with his sharp fingernails; and then suddenly it was over. He withdrew, leaving her sore and bleeding. She screwed up her eyes and pressed her lips together, trying not to cry.

He glanced over his shoulder and buttoned himself up. 'Told you nobody would come, didn't I?' He laughed. 'Good thing my wife isn't on board!'

'Bastard!' she muttered.

He grinned. 'Well I enjoyed it. Haven't been with a virgin in a long time.' He flicked imaginary specks from his jacket. 'I honestly thought you were on the game. I didn't believe that tale about your sick auntie. Or your Irish accent! I could meet you again, if you like.' He put his hand in his pocket and drew out a sixpence. 'Here,' he said. 'Go and treat yourself.'

'And you can jump up and bite your arse,' she hissed at him, but snatched the coin from his hand. 'You forced me. I would have paid you back.'

85

He pinched her cheek. 'I don't think so,' he said. 'And as for forcing you, I reckon you didn't need much forcing. You were ripe for it. I just happened along at the right time.' He straightened himself up. 'Cheerio,' he said. 'Be seeing you.'

'Not if I see you first,' she retaliated. 'Get lost!'

When he had gone, Bridget staggered to the rail and leaned over it, breathing in great gulps of air. She felt sick and very sore. *I didn't know it would be like that. I thought it would be thrilling and passionate. Perhaps it is with somebody you care for or maybe it's always like this 'first time.* Her eyes prickled with tears. She had enticed men before but had never allowed them to go too far. *It's your own fault, Bridget Turner,* she thought pragmatically. *It was bound to happen sooner or later, but I'd like to have chosen with which man. But there, it's done with now. I'm a woman not a girl.*

She spent ten minutes or so composing herself and then sauntered round the deck, coming across Mikey leaning on the ship's rail. 'Hello, Mikey. Fancy seeing you here!'

He turned, reluctantly it seemed to her. *Perhaps he'd seen her come aboard with a man. Maybe he's jealous,* she thought hopefully.

'You can't come wi' me, Bridget,' were his first words. 'I told you I was going to look for work.'

'I know. I know!' she said. 'But I'm seeking work too so we could travel together. You don't have to watch out for me,' she added. 'I can watch out for myself. I'm older than you.'

He shrugged and turned back to look over the water and the nearing Lincolnshire shore. 'Suit yoursen,' he muttered. 'But I'm heading for London.'

'London! That's miles away! I could come wi' you,' she said, as he knew she would. 'Go on, Mikey,' she urged. 'Let me. I won't be a bother and I'd be company for you.'

'I said suit yoursen, didn't I?' he said irritably, but a small part of him thought that it would be quite good to have company, though Bridget wouldn't have been his first choice. 'But you'll have to fend for yoursen.'

'I will,' she said. 'I know how.' She sat down on the bench near him, wincing and giving a small gasp as she did so.

He looked down at her. 'What's up?'

She shook her head. 'Nowt. I'm a woman, en't I? Sometimes we get stomach cramps.' She gave a dismissive gesture. 'We cope wi' it.'

'Have you got any money?' he asked, as the ferry docked at the end of the journey.

'A tanner,' she said, fingering the sixpence the stranger had given her. 'And a few coppers.'

'Shan't get far wi' that,' he muttered.

'No,' she said vaguely as she spotted the stranger waving to a woman on the shore. 'But I might be able to get some more. Wait for me, Mikey,' she said urgently. 'Wait on 'dockside. Don't go wi'out me.'

She dashed away and he saw her weaving her way through the passengers waiting to alight. What's she up to, he wondered. Where's she going?

'Hello again,' Bridget said, and the man jumped, startled, as she came next to him.

'What do you want?' He glanced nervously towards the dockside. 'I'm in a hurry.'

She linked her arm in his. 'You know when you said we could meet again? Well, perhaps I'd like that, after all.'

He shrugged her off. 'Yes, but not now,' he muttered. 'I'm being met.'

'Really?' She affected surprise. 'Your wife, is it? Perhaps you'd introduce us.' She gazed up at him. 'What would she think, eh, if she thought you'd been – you know? Wi' me?'

He stared at her, a horrified expression on his face. 'She – you wouldn't,' he blustered. 'She wouldn't believe you.'

Bridget pouted. 'She'd wonder though, wouldn't she? No smoke wi'out fire? And that crewman that went by, he'd know it was true. He wouldn't know you'd forced me, of course; I'd have to admit to that.' Her mouth turned down and tears filled her eyes. 'And me a good Catholic girl.'

There was a thud as the gangplank hit the ground. 'All right,' he said hastily. 'How much?'

She made a moue. 'Five bob?'

He took a breath. 'It wasn't worth that much!'

'It was to me,' she said. 'You took my virginity. It was worth all of that.'

He fumbled in his pocket as he was jostled by people anxious to be off, and looked down at the coins in his hand. 'Four shillings,' he said. 'That's all I've got.'

She took the silver. 'Look in your other pocket,' she said nonchalantly, as if she had all the time in the world.

Muttering, he did so and brought out sixpence and a silk handkerchief.

'That'll do,' she said, taking them both. 'Go on then.' She smiled sweetly. 'Go and meet your lady wife, and don't forget to look behind you.'

He hurried off and Bridget laughed as she saw him dash down the gangplank and greet the woman, then glance behind him before urging her away towards a waiting cabriolet.

Bridget ambled down to the dockside and then began to hurry as she saw Mikey pacing impatiently. 'Mikey,' she called. 'I'm here. Sorry. Had a call o' nature.'

'Come on then,' he said. 'Let's be off. I'd like to be in Lincoln by nightfall.'

'He's coming, poor lamb.' Nanny peered from behind the window drapes as the chaise drew up at the door. Simon had suffered the ignominy of travelling by public coach from school to the railway station, and now a hired vehicle was transporting him and his luggage on the last lap of his journey.

Eleanor peered from beneath Nanny's arm. 'I hope Papa doesn't beat him,' she said softly. 'I so hate it when Simon cries.' And he takes it out on me sometimes if he thinks I've heard him, she thought. The last two times Simon had been beaten by his father he had held Eleanor against the wall afterwards and punched her in the stomach and warned her not to tell anyone.

'We must be patient with him,' Nanny said. 'Though it will be difficult if we can't speak to him.'

Eleanor opened the door to her room just a crack and listened intently for the sound of voices. She heard her father giving terse instructions and she could imagine him standing in front of Mary telling her that the servants mustn't speak to Simon either. Then she heard her brother dragging his bag up the stairs. She turned a tearful face to Nanny. 'Poor Simon,' she said. 'Whatever will he do?'

Simon passed her door and looked in. He lifted his top lip sneeringly. 'I'm to unpack, wash and change and then go down for a beating,' he muttered and, as Eleanor took a gasping breath, added scornfully, 'Nobody need think I'm scared of that, because I'm not.' He glanced at Nanny, and Eleanor saw him give a hard swallow and blink his eyes before moving on.

Nanny tutted and shook her head, then sighed. 'Nothing we can do, my dear. I'm afraid he's brought it on himself.'

Eleanor hung about the landing, unable to concentrate on anything but Simon, even though Miss Wright had set her some schoolwork. If only I could speak to him, she thought, I would tell him that I am his friend as well as his sister. What would I do, I wonder, if this was happening to me? I would be very unhappy, I know that. And I think – yes, I know, she mused, that I would probably run away.

Simon's door opened and closed and Eleanor waited as he came towards her. He put his face close to hers. 'Going to listen for me crying, are you?' he hissed. She shook her head and mouthed *no*. Then she put out her hand to his. For a second he looked at it and then dashed it away. 'Don't need your pity,' he muttered. 'Don't need anybody's.'

She watched him walk defiantly down the stairs and then went back into her room and closed the door.

I'll not cry, Simon thought. I'll not give him that satisfaction. Right now he hated his father. He hated his teachers too. Especially those who he knew enjoyed giving physical pain.

Why should I be beaten because I can't answer a question? He had on occasion challenged his tutors, which had led to another stroke of the cane. I'm not academic, not scientific. I like art. I'd like to paint. But that isn't considered a suitable profession for the only son of a lawyer.

His father waited for him in his study. On his desk was a black cane Simon hadn't seen before. A small frown creased his forehead. Surely it hadn't been purchased especially to punish him? He watched as his father picked it up from the desk, testing its strength by flexing it between his hands. Then he thwacked it in the air with a swift whistling stroke, making Simon flinch.

'So have you anything to say in mitigation before I use this deterrent?' he asked coldly. 'Can you give me any reason why I should not punish you? I have received nothing but bad reports from your headmaster. They do not want you there any longer.'

'Good,' Simon said rebelliously. 'I'm glad to leave, Father. I hated it there and always did. I begged you to let me leave.' His voice cracked, his resolve failing as he saw his father's face redden.

'How dare you?' his father bellowed. 'How dare you question my judgement?'

Simon remained silent. His father didn't want an answer. He only wanted submission. Best to get on with it.

'I have ordered everyone in this household not to speak to you.' His father's voice was barely controlled, trembling with anger or passion. 'You will be sent to Coventry. No one must speak to you, and you must not speak to them. Is that understood?'

Simon merely nodded, understanding now why Eleanor was acting so strangely.

'Yes, Father,' he answered.

'And you will come down here every morning before you are sent to your new school and I will decide what form your punishment will take. Now. Hold out your hands.'

CHAPTER TWELVE

Simon's palms were cracked and bleeding. Never had he felt such pain. He wept when he got back to his room, and buried his face in the pillow. 'He's a sadist. And he said I shall get this again tomorrow unless I mend my ways. Well I shan't,' he sobbed. 'I shan't.'

The door opened quietly but he didn't look up. It's Eleanor, he thought. Come to gloat. But it was his mother, not his sister, who knelt by the bed and put her arm over him, her head close to his. He turned over and submitted to her tearful embrace. She can't speak to me, he thought, but she's here. He felt the comfort of her lips as she gently kissed his bleeding hands.

She got up and went out of the room and a few minutes later came back with a cloth and a bowl of warm water. She tenderly bathed his palms, which stung as she wet them, then covered them with salve. She tapped her mouth with her finger to acknowledge her silence, then blew him a kiss as she left.

A few minutes later the door opened again, and Eleanor slipped inside. 'I'm not supposed to speak to you,' she whispered. 'So you must promise not to tell. I'm so sorry, Simon.'

'No, you're not,' he muttered. 'It's all right for you being at home. You don't have to go to school.'

She shook her head. 'It's not all right,' she said in a low voice. 'It's quite hateful really.'

As they sat together, not speaking, the door suddenly crashed open and their father stood like a demon in the doorway. 'I knew it,' he bellowed. 'I knew I would be disobeyed. Get out of here.' He glared at Eleanor and pointed to the doorway.

'Father, I only came to see—'

'Out, I say.' He looked so angry she was afraid that he would lash out at her. She cast a scared glance at Simon and scurried out.

'Did she speak to you?' his father demanded.

'She only came to see if I was all right,' Simon muttered, his face and neck flushing.

'Did she speak to you?' he repeated. 'Stand up when I'm talking to you!'

Simon cowered, trembling, in front of him. 'No,' he lied. 'She just came to look at me.'

'Liar!' His father's hand struck so hard across Simon's face that he staggered. 'Did she speak?'

Simon nodded, holding his cheek, unable to hold back the tears. 'Yes,' he mumbled. 'But you're not to hit her.'

'I don't hit women or girls,' his father retaliated grimly. 'I shall find some other punishment for her; and as for you, it will be bread and water for the rest of the day and you can look forward to another taste of the cane in the morning.'

He turned on his heel and left, leaving Simon sweating over the promised punishment and full of shame for letting his sister down.

Eleanor was summoned to appear in the drawing room. She was very afraid. Her father, she knew, would have tried to winkle out of Simon whether she had spoken to him. She clasped her fingers together. Will he have told? Will I get the cane? She had seen Simon's red hands though he had tried to hide them from her. She knocked on the door and waited for permission to enter.

Her mother sat on the sofa. Her face was white and strained-looking and she didn't look up as Eleanor entered. Eleanor dipped her knee to her father, who was standing by the fire-place.

'I have been disobeyed,' he said without preamble. 'My

instructions were that your brother was not to be spoken to. You wilfully flouted or sought to ignore that command.'

Eleanor hung her head. So Simon told of me, she thought. How could he? She didn't speak. She now knew well enough that if she did she would be in even more trouble.

'You will of course be punished,' her father went on. His voice was cold and unflinching, which she thought was more terrifying than when he shouted.

'I have told your mother that, like your brother, you will be given bread and water and not be allowed contact with anyone until such time as I decide.'

Eleanor lifted her head, her lips parted. No supper? And I'm so hungry. 'Yes, Papa,' she murmured.

'And,' her father continued, 'don't think that is the end of the matter. You are to come with me.' He marched towards the door and Eleanor cast an anxious glance at her mother. Where am I to be taken? Her mother lifted her head and in answer to Eleanor's unspoken plea shook her head, causing tendrils of hair round her face to tremble.

She was ushered up the stairs. They went up one flight to the bedrooms and then up another to the schoolroom floor and then up again to the top attic. Where are we going, she wondered, thinking that there was only the maids' room up here. But on her previous visit she had missed seeing the low door on the landing.

Her father took a key from his pocket and bent down to unlock it. Eleanor peered inside. There were piles of papers and files stacked from the floor to the top of the eaves into which the cupboard was set. She looked enquiringly at her father. Was it her task to sort through the papers? Not a punishment, she considered, for she would quite enjoy doing that. She thought that perhaps they were legal documents, for some were of thick yellowing parchment.

'You'll stay here until bedtime,' her father said. 'And you will not make a sound. If you do you will be here until morning.'

She looked at him. What did he mean?

'Get inside,' he commanded. 'Go on.'

'Inside?' she said. 'But how? There's not much room.'

He took her by the arm and pushed her in. 'It's not meant to be comfortable,' he said. 'It is meant for your discipline. You can reflect on your disobedience whilst you are in there and consider that even if I do not succeed in breaking your brother's will, I shall most certainly break yours.'

She could barely turn round. 'Papa!' she protested. 'I don't like the dark. I shan't be able to breathe.'

'Nonsense,' he said, closing the door on her. 'Of course you can.'

Eleanor heard the key turn in the lock. 'Please, Papa. Don't lock me in. I promise I'll be good.'

'I have just said that you must be quiet,' he thundered. 'Or you will be here until tomorrow.'

She heard his footsteps on the uncarpeted floor of the landing, and then going down the stairs, and then she could hear nothing, only feel the pounding of her beating heart. She began to panic. Suppose I suffocate? No one would know. If I scream who would hear me? Not the maids down in the kitchen. Not Nanny, because she's deaf, and even if she did, what could she do? And Mama will be too frightened to ask Papa where I am.

Tears rushed down her face as she began to sob. The whole of her body heaved and shook as she curled in the small space. 'I don't like the dark,' she whimpered. 'I'm frightened.'

A little later there came a soft tapping on the door and a whisper of words. Eleanor tried to control her weeping. 'Wh-who is it?'

'It's me.' Her brother's voice was low. 'Sorry, Eleanor. I didn't mean to tell of you.'

'I'm frightened,' she said. 'I might die.'

'No, you won't,' he whispered back. 'There's a gap in the eaves where a draught blows through. I was put in there when I was about eight, just before I was sent away to school. That's how I knew where you'd be.'

'It's dark,' she protested. 'I can't see.'

94

'Yes, but some light creeps under the door. You'll get accustomed to it eventually. Listen, Eleanor, I want to tell you something.'

'No. Don't tell me,' she said quickly. 'He'll get it out of me.'

'Oh!' He sounded disappointed. 'I suppose you're right. I don't want to get you into any more trouble.'

'No,' she said tearfully. 'I'm to miss supper, and can only have bread and water.'

'Me too,' he murmured. 'I've got to go, Eleanor, before I get found out. Keep your pecker up.' She gave a hiccuping sob as she recognized one of Nanny's favourite sayings.

Simon was right about the light. A pale strip of light slid under the door, but it didn't last for long as the window on the top landing was small and the light outside was fading fast. Soon she was in total darkness. She shuffled about, feeling the stacks of papers, and lifted a pile of them down to make a cushion, for the floor was hard and uncomfortable. She had to sit with her knees either up to her chin or else tucked under her, as there wasn't enough room to stretch out. She leaned back against the wedge of files and bound documents and waited. And waited.

In spite of the slight draught which came in as Simon said it would, the stack of papers insulated the cupboard, making it quite airless. She dropped into an intermittent doze, waking up from time to time with cramp in her legs, needing to shift her position. I've been here for hours, she thought. Has Papa forgotten me? She heard the clatter of footsteps running upstairs and listened intently. It's not Papa; his shoes don't make that sound. Not Simon either as he'll be wearing his indoor slippers. One of the maids then?

She put her ear to the door; yes, the door to the maids' room opened and closed and then a few minutes later opened and closed again and the clatter of boots sounded down the stairs. Eleanor sighed. One of them must have forgotten something and had to come upstairs for it. She occupied some time wondering what might cause the maid to run upstairs at that time of the early evening. A clean handkerchief perhaps? Or maybe she had torn a stocking and had to come up for another. She wasn't upstairs long enough to darn it. Or perhaps she was going to serve supper and needed a clean cap. I wonder what they are having for supper. I'm so hungry. And thirsty.

Eleanor slept and then woke again. Her throat was parched and she wanted to use the lavatory. I don't know how much longer I can wait. She began to cry, dry racking sobs. They've forgotten me. I shan't be missed until breakfast when Nanny will wonder where I am.

A door banged downstairs. The front door? Who would bang it like that? What was the time? Had they had supper? The door banged again and she could hear someone shouting. Her father? It had to be; no one else in the household shouted like that. Running footsteps came up the stairs and she heard the maids' breathless voices.

'I've already looked, I told you,' one of them said. 'I even looked under 'bed.'

'Well we have to look again. And if he's here you're in right trouble.'

Eleanor heard the door to the maids' room open again, the sound of furniture being moved, and then their voices. 'Well, I don't know,' said one. 'I can't think where else to look.'

They paused outside the cupboard door and Eleanor held her breath. 'Can't be in there, it's allus kept locked,' the other girl said. 'And we don't have a key. Come on, we'd best get down or we'll be in bother.'

'No. Wait!' Eleanor called, desperate at last to break the silence. She banged on the door. 'Please! Ask my father to let me out.'

'Who's that?' Eleanor felt that someone had bent down to peer through the keyhole. 'Who's in there? Not Miss Eleanor?'

'Yes,' she wept. 'I'm locked in. Please ask my father to let me out.'

There was a shocked silence and then one of the maids, Eleanor thought it was Mary, said, 'Who put you in there, Miss Eleanor?'

'My father.' She could barely speak. 'Tell him I'm sorry and I'll never disobey him again.'

'Poor little lass,' the other maid said in a whisper, but loud enough for Eleanor to hear. 'What a way to treat a bairn.'

'We'll fetch him, Miss Eleanor,' Mary said. 'But be prepared. He's in a foul temper. Your brother Simon has disappeared.'

Her father came storming up the stairs a short while later. He rattled the key in the lock and opened the cupboard door. Eleanor fell out, ashamed and upset as the stench of urine on the parchment and her soggy clothes followed her. Her father stood back, wrinkling his nose in distaste. 'Prepare a bath for her,' he ordered Mary, who had followed him upstairs. 'And then,' he told Eleanor in a cold, severe voice, 'you will come down to the drawing room. I want a word with you.'

Eleanor licked her dry lips. 'Yes, Papa.' She tried to stand but her legs gave way beneath her and Mary bent to help her up as her father turned and went downstairs.

'Whatever have you been up to to deserve such a punishment?' the maid whispered. 'You must have been really naughty.'

Eleanor shook her head. It was too much effort to speak, her throat was so dry. 'Water,' she rasped.

'Let's get you back to your room and then you can have a drink. Nanny'll look after you. She's been down to 'kitchen several times, asking where you were.'

Nanny gave her a long drink of water and a slice of raisin bread, and then Eleanor succumbed to her ministrations, weeping copious tears as the old lady helped her into the bath and washed her red and swollen face, then put her into her night clothes. 'You can go downstairs in your dressing robe just this once,' she said. 'And tell your father I said so,' she added firmly. 'Locking a child in a cupboard!' she tutted. 'I've been looking all over the house for you.'

A few minutes later, Eleanor stood before her father. He was alone in the drawing room. 'I'm sorry, Papa,' she murmured. 'I'll never . . . never . . .' What was it I did, she thought, confused and fearful. 'I'll never disobey you again.'

Her father nodded, but didn't look at her. 'I trust you have learned your lesson.' He lifted his chin. 'But what I want to know now, and remember the punishment if I should find you lying, is do you know where your brother is?'

Eleanor shook her head. 'In his room?'

'He is not in his room! Did he come upstairs? Did he tell you where he was going?'

Her lips parted. Simon had wanted to tell her something. What a good thing she had told him not to. 'I don't know what you mean, Father. I haven't seen Simon since we were in his room. Before my punishment, I mean.'

That bit was true. She hadn't seen anyone from the pitch black cupboard. And Simon hadn't told her where he was going. 'Where can he be, Father? Doesn't Mama know?'

'Your mother has gone to lie down. She is unwell. Your brother, Eleanor, appears to have run away.'

CHAPTER THIRTEEN

They didn't reach Lincoln that evening. Mikey had had no idea that it would take so long, and he thought, to be fair to Bridget, that she hadn't held him up at all, even shortening their journey by flagging down a waggon and asking for a lift. She'd waved to the driver and shouted hello, giving her most winning smile and asking if he would give her and her brother a ride. 'Our ma will be having a duck fit,' she'd said. 'She expected us home hours ago.'

'Why did you say I was your brother?' Mikey asked after they had got down and waved the waggoner goodbye.

'Because otherwise he might have thought we'd run away.' She smirked. 'You know. To be together.'

'Rubbish!' Mikey said. 'Why'd he think that? He'd see we're not old enough.' Though as he looked sideways at Bridget, he thought that perhaps a man wouldn't be able to guess her age.

It was almost dark by the time they arrived in the medieval town of Lincoln the next evening, and the towering cathedral was etched against the night sky. They were very tired, having slept in a spinney the previous night and been awakened early by the cucketing cry of pheasants; they were also very hungry, having eaten only bread given to them by a villager whose door they had knocked on begging for water.

They wandered about, not knowing which direction to take, but needing food and shelter for the night. 'We'll go up to

99

'cathedral,' Mikey said. 'We should be able to find somewhere to sleep there.' He was thinking of his former bed beneath St Mary's arch. 'And then we'll move on in 'morning.'

'I want summat to eat first,' Bridget moaned. 'I'm starving.' She looked about her. 'Over there, look. See that old bridge with shops on it? You stop here, and I'll go and get us some food.'

Mikey waited, looking about him at the timber-framed buildings and the people scurrying about their business. It's just 'same as at home, he thought. I suppose life is 'same wherever you are. You've got to work and you've got to eat.

Bridget returned in triumph ten minutes later. 'I've got a penny loaf, half a meat pie and two slices of sweet cake.'

Mikey's jaw dropped. 'You said you'd onny got a tanner.'

She gave a little shrug. She hadn't told him about the black-mail money the stranger had given her. 'Baker was shutting up shop,' she said. 'He wanted rid of 'em. Come on, let's find somewhere to sit and eat.'

They traipsed up an extremely steep hill towards the cathedral. Both puffed and panted, their lungs bursting and their legs aching, being used only to the flatness of the Hull streets.

'I shall have to stop,' Bridget gasped, halfway up. 'I've no breath left.'

'Nearly there,' Mikey wheezed. 'Come on. We can lean against 'wall. Think of all that feasting in front of us.'

Neither of them could speak when they reached the top and collapsed on the ground to lean against a wall outside the cathedral.

'I need a drink,' Mikey said at last. 'There'll be a pump somewhere.' He went off to look and came back shortly with his face wet. 'Just over there.' He pointed. 'Go on, tek a drink and then we'll eat.'

Bridget did, but first relieved herself in some bushes. 'Oh!' she sighed, blowing out her lips. 'That's better.'

They ate their fill, leaving one slice of sweet cake for the morning, and Mikey said it was the best meal he had ever

100

tasted. Bridget looked smug, but didn't comment that he might have gone hungry but for her.

The night was damp, but they found shelter in a walled area within the cathedral grounds and were so tired they fell asleep almost immediately. They awoke to birdsong, and after drinking from the pump they shared the slice of cake.

'I think we should move off now,' Mikey said. 'With a bit of luck we might get another lift, like yesterday.'

Bridget agreed. She'd done a mental calculation of the money she had left and knew there wasn't enough to pay for transport, so they'd have to beg a lift. On their wanderings round the town when they'd arrived last night they had seen people scurrying towards the grey brick station with its tall ornate chimneys, but they knew that such travel was for the well-off, not for urchins such as them.

They saw the town gate as they moved off; the Stonebow, it was called, and the guildhall was above it. Bridget crossed herself when she saw the stone figures of the Archangel Gabriel and the Virgin Mary in the niches in the wall. She generally pooh-poohed any form of religion, but thought that perhaps it wouldn't do any harm to show a little respect under the circumstances.

'We'll make for Nottingham,' Mikey decided. 'I don't know where next.' He wasn't confident about the rest of the journey. 'We'll have to ask 'way to London.'

Bridget had no idea at all of geography. Her life had been spent in Hull and she could find her way blindfolded down every street and alleyway of that town. She had known that Lincoln was across the estuary and London was a long way off. Of anywhere else, she knew nothing.

'We'll have to look at 'milestones, Mikey,' she said. 'They'll tell us how far it is.'

They passed through quiet villages and deserted hamlets, past ancient churches, old farmhouses and country inns; skirted streams and duck ponds, and travelled along country roads and lanes. They saw few people and didn't speak to any, though they saw farm workers out in the fields gathering in the harvest.

'Lincolnshire is isolated,' Mikey commented as they sat on the verge to rest their feet. 'It's like East Yorkshire. Folks don't travel through. They onny come if they want to be here.'

Bridget turned a weary expression to him. 'How do you mean?'

'Well.' He struggled to explain the conclusion he had come to. 'Folks coming into Lincolnshire from 'south get as far as 'Humber estuary, and have to stop or else cross over it. And if they cross it, say on 'ferry, they come into East Yorkshire and if they keep going they'll reach Spurn Point and 'sea. They can't get any further, you see, unless they tek a boat.'

'Oh,' Bridget said. 'So those who live here must really like it, mustn't they?'

Mikey nodded. 'Yeh, I suppose so. Unless they were born here and nivver moved.' He got to his feet. 'Come on. We're not going to mek our fortune here, not unless we become farmers.'

'Farm labourers, you mean.' Bridget pointed across meadow land to a great house in the distance. 'Look at that acreage! How could anybody be so rich as to own all of that?'

'Lucky, I suppose,' Mikey said. 'Or else have a rich da or grandda. It's lovely,' he murmured. 'So peaceful.'

'And boring,' Bridget scoffed. 'What do folk do all day?'

'They work!' Mikey was indignant. 'They don't just look at 'scenery all day. They work on 'land, no matter what 'weather's like, or dig ditches and drains and look after hosses. All sorts of jobs.'

'How do you know?'

'I just do,' he muttered. 'Somebody's got to grow corn and vegetables and keep pigs and cattle. How would we eat other-wise?'

Bridget shrugged. 'Don't know,' she said. 'Hadn't thought about it.'

The traffic became heavier as they approached Nottingham, many vehicles overtaking them as well as coming towards them; some of the vehicles coming from Nottingham were waggons pulling animal transporters or trailers piled high with machinery, or donkey drays loaded with canvas. There were also several horseback riders.

'They've been to 'Goose Fair! We'll miss Hull Fair,' Bridget complained. 'That's where they're heading. I allus go. Never missed afore!'

'Well, ask if they'll give you a lift back,' Mikey said grumpily. 'You don't have to come wi' me.'

A young dark-haired girl riding a Pinto waved to them and called hello. Mikey waved back, but Bridget only scowled. 'Is she a gyppo, do you think?'

'Romany, you mean. Yes, I think so.'

'Anyway, I didn't say I didn't want to come wi' you,' Bridget continued. 'I onny said we were missing Hull Fair.'

Mikey didn't answer. Seeing the fair folk reminded him how he too always went to the fair with his mother and brothers and sister. They had little money to spend but that didn't matter as they soaked up the atmosphere of music and drumbeat and rifle shot, the trumpeting of elephants and the roar of tigers. Dancing girls in bright costumes enticing visitors in to see their show, showmen cracking whips; such sights and sounds were all for free and the memory of them saddened him.

It was a warm dry night and they slept in the open again, but the following morning, as they began the next leg of their journey, the rain began; light drizzle at first but then increasing to a downpour. They became so wet that they hurried off the road into a plantation of oak trees to shelter beneath the canopy, where the rain didn't penetrate.

'We're miles and miles away from London, aren't we?' Bridget shivered. 'When do you think we'll get there?'

'Dunno.' Mikey was despondent. 'I've been wondering whether to try for a job o' work in Nottingham. Just to tide us ower, you know. Mebbe earn a copper or two to afford a bit o' dinner.' He only had a few coins left of the money that Milly had given him. He'd save it for a rainy day, he'd thought, but it was raining now. Bucketing down.

'I've got some money left,' Bridget admitted. 'When we get to Nottingham we'll spend it on a hot dinner.'

Mikey was about to ask where the money had come from when she suddenly called out, 'Look, there's a waggon coming over.'

He looked up to see a two-horse waggon trundling towards them. The driver sat in front, his shoulders covered in a waterproof cape, and in the back of the waggon someone was sitting hunched up under a sack.

'Hey up!' the driver called to them. 'Room for us?'

'Plenty,' Mikey called back. 'You going far?'

The driver wiped his streaming face with his soft hat. 'Aye. To Nottingham town.' He indicated the back of the cart with his thumb. 'But this young feller's getting soaked so I said I'd stop until the rain eased up a bit.'

The sack was thrown off and a fair head appeared. A youth of about Mikey's age looked out at them. 'I'm wet through,' he said. 'I should have brought my mackintosh.'

A swell, Mikey thought, noting the boy's accent and the fact that he could afford a proper raincoat. 'Where're you heading?' he asked.

The youth hesitated. 'I'm hitching to see my aunt in Nottingham.' He glanced towards the driver. 'My parents are dead and I'm hoping she'll let me stay for a while. What about you?'

'We're going to London,' Bridget interrupted.

The boy jumped down from the waggon and stretched himself. 'I'm going to London too as a matter of fact,' he murmured, his back to the driver. 'But I don't want to tell the driver in case anybody questions him about me.'

'Who would do that?' Mikey asked. 'Are you in trouble?'

'I will be if my father finds me,' the boy muttered, his voice full of cynicism. 'I've run away from home. Have you? Is that why you're on the road?'

'No,' Mikey said. 'I haven't. I haven't a home to run from, and Bridget . . .' He hesitated.

'I haven't run away.' Bridget tossed her head. 'I left a message for my ma that I was going away for a bit. But I'm old enough to leave home anyway,' she added truculently.

'Well, if this waggoner'll give us a lift, we could mebbe travel together?' Mikey suggested. 'Or do you prefer to be on your own?' he added, recalling how reluctant he had been to have Bridget tagging on.

The boy shook his head. 'No, I don't. It would be good to have company. What's your name?'

'Quinn.' Mikey told him. 'Mikey Quinn. What's yours?'

'Simon,' he said. 'Just Simon.'

They left the thick woodlands behind and entered the teeming, congested textile town of Nottingham. Mikey and Bridget put their remaining money together and had just enough for a night's lodgings. Bridget slept in a dingy rooming house and Mikey shared a hostel dormitory with working men. He reflected that the slum dwellings here were on a par with many in the back streets of Hull. Simon said he would find his own accommodation and meet them the next morning, which he did.

He told them about the hosiery and lace-making in Nottingham and how the merchants were moving further out of the town as it grew bigger. 'Much the same as in Hull,' he said airily. 'The merchants don't want to share the same air as their workers.'

'How come you know so much?' Bridget asked pertinently. 'Did you go to school?'

Simon gave a disdainful laugh. 'Of course I went to school! But I was expelled. That's why I've run away.'

'Expelled? What does that mean? Were you at Hull Grammar?' she asked.

'No. Boarding school, of course. I was sent away when I was eight. Hated it,' he said with venom. 'Hated it! I was always in trouble. The masters beat me and the other boys bullied me when I was young, and I was expelled – asked to leave because I beat up another boy. He deserved it, though.'

'But why have you run away from home?' Mikey asked.

105

'Were you lying about your parents being dead? Won't they worry about you?'

Simon held out his hands, palms uppermost. 'Look,' he said. 'My father did that.' His palms were cracked and swollen. 'He was going to send me away to another school. A much stricter one than the other.' He took a deep breath. 'And he promised me a beating every day until I agreed to mend my ways.'

'Haven't you got a mother?' Mikey asked, thinking how horrified his own mother would have been. The only punishment she ever meted out to him and his brothers was the sharp end of her tongue. 'Won't she be worried about you?'

Simon swallowed and blinked, and when he spoke again his voice cracked. 'I expect she will be, but she's afraid of my father. He wouldn't beat her, of course,' he added hastily. 'He doesn't beat women; though he locked my sister in a cupboard for speaking to me when I was sent to Coventry. But he would find a way of punishing my mother if he thought she was favouring me.'

Seems to me that there's not much difference between rich and poor if you're in a family like that, Bridget thought. Her father was a bully and her mother always had to appease him, whilst the children kept out of his way, especially when he was drunk. Perhaps Simon's father drinks a lot, like mine, and that's why he beats him.

My father wouldn't have beaten me if he'd been alive, Mikey thought. Not to make my hands bleed like his. Ma said Da was a good man. She allus said that; but even if he had done, Ma would have stuck up for me – for all of us. She wouldn't have allowed anybody to bully us, but neither would I have run away and left her to face such a man by herself. Simon's ma must be very frightened on her own. Seems to me that it's harder being rich than it is to be poor.

Simon hoisted his knapsack further up his back. He thought that he was luckier than the other two. He had a clean pair of socks and another pair of trousers in his pack, whereas they were a scruffy-looking couple and carried no luggage. Not two halfpennies to scratch together, I bet, he surmised. He had enough money for food and lodgings, though the accommodation last night had cost more than he had anticipated. London was where he was bound and he considered himself fortunate to have company for the journey. It's safer to travel with someone else, he thought, but I'll ditch them as soon as we arrive.

CHAPTER FOURTEEN

Tempers had been simmering for days. Each nightfall, or even before it was dark if they were very tired, Mikey and Bridget would search about for somewhere to sleep – a shop doorway, beside a brick wall or even beneath a tree if it was dry – whereas Simon would sidle away, murmuring that he was going to take a look round. He wouldn't come back until the next morning when he would reappear looking clean and refreshed.

'He's stopping somewhere,' Bridget grumbled as they watched him amble off early one evening. 'He's got some money but he's not sharing it wi' us.'

'That's what I think,' Mikey said. 'Not much of a pal, is he?' Then he grinned at Bridget. 'Not like you, using your money to buy food for both of us.'

She shrugged. 'But we knew each other before, didn't we? Perhaps he doesn't trust us.'

'Mebbe,' Mikey said thoughtfully. He got up from where they were sitting by a bridge in a village. 'Come on,' he said. 'Let's be off.'

'What? I'm tired,' Bridget complained. 'We've been walking all day. Besides, what about him?' She jerked her head to where Simon was heading down the village street.

'We'll not go far,' Mikey said. 'Just a couple o' miles to 'next town or village. And we'll let him find us. See how he likes being on his own.'

'All right,' she said. 'Serve him right.'

They walked down the road for another two or three miles, travelling through dense woodland and coming to the town of Retford, which was split in half by a river. There was a market fair in the town square and many of the traders were packing up for the night. Some of the stalls had been selling food cooked on braziers whose coals were now burning low.

'Come on, young feller, and you, young lady,' a stallholder called to them. 'Last of the sausages and bacon. Don't let 'em go to waste.'

'No money.' Mikey walked up to him. 'Can I do any jobs for you to pay for 'em?'

'You can help me pack up if you like. I'm moving on tonight. Help me strip down the stall and you can have what's left.'

'What can I do?' Bridget said eagerly. 'Can I help? I'm starving!'

'Starving! You don't know what starving is. All them curves on you.' He winked. 'I can see you've been well fed.'

'Shall I try to drum up some customers?' She smiled at him, dimpling her cheeks.

'Aye, you can do. Save some for the two of you, but there's hot meat pies left, and a pan o' peas.'

Bridget cleared her throat. The smell of the food was making her salivate. 'Come on, folks,' she called to passers-by. 'Special price, don't miss a bargain. Hot pies and peas for supper! Warm bread cakes.' She'd noticed the bread in a basket and put some to heat up by the brazier, keeping the rest on one side for her and Mikey.

A group of soldiers came along and she called to them. 'Come on, lads, what do you fancy?'

'Well, I wouldn't mind a kiss,' one of them grinned. 'How much for a kiss?'

'More'n you can afford,' she teased.

'Go on,' he said, egged on by his companions. 'How much?'

'A tanner then,' she said and held her cheek towards him. 'Let's see your money first.'

He fished in his trouser pocket and brought out a shilling. 'Two kisses please,' he said, rather sheepish now as his friends hooted.

She allowed him to kiss her on each cheek and then she smiled and kissed him on the mouth. He was a good-looking fellow, she thought, and it was no hardship.

He pretended to swoon and then put his hand in his pocket again and brought out sixpence. 'Now I'll have a bacon sandwich,' he said huskily. 'You've given me an appetite.'

'But for what!' one of his fellows exclaimed, then he too put his hand in his pocket for a sixpence.

'Bacon sandwich?' she enquired saucily.

'A kiss,' he said, and put out his arms.

She was glad that the brazier was between them, for this soldier had a gleam in his eye. She leaned her cheek towards him, taking his sixpence as she did so. 'That's it,' she said. 'I'm right out of kisses now. Onny hot pies and bacon left.'

They all bought something, all anxious to persuade her to give them the pleasure of her company, until she finally said, 'That's it, lads. Nowt left now. All 'rest is for our supper.'

'Who's yon feller?' one of them asked. 'Is he with you?'

She nodded. 'Yeh. My brother. We're mekking our way to London. Going to seek our fortune.'

One of the soldiers leaned towards her and whispered, 'You'd make it quicker without him, darling.' He winked. 'Could make a fortune all of your own.'

She smiled sweetly. 'But all my other brothers would come after me,' she said. 'And they're all huge.' She lifted her hands on either side of her shoulders to indicate their size. 'I just couldn't risk it.' She blew them all a kiss and turned away.

The stallholder gave Mikey sixpence for helping him, and when Bridget handed over the money for the sales she had made he was well pleased. 'Here,' he said, giving her a copper. 'And finish what's left of the food. It won't keep, and I only cook fresh.'

Bridget piled bacon into the bread cakes and they ate the last few sausages with their fingers, then Mikey asked the

110

trader if he knew where they could get a cheap bed for the night.

'Try Granny Hargreaves,' he said. 'She'll put you up if she has a spare bed.'

He told them where to find the landlady and, with all of his belongings packed in a handcart, he trundled away, calling out his thanks. They grinned at each other, feeling satisfied with the food and with earning it, and set off to find the lodgings.

The terraced cottage was down a narrow lane. A low light was burning in the window and the door was slightly ajar.

Bridget knocked. 'Is anybody there?' she called through the gap. 'Is this Granny Hargreaves's house?'

'Who is it?' an old querulous voice wavered. 'Are you selling summat?'

'No,' Bridget answered. 'One of 'market traders said you might have lodgings, just for tonight.'

'Come in. Come in,' the woman called. 'I can't get up, me back's gone.'

They walked into the dim room. The lamp in the window was the only light, as the fire had burned low. An old woman was sitting by it with a shawl round her shoulders.

'Can you turn the lamp up a bit?' she said. 'Not too much,' she added sharply as Mikey turned the wheel. 'I'm not made o' brass. Now then.' She peered at them. 'Who are you? Do I know you?'

'You don't know us, but we were recommended to come to you,' Bridget said. 'We need beds for tonight.'

'I've one spare, but I can't get up to make it. You'll have to get 'blanket out of the box yourself.'

'Where will you sleep, Mrs Hargreaves?' Mikey ventured. 'Can't you get into bed?'

'No, I can't. Not unless somebody helps me. I'm stuck in this chair till morning when me daughter comes.'

'We'll help you,' Bridget put on her sweetest voice. 'Won't we, Mikey?'

'Mikey?' Mrs Hargreaves said sharply. 'Is that a young fellow? I'll not have a young fellow helping me into bed!'

'I can help you out of 'chair though, can't I?' Mikey said. 'And I'll mend 'fire if you'll tell me where 'coal or wood is.'

'Ah. Well, that's how me back went, you see,' she said. 'I was shovelling a bucket o' coal and I felt it go. I got inside to me chair but then couldn't get up. I'm dying for 'privy 'n' all.'

Bridget pulled a face behind Mrs Hargreaves's back. This wasn't what she'd expected, but at least they were inside with a promise of at least one bed for the night.

Together they helped the old lady out of the chair and got her to the back door. 'I'll not mek it to the bottom of the garden,' she wailed. 'You'll have to fetch me a pail.'

Mikey turned away with a grin as Bridget ran off to fetch a pail as instructed. He picked up the poker and riddled the fire, bringing the coals to life, and thought that to sleep on the rug in front of it would be luxury. When Bridget and Granny Hargreaves came back into the room, he said, 'I'll fetch some coal and wood in, shall I? You'll want to keep 'fire in overnight?'

'Aye, I will.' The old lady gave a relieved sigh. 'I charge, you know, for a bed. You can't stop for nowt.'

'We realize that,' Bridget said softly. 'But we don't have much money. Onny what we earned from 'stallholder.'

'Was it the hot pie man?' she asked. 'He sometimes sends folk to me.'

'Yes,' Mikey said. 'He said you were 'best and wouldn't rob us.'

'Did he?' The old woman wrinkled her nose. 'Aye, well, I do a good turn now and again, if I'm treated right.'

'I'll help you into bed, if you like, Mrs Hargreaves,' Bridget said. 'Can me brother sleep on 'floor?'

'Your brother, is it?' the old woman said. 'Well, he can share your bed if you've a mind.'

'No,' Mikey said swiftly. 'We're too old for that. Not like when we were bairns.'

'Where you from?' she asked. 'You're not local.'

'We're from Hull,' Bridget answered. 'But we're on our way to London.'

'Ah, you young folk,' Mrs Hargreaves grunted. 'You all think London's paved wi' gold. But it's not, you know. You'll not find owt different from what you've had at home. But there you are, you'll not be told. Help me into bed,' she said to Bridget. 'And then you can take 'truckle bed. You'll find a blanket each. But there's no food, mind. I onny do bed, not board. But you can make a hot drink if you like. And I'll have one as well.'

They assured her they didn't need food, and after she was tucked in to her cot in an alcove behind a curtain Bridget filled the kettle from the outside pump and swung it over the fire whilst Mikey loaded two coal scuttles and brought in a pile of wood, which he placed in the hearth.

'What luxury!' He stretched his arms above his head and then sat cross-legged on the floor. 'I'll sleep like a log to-night.'

Bridget was searching in a cupboard. 'There's some cocoa,' she said. 'Shall I mek that instead of tea?'

Mikey agreed and she soon had three steaming cups of cocoa ready. She took one to Granny Hargreaves, but came straight back from behind the curtain, whispering, 'She's asleep already. We'll have to share this.'

'No hardship,' Mikey said quietly, with frothy cocoa over his mouth. 'She's very trusting, isn't she? We're complete strangers and yet she's let us into her house.'

Bridget glanced round. 'She's not got much to steal, has she?'

'Mebbe not,' Mikey said. 'But even so, she's willing to share it.'

'Yes,' Bridget said thoughtfully. 'Not like Simon, who's keeping whatever he's got to himself.'

They were both instantly asleep, Bridget on the truckle and Mikey on the rug, and neither woke until someone opened the front door.

'Who are you?' A woman stood over them. 'Where's my ma?'

Mikey sat up, rubbing his eyes. 'Lodgers,' he mumbled. 'Granny Hargreaves is in bed.'

113

Bridget murmured something and turned over, falling asleep again.

'I'm in here,' Mrs Hargreaves called out. 'Where do you think I am?'

'I've telled you before, Ma,' the woman said, opening the bed curtain. 'You shouldn't let strangers into the house. You'll be robbed and murdered in your bed.'

'Course I won't,' the old woman spluttered. 'They were recommended anyway. Hot pie man sent 'em.'

'Oh, well that's all right then,' her daughter said sarcastically. 'And I expect they've eaten all your bread and drunk your tea.'

Bridget sat up and gazed sleepily at the woman. 'No,' she said huskily. 'We had a drink o' cocoa, that's all, and I washed 'cups up,' she added. 'We onny needed a bed for 'night. We're on our way to London.'

'Are you?' she answered sharply. 'Well, if you see my lad, send him home, will you?'

Bridget nodded. 'What's his name?'

The woman gave a grim laugh. 'It's a big place is London. You're hardly likely to meet him.'

'We might,' Bridget said. 'What's his name?'

'Tony. Anthony Manners,' she said. 'Tell him I need him back here sharpish!'

They paid Granny Hargreaves sixpence, which was all she wanted. She said they had saved her life by getting her to bed and because Mikey had filled two coal hods for her. 'Call again,' she said, 'and welcome.'

They wandered round the town, killing time to give Simon chance to catch them up, but by eight o'clock he hadn't come so they decided to move on.

'Knowing him he'll be hitching a lift wi' a waggoner,' Mikey said. 'He'll probably overtake us.'

'Yeh, and he'll have had a good breakfast as well, I bet,' Bridget said. 'I'm hungry again.'

'Let's keep walking till dinner time,' Mikey said. 'And

if we eat then it'll mebbe last us 'rest of day.'

But they had gone no more than a mile when they heard someone calling their names. 'Mikey! Bridget! Wait!'

They turned round and saw Simon waving. 'Wait,' he shouted. 'Please wait.'

'Shall we?' Bridget teased. 'Or shall we let him run to catch up?'

'He's running anyway,' Mikey said. 'We'd best wait on him.'

Simon was breathless and red-faced by the time he reached them. 'Oh!' he gasped. 'I thought I'd lost you. Phew! Where did you go? I looked all over for you. Why didn't you wait?'

'What happened to your face?' Mikey ignored his questioning. 'Have you been in a fight?'

'Yes.' Simon breathed heavily. 'Last night. I – er – well, I fancied a proper bed and as I had a bit of money left' – he didn't look at either of them as he spoke – 'I thought I'd try for lodgings.'

'Oh, really?' Bridget put her hands on her hips. 'Didn't bother about us, then! Didn't I say, Mikey, didn't I say that he'd gone looking for somewhere to stop 'night?'

Mikey nodded. 'You did say that, yes. So where did you go?'

'I went to a hostelry and asked if they'd a room.' Simon was shamefaced. 'But they were full up and the landlord suggested I went somewhere else. There were two or three fellows in there, older than me, who must have heard him. They followed me up the street, pushed me into an alleyway and told me to hand over my money. Well, I wasn't going to do that without a fight, but they gave me a beating and made me hand it over.' He put his hand over his mouth and muttered thickly, 'It was just like being at school again.' He blinked rapidly but Mikey and Bridget saw the tears. 'And then they started kicking me, saying I was a rich bastard, but then this apparition dressed in black suddenly appeared and frightened them to death. He set about them with a great wooden stick and they scarpered. I spent the night in a doorway and as soon as it was light I set

115

off to find you. I thought you must have had a lift,' he added, 'and I'd have to travel on my own.'

'So who was it who rescued you?' Bridget asked curiously.

'He didn't say his name, but when I said I was with some friends and we were going to London, he said that he was heading that way and would catch up with us.'

'He'll have a job,' Bridget said scornfully. 'We're miles ahead.'

'He said he was getting a lift,' Simon said. 'Something about somebody owing him a favour.'

'Come on then,' Mikey said, 'let's get moving. We can't stand round here all day.'

Simon groaned, saying that he ached all over, but Mikey and Bridget ignored his complaints. Sleeping in doorways wasn't comfortable, they both knew that. Last night was the best night's sleep they had had since setting off on this journey.

The traffic on the road was heavy and they managed lifts several times in waggons and carriers' carts. It was close on midday when they were dropped off from a waggon which was turning in another direction. They trudged on, and hearing the sound of fast-moving hooves behind them looked round hopefully. But it was a four-wheeled clarence coming towards them and they knew that it wouldn't stop to pick up wayfarers.

They continued on, agreeing that they'd stop as soon as they came to a cottage or village to beg a sup of water or maybe buy a loaf with the money they had left, but they turned round again when they heard the hooves bearing down on them.

'Idiot,' Mikey muttered when he saw the driver standing up in his seat with his black coat billowing behind him and his whip raised, lashing the horses on. 'He's in a mighty hurry.'

Then the carriage slowed as it reached them. It was very shabby though once it had been smart; the red varnish was peeling, and the brassware was in need of polishing.

116

'Hey up, lads and lassie,' the driver called out. 'Do you want a lift?'

'Yes, please.' Simon rushed forward. 'I'm glad you caught us up.'

'Thank you,' Bridget said, following quickly.

Mikey held back. He took a breath. He would have known that mean face, the long nose and wild black hair, anywhere. This was a man he had hoped never to see again. Tully.

CHAPTER FIFTEEN

Mikey would have been the first to admit that without Tully they might not have got to London. Might even have died on the journey, for the weather had become cold and wet and the chances of work would have been minimal. Besides, the only thing he could offer to do for anyone was chop wood or bring water in from the pump. I'm useless, he had thought. No skill at anything.

Tully had grinned down at them from his perch, but hadn't at first recognized Mikey. They'd climbed aboard the rocking old carriage and had been hurled from one side to the other as Tully continued his nightmarish driving. Night was falling as they reached the outskirts of a town and Simon, hanging on to a leather window strap, peered out and said, 'Coventry. I wonder why he's come this way.'

'Coventry?' Bridget looked and felt sick and had been lying across one side of the carriage, leaving the two boys to sit at the other. 'Of course, you've been here before, haven't you?'

He turned to glance at her. 'No. Never,' he said, before turning back to the window.

She sat up and leaned on one elbow. 'You told us you had,' she said thickly. 'You said you'd been to Coventry.'

Simon snorted. 'I didn't mean I'd actually *been* here! It's a saying. *Sent to Coventry*. It means that nobody is allowed to talk to you.'

'Why?' she asked scornfully. 'That's stupid!'

He shrugged. 'I don't know. Something to do with the Civil War, I think. Don't ask me. I think that soldiers were sent to Coventry and no one would speak to them.'

Bridget lost interest and put her head down again. 'I wish we could stop,' she said wearily. 'I'd rather be walking.'

Mikey had been quiet on the journey. How was it that Tully was out of prison so soon? How had he been able to beg, borrow or steal a carriage? And if he had stolen it were the three of them implicated? It was too depressing to think about as he remembered his time in prison. He put his head back against the worn upholstery, closed his eyes and didn't open them again until he heard Simon and Bridget squabbling over Coventry.

The carriage slowed as it travelled through the town, and once or twice Tully stopped to ask directions. Finally he drew to a halt outside an inn with a swinging sign proclaiming it was the Town Wall Tavern.

'Come on,' he called to them, opening the carriage door. 'We'll stop here. Clear off and make yourselves scarce for an hour. I've some business to attend to.'

Simon got out of the carriage first, then Tully made a great show of helping Bridget down, but as Mikey stepped down Tully grabbed his arm. 'Hold on, feller-me-lad. Where've I seen you afore?'

Mikey swallowed hard. Would Tully remember if he didn't tell him? But he did remember. He suddenly shouted, 'Hah!' and pointed a bony finger. 'Course! Kingston Street. Quinn! What 'you doing so far from home? What's your ma going to say about that? Wise woman, your ma, if I recall.'

'She died,' Mikey told him miserably. 'I never saw her again.'

Tully patted his arm in a show of compassion which didn't fool Mikey at all. 'Tell you what, Quinn,' he said. 'You stop wi' me and I'll see you all right. You and your pals.' He winked at him. 'We'll mek our fortune in London, believe me.'

Tully spoke to Simon before going into the tavern, having

119

tied the horses to a lamppost which couldn't possibly have contained them if they had seen fit to bolt, but the horses seemed as weary as Mikey felt and stood with their heads and necks drooping towards the gutter.

'Come on, Mikey,' Bridget called to him. 'Tully's given Simon some money for us to buy food and a drink, and he says we can travel to London with him. For free!'

For free, Mikey pondered. I don't think so!

An hour later, having had bread and cheese and a glass of ale each, they returned to the carriage. Tully wasn't there but two small boys were. They said they were brothers. One said his name was Sam and he was seven. He didn't know how old his brother William was, but he was younger than him and they were waiting for Mr Tully.

The carriage door was open so they all piled in. Mikey questioned Sam but couldn't get much sense out of him, except that Mr Tully knew his uncle and that he was going to look after them. 'He give 'im five bob,' he piped.

'Who did?' Bridget asked.

'Uncle Walter gave it to Mr Tully. It's for our board and lodgings.'

Tully came back with a short thickset man who didn't speak but climbed aboard beside Tully. The journey wasn't quite as hazardous as it had been before and they guessed the horses were too tired to go any faster with the extra weight. They made several more stops over the next three days, changing the horses once, and eventually reached the outskirts of the capital. Tully stopped the carriage at a tavern and they all trooped in to have more bread and cheese and stretch their legs. The two small boys were almost crying with tiredness and Mikey thought of his brothers and wondered how they were coping with life in the Hull workhouse.

'Next stop London,' Tully told them. 'It'll be dark when we get there and I want you all to be quiet. Do you hear?' William was snivelling and grousing and Tully frowned at him. 'Do you hear?'

Sam nudged his brother and the younger child raised his

dark-shadowed eyes to Tully and nodded. Then he put his dirty thumb in his mouth and sucked furiously.

'We'll stay wi' a friend for a few days,' Tully said, 'and then we'll go to more permanent lodgings as soon as I've made contact with my associates.' He rubbed his mittened hands together. 'Then we'll start work.'

'What kind of work?' Mikey asked.

Tully patted his nose with a finger. 'Can't say just yet,' he said furtively. 'It's all hush-hush.'

The friend apparently lived in Whitechapel, which they approached as evening was drawing on. A fine drizzle was falling, which only added to the misery and degradation they saw around them.

'I say,' Simon whispered. 'I hope he's not expecting us to stay round here.'

'It's worse than 'back streets of Hull,' Bridget said in a low voice. 'Far worse.'

Although they were travelling in on the main road they could see blackened dwelling houses down the side streets, as well as mud-filled courts and alleyways, and in all of them shadowy groups of men, women and children, the men leaning against the walls, the women standing talking in their tattered clothing, their arms folded in front of them and their children, barefoot and half naked, playing in the dirt.

Mikey said nothing, only stared out of the window. So this is London. Here is where we are going to make our fortune. Doing what? It can only be illegal. This is why Tully's come here. He's too well known in Hull. London is so vast he can escape 'law. He'll hide like a rat in a warren and nobody'll ever find him.

The horses slowed and pulled to the left, and they were driving down a dark and narrow street. There were no gas lamps to light the way and Mikey wondered how Tully knew the directions, but then he realized that the friend they were staying with was probably the man riding at his side. Another thief, he thought cynically. We shall be in a den of thieves.

They drew up outside an unlit dwelling house which had an

iron staircase at the front of it. They were ordered out of the carriage and told to wait, which they did, fearful and shivering, the two younger boys crying with wretchedness, whilst Tully and his associate drove the vehicle away.

Mikey took William by the hand and drew him close. 'It's all right,' he told him quietly. 'We'll be inside in a minute.'

'It's dark.' Sam came to stand beside him. 'William doesn't like it when it's dark.'

'I don't like it much either.' Bridget's voice came eerily out of the gloom. 'Where do you think Tully's gone?'

'Gone to bed down the horses, I should think,' Simon answered gruffly. 'This is a rum do and no mistake. I'm beginning to wish we hadn't come with him.'

Ten minutes later they heard the sound of boots and the murmur of voices and Tully and the man came back.

'Come on,' Tully said in a low voice, 'and no talking till we get inside. 'Lead on, Gilby.'

They followed Gilby up the staircase, scrabbling to find their feet on the slippery metal steps and holding on to the handrail, which was cold and wet to the touch, until they came to the top. Gilby fumbled with a key and opened a door, and a moment later lit a match which he put to a candle. They saw the interior of a room rather like a hayloft, with no window but half a dozen or so straw mattresses on the floor.

'You're not expecting us to stay here,' Simon began, but Tully hushed him, his finger raised.

'Onny for a night or two,' he said placatingly. 'I realize you're used to summat better, young sir, but good accommodation is hard to find just now. A few days more and we shall have somewhere more to your satisfaction.'

His eyes narrowed as he looked at Mikey and gave a sly grin. 'Better'n Kingston Street though, ain't it, Quinn?'

Mikey shook his head. 'Kingston Street was clean,' he muttered. 'This is filthy. You wouldn't keep a dog up here.'

'Well we ain't got no dogs,' Tully snarled. 'So you've to mek 'best of it.'

'Where's 'privy?' Bridget asked.

Tully nodded over to a corner where a metal pail was standing. 'That's for you fellers,' he said. 'And you empty it yourselves in 'morning. You, lassie, come wi' me and I'll show you.'

Bridget bit her lip and looked at Mikey. 'Come down wi' me, Mikey, will you?' she asked.

Tully leered at them both. 'How touching,' he mocked. Then he went to the table where the candle burned, picked up another stub and lit it from the first, then handed it to Mikey. 'At 'bottom of 'stairs turn left into 'alley and you'll see 'privy at 'bottom near to 'wall.'

Mikey took the candle and cupped his hand round the flame to prevent it from blowing out. They went back down the stairs.

'I'm scared, Mikey,' Bridget whispered. 'What does he want wi' us? Or wi' young bairns?'

'I don't know,' Mikey said. 'No idea. I onny know that we don't have to stop. As soon as it's light in 'morning we'll have a look round, see where we are, and if we don't like what we see, then we'll be off.'

'But what about them bairns?' Bridget felt about her for the wooden box which held the privy. They knew they were there by the stink emanating from it. 'What'll we do about them?'

A wind suddenly gusted and blew out the flame. Mikey's low voice echoed in a ghostly whisper as he answered, 'We'll tek 'em wi' us.'

Only the young boys slept well that night. Mikey, Bridget and Simon tossed about on the prickly straw and whispered to each other, conscious of Tully and Gilby, who had gone out and then come in again at about midnight to sit at a rickety wooden table sharing a jug of ale and muttering and grunting together until the early hours.

It was raining the next morning. They could hear it rattling on the tin roof of the building and gushing over the broken gutters. Bridget opened the door and peered out and then made a dash down the steps to the privy. By the time she had splashed through the puddles to reach it she was soaked to the skin. The men and boys all used the convenience of the open doorway to save getting wet.

Bridget shivered and squeezed the water from her skirt when she came back. Tully magically found a piece of dirty sheet which he handed to her and she rubbed at her hair. 'I'll get my death,' she sniffled. 'I wish I was at home.'

Mikey nodded. So did he. But would he be any better off? Would he still be sleeping under the arch of St Mary's? It would be as cold and wet there as anywhere else.

CHAPTER SIXTEEN

It rained for a week. It seeped in under the door and poured in torrents through the roof. Mikey thrust the pail beneath one gushing downpour only to find another spouting through a fresh gap, and then another and another. Tully searched about for bowls and tins and jars to catch the rainwater and they were all kept constantly dashing to throw the contents out of the door into the yard below.

The two young boys thought this a great game to begin with and it kept them amused for hours, until they could no longer empty the containers fast enough and the water ran in rivulets across the floor, spreading out towards the mattresses and soaking their boots. Then the dampness clung to their thin clothes, their hands and feet were red with cold and they shivered uncontrollably. They were hungry, too. Tully went out once a day and brought back stale bread to share between them.

We'll never get out of here, Mikey thought. How can we leave and look for somewhere else to live or work in weather like this?

The building in which they were living was unoccupied except by themselves, although it was large enough to house half a dozen families. Yet they neither saw nor heard anyone else about. No neighbours, no cats or dogs, no horses or carts.

'Where are we exactly, Tully?' Mikey asked. 'How is it there's nobody else living here, yet we saw crowds of people as we came down the road?'

He knew that as soon as a house was vacated in Hull it would be immediately occupied again, legitimately or not.

Tully chewed on his lip. 'Don't know,' he muttered. 'Gilby found it.' He glanced at Mikey. 'Won't be for long. As soon as it stops raining we'll be off.'

'Where to?'

'Shut your face, will you? Forever asking questions! You're in London, aren't you? Where you wanted to be. You wouldn't have been here but for me.'

'I know that,' Mikey retaliated. 'But we're not doing owt. We're just stopping here, twiddling our thumbs, and we're all hungry. We need to work to be able to buy food. Who's paying 'rent?' he asked suddenly. 'Or are we just dossing here without 'landlord knowing?'

'Might be,' Tully said. 'Just mind your own business. We'll move when we're good and ready. Tell you what, Quinn,' he added slyly. 'You go out and fetch 'bread 'stead o' me.'

Mikey could hear the rain on the roof, but he agreed. Anything, he thought, just to get out of here. 'I've no money,' he said.

'Well, well, well! Fancy that,' Tully said sourly. 'So who's going to pay for it?' He put his face close to Mikey's. 'Same fellow who's paid for it afore, eh?'

Mikey nodded. 'I know,' he conceded. 'I know that you've paid for it. So what do you want back from us, Tully? You're not feedin' 'n' sheltering us from 'goodness of your heart, are you?'

Tully patted Mikey firmly on his cheek. 'Quite right, Quinn. I'm not. But you'll have to wait 'n' see, won't you?'

Mikey turned up his collar as he went down the steps. It was still raining, a heavy drizzle, though the sky seemed a little lighter than it had been. I'm frozen, he thought. I'd give owt for a bowl of hot soup. I wonder if there are any soup kitchens about. It's a run-down area. I'll ask if I see anybody.

He had only had a bird's eye view of the street from the

126

loft, and then only a corner of it. It had been dark when they had arrived and so now, when he turned the corner into the street, he was shocked by the filth and dereliction of the muddy sewage-strewn road and the boarded-up, blackened brick buildings.

'There's nobody about,' he muttered. 'Where is everybody?'

He peered through a gap in a door of one of the buildings. It had obviously been some kind of workroom, for there were bits of machinery scattered about. That could be sold for scrap, he thought. Why has nobody taken it out? He followed the directions given to him by Tully. The houses he passed appeared unoccupied, though as he glanced at one or two of them he thought he saw eyes peering out at him. They disappeared so swiftly that he decided he was mistaken, and it was only his imagination that made him see faces behind the torn and tattered cardboard which filled the window frames.

Eventually he came to a row of shops which were little more than single rooms, in front of a court of a dozen or so houses. The houses in the court were occupied, or they would have been except that the occupants were standing outside, in spite of the drizzling rain which ran down the walls of their dwellings from broken gutters and rattling drainpipes.

He went into one of the shop doorways. 'Have you got any old bread?' he asked the woman behind the crate which served as a counter. 'I've not got much money.'

'Nor have I,' she answered, and Mikey blinked at her accent; it was the first London voice he had heard, as even Gilby, on the rare occasions when he had spoken, had a northern voice.

'Where you from?' she asked. 'I 'eard somebody talk like you only the other day.'

'We're in lodgings just along 'street,' he said evasively. 'We're not stopping long. We're looking for work,' he added.

'So's everybody.' She sniffed. 'How much bread do you want? I can let you have one of yesterday's loaves and one of today's. Penny ha'penny,' she said, holding out a dirty, wrinkled hand.

He handed over the money and she thrust the unwrapped bread at him. 'Where did you say you were from?' she asked again.

'From the north,' he said. 'From Hull. It's a port,' he added.

'Aye, I know it is. My old man used to go there when he was in work. On the barges,' she said. 'So where are you lodging?'

He described the street and the empty building. 'There's nobody else living round there,' he said. 'Place is deserted.'

She gave a cackle and took a step back. 'There's no wonder,' she croaked. 'Them buildings have been condemned. They'll be pulling 'em down any time now. Haven't you noticed the stink? The stink o' death?'

Mikey shook his head. 'No,' he gasped. He was used to noxious smells, and wouldn't have noticed.

'Cholera,' she stated. 'Folks round there died of cholera. Dozens of 'em had it. They reckoned one of the dock workers brought it home with him. He'd been handling cargo from Asia.'

Mikey swallowed. What if someone living in the hayloft had had cholera? Could you catch it from floors and walls? Who had been sleeping on the straw palliasses? He thanked the woman and turned to leave, and then asked in a dazed manner, 'Are there any soup kitchens round here?'

She nodded. 'Later, about four o' clock, the parson and his wife set up a stall. You'll need to queue up. There's always a lot o' folk waiting.'

She gave him directions to the nearby church and he thanked her. Then she called him back. 'Here,' she said, handing him a currant bun. 'Take this. It's yesterday's and a bit dry but it'll mebbe fill a corner.'

He thanked her profusely and bit into it as he walked back. It was dry but the currants were still soft and partially satisfied his craving for something sweet.

When he got back to the hayloft, Sam and William rushed towards him and Bridget and Simon looked at him eagerly.

'Did you get owt, Mikey?' Bridget licked her dry lips. 'I'm that hungry.'

He shared out that day's bread between the five of them and the old bread between Tully and Gilby, first tearing off the crust and giving it to William, who he thought didn't look well. His hands and lips were blue with cold and he shivered constantly.

'There's a soup kitchen at four o'clock,' he told them. 'We'll all go. We need summat hot to warm us up.'

Tully objected. 'No,' he said. 'I want you all to wait here. We might have to move off at a minute's notice.'

'It won't tek us long,' Mikey insisted. 'We'll come straight back.' He stared at Tully. 'Did you know why this place was empty? Why there's nobody else about?'

Tully's lip quivered. 'Might have done,' he muttered. 'My contact said it was all right, we'd come to no harm.'

'What?' Bridget and Simon spoke together. 'Why is it empty?' Simon asked.

Mikey flashed a glance at Tully. He didn't want to frighten everybody. 'It's going to be pulled down,' he compromised. 'The wreckers are due in any time.'

'Crikey!' Bridget said. 'Hope they don't do that while we're still in it.'

'We shall have gone.' Tully said. 'Tomorrow, at 'latest, we'll be off somewhere else.' He rubbed his hands together and thinned his lips in what might have been a smile. 'Then we'll be off to mek our fortune.' He tapped his long nose. 'Mark my words.'

It began to get dark quite early; heavy clouds hung low and there was not a patch of sky to be seen. Tully and Gilby said they wouldn't go out in case their contact arrived. Mikey was beginning to think that this contact was mythical, but he and the others decided to set off and be the first in the queue for soup. Sam and William became quite excited at the thought of it and Bridget asked if there would be bread as well.

'I find this very degrading,' Simon declared. 'If I'd known—'

'What?' Bridget was scornful. 'You'd have done what? You'd

have perished,' she told him. 'You got beaten up and had your money stolen. You wouldn't have survived, and none of us would have been anywhere near London wi'out Tully. He's got some sort o' plan for us. He wouldn't have asked us to come along otherwise.'

Yes, Mikey thought as they trudged down the wet street. But what exactly is his plan? William came up beside him and put his small hand into his. What does Tully want with us? He recalled the police constable in Hull warning him to keep clear of Tully, or he'd be in even worse trouble. He squeezed William's hand. 'Nearly there,' he said cheerfully. 'And then a bowl of hot soup.'

There was already a group of people clustered round a wooden stall, where a woman and a man in a shabby overcoat and a clerical collar were attending to a heated brazier with a cauldron on it.

'It's not ready,' the man called out. 'You're all far too early. Now then,' he said on seeing the newcomers. 'We haven't seen you before.'

'We've just arrived in London,' Simon said. 'And we've found ourselves without decent lodgings.'

Some of the people in the crowd nudged each other as Simon spoke and Mikey wished that he hadn't. With his voice nobody would guess that we were down and out. He glanced round at the crowd. There were men, women and children wearing little more than rags; the children were mostly barefoot, their dirty toes curling up against the cold.

'We've come looking for work,' Bridget said. 'There's none where we come from.'

'You'll not find it here,' a woman called out. 'There's no work for us as was born here, let alone foreigners.'

'We're not foreigners,' Bridget objected. 'We're from Hull.'

'That's foreign,' the woman replied. 'Sounds foreign anyway,' she muttered.

'Well, there'll be enough soup for all of you,' the parson said in a forced jolly manner. 'And who knows what tomorrow will bring? The good Lord will take care of us all, and if we pray together He might have work for everyone who looks for it.'

He put his hands together, as did his wife, and they both closed their eyes. 'Shall we give thanks,' he intoned, 'and thank Him for the food we are about to eat.'

Bridget sighed and crossed herself, and the two small boys squeezed their eyes tight and clasped their fingers fervently. Mikey and Simon glanced at each other, and although both made a token gesture of putting their hands together, neither of them prayed aloud as the rest of the crowd were doing. I'll say my thanks when I've eaten, Mikey thought. Not before.

The potato soup was hot and filling and they were given a slice of bread to dip into it. They all rubbed their noses and sniffed as they drank from the bowls, then wiped the bread round them to take up every last drop.

Sam licked his lips. 'Best soup I've ever had,' he said. 'I wish I could have some more.'

The parson heard him. 'Sufficient unto the day,' he said, then bent down towards him. 'Were you very hungry, boy?'

Sam nodded. 'We both are,' he said. 'Me and William.'

'And what are you doing here so far from your home? Who brought you here?' He looked at Mikey. 'Is this your brother?'

'No.' Mikey shook his head. 'The man we're travelling with collected them from Coventry.'

The parson frowned. 'For what purpose?'

Mikey shook his head. 'Don't know, sir.'

'Is he a relative, this man you're travelling with?' the Reverend asked solemnly.

'Not of mine, sir. We met him – well, knew of him.' Mikey baulked at lying to the parson. 'And then he offered us a lift to London and promised us work.'

'Do I detect a northern accent?' the parson's wife asked. 'Yorkshire perhaps?'

William pulled on Mikey's arm before he could answer. 'Can we go now?' he said. 'If there's no more soup.'

'Come again the day after tomorrow,' the woman told him. 'We're here three evenings a week.'

131

The parson delayed Mikey for a moment before they left. 'If you should have cause for concern about the youngsters,' he said in a low voice, 'my wife and I run a school for destitute boys. We teach them to read and write and give them a hot meal every day; alas, we don't have room to let them all stay overnight, but they have the advantage of a Christian education.'

Mikey thanked him and as he walked away he deliberated on the usefulness of such a scheme if the boys had to spend nights without shelter.

His spirits sank as they approached the derelict building which was their temporary home. His mother had always had a fire burning in the grate and the children would never walk past a piece of brushwood or kindling without picking it up to bring home and burn. One of Mikey's regular pursuits was to walk down to the River Hull and search for a washed-up spar or burnable wreckage, and sometimes he would hang about a carpenter's shop in the hope of being given an offcut of timber. This building was cold and damp and dismal with no means of making a fire.

They climbed the steps and opened the door. Mikey ushered in the younger boys and then followed them, Bridget and Simon dragging their reluctant feet behind him.

'There you are, m'dearies,' Tully called to them. 'Come along in. We've got 'news we were waiting for.' He was rubbing his hands together and leering at them in an over-friendly manner which instantly made Mikey suspicious.

A lamp had been lit which threw long dark shadows about the room; Tully's, Gilby's and a stranger's. Mikey gazed keenly at the newcomer. Was this the contact that Tully had been speaking of? He was younger than Tully by far, perhaps in his late twenties. Tall, long fair hair and an open generous expression which perhaps with slight reservation you might trust.

'How do?' he said, coming towards them. 'I hear we're going to work together. You're Quinn, I gather? My name's Tony Manners.'

CHAPTER SEVENTEEN

'Tony Manners!' Bridget exclaimed. 'We met your ma! Didn't we, Mikey? And your gran as well.'

Tony Manners frowned. 'How come?'

'When we were travelling,' Mikey broke in, thinking that perhaps Tony Manners might not want everybody to know he was from Retford.

'We stopped wi' your gran,' Bridget butted in, 'and met your ma. She said if by chance we should run into you to tell you to go home.'

Tony Manners laughed, his full cheeks dimpling. 'Fat chance of that. Do this, go there, get a proper job. No fear. I'm doing all right on my own thank you very much.'

Mikey shrugged. 'Well, we've passed 'message on. What is it that you do exactly and how do we fit in?'

Manners glanced at Tully, who shook his head. 'I'm in 'import business,' he said. 'I've got a warehouse near to the docks and I need some extra staff. Tully said he had two lads who'd fit the bill.'

Simon chewed on his lip and then said. 'Not labouring work, I hope, because I'll not do that.'

'Ah.' Manners nodded at Simon. 'You'll be the educated one,' he said. 'No, I need somebody like you to look after the books and organize deliveries and such, whilst you, Quinn . . .'

I'll get 'labouring jobs then, Mikey thought with a degree of bitterness. Cos I'm not educated.

133

'I need somebody sharp-witted to help me run things,' Manners went on. 'You know, keep an eye on the men to make sure they're not helping themselves to stuff.'

Tully's told him that I've been in prison, Mikey thought resentfully. He's told him that I stole. It takes a thief to know another. Will my reputation always follow me? Will I never shake it off?

'What about me?' Bridget piped up. 'What am I to do?' She looked anxious; worried that she might be left behind.

'I've got something in mind for you, m'dear,' Tully chipped in. 'Something special up 'West End.'

'West end? What's that?' she asked. She narrowed her eyes. 'Doing what?'

'I'll tell you later,' he mumbled. 'Now then.' His voice rose. 'Come on, let's get started. We're moving off to the new lodgings which our friend here has kindly found for us. Get your gear.'

They'd nothing to take. None of them had any possessions except for Mikey, who still had Mrs Turner's blanket, which he had used to cover Sam and William when they were sleeping on the cold floor. He picked it up and slung it over his shoulder.

'What about these bairns?' he asked Tully. 'Where are they going?'

'Why, with us!' Tully feigned astonishment at the question. 'O' course they come with us. Would we leave 'em behind?' He patted William on the head. 'We've got plans, haven't we, William? Great plans for you two and Bridget.'

William looked up, his eyes large in his dirty face. He licked his lips. 'Can we go home?' he said plaintively. 'I wish we could.'

Sam took his hand. 'We ain't got no home, William. Not any more we ain't. We've to go wiv Mr Tully. He promised Uncle Walter he'd tek care of us.'

Bridget glared at Tully. 'Don't think I'm going to be nursemaid to 'em,' she told him. 'I'm not cut out for that. I've had enough of lookin' after 'bairns in my own family without anybody else's.'

'No, no,' Tully soothed her. 'It'll all be explained in due course; now come along.' He ushered them all out of the door. 'Let's be off.'

There was a single-horse open waggon tied up outside. Manners unfastened the rope and urged them all to climb aboard. Then he climbed up on to the raised metal driving seat and shook the reins and they were off, six of them plus the two children.

They travelled for over an hour; the rain was coming down in a fine steady drizzle and for much of the time there were no street lights until they came to a long road which was better lit, the gas lamps flickering yellow through the mist. Manners called out to them that this was Commercial Road and that they would soon arrive in Wapping, their destination. The two young boys were grizzling; they were cold and wet, even though they were huddled together under Mikey's blanket.

They passed many long side streets filled with houses and there were lots of people about; most looked like labouring men coming home from work, but there were women too dressed in grey shawls and shabby skirts. Shops were open and some houses had stalls and wheelbarrows and large cane baskets containing fish or fruit outside their doorways. Mangy cats and scratching dogs hung about and small children played in the gutters.

'This is no better than the other place,' Simon whispered to Mikey. 'It's total degradation. What are we doing here?'

Mikey silently shook his head. He was tired and hungry and felt utterly defeated. I should have stayed in Hull, he thought. At least I would have been with people I knew, even doorways I was fond of. He thought with affection of St Mary's archway. Looking back, the paving didn't seem to have been so very hard.

He recalled the excitement he had felt as he'd travelled on the ferry on the first leg of his journey from Hull. Everything seemed rosy then, he thought. I was off on an adventure. I made the wrong decision, and because of that, so did Bridget. She wouldn't have come if it hadn't been for me. But we have to make the best of it, and then as soon as we can, with money in our pockets, we'll make our way back. He was about to say as much to Simon and Bridget when the waggon drew to a halt and Manners called out that they had arrived.

A tall warehouse down a side street and round the corner from a seedy public house was their destination. They drew into a large yard, and from the outside the building didn't seem very different from the one they had vacated in Whitechapel. Large wooden doors fronted it, and there was a side door which Tony Manners unlocked. He lit a lamp on a shelf inside and they saw a steep and narrow staircase.

'Come on up,' he said. 'Gilby, lock the door behind you.'

They followed Manners up the stairs, which opened into a large room. There was a table and several chairs, and along one wall were alcoves containing mattresses. A sink was set in one corner and almost at the end of the room was a stove with a metal chimney. They all rushed towards it and put out their hands. It was warm.

Tony Manners opened a wall cupboard and brought out bread and cheese and a bag of tea, and set a kettle on top of the stove. They all silently watched him, hardly daring to hope that food and drink was about to be served. William began to cry and Sam hushed him. 'In a minute,' he said. 'In a minute.'

They were reluctant to leave the warmth of the stove, but Manners told them to sit at the table and eat the bread and cheese, promising that he would go out and buy a meat pie as soon as the tea was brewed.

'You see how well my ma brought me up,' he grinned. 'Not many men know how to make a pot o' tea.'

I know, Mikey thought, but I'm not going to tell him or else it'll be my job from now on.

Whilst they were eating and drinking their tea, Tony Manners slipped out and within ten minutes was back with enough steaming hot meat pie for them all, including Tully and the ever silent Gilby. They ate hungrily, stuffing the pie into their mouths with their fingers and greedily licking off the gravy. Then William put his head down on the table and fell asleep.

'Put him to bed. Put him to bed,' Tully said to no one in particular.

Bridget glanced down at the sleeping child and went on eating as if she hadn't heard, and it was Mikey who picked him up and carried him across to one of the mattresses, where he curled up with his knees to his chest.

Sam rose from the table. He had gravy on his chin. 'I'll sleep wiv him,' he said. 'Cos he'll wake up and not know where he is.'

'Good boy.' Tully nodded approvingly. 'You look after your brother and tomorrow we'll go out on a treat.' He winked at Bridget. 'We'll tek a look at 'shops in 'West End, shall we, m'dear? You'll like that, I'll be bound. Don't she look like a young woman who'd like that, Tony?'

'Certainly does,' Tony Manners agreed. 'Yes, you go off and enjoy yourselves and we'll hatch out a working plan, eh, fellows?' he said jovially to Mikey and Simon.

'Sounds all right to me,' Simon said. 'I shall be ready for anything now after food and a good night's sleep.'

'Quinn?' Manners raised his eyebrows in Mikey's direction. 'What do you think?'

Mikey nodded. 'Yeh. What did you say you were importing?'

Manners's friendly face creased about the eyes and his mouth set. 'I didn't,' he said. Then he smiled. 'We'll discuss it in the morning.'

Tully roused them early the next morning. It was still dark, and the sky was obscured by heavy rain clouds. They breakfasted on bread and tea and then he told Bridget and the younger boys to come out to the yard in ten minutes. When they came down the steps he was sitting in the driving seat of the waggon waiting for them.

'Just borrowing this for today,' he explained. 'Manners doesn't mind. I'll get another hoss by tomorrow.'

'Where did you say we're going?' Bridget asked again.

'Told you,' he said irritably. 'Up to 'West End.''

'But what is it?' she asked. 'West end of what?'

'It's called 'West End,' he said. 'It's where all 'best shops are. And parks,' he added.

She had to be satisfied with that, for he was obviously not going to tell her more, but she was anxious about her role. Mikey and Simon had gone off with Tony Manners, down to the wharves, he'd said, but they were as ignorant as she was about what they were to do to earn their living.

They drove past dismal streets of blackened terraced housing. Some of the courts and yards contained pigs which seemed to have free access to the open doors of the dwellings. Behind these buildings were other alleys, some divided from their neighbours by stinking drains. A constant stream of workers trudged along with bent backs, their eyes lowered to seek out broken paving and mud-filled potholes. When she asked Tully where they were going he simply grunted, 'Dock workers.'

Presently, as a watery sun came up, she saw that the housing was slightly improved. Terraced houses stood to either side of the road and although some were boarded up, there were others with lace curtains and potted plants in the windows and clean-scrubbed doorsteps. Here and there in the gaps between the terraces were strips of turned land showing lines of cabbages. Some had wooden huts on them and others a goat or a cow.

It was almost midday when Tully said, 'Nearly there, missy. Primp yourself up a bit.'

Bridget had been admiring the changing view. The terraced housing they were passing now was tall and imposing, often with ornamentation, pillars and wide steps to the heavy front doors. Many of the dwellings had carriages or dog carts waiting outside, their drivers dressed in smart clothing. There wasn't a sign of a privy or a pump, and tubs outside the doors were set with small green trees.

She looked up at Tully. Primp yourself up! Though she had

washed under the pump this morning, she was wearing the same clothes that she had worn to set off on the journey from Hull.

'How?' she asked. 'How can I do that?'

'En't you got a comb?' he said. 'No? Well, run your fingers through your curls then. I don't know,' he chuntered. 'What do girls do?'

'I need another skirt,' she said. 'You said we were going to look at 'shops.'

'We are.' He raised his whip. 'Look at that. Never seen owt like that afore, have you?'

She hadn't, and the spectacle before her drew her breath away. A large grass square was surrounded by elegant houses as big as palaces; riders, the men in top hats and the women in riding costume, were trotting along the clean neat paths below overhanging trees; through the bare branches, she could see white marble statues gleaming in the midday sunshine.

This is for me, she breathed. This is where I want to live. The two boys lifted their heads above the rim of the waggon.

'Ooh,' William said. 'Are we in heaven?'

'I think we might be.' Bridget smiled. 'As near as we're likely to get, anyway. Where are 'shops?' she called to Tully. 'There are none here.'

He drew up at the side of the road and turned towards her. 'We have to go and see a mate o' mine first. His wife has a shop – o' sorts. We'll get you summat from her.'

'How come you know folk in London?' she asked. 'I thought you were from Hull? You talk like Hull.'

'Been around a bit,' he said. 'Lived all over. Born in London I was, but moved north when I was just a nipper.' He leaned down and lowered his voice. 'Don't tek offence now, will you, but I need to know. Are you a gay gel?'

'What do you mean?'

'You know!' He lifted his shaggy eyebrows. 'Do a turn for a tanner or two?'

She stared at the suggestive grimace on his face. 'A

139

prostitute? Is that what you mean?' When he nodded, she said indignantly, 'No, I'm *not*.'

'All right,' he said, taking up the reins again. 'Onny wondered. Have to try summat else then.' He urged on the horse.

The something else, she discovered after having swapped her skirt and blouse for others, marginally cleaner than her own, from Tully's mate's wife, who ran a second-hand clothes shop in one of the back streets, was detaining gentlemen to ask them the time or for directions. As she did so, Tully would appear and crash into them, and as the gentlemen helped Bridget to her feet, with many apologies and a tilt of their hats, he would disappear along the street taking with him a shiny fob watch or a leather wallet.

So be it, she thought as she made her way back to where Sam and William had been positioned by an expensive-smelling shop doorway. They both had dirty faces and Tully had taken away their worn boots and left them in the waggon. Sam was to place his hand on William's shoulder and beg for both of them. 'Spare a copper, sir, madam. Me bruvver's hungry.'

I wonder what Mikey is doing to earn his living? She glanced at her reflection in a shop window. I look all right, she thought. I think I might do well here.

Tony Manners led Mikey and Simon towards the river. 'I work from the wharves,' he said. 'Commodities – tea, coffee, spirits, that kind of thing. The dock company have taken some of our trade, but there're still plenty of supplies coming in cos of the free water access for the lighters.'

'How do you mean?' Mikey asked.

'No charge to the lighters when they bring goods in from the ships.' Tony Manners gazed acutely at Mikey, as if he was weighing him up. 'But you won't need to bother about that. Most of our stuff comes in late at night. Cos of the tide, you know. So I'll want you to work in the warehouse and repack it to send off to our customers. They only want small quantities, not huge crates of it. And you,' he turned to Simon, 'I want you to mark off what comes in and what goes out.'

'An inventory?' Simon said knowledgeably. 'Taking stock.'

'That's it.' Tony Manners seemed pleased with the way his plans had been accepted. 'Here we are.'

They turned off the road and headed towards the wharves. There were hundreds of warehouses, sheds and other buildings as well as masses of crates, barrels, baskets and loading trolleys outside them. No one had challenged Manners as to their business there, and Mikey guessed that he was probably well known in the area. He looked every inch a working businessman as he marched confidently forward. He was dressed in a plain coat, waistcoat and trousers and wore a rather battered top hat. He had given Mikey and Simon each a soft hat to wear, which seemed to be standard for other men going about their business on the wharves.

Manners took a heavy iron key from his waistcoat pocket as he walked towards a building which was approached by a narrow opening between two other warehouses. From the front it couldn't be seen as one of the other warehouses obscured it.

Just the place for dealing in illicit goods, Mikey thought cynically. He wasn't convinced that Manners was totally honest, and was watchful as he opened the door. There were two youths inside already, younger than himself, he realized as they stood up from their task of emptying a crate.

'This is Smith, and this is Brown,' Manners said casually. 'Quinn and Simon,' he said to the youths. 'They're going to run things; get a system going,' he added.

The youths stared at Mikey and Simon but didn't say anything, and Mikey concluded that perhaps they weren't very bright. He walked over to look in the crate. Tea, with the sacks already opened. He breathed in the aroma. How my ma would have loved to see this, he thought.

'We've started repacking it, Mr Simon,' Smith said. 'We've spilt a bit but we'll sweep it up.'

'I'm Quinn,' Mikey said. 'He's Simon.'

141

'If there's any spilt, it goes into a separate bag.' Manners came over. 'That's sold off cheap. But be careful not to spill much,' he warned the two youths, 'or I'll have to stop it out of your wages.'

Mikey looked round. There were crates stacked high to the ceiling and other smaller boxes in stacks of three or four placed against the walls. Well, it's a job of work, and there's nothing else on offer, he thought. Manners hasn't mentioned wages yet or what he's going to charge for our bed and board. Will I make my fortune here? He gave a sigh. I don't think so, but if I can keep body and soul together then it will do for 'time being. I've just got to make 'best of it.

CHAPTER EIGHTEEN

Hull 1857

Eleanor gazed out of the drawing room window at the bustling High Street below. She was alone in the house, apart from the servants; her mother had left that morning on a visit to her sister, who lived in Nottingham. Eleanor had asked if she could accompany her, but her mother had become very flustered and said no, it wouldn't be convenient. Eleanor couldn't think why. She understood that Aunt Maud had a very large house, though she had never been, and on the two occasions when her aunt had visited Hull she had been very friendly towards Eleanor.

It is a very dreary life, she thought, with little to entertain me. There were only books and sewing and today she was bored with both; the thought of her father as her only companion when he returned from his office filled her with dread.

Since her brother Simon had run away five years ago, her mother had spent more time with her. Nanny had gone to live with a relative but had died shortly afterwards; Miss Wright had left and been replaced by other governesses until a year ago, when Eleanor's father had decreed that she no longer needed schooling. Her mother could teach her all there was to know about running a household, and that would be much more useful than learning French or mathematics.

So her mother had taught her how to fold table linen and

arrange flowers, and had shown her a cookery book describing different kinds of meat – beef, pork, venison and so on – the various joints to be obtained from them, and how to cook them. Not that you are likely to have to cook them yourself, her mother had emphasized, but you need to be able to recognize that they have been cooked properly, and to know the kind of sauce which should accompany them.

Eleanor found it quite interesting and would have liked to put the instruction into practice, but her mother said that under no circumstances must she upset Cook by asking, as cooks were very hard to come by and the one they employed now understood exactly how her father liked his food.

Her mother began to attend meetings of societies which had been established for the greater understanding of the complexities of urban life, for once in her married life defying her husband, who had said she wasn't at all the kind of person who would be able to contribute anything to such gatherings. After her first meeting she had come home flushed and animated, ready to pour out all she had heard, but Mr Kendall had told her coldly that he heard such nonsense every day and didn't wish to hear it at home.

Eleanor often wondered where her brother had gone and what he was doing. The police had been informed of his flight at the time and posters put up in the streets of Hull, but there had been no response. Mrs Kendall had written to her sister telling her of his disappearance, and pleading that if by chance she should hear anything of a runaway boy in Nottingham she should enquire immediately to ascertain whether or not it was Simon.

'He will not come here,' Maud had replied. 'The poor boy would know I was duty bound to return him to his home. To a home, I might add,' she had written, 'where he is patently unhappy.'

Kendall, on reading the letter, had thrust it back at his wife, muttering that Simon would find that he had something to be unhappy about when he did eventually return.

This morning, on impulse, Eleanor put on her bonnet and

outdoor coat. There was no one to tell her she shouldn't go out. She had already spoken to Cook about the evening meal and her father had informed her that he wouldn't be coming home at midday, as he usually did when her mother was at home. I will go for a walk, she thought. I do not need a companion and shall be perfectly safe on my own. I have often seen ladies alone in the street without a maid, and I shall not need one to carry my purchases as I haven't any money to buy anything.

After Simon had run away, it was discovered that money was missing from his father's desk drawer. Mr Kendall immediately assumed that his son had stolen it as it had been there when he and Mrs Kendall had gone in to supper. The maids only entered his room in the morning, to open the curtains and clean the grate, and, he had determined, they wouldn't have had time to slip off whilst serving the meal; and as Eleanor was locked in the cupboard, Simon alone must be the culprit. It was following this incident that all money was locked away and Eleanor had to ask her father or her mother for money every time she wished to make small personal purchases, which was not often.

Eleanor quietly closed the front door behind her and took a deep relieving breath of freedom as she stepped down on to the footpath. She glanced up at the drawing room window but there was no one to look out and she gave a little smile of satisfaction that she was free of constraints. A brisk breeze blew, whipping her coat around her ankles and tossing her fringe beneath her bonnet, but she wasn't cold. In fact she was quite exhilarated, and wondered if this was how Simon had felt as he escaped from home.

The High Street was a narrow cobbled street close by the River Hull in which many eminent merchants and shipping magnates lived and worked. However, Mrs Kendall had often asked her husband if they might move away to the country as the area also housed many run-down courts and alleyways where it was not safe to walk at night.

He had always refused, saying that his work was here

amongst the shipping and corn merchants, but she knew the real reason was that there was a certain distinction and esteem to be gained from living so near the mansion where Charles I had been entertained by Sir John Lister and, a century later, the emancipator William Wilberforce was born; in the same street, Henry Maister, head of a leading merchant family, had made his home, as had the noble family of De la Pole.

Eleanor knew these famous names from her history lessons, and she had also walked by the side of the Old Harbour with her several governesses and been told of the vast fishing industry which serviced the town of Hull. Now, though, she was anxious to leave the street and explore the rest of the town, although she would avoid at all costs cutting through Bishop Lane, where her father's office was situated.

She scurried across the top of it, glancing anxiously down as if her father would be looking out for a miscreant and might instead find her. The lane was crowded. It was so very narrow that there was room only for one cart or waggon to traverse it, and as she gazed down she saw that a covered coach appeared to be parked there, with a number of uniformed policemen standing by it.

A criminal, she mused, waiting to see a lawyer, for there were several law offices in the lane as well as commercial premises. She made a cut through Scale Lane into the main thoroughfare of the Market Place. It was a Tuesday, one of the market days, and the area was buzzing with people, buying from the traders.

I must ask Papa for some money, she thought, for I could buy some bargains. There were stalls selling hot pies, vegetable and fruit stalls, fish stalls and flower stalls, and she would have loved to carry home a sweet-smelling posy or a bag of rosy apples.

There was also a hum of anticipation in the street and she watched a group of ragged children who in turn were watching a group of men putting up a canvas shelter. Of course, she thought, it's Hull Fair time. She remembered full well hearing the sounds of the fair arriving the week her brother ran away, as she sat alone in her room: the trumpeting of elephants, the drumbeats and penny whistles, the clatter of hooves on cobbles, the shouts of children. But most of all she remembered hearing her mother sobbing and weeping and knowing that she could not comfort her, for Simon was and always would be her mother's favourite child.

A thin-faced young man passing by raised his hat. 'Good morning, Miss Kendall.'

She turned to him. Who was he? She inclined her head, and he hesitated in his stride and turned back. 'You perhaps don't remember me, Miss Kendall. Percy Smart. I'm one of 'junior clerks in your father's office.'

'Oh, yes,' she said. 'Of course.' She did remember him now. He had called at the house on several occasions to bring her father some urgent papers. She had always thought him a servile, oily individual, but her father seemed to think well of him, perhaps, she thought ungraciously, because Smart toadied up to him.

'It's a nice day for a walk.' His eyes appraised her shiftily. 'I found an excuse to come out. The office is so full of officials, inspectors and administrators that I thought I wouldn't be missed.' He tapped the side of his nose. 'I'm sure you won't give me away.'

'Indeed not, Mr Smart.' She raised her eyebrows. 'And if you hadn't alerted me to your presence I would have been unaware of it.' Perhaps I am being rude, she thought. But why tell me something only to ask me not to reveal it?

He nodded his head, smiling in a foppish way, and added, 'Well, I suppose everything will be sorted out sooner or later. People don't understand how many complications there are in dealing with legal affairs.'

'I know nothing about that, Mr Smart, and if you will excuse me I must be getting along.' I don't know what he is talking about, she thought as she took her leave and he again tipped his hat to her. But whatever it is I don't think he should be discussing it with me.

She spent another hour looking in the shops and reading

the posters advertising the coming attractions, the circus, the travelling theatres, the two-headed dogs, the thought of which made her shudder, and then decided she had better return home for luncheon or Cook would not be pleased. She strolled back down the High Street, and just before she reached the top of Bishop Lane she saw her father turn out of it and head towards their house.

He's coming home after all! I hope Cook has done enough food. I said I would just have a light repast. She became agitated. He will have to have mine. I'll say that I'm not hungry. Why is he coming home? Is it because, as Mr Smart said, there are too many people there? Has something gone wrong? But surely, as a senior partner, my father would be needed.

It was of no use surmising or second-guessing. If her father wanted to tell her, he would, but more than likely he would not. He was putting his key in the lock as Eleanor approached.

'Hello, Papa,' she said in as bright a voice as she could muster. 'Have you come home for luncheon after all?'

He turned and looked down on her from the top step. Her heart skipped a beat at his frown. I can surely go out when I want to, she thought. And I'm too old and too big to be locked in a cupboard. The memory of it still gave her nightmares.

'Eleanor?' It was as if he hadn't seen her in a long time. He gave a little shake of his head. 'No,' he said. 'No, I don't want anything to eat.' He pushed open the door and entered, holding it ajar for Eleanor to come in. 'I'll just have a jug of coffee. Tell your mother I want to speak to her straight away.'

She stared at him. 'But she's not here, Papa! She's gone to stay with Aunt Maud.'

He gazed back, his forehead creased. 'Oh! Yes. I'd forgotten. Was that today?'

'Yes, Papa. Just this morning. She caught an early train.'

He grunted. 'Then I will write and tell her she must come back immediately.' It was as if reason had come back and he was himself again. 'She's needed here.'

'But . . .' She was confused. 'Mama will not yet have arrived in Nottingham. She was expecting to stay at least a week.'

Though as she said it, Eleanor recalled that her mother had been very vague about the date of her return.

'Never mind what she was expecting,' he answered brusquely. 'She must return at once.'

'Has something happened, Papa?' she dared to say. 'Is something wrong?' Her thoughts flitted to Percy Smart, who had sneaked out of the office.

Her father gave her a sharp glance. 'What? What makes you say that?'

'N-nothing, except that – you seem upset over something,' she said lamely.

'I am not upset.' His eyes flickered about the hall and up the stairs. 'I shall go to my room. Send for my coffee straight away.'

'Shall I ask Cook to send in a slice of bread and beef?' she asked.

'No!' he bellowed. 'Do not trouble me with such insignificances.' He marched away to his study just off the hall.

Eleanor shook. Something's happened. Whatever it is, will he take it out on me? She knew her father's idiosyncrasies very well. If he had had a problematical day at the office, she and her mother tried to keep out of his way, and the maids became invisible, disappearing down the kitchen stairs or into the laundry room when he was having what Eleanor had once overheard Mary expressively describe as 'Master's strop'.

She slipped down the back stairs to the kitchen. On the table her own luncheon was being prepared. Cook was standing by the range stirring something in a pan and a maid was washing up in the sink.

'Cook!' Eleanor said quietly, for the opening of the door had gone unheard.

The cook turned round, startled to see Eleanor in her kitchen. 'Miss! Is something wrong? They're just about to bring up your luncheon. We're not late?'

'No, no,' she assured her. 'It's just that my father has arrived home unexpectedly. Will you ask Mary to take him a large pot of coffee, please? He doesn't require anything to eat—'

'Oh, surely just a morsel—' Cook began.

'Nothing!' Eleanor emphasized. 'Please don't press him.'

'No, Miss Eleanor.' The cook nodded. 'If that's what he said. And we'll send yours up in just a minute.'

'Thank you. Will you ask Mary to bring it to my room? I won't eat in the dining room as I'm alone. Just on a tray. Please!'

She slipped back upstairs to the hall and then up the two flights to her own room. She still used the old nursery, for she felt very comfortable there. It was her own private place where she kept her books and writing materials and the maid lit a fire every day so it was always cosy and warm, but best of all no one ever bothered her, least of all her father.

CHAPTER NINETEEN

Eleanor stayed in her room for three days, coming down only for breakfast and having her lunch and supper brought to her upstairs. She saw her father only twice in that time and was surprised to see him then, for on both occasions it was during the morning when he should have been in his office. He was plainly not intending to leave the house, for he was unshaven and without his jacket, and wore an old knitted garment on top of his shirt.

She asked him no questions but simply greeted him and said she hoped he had slept well; in answer he only grunted. On the fourth day he was waiting for her in the breakfast room and without any preamble asked if she had heard from her mother.

'No, I haven't,' she said. 'Perhaps there will be a letter to-day.'

'The first post has been already,' he muttered, 'and there was no reply to my letter.'

She bit on her lip. 'Second post,' she said nervously. 'It generally comes just after lunch.'

'I am aware of when it comes.' His manner was sharp. 'I receive post every day.'

She crossed to the sideboard. 'May I serve you some bacon, Papa?' she asked. 'Or scrambled egg?'

'No. I'll have toast and marmalade. And coffee,' he added.

Eleanor served him and then helped herself to eggs. She

was hungry but didn't have bacon or kidney as she knew she would choke on it; she was so nervous that her throat was tight.

Her father drank his coffee and nibbled on the toast, glancing at her from time to time but not speaking. Eleanor kept her eyes lowered so as not to confront him. Finally he spoke, after loudly clearing his throat.

'What were your mother's plans for Nottingham?'

She looked up, her lips parted. 'Plans, Father? I didn't know she had made any.' Eleanor swallowed. 'I assumed that she was only visiting Aunt Maud. It is a while since they last met.'

'Hmph! That is what she told me. Why she should want to visit that harridan I can't imagine.'

Eleanor was shocked at his language and could think of no reply.

'Do you think she has news of your brother?'

'I – I don't know. Mama never said that she had.' Eleanor pushed her plate away, her appetite failing. Surely her mother would have confided in her if she had heard tidings of Simon.

Her father rose from the table, taking his cup and saucer with him. 'I shall be in my study,' he announced. 'I am not going to the office today.'

Nor did you go yesterday or the day before, she thought, and ventured, 'Taking a little holiday, Papa? You rarely do.'

He turned towards her and for a moment she thought he was going to say something, but he appeared to think better of it and gave a shake of his head. He looks so pale and unwell, she thought. He is surely not fretting over Mama.

At mid-morning she decided to take a walk, even though it was wet and windy. She put on her outdoor cloak and fastened the hood over the top of her deep-brimmed bonnet, then picked up an umbrella from the hallstand.

Her father appeared at the study door and looked questioningly at her. 'I'm just going out on an errand,' she explained. 'I need embroidery silks.'

'Ah,' he muttered. 'I thought I heard the post.' He turned back into his room again.

I ought to buy some silks now, she thought, or be found out in a lie. But I don't have any money. I will have to place them on account at the haberdasher's. That is what her mother always did and the account was then sent to her father. Mama never has any money either, she realized; I don't think I have ever seen her with anything in her purse. It would be so nice to have just a little allowance to spend as I pleased. Perhaps, could I, dare I ask Papa?

She purchased silks, ribbons and a few reels of cotton, just to make the sale worthwhile, and bidding the saleswoman good day she stepped outside again. The rain was coming down in torrents, and after battling unsuccessfully to keep her umbrella from blowing inside out she decided to return home.

As she waited for someone to open the door, she glanced down the street. The postman was heading this way. 'Do be quick, Mary,' she implored beneath her breath. 'Let me in.' When the door was opened, she kicked off her shoes in the hall and gave the maid her wet cloak to take away and dry, and ran upstairs. She didn't want to be there when her father collected the post. If her mother hadn't written, he would be in a fearful mood.

She put on her indoor slippers and tidied her hair. She still wore her hair loose as her parents didn't consider her old enough yet to put it up. She searched in a drawer for a lace cap and was pinning it on her hair when she heard her father roar.

'Eleanor! Eleanor!'

She dashed out of her room and along the landing, and peered over the banister. Her father was below, looking up. In his hand he held a letter.

'Yes, Papa?'

'Come down here at once!'

Oh, she thought, he sounds so angry. What have I done? Is the letter from my mother?

She ran down the stairs, lifting her skirt so that she didn't fall. 'What is it, Papa? What has happened?'

Mary appeared at the top of the servants' stairs as if in answer to an urgent summons, but she was brusquely shooed away by Mr Kendall.

'What's happened? What's happened?' He took Eleanor by the arm and pushed her into his study. She never came in here. This was her father's private sanctum. 'You might well ask what's happened!'

Eleanor stood trembling, waiting for an explanation. She clenched and unclenched her hands, then clasped them together. 'Mama is not sick, is she?' she whispered. 'Or is it Simon?'

'No, it is not Simon,' he roared. 'This is a letter from *your mother!*' He emphasized the relationship so firmly, it was as if whatever was amiss was Eleanor's fault for having such a mother.

'Tell me what it is, Father,' she implored. 'Have I done something wrong that Mama has told you about? I assure you that whatever it was—'

'Not *you*,' he interrupted fiercely. 'This is not about *you*. This is from your mother. My wife! Telling me that she is not coming home. *Ever!*'

Eleanor was thunderstruck. Not coming home? But what about me? Am I to stay here? With my father?

Her father turned to his desk and picked up another envelope. 'This is addressed to you. It is marked personal and private; otherwise I would of course have opened it.' He stared at her. 'It is within my rights to do so. You are not of an age to receive correspondence without my reading it, but as it is so obviously your mother's writing, you may see it first.'

She took it with trembling fingers. 'Thank you,' she whispered. 'May I sit down?'

He waved her to a chair, but he remained standing by the fireside, tapping a foot on the carpet and banging one fist into the palm of the other.

Eleanor struggled to open the envelope and then, in a small, cracked voice, asked if she might borrow a paper knife. Her father handed one to her without a word; she slit the envelope and withdrew the letter.

My dear Eleanor [her mother wrote in her fine neat handwriting],

This letter may come as a shock to you, but on the other hand your father might by now have acquainted you with the contents of the letter I have sent to him. In short, my dear, I have left your father and am now living with my sister Maud and her husband, Mr Morton James. They have been very kind and considerate to me, and although I do not envisage spending the rest of my life with them, they have offered me shelter for as long as I require it.

I have been very unhappy for many years, particularly since your brother ran away, and although I have tried hard to be a good and faithful wife, I cannot any longer live under the same roof as your father. I am very sorry to leave you behind, but I have no wealth of my own and although our house was mine, bequeathed to me by my father before my marriage, it is now of course, in law, the property of my husband. Your father therefore can offer you more materially at the present time than I can and also of course insist that you stay with him.

I know that your father will be angry with me, but I hope he will allow you to write to me care of Aunt Maud and that you will be able to receive my letters. I shall think of you often, my dearest child, and send my fondest love.

I am your affectionate mother,
Rosamund Kendall.

Eleanor swallowed hard for a moment and dared not lift her eyes to look at her father. At last she raised her head and saw him looking at her with narrowed eyes.

She whispered, 'How can we get her back, Papa?'

'She does not want to come back,' he said in such a vicious tone that she trembled. 'She has left without a penny to her

155

name and with only the clothes she was wearing. And,' he added, 'even those I paid for. Every bill your mother incurs comes to me.'

'I know,' Eleanor said. 'Mama always said we must not be extravagant; that we must always remember that you are responsible for us.'

'Did she indeed?' Her father was brusque. 'And did she tell you that I am still responsible for her, even though she has left her marital home?'

'No, Father, she didn't.' Eleanor knew now, with a sinking feeling, that her mother had always been under her husband's domination. And is that what will now happen to me, she thought. Is that my lot in life? Will I now have to take my mother's place and be under my father's rule? Never to live a life of my own?

The thought of it filled her with despair. She had always had a quiet childhood. Her friends, if they could be so called, had been carefully chosen for her; a select few who were considered suitable companions and who had had as little say in the matter as she had.

'No, I thought not,' he muttered. He began to pace the room, holding his chin in his hand and chewing on his lip. Then he stopped in front of Eleanor. 'Until your mother comes to her senses,' he announced, 'you must run the household. You should know enough by now to organize Cook and the maids. We will eat together as if nothing unusual has happened.'

'Yes, Father,' Eleanor murmured. She had been allowed to join her parents for their evening meal for quite some time now and had considered that changing into evening attire was very tiresome when there were just the three of them. Her mother always dressed very properly, usually in watered silk or georgette, and wore pearls in her hair or round her neck, Eleanor often flouted convention and merely donned a pretty shawl over her day dress, or perhaps a fichu of lace at the neck, and hoped her father wouldn't observe it. Usually he didn't. Now, she reflected, he was sure to notice.

'Will you travel to Nottingham, Father?' she asked. 'Perhaps

Mama is unwell and only needs a short time away from home.' Even as she said it she knew it wasn't true.

'I cannot travel anywhere at the moment.' He spoke abruptly. 'There is an inquiry at my place of work and I must be available.'

'Oh?' Eleanor raised her head but the look on her father's face defied her to question him. An inquiry? She recalled the police carriage in Bishop Lane, and meeting the unctuous Percy Smart who had slipped out of the office. I do hope Papa isn't in any kind of trouble. He can't possibly be; he's always so punctilious, such a purist. Yet a flash of memory recalled an occasion when Simon had clashed with him and their father had bawled, 'Do as I *say*, not as I do!'

I wish Mama was here. She would know what to do. She would know how to act normally and go about the everyday tasks, as if everything was all right. Yet it's not all right. I feel unsure and anxious, as if my world is falling apart.

She blinked; tears were not far away. I'm a prisoner. She watched as her father continued his pacing, muttering, occasionally clenching his fists and shaking them as if making a point. A prisoner and my father is my jailer, she thought. I would run away, but what would I do for money and where would I go?

That evening, before supper, Mary came to tell Eleanor that her father wished to speak to her. When she came downstairs he was seated at his desk but she was surprised to see him dressed in smart outdoor attire. He was shaved, with his hair pomaded and his side whiskers trimmed.

'I have to go out,' he said. 'I won't be back for supper.' He finished whatever it was he was writing and turned to her. 'I have put money in the cash box for any incidentals that you might need. Please ensure that you obtain a receipt for anything you spend. There should be enough money to last a week. I don't suppose you'll need much, but accounts for the butcher, grocer and so on should be sent to me as usual.'

He stood up. His colour was high and he seemed agitated. 'I'll see you at breakfast.'

She was relieved to see him depart, but curious about where he was going. To meet friends perhaps and discuss his current problem, whatever it was. She ran upstairs to look out of the top window to check on his direction. At first she couldn't see him. He wasn't heading towards the office or the town with its inns and coffee houses, but then she turned her head and glanced the other way and saw him walking briskly in the other direction towards the opposite end of the High Street.

Wherever is he going, she wondered. There's nothing up there to interest him. Only dilapidated dwelling houses and disreputable taverns. She had been told often enough not to travel that way, especially not after dusk. But her father was walking steadily as if he knew exactly where he was going.

Why am I so uneasy, she thought. Papa used to go out quite a lot in the evening at one time. He was also often late home from the office and Mama would pace about wringing her hands. She never would say why she was worried. A distant memory of her parents' raised voices came to mind, her mother's piteous and accusing, her father's arrogant and overbearing. It was around that time that her mother seemed to withdraw into herself, and it was as if they began to live separate lives.

I can't live like this. The feeling of being trapped, a virtual prisoner, began to overwhelm her. She thought of the money in the cash box. Enough for a week, he'd said. That wasn't enough. I'll save it, she decided. I'll save it until there's enough to take me to Nottingham and then I'll leave.

CHAPTER TWENTY

It took Eleanor three weeks to save what she considered to be sufficient money for a journey, but she had to practise deceit, for her father had asked for receipts for everything. She had previously received slips of paper from the haberdasher's itemizing articles purchased on credit. These she carefully copied, and for small items such as silks or ribbons she wrote 'Paid with thanks' at the bottom, with an undecipherable signature. On other slips, she wrote 'For personal items', hoping that her father wouldn't question them, which he didn't.

At the end of each week, she left a few coins in the cash box to show that she wasn't overspending and on the third week-end she noticed that her father counted out the same amount of money without checking the contents of the box. Another week, she contemplated, and then I will make plans.

On the following Monday she and her father were finishing breakfast when there came a hammering on the front door. Her father frowned; he faltered over his bacon and dropped his knife on the floor.

Eleanor rose to get him another, but he barked at her, 'Leave it. Leave it.'

She sat down again and saw that he had grown pale and was biting nervously on his lip. 'Who might it be, Papa?' she asked tremulously. 'Is it bad news?'

'I think possibly so,' he muttered. 'And if it is, then you must get in touch with your mother immediately.'

She was about to ask him with what intention when Mary knocked and came into the room. 'Beg pardon, Mr Kendall. Two . . . gentlemen,' she hesitated over the word, 'two people to see you privately.'

Mr Kendall rose to his feet, scraping the chair legs on the floor, and Eleanor rose too.

'In my study,' he said. 'Take them in there.'

'Father, what is it? Who is it who's come?' Eleanor screwed and knotted her table napkin.

'The police, I think,' he said, quite calmly. 'They will want to ask me some questions regarding the office inquiry.'

'Police! What's wrong? Is there something missing?'

'Yes.' He was abrupt. 'There is money missing from a client's account, and I have been accused of misappropriating it.' He walked briskly towards the door. 'Finish your breakfast.'

She sat down with a thud. Surely her father wouldn't do such a thing. He was in a position of trust, and had been with the same firm of lawyers for years. It must be a mistake. Her mouth was dry. She picked up the teapot to pour more tea into her cup but her hand trembled so that she couldn't hold it.

Mary came back into the room. 'Shall I clear away, Miss Eleanor, or would you like something else?' She spoke quietly and seemed anxious.

'Would you bring me some water, please?' Eleanor's voice cracked. 'The bacon was very salty.'

They'll be discussing it in the kitchen, she thought. Mary will have told Cook that the police have come to the house. They'll be worried that they might lose their jobs. Which they will, she realized, if Papa should be found guilty and lose his position at the firm. Who would pay their wages? Her mind raced on. Suppose he went to prison? Not that he would have done anything underhand, of course he wouldn't. He was so opposed to wrongdoing.

Her father never discussed his work or his clients, but with a sudden clarity she remembered the rabbit boy from all those years ago. A criminal, her father had called him, and stated

160

that he should be punished by a spell in prison to teach him the error of his ways.

It must be a mistake. Papa is a pillar of society. An upholder of what is right. She also recalled the outcry when her father discovered that Simon had stolen money just before he ran away. She put her hand to her mouth. Whatever would he say if he realized that she too had taken money from the cash box for her own use?

Mary came back with a jug of water and poured Eleanor a glass, then quietly cleared away the breakfast dishes. 'Can I get you anything else, Miss Eleanor?' she asked, and when Eleanor shook her head she went out of the room.

She sat for nearly half an hour, sipping water, meditating and making plans for all eventualities, and then got up and went to look out of the window. Outside their door was a black carriage. She took a sudden intake of breath. It was an enclosed two-horse vehicle with small barred windows at the side and a door at the rear, just like the one she had seen outside her father's office. Sitting at the front was a uniformed policeman.

Eleanor turned as the door opened. She felt very faint and giddy. Her father stood there, his face even paler yet wearing an expression of disdain.

'Eleanor, I have to go with these officers to answer some more questions.' He hesitated. 'I might not be back tonight. Will you pack a bag with a towel and my shaving things?'

She stared at him, then licked her dry lips. He looked away from her. 'Would you hurry, please? These people are very impatient.'

'Yes.' She galvanized herself into action. 'W-will you be gone for long?'

'I don't know.' He was abrupt, as if he didn't want to speak or think about it. 'Write to your mother and tell her to come home. There are arrangements to be made.'

Tell her, she thought as she ran upstairs. How can I *tell* my mother to do anything? If she had decided to leave, why would she change her mind and come home to a position of shame?

For that is what it will be, even if my father is innocent and proved so. Mud sticks and there will always be some who will say that there's no smoke without fire.

She went to the linen cupboard and selected a towel, and then took out a second. He might be there longer than a day and a night. Will someone do his laundry, I wonder? She realized that her knowledge of court or prison procedure was woefully inadequate. In her father's dressing room where his zinc bath and washstand were, she found his dressing gown, razor blade, shaving brush and soap and hunted in the bottom of the wardrobe for a small travelling bag which he occasionally used if he was away attending an out of town client. She unearthed it and began to pack, taking out a journal to make room.

Then she thought he might welcome something to read, and flicked through the pages. She dropped it with a gasp. There were pictures of women, not ladies, in it, most of them in various stages of undress.

'Oh,' she breathed. 'However did that get there?'

She hurriedly hid the journal in the wardrobe and placed a pair of shoes over it. I'll have to hide or burn it later, she thought. I can't risk Mary finding it.

A voice called up the stairs. It wasn't her father but one of the policemen. 'Come along, miss,' he bellowed. 'We haven't got all day.'

She burst into tears as she ran downstairs and handed over the bag to her father. He took it without a word, but a frown creased the top of his nose and his eyes narrowed as he opened it.

'I shan't need this.' He handed the dressing gown back to her and one of the policemen sniggered. 'Was there anything else in the bag?'

'No, Father,' she lied. 'It was empty.'

His face cleared. 'Thank you, Eleanor. Write to your mother,' he said again. 'Goodbye.'

And he was gone. She stood by the closed door and stared through the top half, which was of stained glass in the shape and colours of a sunburst. She saw the top of her father's head suffused with yellow and his jacket with purple as he climbed the steps into the police van.

Eleanor wiped away her tears and turned as she heard a sound at the top of the servants' stairs to the basement. Mary was standing there. 'I hope it's not trouble, miss,' she said. 'Cook and me are right worried.'

Eleanor swallowed. 'I'm sure it's not,' she said bravely. 'It's some kind of misunderstanding, I believe. That's why my father has gone with those men. To try to shed some light on the matter. I expect him to be home in a day or two. In the meantime we must carry on as usual.'

Mary nodded and dipped her knee, but looked doubtful. 'Yes, miss,' she said. 'Will you be wanting luncheon?'

Eleanor took a deep breath. 'I don't believe I will,' she said. 'I'll have coffee and some bread and cheese in my room at midday. I'm going out now. Would you get my coat and hat from upstairs, Mary?' She suddenly felt she hadn't the strength to climb the stairs again, but she was desperate to get out of the house.

As she waited for the servant to come back, she fought to keep back more tears. I mustn't cry in front of her, she thought. She will know there is something terribly wrong if I do.

Mary helped her on with her coat. 'You'll ask if there's anything we can do, Miss Eleanor? We'll be onny too pleased to help.'

'Thank you, Mary,' she murmured. 'But I'm sure everything will be all right.'

'Perhaps you should write to your mother,' Mary said kindly. 'You're very young to be left alone. It don't seem right.'

Eleanor nodded. 'Yes,' she agreed. 'That is what I'll do as soon as I come back.'

She walked without any real idea of where she was going. She wandered the length of the High Street, pausing to gaze down at the Old Harbour from Rotten Herring Staith, but not staying long as the men working at the warehouses looked at

163

her curiously. She crossed over Blackfriargate and from there she turned into Humber Street and Queen Street and came to the pier.

She leaned on the rail and gazed down into the choppy water. The tide was high and the waves threw fine spray into her face, which hid the tears which she hadn't been able to control as she walked. She fished for a handkerchief, patted her eyes and then blew her nose.

'Good morning, miss!'

She turned abruptly; she was sure there had been no one near her as she'd walked across the wooden planking, but now the abominable Percy Smart was standing close beside her. Had he been following her, she wondered.

He touched his hat. 'Sorry to hear about your pa,' he said, and she thought that he didn't look sorry, and in fact had a gloating smirk on his face which he didn't attempt to disguise. 'Your ma'll be worried, I expect. All sorts of details come out in a case like this. Things to do with character, you know, not 'business in hand.'

'I don't know what you're talking about,' she retorted. 'There is nothing about my father's character that has anything to do with anyone else. Now will you excuse me? I'm sure you have other business to attend to.'

She turned away, but not before she saw his sly grin as he touched his hat again.

'No,' she heard him say. 'I'm excused the office for 'time being. I work closely with Mr Kendall, you see, so I'm to appear in court for 'prosecution.'

Slowly she turned to face him. 'Prosecution?' she said huskily. 'But – but he's only gone to answer some questions. Nobody said . . .' Her voice tailed away.

'No, miss,' he said. 'I think you'll find he's not coming home for a bit. From what I gather, Mr Kendall will be charged with embezzlement.' He nodded solemnly. 'That's a prison offence – or worse.'

Eleanor turned giddy and leaned against the railings. What was she to do? Whom could she turn to?

'Can I walk you back home, miss?' Smart held out his arm, elbow akimbo. 'You don't seem well. Hope I haven't upset you?'

She put up her hand to ward him off. 'No. Please leave me alone.'

Smart tipped his bowler again and gave a slight bow. His manner seemed arrogant now, as if he'd got the better of her. 'I'll wish you good day then,' he said, and he turned and walked away.

She was trembling, her legs wobbly, and she wished she had never left the house. Then across from the pier she spotted a coffee house and two ladies going into it. She took a breath. Could I go in alone? Would it be all right? Not unseemly? She decided that she would anyway, whether or not it was unconventional.

Another two ladies were entering as she reached the door, and they held it open for her. They both smiled and said good morning, and she thought that perhaps this was something which ladies did, though she couldn't recall her mother ever going out to a coffee house; but then, she thought, as she took a seat at a table in the corner, perhaps she did and never mentioned it. Father wouldn't have approved.

My father disapproved of so much. Eleanor gazed down at the plain white cloth and waited for a pot of coffee which she had ordered. And yet he went out. He went to his club quite often and came home late, yet he didn't like her mother to go to her meetings. Why was that? She frowned. Her head throbbed and she pressed her fingers to her temples. Was he afraid of gossip? Of her mother hearing gossip, even? And where had he been going the other night when he had gone off without supper and not in the direction of his club?

I don't know my father, she thought, as she gratefully sipped the steaming coffee. There are aspects of him about which I know nothing. Did my mother really know him? Is that why she went away? Did she suspect that all was not well? She was suddenly stung by the possibility that her mother suspected that something might be wrong and had therefore left. But why did she leave me? Why was I left behind to face this disgrace? She felt the hot sting of fresh tears. I shall ask her, she thought. I won't write. I shall go to Nottingham to seek her out and I'll go tomorrow.

CHAPTER TWENTY-ONE

Eleanor looked through her mother's housekeeping books to find out when the servants were due to be paid. Cook, who was aged about thirty, would expect to earn twenty pounds if she was kept on, and Mary, who was a general maid, would expect about the same, give or take a shilling or two. They were paid annually at the end of November so were due to be paid in about two weeks. I will be there and back within that time, Eleanor reckoned, and if Mama returns with me, then she can decide what is to be done. If the worst happens and Father is imprisoned, then Mama and I won't need so many servants. We could manage without a cook, at any rate.

It wasn't that she was convinced that her father was guilty or not guilty; she had no idea at all how he could have embezzled money, but had decided to keep an open mind. I fervently hope that it is all a big mistake, for it would be so shameful. How would we ever hold up our heads again if it is true?

Next she looked round the house for items she could sell to supplement the money she already had. She secreted the objects already earmarked into a carrying bag, found a pair of sugar tongs which were hardly ever used, half a dozen silver teaspoons and an elaborate epergne which she knew her mother hated; it had been given to her on her marriage by a maiden aunt of her husband's who had disapproved of her.

Once again she put on her coat and hat and sallied forth,

167

this time to find a jeweller or silversmith who might buy the silver from her.

'My mother no longer has need of these,' she told the first shop owner, 'and wonders if you would be interested in buying them from her?'

He looked at her from over the top of his round spectacles. 'Do you have proof of ownership, young lady?' he asked, though not unkindly.

'W-well, no,' she said. 'My mother was embarrassed about coming, which is why I am here.'

'Mm,' he pondered. 'I don't usually buy in this way, but they are quality pieces.' He offered what she considered to be a low price for the silver spoons and didn't want the epergne, so she thanked him and to his surprise put them back into the carrying bag and said she would try elsewhere. Then she walked to Silver Street and chose at random a silversmith's which had similar pieces in the window.

She gave the same patter as before and this time the jeweller didn't question the origin of the items until he had carefully examined them. Then he gazed at her very solemnly and asked her the same question as the other had.

'They belonged to my mother,' she said plaintively, 'but she has no need for them now, and I'm ashamed to admit that I am in dire straits.'

'I'm so sorry to hear it,' he said, his face creased with sympathy. He was an older man, old enough to be her grandfather, she thought, though she didn't remember either of her own. 'These are difficult times for such a lot of people.' He sighed. 'But they are good pieces and I can certainly sell them, though perhaps not offer you as much as you would like. Do you have someone you can go to? Some relative?'

She bit her lip and then spoke huskily. 'To my aunt. I think she will give me a home.'

He nodded, and then said he would take all the silver, and offered her considerably more than the previous shopkeeper had done.

She tried to hide her delight; there would be enough now

to take the train to Nottingham and some left over. 'You're so kind,' she told him. 'I can't tell you how grateful I am.'

He counted out the money in front of her and then added another crown. 'I'm always beguiled by a pretty young face.' He smiled. 'But not a word to my wife!'

Eleanor thanked him again and went out of the shop with a great sense of relief. She decided there and then to buy a train ticket to Nottingham for the next morning. It was quite a distance across the town to the railway station, but she didn't want to waste any of her precious money on a cab. The walk will do me good, she thought, and I can plan what to say to the servants to explain my absence. I feel so much more positive now that I'm actually doing something.

Later that day she packed a small bag of clothes and personal belongings and hid it in her wardrobe. Then she put money into an envelope to give to Cook to pay the tradesmen's bills.

She hardly slept that night. Too many things were going round in her head: what she should say to Aunt Maud when she turned up on her doorstep, how she would explain to her mother that Papa had been taken into custody, what she should say in order to persuade her to come home.

She rose early the next morning, washing and dressing without waiting for Mary to knock. Her train was at nine fifteen and as her bag was quite heavy she had decided to ask Mary to run out and get a cab to take her to the station. She picked up the bag and her coat and hat and went down to the dining room, where Mary was laying out the sideboard with bread and hard-boiled eggs and a dish of marmalade.

'Why, miss,' Mary said. 'Why ever are you up so early? It's not yet eight o'clock.'

'I've decided to go to Nottingham,' Eleanor said brightly. 'I thought of it all last night. There is no need for me to stay here alone, so I shall visit my aunt and return with my mother when she is ready to come.' She handed Mary the envelope with the tradesmen's money. 'Will you give that to Cook, please? I don't know if we owe anything for food purchases, but if we do then there should be sufficient there. Please ask her to obtain receipts. My father is most particular about that,' she added, hoping to indicate that her father was still in overall charge of the household accounts.

'Yes, miss.' Mary stared at her, plainly bemused. 'Is there anything we should be doing whilst you're away?'

'Erm.' Eleanor considered. What would her mother have said? They rarely went away, so it had never been an issue. 'Perhaps you could bring the sweep in to do the chimneys whilst there are no fires being lit, and then of course there will be the cleaning up after him. Have you plenty of sheets to use?'

'Yes, Miss Eleanor. I was saying onny 'other day that it was time to have him in before 'winter sets in.'

'Then it's a good opportunity,' Eleanor agreed. 'Send for him to come as soon as possible, for I don't suppose we shall be away for more than a week or two.'

'Very good, miss. I'll ask Cook to pack you some luncheon, for I dare say it will take some time to travel all that way. And shall I find a cab to take you to 'station?'

'Oh, yes please, Mary. Say in about forty minutes? Then I've time for breakfast.'

She ate a good breakfast, for Mary was quite right: it was a long journey to Nottingham and she would be hungry before she got there. And of course she would be unexpected, though she was sure her aunt would offer her a late supper.

At the railway station she tipped the cab driver and gave the porter who carried her bag a threepenny bit, not knowing what he would expect. He plainly expected more, for he said, 'Second class, is it, miss?' and she agreed that it was. She had decided when buying her ticket that first class was more than she could afford. Second class carriages were no longer open coaches but closed against the weather, and although she guessed that the seating would perhaps be less comfortable than first class she was prepared to put up with that for the sake of saving money.

It would be nice to be extravagant once in a while, she mused, as she settled into her seat for the first part of her journey, but somehow I don't think that I will have the opportunity for some time to come, indeed if ever.

Late in the afternoon, she was roused from slumber by the train screeching to a halt and a porter on the platform calling out, 'All change.' She hurriedly picked up her bag, and her hat which she had taken off, and spoke to the other passengers in her carriage who were waiting for the door to be opened. 'Is this Nottingham?' she asked someone, her voice thick with sleep. 'Excuse me, is this Nottingham?'

The other passengers nodded and told her it was. One man offered the information that this was the new station, not the old one in Carrington Street. She stepped down on to the platform and gazed round. It was a large station, recently expanded by the Midland Railway, with links to Lincoln and London.

She was very tired and looked for a porter to take her bag and find her a cab, but all was hustle and bustle as passengers jostled each other to reach their destinations. Eventually she managed to find one and hurried after him towards the queue for horse cabs. Twenty minutes she waited until it was her turn; she gave the driver her aunt's address, which seemingly was a good way out of town, and they set off. It was dark by now and she couldn't see where they were going, although gas lighting cast an eerie yellow glow over some of the streets.

Eventually, the driver drew to a halt outside a redbrick house with an iron railing round the front garden. There was a double gate, which was closed. The cabbie opened the cab door for Eleanor and she stepped out and paid him. 'Will you be all right on your own, miss?' he asked. 'I'll wait if you like, though there's a light showing.'

'Thank you, I'll be quite all right,' she told him. There was a light in the basement, another in one of the front windows and one upstairs. 'I am expected,' she lied.

He tipped his hat and drove off. Eleanor mounted the front steps to the house and rang the bell, which she heard echoing down the hall. In a minute or so a maid opened the door.

'Oh,' she said. By her expression she was expecting someone else. 'Good evening, miss.'

'Good evening,' Eleanor replied. 'May I speak to Mrs Morton James, or Mrs Kendall?'

'Please step inside, miss. Who should I say is enquiring?'

'Eleanor Kendall,' she said faintly. She was very tired after the journey, and felt quite weepy when she thought of what she had to tell her mother.

The maid knocked on a door off the hall and stepped inside, and a few minutes later came out again, followed by a rather large lady done up in purple velvet and strings of pearls. She came fluttering along the hall towards Eleanor whilst the maid ran upstairs.

'My dear girl, whatever has happened to bring you here? And alone!'

Eleanor barely remembered her aunt, though as she submitted to a kiss on her cheek and dipped her knee, a faint recollection came to her of overpowering perfume and being dandled on her knee.

'Is Mama here?' she asked. 'I must speak to her, Aunt Maud, and beg her to come home.'

'Eleanor!' Her mother was hurrying down the stairs. 'What are you doing here? You haven't – your father hasn't brought you?'

'No, Mama.' Eleanor felt a build-up of emotion on seeing her mother, who looked lovely, dressed in a flowing lilac gown which Eleanor had never seen before. Her hair was dressed with pearls and she looked as if she was about to go out to the theatre or to supper. 'Papa . . . Papa is not at home.' She felt faint with tiredness and hunger and swayed on her feet.

'Come inside. Come inside,' her aunt said. 'Rosamund, this poor child is exhausted.' She clapped her hands. 'Letty. Bring tea and cake at once.'

The maid, who had been hovering, darted off below stairs and Eleanor was shepherded into the drawing room, where a man was standing with his back to the fireplace.

'This is your uncle, Mr Morton James,' Aunt Maud said. 'Move along, dear, and make room for this young lady.'

Obediently he did. He seemed to be the kind of man who would always obey his wife, and he plumped up a cushion on the sofa for Eleanor to sit down.

'Where is your father, Eleanor, if he is not at home?' her mother asked. 'I'm surprised that he allowed you to travel all this way alone.'

The doorbell rang as she spoke and she looked significantly at her sister.

'He doesn't know I've come,' Eleanor said, and wondered how much she should say in front of her aunt and uncle. She swallowed and looked from one to another. 'It's a very private and difficult matter, Mama.'

'You may speak in front of your relatives, Eleanor. I have no secrets from them.'

Eleanor's uncle harrumphed as if he wished she had, and turned to gaze at the window, though he could see nothing but the reflection of the room and the people in it.

'I rather fear,' Eleanor began, 'I rather fear that Papa is in some kind of trouble. I've come to ask you to come home.'

'What?' her mother said hoarsely. 'Never.'

Eleanor heard the knock on the door and knew that Letty was about to announce another visitor. 'I think he's been arrested,' she said hurriedly, in a low, trembling voice. 'He went away with some police officers and took a night bag with him.'

Her mother gazed at her, her face tense, and then turned to greet the man who had just been announced. He bowed to Aunt Maud and her husband, and then, smiling, he took her mother's hand and put it to his lips.

'Rosamund,' he said. 'How delightful you look.'

She gave him a faint smile and clutched her throat. 'My dear,' she said, 'this is my daughter, Eleanor. I'm afraid she has brought disturbing news.'

Eleanor knew she should rise to greet the gentleman, but she was rooted to the chair. Her mother had called him my

173

dear! Eleanor could not recall her ever saying that to her father.

'Eleanor,' her mother said, and she had a nervous though slightly defiant expression on her face. 'I would like you to meet my good friend, Mr Timothy Walton.'

Eleanor wet her lips with the tip of her tongue. I didn't know that married women could have men as good friends. She gazed at Mr Walton. He was dark-haired and had an aristocratic face which just now wore an amused expression as he gazed back at her and gave a bow.

He's my mother's lover, she realized, and almost choked at the idea of it. Her paramour!

CHAPTER TWENTY-TWO

Eleanor was shocked to the core. Horrified. It wasn't possible;
not her mother and this man. This stranger who was gazing at
her with an amused smile as if she was just a child without any
understanding. Who was he, anyway, and how did her mother
know him? She had been staying with Aunt Maud for such a
short time that it wasn't possible that she could have become
so familiar with anyone. Not even a female, let alone a man.
I won't honour him with the term of gentleman, she thought,
for he certainly isn't one.

'I am delighted to meet you, Eleanor,' he was saying. His
voice had a deep, velvety timbre. 'Your mother has spoken of
you, and of your brother Simon.'

Eleanor rose unsteadily from the chair and gave a slight
dip of her knee. 'Sir,' she said, and stood with her eyes
averted.

'Eleanor,' her mother said, 'we need to talk, but I – we
– are on our way to the theatre.' Her cheeks were flushed.
'Your arrival was quite unexpected and I cannot cancel.' She
glanced at Mr Walton. 'But we shan't be late back. It isn't a
long performance.'

'Eleanor will be quite all right with us, Rosamund,' Maud
broke in. 'She can change and rest from her journey and then
we'll have supper.' She beamed at Eleanor. 'And we can catch
up with news. It's such a long time since we last met.'

Didn't they understand? Eleanor gazed from one to another.

I've just given them shattering news about my father and it's as if they haven't heard me.

'Yes,' her mother said. 'And then later you can tell me what has happened.' She gazed at Eleanor. 'I'm not wholly surprised, Eleanor,' she said softly. 'I knew that one day there would be repercussions.'

'Off you go, my dears,' Maud said brightly. 'Do have a lovely time. We'll get a room ready for Eleanor in no time at all.'

Eleanor's mother gave her a hesitant smile as she left, but Eleanor didn't respond. Have I come all this way for nothing, she wondered. What am I to do? Do I go home alone? Who will pay the servants or the household bills?

The maid brought her tea and cake, which revived her, and then her aunt took her upstairs to where a room had been prepared.

'I always keep a room in readiness,' Aunt Maud said breezily. 'We only need to put a match to the fire and a warming pan in the bed and it's ready for occupation.'

'Aunt Maud,' Eleanor said impulsively. 'Who is Mr Walton? How does Mama know him?'

'Ah!' her aunt said cautiously. 'Well, your mother has known Mr Walton for some considerable time; but she didn't meet him here, if that is what you are thinking. Oh dear no! Indeed not. My dear girl, your mother has been very unhappy for a number of years, and at last she has had the courage to escape.'

'But – but she's married to my father!' Eleanor exclaimed. 'She shouldn't be seen with another man. People will talk!'

Her aunt shook her head. 'People round here don't know your mother or Mr Walton either,' she said. 'And although I do not condone social intercourse between gentlemen and ladies who are not married to each other, I feel that in view of your father's unfortunate circumstances, your mama does deserve a little happiness.'

'But you didn't know about my father until I told you,' Eleanor said heatedly, 'and they had already made arrangements to go to the theatre together. And how does she know him? Mama never goes anywhere except to her meetings.'

Her aunt nodded slowly. 'Indeed!' She took a breath. 'How old are you, Eleanor?'

'Sixteen.' Eleanor's lip trembled. She felt about six, unsure about everything. Wanting to do right but knowing she would do wrong.

'Then you are old enough to know.' Aunt Maud meditated. 'What I meant about your father's circumstances wasn't anything to do with the tidings you have brought, but a matter I was already privy to.'

Eleanor waited. What was her aunt about to tell her? There couldn't be anything worse than her father's being arrested.

'Your father is a tyrant,' Maud began. 'Harsh and unyielding. He always has been, though we didn't know it when he first met your mother. Our father, mine and your mother's, didn't care for him. He was against the marriage to begin with but was persuaded by our mother, who was a very foolish woman, though I say it who shouldn't, that it was a very good match. Your father had an excellent career ahead of him, but unfortunately he also had an exceedingly large appetite.'

Eleanor frowned. Her father was a very picky eater and only ever ate lightly.

Her aunt raised her eyebrows. 'For the ladies,' she said softly. 'He had an eye for the ladies.'

'I don't understand,' Eleanor said. 'I don't know what you mean.'

'Well, of course you don't, child,' Aunt Maud said. 'But it's time that you did. Edgar Kendall strayed from time to time. First it was with servant girls, who could hardly refuse him, but then his tastes became more varied and he began frequenting houses of ill repute, and this, I fear, has led to his downfall. He spent more and more money on entertaining these girls, or perhaps I should say being entertained by them, and I suspect that he has looked for illicit means to fund that pleasure.'

Eleanor was silenced. She couldn't comprehend that her strait-laced, moralistic father, who regularly beat Simon for misbehaviour, could possibly have sunk so low.

177

'He has an unhealthy appetite for these so-called ladies of the night,' her aunt murmured.

'Stop!' Eleanor cried. 'I don't want to hear any more.' She felt sick and angry. Hot furious anger, torn between the loyalty she thought she should feel for her father and her dismay at the betrayal he had wrought on her mother, her brother and herself. Yet her mother had betrayed her, too. She had left her behind knowing her father's character, and what was worse she had probably planned to meet Mr Walton here.

'You said that Mama had known Mr Walton for some time, and that she hadn't met him here; does that mean that they travelled here together?' Her voice was shaky as she asked the question.

'Not to my knowledge. Mr Walton called last Tuesday and left his card. He came to visit your mother yesterday and they walked in the garden. They were within my sight the whole time, and then he came in and took tea with us. Tonight is the first time they have been out together. There is no harm in it, my dear.'

Eleanor began to pace the floor. 'I beg your pardon if I appear rude, Aunt Maud. I came here uninvited but I didn't know what else to do or where to go. I wanted to see Mama. I was so sure that she would know the answer to our dilemma, but now I think that she will wash her hands of it and won't come back home.' Tears trickled down her face. 'She doesn't care about me or what becomes of me. She never has; she only really cared for Simon, and we don't even know where he is. He hated my father too.'

'I'm sure you are wrong, my dear,' her aunt said in a conciliatory tone. 'Of course your mother cares for you, but mothers and sons, you know, have a special relationship.' She hesitated and pressed her lips together. 'On the subject of Simon, I could enlighten you, but I think it best that your mother should do so.'

'Enlighten me?' Eleanor wiped her eyes. 'Have you heard from him? Is there word?'

Her aunt gave a slight nod. 'Your mother must tell you. It's not my place.' She wouldn't be drawn further and left Eleanor to wash her hands and face and prepare for supper.

Eleanor flung herself across the bed after her aunt had left. She still felt full of tears and yet she was so tense, so knotted up with anger, that she couldn't cry them out. What am I to do? Do I go back home? How will I live?

Then she took stock of the situation. Perhaps Papa wasn't guilty of any charges; perhaps what Aunt Maud said was untrue; after all, how would she know? She rarely saw her father.

Simon! So has he written to Aunt Maud? He would never write to Mama at home for fear of Father finding the letter first. It's five years since he left; why write now? He will be eighteen – a man! Perhaps he is no longer afraid of our father, or perhaps he has done well for himself and wants to tell us.

She sat up. I could go to him! If he has a house he would give me shelter until such time as Papa is exonerated. She still clung to the belief that her father must be innocent, even though the facts seemed to show that he wasn't.

She would speak to her mother when she came back and find out what Simon said. Perhaps her mother would let her read the letter. Eleanor felt a flutter of excitement. If I read it and there's an address, then I'll go to him. I'll turn up on his doorstep just as I have done today at Aunt Maud's.

She rinsed her hands and face and brushed her hair and went down to supper.

'You seem a little calmer, Eleanor.' Aunt Maud smiled. She was wearing a shawl over her gown and a lace cap on her head, and was presiding over the supper which had been laid out on a small table in the drawing room. 'I thought that you and I would eat in here, dear,' she said. 'Uncle Morton has gone to his club so there's just the two of us. I always think it's such a waste of effort using the dining room for a simple supper.'

'I agree, Aunt Maud,' Eleanor said. 'Papa always insisted that we eat at the dining table even if we were only having a cold supper.' She paused and thought too about the ritual of dressing he demanded. How very proper he always is – *was*,

179

she amended – and yet they are saying he has done such unspeakable things.

She shut her mind to it and concentrated on her plate, but although the cold chicken, boiled ox tongue and crusty bread was satisfactory, her appetite was minimal and she simply toyed with the food, despite Aunt Maud's urging to eat more.

After supper was cleared away, her aunt yawned and Eleanor fidgeted as they made desultory conversation. She felt very tired and her body ached. She was trembling and shaking, just as if she was still travelling on the train.

Finally her aunt said, 'If you will excuse me, Eleanor, I'm going to my bed. Stay here by the fire by all means, if you wish to wait up for your mother. There are magazines in the rack and Uncle Morton's newspaper if you wish to read.'

Eleanor thanked her and rose to her feet as her aunt stood up. 'Thank you for your kindness, Aunt Maud,' she said. 'I'm sorry to have descended upon you without warning.'

Her aunt tut-tutted and said it was nothing. 'You are always welcome, my dear,' she said, giving her niece a peck on her cheek. 'Such a pretty girl you have become. I'll see you in the morning, but not too early. I never rise before nine.'

Eleanor sat again after she had gone and gazed into the fire. She didn't want to read, but only to think of what Simon might have said, and what action she could take.

After a while, her eyes closed and she drifted off into a light doze. The house was quiet and she heard the clock strike but lost count of the chimes. Was it nine or ten? She thought she heard the whistle of steam and the slam of carriage doors, and felt the sway of the train as it rattled along the track.

'Eleanor! Eleanor!' Her mother shook her gently. 'Wake up.'

'Mama!' Eleanor roused herself. 'What time is it?' she said thickly.

'Time you were in bed,' her mother said. 'We'll talk in the morning.'

'No.' Eleanor cleared her throat. 'Now. I'll never sleep otherwise. Aunt Maud said you'd heard from Simon.'

Her mother looked slightly cross. 'Yes. There was a letter waiting for me when I arrived here. Simon had written and asked your aunt to send a message to me.'

'Oh,' she said. 'So is that why you came?'

Her mother sat beside her. 'That was not the only reason,' she said. 'I had already decided to leave your father; but when Maud wrote and invited me to stay, and implied that it would be a good time for me to come, I knew that he had been in touch. I have waited and waited for a letter from him, and I always knew that he would write here rather than to home.'

She gazed at Eleanor and swallowed. 'It was an opportunity for me to do what I had planned to do for a long time, which was to leave your father.' She looked down at her lap and went on, 'I will be considered an outcast, I know, but I can't help it. I cannot live any longer as I was doing. I can't tell you how dreadfully unhappy I have been for years and years, and how much I have longed for my freedom.'

'But – Mr Walton?' Eleanor asked. 'How do you know him?'

A deep flush suffused her mother's cheeks. 'I met him in Hull,' she said quietly. 'At one of the meetings I attended. He introduced himself and we found we had a lot in common. We used to sit together, until people remarked upon it, and then we sat apart but within the same social circle. Then one evening I couldn't get a cab and he offered to walk me home. We became friends,' she said simply. 'He's a widower, a kind, sympathetic man, and I confided in him.'

She lifted her eyes to Eleanor, and it was as if she was about to say more, but then changed the subject. 'But let me tell you about your brother. He is well and living in London and apparently in a good position with a wholesale import company.'

'May I read the letter?' Eleanor begged. 'Please. It has been so long.'

'Of course.' Her mother opened her purse. 'I carry it everywhere with me.' She smiled. 'I'm so happy to know where he is.'

Eleanor opened the letter and glanced at the contents. There was no address. She scanned it through and learned that her brother was working at one of the riverside wharves in the port of London, where he dealt in commodities.

'We can't write back,' she said. 'He hasn't given an address.'

'No. That's rather strange, isn't it? But I thought that perhaps he was worried that his father might be able to trace him. However.' She fished about in her purse again and brought out a slip of paper with a name on it. *Manners Inc.* 'This was inside the envelope,' she explained. 'Whether by accident or design I can't say. But there's still no address, so I can't write to tell him.'

'To tell him?' Eleanor looked up. 'To tell him that you received his letter?'

Her mother shook her head, and now, instead of being flushed, her countenance was very pale. 'I'm sure you will be all right, Eleanor.' Her voice trembled as she spoke. 'You were always such a sensible child and your father was fonder of you than he was of Simon. He always said that I spoiled him. And there's always Maud if you should need advice.'

Eleanor was bewildered. 'Why should I ask Aunt Maud for advice? Will you not come home with me, Mama?' she said tearfully. 'I'm sure it's a mistake about Papa.'

'It is not a mistake, Eleanor,' her mother said softly. 'And I'm not coming home.' She lifted her chin. 'I'm going away. To Canada. With Mr Walton.'

CHAPTER TWENTY-THREE

Eleanor gasped. 'Oh! How can you say such a thing?' She couldn't believe that her mother would utter such a sinful statement. It was dreadful. Unthinkable. Immoral! Not her mother, who behaved with such decorum; her mother who was always so ladylike and proper; who had always insisted that Eleanor behave in a modest manner, even when she was very young, and had taught her not to show her ankles and to sit with her knees together and her hands folded neatly in her lap. And now she was saying that she was going away – with a man!

Eleanor burst into tears. 'Mama! You can't do this. Papa would divorce you.'

'I sincerely hope that he does,' her mother said calmly. 'I have found an inner strength and I cannot waste the rest of my life with a man I hate, who is cruel and unkind, when I have the chance of happiness with another.'

Eleanor sobbed and sobbed as if her heart would break. She was devastated, her desolation complete. 'You don't care what happens to *me*,' she wept. 'I shall have no one. No one! Papa will be in prison and you – and you . . . No one will ever speak to you again,' she raged. 'You'll be an outcast!'

'I know, and that is why we are going to Canada. No one will know us there. Eleanor,' her mother said softly, and stroked her head. 'Please don't think that I don't care what happens to you. I do care, very much. But I am powerless. I can't take you with me. Your father wouldn't allow it. He will ban me from seeing you, just as he banned me from trying to find Simon. Even if he is imprisoned, I am not allowed to make any decision over your life. That is a woman's lot, until such time as the law is changed, and it will be,' she said determinedly. 'It will be, one day. And then women can take control of their own lives and those of their children.'

'But I won't ever see you again.' Eleanor began to weep once more.

'You will,' her mother assured her, and her eyes were wet. 'As soon as you're of age, you can come out to join me – us,' she added. 'Unless, of course, you should wish to marry and be under another man's domination instead of your father's.' She looked pensive. 'But you must be sure that that is what you want. Don't be persuaded against your will.'

Eleanor wiped her eyes. 'I won't ever marry,' she said. 'If it is as bad as you say.'

'It's not bad for everybody.' Her mother gave a hint of a smile, although she seemed very downcast. 'Aunt Maud is happy enough.'

Eleanor sniffed. 'But Uncle Morton is so very boring, isn't he?' She gave a hiccuping sob.

'Come now.' Her mother rose to her feet. 'We'll talk again in the morning about what you should do when you return home.'

But I don't want to go home, Eleanor thought as she lay in the deep feather bed. There is nothing to go home for. Perhaps Aunt Maud would let me stay here, but Papa doesn't like her so he wouldn't allow it and besides, what would I do all day? She thought nostalgically of her own room, her own haven with her books, her writing and drawing materials, the personal belongings and childhood toys which she clung to. And the servants will leave, she thought. They won't stay just to look after me, and who would pay them in any case? So I shall be quite alone.

She heard a clock strike one, and then two, and drifted off to sleep, and then she heard the strike of four and was wide awake. Why should I go home, she thought petulantly. Mama must think that she can leave the running of the house to me whilst she goes jaunting off to another country. Well she can't. But then there's Papa. Who will look after him when he comes home?

She sat up in bed. He'd get another servant, I expect, but he'd expect me to organize everything just as Mama has always done. Well I won't. Tears rushed to her eyes, but they were tears of temper and anger, not sorrow or misery at her lot. They've let me down. Both of them.

She pushed back the covers and swung her legs to the floor, searching for her slippers in the half-light of dawn. I'm leaving, she thought. Leaving before I'm persuaded otherwise. I'll go to London and find Simon. I think I have enough money left to get there. She paused. Was she being hasty? Should she ask her mother for some money? But no, she'd only be suspicious.

She washed her face and hands, quickly dressed and repacked her bag, leaving behind the things she didn't think she would need, like her extra pair of boots, which she pushed under the bed. Should I leave a note, she wondered. Will Mama assume I've gone back home and therefore not search for me? Not that I think she will, anyway, she reflected. I'm a liability to her. No, she decided. I'll just leave. The servants won't be up yet and I'll walk as far as I can and then hail a cab.

She crept downstairs, unbolted the front door, turned the key and slipped outside. It was a grey morning with a fine drizzle but she stepped out smartly, leaving the house and street behind and hoping that no one had seen or heard her go.

After a half-hour when she was beset with anxiety as to whether she was going the right way, she heard the clop of horse hooves and the rattle of wheels and turned to see a carrier's cart coming towards her. She hailed him and asked if she was on the right road to the railway station. He said that she was and asked if she would like a lift.

Eagerly she climbed up beside him and he asked where she was off to.

'I'm going to London,' she said, 'to stay with my brother.'

'Ah,' he said. 'I didn't think you were going job-hunting. Not a servant lass, I could tell that straight away. But should you be going on your own, miss?'

Eleanor wished then that she had made up a story to tell him. Suppose he called at Aunt Maud's house and told someone he had given a young woman a lift.

'I'm only breaking my journey with him,' she told him. 'Then I'm going to . . .' she sought in her head for a place name, but could find none, 'then I'm going to be a governess.'

He nodded his head but asked her no more and dropped her within a ten-minute walk of the railway station.

The booking office didn't open for another hour and so she sat and waited. It was cold on the concourse and she was hungry and beginning to wish that she had waited until after breakfast and slipped out then. I was hasty, she thought, but making my own decisions is all new to me so I expect I will make mistakes. She thought of her brother and how she would find him.

I expect the London docks will be much bigger than the ones in Hull, she mused. But everybody will know everybody else, so I'll soon be able to find this Manners company where he works. She took a breath. At least I hope so.

The London train, when it eventually arrived, was very slow and stopped at almost every station, but when Eleanor stepped on to the platform at her destination she was overwhelmed by the number of travellers, so many more than in Hull or Nottingham, all pushing and shoving and talking and shouting until she wanted to shut her ears.

She found a policeman and went up to him. 'Excuse me,' she said, looking up at him. 'I've come to see my brother and I've lost his address. He works at the wharves. Do you know how I would set about finding him?'

The policeman pushed up his helmet and laughed. 'Do you know how many wharves there are in London, miss?' When

186

Eleanor shook her head, he bent towards her and said, 'Over two hundred to my knowledge. What kind of business does he work in? Specialist or general?'

Eleanor bit her lip. How stupid she was. She should have known better. She should have had more information. 'Commodities, I think,' she said.

'Mm,' he said. 'You've got a job on, miss. Commodities go from the Pool of London right the way to Greenwich. There's the Free Trade wharf, Butler's wharf, that's the old one, Hay's wharf, that's the new one . . . there's any amount of wharves. Don't you know the name?'

'Manners,' she said miserably.

'What?' He frowned.

'Manners Incorporated, that's what it's called. I think,' she added.

He gave her general directions towards London Bridge, but told her that she should catch a horse bus. 'You can see the wharves along both sides of the Thames, but they're difficult to get at because of the warehouses behind them, and they might not let you on, o' course,' he said. 'They don't like strangers pottering about.' Then he grinned. 'Not that you look like a villain up to no good, miss. Ask another copper if you see one,' he added. 'They might be able to put you right.'

By now it was well after midday and Eleanor was fainting with hunger. There was a pie and pea stall outside the station and she put her pride in her pocket and bought a portion and wolfed it down. She gave a great sigh. How good that was. How dreadful, she thought, to be always on the verge of hunger. She saw several children, barefoot and thin, hanging about the station and many were begging.

I'd give them something if only I dared, she thought. But I don't have very much money and if I don't find Simon today, I must keep something for a bed tonight. She was in a situation totally unfamiliar and strange, and was gradually realizing that she had no knowledge or comprehension of how she would obtain suitable accommodation where she would be safe.

She stood for a few moments looking about her and

wondering where she would get a horse bus. Everyone seemed to be bustling about as if they knew where they were going, and she was hesitant about asking for directions. But she plucked up courage and spoke to an old woman.

'Cross the road, dearie,' the woman said, when Eleanor asked the way to the Pool of London, 'and catch a bus to London Bridge. Best view in all of London that is.' She had a funny kind of accent, Eleanor thought, and was dressed completely in black. Black skirt, black coat, black hat with a bedraggled feather in it. She was carrying a shopping basket containing limp cabbages and black-spotted carrots.

Eleanor hopped on the next omnibus to come clattering towards her with a sign for London Bridge on the side. She felt nervous but excited; perhaps after all it wouldn't be long before she found Simon and then he would take charge. She would be able to stay with him, and she supposed she would have to find some kind of employment. I can't really expect him to finance me. But we'll be able to discuss the situation and decide what to do for the best. When I explain about our father, Simon will be on Mother's side of course and will have no sympathy with Papa at all.

'London Bridge. Pool of London,' the conductor called out as she was busy meditating and gazing out at the busy streets; at the tall new buildings which were being built not just in brick but in glass and iron and stucco, with marble façades; at the hundreds of people who were scurrying along the pavements, the horses and carts, the omnibuses, the waggonettes and carriages; such a noisy bustle as she had never seen before. Hull was a mere little town in comparison.

'London Bridge! Pool of London!'

This was it; hurriedly she rose from her seat and joined the queue of passengers waiting to exit the vehicle.

The Thames lay before her and she was astonished at the mass of shipping lining its banks on either side. She wanted to linger awhile along the edge to look across the river, but found she was being carried like flotsam by the flow of people who were surging towards the granite bridge which spanned it.

Everyone was rushing with a swift intensity and she realized that they were probably on their way home from work, although there was a good deal of activity still going on down below on the ships. She followed the crowd, or rather was pushed along with it, on to the bridge where some were hurrying whilst others stopped and lingered, leaning over the railing to gaze down into the river, which rippled and glistened with a silvery light.

Eleanor took in the scene. She was overwhelmed by the sheer size of the bridge with its five arches, but although she was mesmerized by the view she was also overcome by the unlikelihood of finding her brother, a task which she now rather thought was an impossibility. So many people, so many grand buildings, warehouses, wharves, and storage sheds. Where to begin? She glanced round the crush of people to see if she could find a police constable as the other officer had suggested, but she couldn't see anyone resembling a person in authority. Down below there were wharves on both sides of the river, so she would have to start on one side and work along it. It was growing dark; gas lights were being lit in the buildings and were reflected in the water, showing a million twinkling stars.

She was scared. Scared by the number of people milling around, scared by the vastness of the area, by the noise and shouting of the men working below, and most of all by the gloomy darkness which was descending ever faster. What will I do when everyone has gone? Where will I spend the night? I must find lodgings; I can't walk about all night looking for Simon.

Eleanor had never in her life had to plan for eventualities. Her life had been mapped out for her. Breakfast, lunch and supper had been set at certain times. She knew when to get up and when to go to bed, for those times had been rigidly ordained since childhood and only supper time had been extended as she had grown older.

She came back off the bridge and set off along the road, glancing about her. So many tall buildings. They were there, she supposed, to serve the companies of the Pool. Further along and in between the buildings were narrow alleys and courts with ramshackle houses; not much better, she thought, than the shed where their handyman at home stored his tools.

Some of the houses had been turned into shops. I must enquire for information, she thought. Whom should I ask? Not a man, for it wouldn't be proper to approach a strange man and ask a question. And yet I must ask someone. Perhaps a shopkeeper? A woman would be all right. They must be asked questions all the time, for directions and so on. She set off at speed towards the nearest shop, which was selling fruit and vegetables.

A man stood behind the narrow counter and she asked nervously if she might speak to his wife. He grinned at her, showing blackened teeth.

'Ain't got one, darling,' he said throatily, 'but I'm on the lookout.' He winked at her and she beat a hasty retreat. Hurriedly, with a swift backward glance over her shoulder, she continued along the road. It was very dark now, and the road glinted yellow from the oil lamps in the shops and houses.

She approached another open doorway. Outside was a trestle table with vegetables and items of clothing on it. When she entered she was relieved to find a woman of about eighteen standing behind a line of orange boxes which seemed to serve as a counter; a young baby was balanced on one arm and in her other hand she held a scoop which she was dipping into a sack.

'Excuse me,' Eleanor said. 'Could you advise me if there are any lodging houses in the vicinity? Somewhere respectable?'

'Respectable?' the woman queried. 'Why? Ain't we all respectable round 'ere? I'd say as we are. Hey, Ma.' She called out to someone behind a lace curtain which Eleanor guessed might lead into a living room. 'Ma!' she shouted again. 'Somebody here wants somefing. Somefing respectable!'

'I didn't mean,' Eleanor interjected, 'I didn't mean that—'

The girl wasn't listening to her apologies but popping something into the baby's mouth.

'What 'you on about?' An old woman lifted up the curtain, and to Eleanor's surprise she recognized the woman who had directed her to the omnibus. She had shed her coat and was wearing a sacking apron over her dress.

'Oh,' she said. 'Found your way all right then did you, dearie?'

'Yes, thank you very much.' Eleanor gave her a trembling smile. 'I'm sorry to bother you again, but – but . . .' To her horror, she couldn't help but burst into tears. 'I'm – I'm looking for somewhere to stay the night,' she sobbed. 'I'm searching for my brother, and – and it's so dark and I don't know where to start looking.'

'Come now.' The old lady came through and took her by the arm, whilst the young woman, seemingly unconcerned, continued feeding the baby. 'Come through here wiv me and let's find out what the trouble is. Two heads is better than one,' she said sagely. 'And you stop feeding that child wiv biscuits,' she called out to the girl.

She led Eleanor through the curtain into a small room furnished with a table and four chairs. On the table stood a loaf of bread and a jug of milk. In the corner of the room a parrot in a cage was chattering to itself as it preened; the old lady threw a cloth over it.

'He talks non-stop when we have visitors,' she said. 'Can't shut him up. Now then, dearie.' She pulled out a chair for Eleanor and one for herself. 'Sit down and tell Aunt Marie all about it.'

CHAPTER TWENTY-FOUR

Eleanor didn't tell her the full story, of course, but what she did tell Aunt Marie was that she was no longer able to live with her parents and so had come to find her brother who was now working in London.

'What? You've come all the way from the north to find him and you haven't got his address?'

Eleanor shook her head and dried her tears and accepted the small glass of ale which was offered to her. It was her first taste of alcohol and she didn't really like it, but she was thirsty as well as hungry, so she sipped it and eyed the bread on the table.

'You want some of that?' Marie asked her. 'I seen you lookin' at it. You can have a slice and welcome.' She got up from her chair, seized a knife and cut a thick slice from the loaf, which Eleanor took gratefully. There was no butter or jam offered with it and when Eleanor looked about her she saw that there was little else in the room that would serve as an evening meal.

Marie sat down again and placed both hands on her ample hips as she considered. 'Our Josh might know the name,' she said. 'He works below on the wharves. Got a regular job with one of the wharfingers; he's not one of your casual labourers ain't Josh, not one of the butcher, baker, candlestick-maker men down on their luck and desperate to earn half a crown.'

She leaned forward and spoke in a confidential whisper. 'He

was doing all right till he married yonder tuppenny-ha'penny hussy. Caught him in a weak moment she did, flashing her Scotch pegs and getting herself pregnant when he was old enough to know better. Now she spends all he earns.' She sat back, pursing her lips and nodding her head. 'She reckons it's for the child, but I've seen the stuff she brings home, shoes and clothes and what not, and she pays nothing for her board and lodging!'

Eleanor made what she hoped were the right comments, but she really didn't understand half of what Aunt Marie was saying.

'Anyway, Josh might know your brother or the company he works for. He knows most folk hereabouts.' She sighed. 'But where will you stay? We've no spare bed, but you can sit in a chair by the fire, if you've a mind.'

'Oh, yes please,' Eleanor said eagerly. 'I would be so grateful if I could. I don't know what to do or where to go otherwise.'

'All right, that's settled.' Marie got up from her chair. 'Now then, I've to mind the shop whilst Dolly goes out for our supper. Can you manage to entertain the baby for a bit?'

'Oh, I think so. I don't know. I've never done it before.' Eleanor too rose from her chair. 'I'm sure I'll be able to.'

She followed the old lady into the shop and listened as she gave instructions to the girl to get pie and peas for four, and then took the child from her. 'And don't hang about,' Marie added. 'Josh will be here any time now and will want his dinner on the table.'

Dolly stuck her head in the air. 'What he wants and what he gets are two different things,' she said saucily. 'And don't let her drop 'im.' She looked pointedly at Eleanor.

Aunt Marie handed over the child. 'She won't drop 'im,' she said. 'Now go!'

Dolly tossed her head and flounced out of the shop, but then she came back. 'What about money? I ain't got any.'

Marie gave her a mean look and put her hand in her apron pocket. 'You've never spent what Josh gave you?'

The girl shrugged. 'Might have. Nuffink to do with you.'

Marie flung some coins towards her and Dolly had to scrabble on the floor to pick them up. They cast looks of hatred at each other as the girl went out again.

Eleanor took the baby into the other room and sat him on her knee. She had never held a baby before and thought of how many new experiences she was having. He was a sweet-faced boy, although very dirty and not very sweet-smelling. He put up his chubby hand to pat her cheek and when she smiled down at him he gurgled, spouting bubbles from his mouth.

She heard the sound of voices coming from the front shop. The child heard them too and bounced up and down on her knee, clapping his hands. 'Dada,' he chortled. 'Dada.'

A thick-set man with mutton chop whiskers ducked his head beneath the curtain and came into the room. The child held up his arms to be picked up.

'How's my little Tommy then?' Josh said. He was much older than Eleanor had expected him to be, and no matter that, according to his mother, Dolly had inveigled him into marriage, he was clearly delighted with his young son.

He threw the child into the air and Eleanor caught her breath in suspense. Dolly had warned her not to drop him and here was Josh tossing him up and catching him in his brawny arms, to the child's shrieking delight.

'So,' Josh said, looking down at Eleanor. 'You're a stranger to these parts. Come all the way from the north?' The way he said it, it sounded as if she was from a foreign country.

'Yes,' she said. 'I live – lived – in Hull and I've come to look for my brother. He's been in London for about five years, I believe, but we – I've only recently heard from him. His name is Kendall, Simon Kendall, and I think he works for someone called Manners.'

Josh shook his head. 'Never heard of 'em.' He lifted Tommy up towards the ceiling and gave him a little shake. 'You sure it's a legit company?'

'I'm sorry,' she said apologetically. 'I don't know what you mean.'

'I mean is it a proper company and not a fly-by-night? One that operates illegally – you know, handles stolen goods.'

'Oh,' she gasped. 'I'm sure Simon wouldn't do anything like that. He was brought up to be honest.' But as she said it, she remembered the money apparently stolen by Simon from her father's room, and the fact that she had sold some of her parents' silver; and, even worse, remembered why her father was being taken to court, and she flushed deeply.

Josh saw her blushes. 'Don't mean to upset you, miss, but there's always a lot of thieving at any dock or wharf. Folks set up in a warehouse or even in the back of a waggon and call themselves a company. They have men working from ships who offload to them and take a backhander. It's hard to know who's who.'

'I see,' Eleanor said huskily. 'Then I don't know. I only know we found a slip, probably from a packing case, printed with the name Manners Incorporated, and I assumed it was where he worked.'

'I'll ask around tomorrow,' he said. 'Somebody might know. Now then.' He tossed the child into the air again. 'Where's your ma got to with our supper?'

After a supper of meat pie and peas, a few pieces of coal were put on the fire. Eleanor was given a thin cushion to place on her chair and a crate to put her feet on. Josh, Dolly and the child went into the shop with rolled-up palliasses and blankets, and Aunt Marie curled up in a corner on a straw mattress with a blanket over her.

Eleanor was astonished that no one washed or changed their clothing before going to bed, and for her own personal needs she was taken out to a privy in the yard. There was a water tap on the wall beside it and she rinsed her hands before she came back inside.

It's very early for bed, she thought, but there's nothing to read and nothing to do, except perhaps have conversation, and maybe they get up very early. She gazed into the fire and listened to Aunt Marie's snores, and could hear low laughter coming from Dolly in the front shop and the rumble of Josh's voice. Then she heard grunting and banging and thought it sounded like someone in pain. But then she heard a shout followed by a laugh and all went quiet again.

Someone fooling about outside, I expect, she thought, and was comforted by the fact that Josh was so big and strong that he would quell any trouble should it come.

She barely slept, for she was uncomfortable on the straight-backed chair, and began to feel chilled as the fire burned low. There was one piece of coal left in the hearth, but no tongs, so she gingerly picked it up with her fingers and threw it on the fire.

The next morning Josh was up at five o'clock. He came into the room with a bucket of coal and, leaning over Eleanor, who was half asleep, he built up the fire and set the kettle over it, then cut a slice of bread from the loaf which had been left on the table overnight.

'Cup o' tea, miss?' he whispered as the kettle started to boil.

'Please,' she answered croakily. 'That's very kind of you.'

'That's all right. I'm always first up. I start work at half past five, or as soon as it's light, so I get my own breakfast.'

She watched him as he spread his bread with some kind of fat from a jar; dripping, she thought, like Cook drains off the meat. I wonder what it tastes like.

He saw her watching him. 'Want some?' he asked with his mouth full.

She put her finger to her lips. 'Yes please.'

He cut another thick slice of bread and spread it with the fat, sprinkled it with salt and handed it to her, without a plate. As she took it she wondered vaguely if he had washed his hands this morning, but she bit into it and found it strangely satisfying, if rather greasy.

He cut himself another slice and ate it, then stood up and said, 'Must be off. I'll ask if anybody's come across your brother. But if I were you, I'd go down to the warehouses behind the wharves and ask there. You just might find somebody who knows him. Take care, though, and don't take any chances.

Always ask for the manager or wharfinger and don't ask the men.'

She thanked him and he went off whistling, not bothering now about being quiet.

Once Aunt Marie, Dolly and the baby were up and had finished their breakfast of tea and bread, Eleanor said she was going to wander down towards the warehouses as Josh had suggested and make enquiries about her brother.

'You take care now who you're talking to,' Marie said. 'They're not all genuine dock labourers. There are some thieving bank clerks and so-called gen'lemen who are there to make a dishonest penny and would thieve from you as soon as look at you.'

'May I come back?' Eleanor asked. 'If I don't find Simon, I mean. I'm willing to pay you for your trouble.'

'Bless you, child, it's no trouble,' Marie said, but Eleanor noticed that Dolly turned up her nose.

Eleanor walked back towards the Thames. There were still crowds of people there and she came to the conclusion that this was how it always was; today there were stalls set up along the bank selling everything from tarnished jewellery and sweet-smelling lavender to whelks and jellied eels.

Although it was possible to walk along the embankment looking over the Thames, the docks and wharves below were blocked by the warehouses and they stretched for miles. It was like another town with buildings crowded one against the other. Nevertheless, she found her way down there and chose the first passageway between two warehouses. Immediately someone shouted at her that it was private property so she turned back and ventured through another entry.

Some of the routes through went straight down to the river; others were obstructed by buildings or sheds, and she came to the conclusion that these had been built after the larger structures, almost as if someone had come along with a barrowload of wood, found a space and put up a structure.

Someone else called out to her. 'Who you looking for, miss?'

'I'm sorry if I'm trespassing,' she said. 'But I'm looking for Manners Incorporated.'

'Who?' The man took off his cap and scratched his head.

'Manners Incorporated. They're an import company, I believe.'

'Hang on a minute,' he said, and shouted to someone. 'Bill! Do you know anybody called Manners?'

The workman, who was pushing a barrow, called back, 'Never heard of him.'

'Sorry, miss, can't help you. And I have to tell you that strangers are not welcome here.'

'I need to speak to a manager,' she said, remembering what Josh had said, 'or a wharfinger.'

'I am a manager,' he told her and she was astonished, for she thought that a manager would at least wear a coat and trousers and not a pair of greasy breeches and flannel shirt.

'I beg your pardon,' she said, and in a small voice added, 'It's just that I'm looking for my brother and I don't have any more information than that name.'

'Well, I'm really sorry, miss. Try the company offices; they would know.'

She thanked him and turned back and went in search of a company office. But again she drew a blank. No one had ever heard of Manners Incorporated or her brother Simon. Now she was beginning to have doubts. Perhaps after all the slip of paper had got into the letter by mistake and was nothing whatever to do with Simon.

In which case, she pondered, as she walked with aching feet back towards Aunt Marie's house, I'll have to go home. Prudently she had set aside some of the money from the sale of the silver, which would pay for the return journey, but she felt melancholy at the prospect of it. How can I face up to the shame of my father's disgrace and my mother's downfall? Her friends and Mr Walton's will know about it and will be constantly tittle-tattling, and how can I live with that? What do I do about the servants? Suppose we lose the house, and what will I do for money?

Over and over she put the questions to herself, but she found no answers.

She was exhausted by the time she reached the shop; she had walked and walked and had been appalled by the poverty she had seen in the district beyond the port area. Rows of dank, dark, one-roomed cottages, little more than blackened wooden boxes with old women sitting outside, stretching out their hands as she approached. Dirty barefoot children followed her begging for a penny for bread, and men crowded outside beer shops turned to watch as she passed, making her feel uneasy and vulnerable.

She hadn't eaten all day, for she hadn't seen anywhere where she would have wanted to buy food, and had merely taken a drink of water from a pump, but when she walked into the shop she was met by the smell of boiling cabbage and onions emanating from the back room.

Eleanor swallowed. She was hungry, but the stench of cabbage was overpowering. Dolly was in the shop with the baby, but she didn't speak when Eleanor came in.

'Is Aunt Marie in?' Eleanor asked. Dolly tossed her head towards the back room.

Marie was stirring the contents of a pot on the fire and muttering to herself. She looked up when Eleanor came in. 'That young – young,' she took a breath, '*madam*! She's spent every penny our Josh's earned and there's nuffink left till payday. He needs plenty of food for his kind of work and all I could scrounge was cabbage and onions. I sold all that lot I bought the other day!'

'I'll buy something,' Eleanor said eagerly. 'I must pay you back for your hospitality.' She fished into her purse and brought out a shilling. 'Here,' she said, holding out her hand. 'Take this. Please.'

The old lady looked at it. 'A shilling!' she said incredulously. 'A bob! You can't go giving that sort o' money away.' She blew out her cheeks. 'Gimme a tanner if you've got one, that'll be plenty.'

It didn't seem much, Eleanor thought as she put the shilling back in her purse and handed over sixpence, but perhaps I can give her something another day. If I'm still here. If Josh hasn't found out anything about the Manners company, then I'll have to go home. There's nothing else I can do.

CHAPTER TWENTY-FIVE

Josh came in hungry from work and was angry that there was only soup and bread for his supper. He shouted at his wife for being a spendthrift but she shouted back that he should take on extra work seeing as they had to keep his mother as well as themselves and their child.

'Ma makes money from the shop,' he bawled at her and Eleanor cringed. 'We managed well enough before.'

Eleanor was sure he was about to say before he married her, but Dolly picked up young Tommy and said they would go home to her own mother if that was how he felt.

Josh immediately calmed down and Eleanor felt sorry for him. Yet how could Dolly threaten him with taking his son, she wondered, when Mama had said that she had no rights over Eleanor herself? She said I would have to stay with my father. Perhaps it's different with poorer people.

She discovered that Marie took trips into town and scoured the backs of restaurants and cafés asking or sometimes searching in refuse pails for scabby vegetables that had been thrown out.

'Round 'ere, darling, they ain't so particular about a bit o' mould or caterpillar,' she told her, 'but not all of 'em can get on a bus into town. You wouldn't believe what those West End cooks throw out, so I rescue it and sell it on for a copper or two. We ain't poor, but we ain't rich either, so it buys a few extras.'

Marie gave Dolly a penny and told her to go out and get some of yesterday's bread, if there was any left, to augment the soup. Dolly took it sullenly and went out muttering that she hadn't known she was going to be an errand girl or she would never have come, but Marie ignored her comments and poured milk into a cup for Tommy and spoon-fed it into his mouth.

'Did you find out anything about Manners?' Eleanor asked Josh diffidently. 'Did anyone know of them?'

Josh pulled a wry face. 'Well, yes and no,' he answered. 'None of the regular men had heard of them, but we've had a casual labourer working for us and when I asked him he seemed a bit cagey. When I pressed him and said somebody was looking for a relative, he opened up a bit. He said he'd worked at Cinnabar Wharf a few months back, down Wapping way. It deals in tea, coffee, spices, that sort of commodity, not like St Katharine's where I work. We handle valuable cargo: ivory, marble, wines and so on; that's why we have more regular workers. You'd never get on to our wharves, security's that tight.

'Anyway, this fellow said that he'd worked, casual like, wiv a company and he was a bit suspicious as to whether it was a proper set-up, so he left as soon as he'd got a promise of other work. Didn't want any trouble, he said, just a regular job.'

'Oh,' Eleanor breathed. 'And did it have a name, this company?'

Josh nodded. 'It did. When he worked for 'em, it was called Manners Incorporated, but he said it might have changed its name since.'

Eleanor took a breath. So at least the company did exist. But could she find it?

'If you get up early tomorrow morning and come out wiv me, I'll show you how to get there,' Josh offered. 'Maybe get you a lift, cos it's quite a stretch. You must be careful,' he warned her for the second time. 'There are some mean streets round there and the folks working on the wharves and in the warehouses won't be pleased to have a stranger asking questions.'

She agreed that she would be careful and told him how grateful she was.

The next morning they rose at four thirty; Eleanor felt that she hadn't slept all night. Her bones ached with sitting up in a chair for the second time. She gratefully swallowed a cup of tea but refused a slice of bread and dripping. She rinsed her hands and face under the outside tap, ran a comb through her hair and was ready.

It was still dark when they left and in silence she scurried alongside Josh's long stride. They reached the main thoroughfare and joined other workers who were tramping towards their places of work. She felt that they had walked miles but presently she heard the clatter of hooves and the rumble of an omnibus.

'Come on!' Josh urged her, grabbing her arm. 'This one's going to Wapping. Hop on and ask to be put off at Cinnabar Wharf. Ask for directions when you get there. Can you find your way back?' He pushed her aboard.

'Y-yes, I think so. What's the name of your street?' she called back as the vehicle rumbled away and Josh receded into the distance.

'Marble Grove,' he yelled. 'Anybody will tell you where it is.'

The omnibus was only half full and the passengers, she assumed, were clerical workers, for they all wore jackets, shirts and trousers, unlike the men walking to work who wore heavyweight trousers, flannel shirts and waistcoats, with mufflers round their necks and caps on their heads.

The conductor put her off at the nearest stop to Cinnabar Wharf and told her she should walk down to the river via the embankment. 'Then you must ask again,' he called out. 'You might not be allowed on.'

'I know, I know,' she muttered beneath her breath. 'I might not be let on and I must be careful.' But it's broad daylight, she thought. What harm can become of me at this time of day?

As she walked, she was aware of curious glances coming her way. It was mostly men walking to work, and the few women who were there were very shabbily dressed. Eleanor was very conscious of her own warm coat and hat. I'm as conspicuous as a monkey in a cage, she thought. I should have borrowed one of Aunt Marie's shawls; but then she thought that probably the old lady would only have the one and couldn't spare it.

Eventually she noticed that the men were peeling off the road and going towards the warehouses, and that in front of her was a high fence guarding the entrance to the river frontage. She sat on a low wall overlooking the river and contemplated her best course of action.

I'll rest my feet a little, she thought, and wait for the men to get to their places of work. Then in half an hour or so I'll cut back up one of the streets and approach the warehouses from the top.

She watched the shipping on the Thames as she sat, and wondered where it was going. Some of the ships were huge and she guessed they were bound for other countries. She thought of her mother who would soon be taking a ship abroad with Mr Walton. Other vessels were barges carrying goods to other ports; some were laden with cables and heavy industrial material and some were lighters which had offloaded directly from the ships and were now heading towards the wharves to deliver their cargo into the warehouses. On the other side of the Thames it was a similar scene, ships lining the bank, loading and unloading, and she could hear the shouts and calls of the men as they worked.

After a while, she got up and walked back the way she had come to allay suspicion in case anyone had been watching and was curious about her. Then she cut up one of the roads leading away from the river and discovered a whole new world she hadn't known existed.

The buildings were cramped together in what seemed like blackened heaps of brick. Women and children stood in open doorways and portrayed such hopelessness that Eleanor wanted to cry in sympathy.

A woman came towards her with one child in her arms and another she held by the hand. 'Will you take one of my girls,

204

miss?' she said. 'I can't afford to feed 'em all, and I've a child here at my breast and no milk for him.'

Eleanor put her hand to her mouth and stared at the woman. 'I'm sorry,' she whispered. 'I can't! I have nowhere to take her to. I have no parents of my own.' A small stretch of the truth, she thought, but she had no time to explain the situation. 'I'm looking for my brother,' she added. 'I hope he'll be able to help me.'

Tears came into her eyes as the woman turned away. There was no anger, no feeling for Eleanor's predicament, just an expression of apathy as if she hadn't expected anything anyway. 'I'm sorry!' Eleanor cried out, but the woman wasn't listening.

Eleanor continued on her way, but with a backward glance to see if the woman was watching her and half expecting to see a child running after her. How dreadful; how heartbreaking that a mother could give away her own child. Perhaps, she thought, it's the only way she can think of to save her from starvation.

Now she was approaching another block of warehouses, and hesitating for only a few seconds she strode out purposefully as if she knew where she was going. One or two men looked up but she nodded her head and said good morning and they touched their caps and then continued with their tasks. She had all the while been casting glances at the warehouses for the company names above them. There was nothing remotely similar to Manners.

She walked as far as she could until she found her way blocked by a building. She turned about and cut down a passageway between two others and came out into a wider area leading straight down towards the river frontage. Though the day was grey the river was glinting, and where the boats and ships disturbed the water creamy white froth tipped and broke the shining surface. There were far more men working here, many moving crates, some pushing barrows and others loading drays and waggons.

Too many people, Eleanor decided. So far no one had

challenged her but she thought that was sheer luck, so she halted in her stride and, turning, slipped into a slit between two warehouses. It was a long, long passageway and very narrow, but she kept on walking though the earth surface was muddy and uneven and she found it difficult to place her feet without cockling over. The end was a long way off and it seemed as if the buildings on both sides were joined together without any spaces between them.

She began to feel claustrophobic. Trapped. She turned and looked back. It was as far again. She must have come halfway. She marched on but the passageway seemed to be getting narrower, so much so that her shoulders were brushing the walls of the warehouses.

Oh, how foolish I am. Why didn't I look before venturing down? She stumbled out at the other end and crashed into a youth who was walking past.

'Crikey, miss,' he said. 'You made me jump! Wherever did you come from?'

'I'm so sorry,' she gasped, 'I – I came from down there.' She pointed to the opening.

Mikey grinned. 'I thought I was 'onny one who knew about that passage.' His eyes crinkled as he laughed. 'Thought I was 'onny one skinny enough to cut through, too.'

She gave a sudden smile, although a few moments before she had felt like crying. Now she thought how good it was to speak to someone who seemed friendly, and with a recognizable northern accent.

'It was a mistake,' she said. 'I thought I could cut through to another section. I didn't realize it went such a long way.'

'Are you lost?' Mikey gazed intently at her, a little frown wrinkling his forehead. 'This isn't a place for such as you, begging your pardon; not unless you're on some kind of business.'

'Which I am.' Eleanor put her chin up and the youth again gave a small frown.

'Sorry,' he said, touching his forehead; he wasn't wearing a cap and his brown hair curled on his neck. 'I thought I'd seen you afore, miss, though I wouldn't have reckoned on its being round here.'

'Well, you haven't,' she said pertly. 'You can't have done. I haven't been here before.'

Mikey saw the frisky lift of her chin and it stirred a flash of recognition. But who was she? Not anyone he would know, judging by her accent or her clothes.

'I'm looking for my brother,' she said. 'Simon Kendall. Do you know him? I believe he works for a company called Manners Incorporated.'

He gave a start. 'I work for Manners,' he told her. 'And there's a fellow called Simon, but he's never told us his second name.'

Eleanor took a breath. 'What does he look like? Is he fair, like me?'

'Y-yes, sort of; a bit darker mebbe.'

'How old?' she asked eagerly.

'Dunno. Same as me, I suppose. Eighteen – nineteen. We don't bother about ages, or bothdays,' he added.

Her face flushed and he thought how pretty she was, with her wide blue eyes and dimpled cheeks. 'Could you take me to him?'

He shook his head. 'No. We're not supposed to bring anybody to 'warehouse or even talk about work.'

'Please!' she begged. 'I've come such a long way. I arrived the other day and I'm staying with some people I don't even know. They took me in when I had nowhere else to stay.'

Mikey looked puzzled. 'But does your family know where you are? This isn't a safe place for you to be on your own.'

He could see the kind of person she was. A young woman from a good family, unused to being out by herself. Not like Bridget, who had run the streets of Hull even after dark, and now, after five years, was almost as familiar with the streets of London. She was even picking up a London accent, as was Simon. But there was something bothering him about this young woman, some small memory itching away in his brain.

'Won't your parents be worried about you?'

'They're away,' she lied. 'Travelling abroad.' Again her chin went up and her nose tilted into the air. 'That's why I need to find my brother. He doesn't know, and – and there are things, personal matters,' she added, 'that I have to discuss.'

He thought it odd that she should have to seek him out. If Simon was her brother, why hadn't he been in touch with her? And even odder that Simon hadn't ever mentioned that he had a sister. Mikey had talked about his sister and brothers to him often enough. Can't be him, he decided. It's just a coincidence.

'Tell you what,' he said. 'I'll get into hot water if I tek you to 'warehouse, but we've got lodgings. If I give you 'address you could come tonight after we've finished work.'

'But what will I do in the meantime?' There was a break in her voice. 'I've nowhere to go and I can't wait around until then. Besides,' she said, her eyes blinking as if she was holding back tears, 'I'm so hungry.'

Mikey bit his lip. He was already late back from his errand. Tony Manners would have something to say if he didn't hurry up. 'All right.' He made up his mind. 'It's nearly dinner time. We tek ten minutes for a pot o' tea. Wait in that gap so that nobody sees you and I'll send Simon up here. I'll not tell him why, cos there's allus somebody about. I'll think on some ruse to get him here and then you can look out to see if it's him. And if it's not,' he said regretfully, 'you'll have to look some other place.'

'Thank you,' Eleanor said quietly. She was close to tears, he could see that. She looked young and vulnerable and – who did she remind him of? There was something, but he couldn't put his finger on it.

'Do you know where he comes from?' she asked.

'What?' He frowned. 'Yeh.' He nodded. 'Same as me. We arrived together about five years ago. He's from Hull.'

Eleanor burst into tears. 'Then it's him,' she sobbed. 'It's Simon.'

CHAPTER TWENTY-SIX

Mikey patted Eleanor's arm. He didn't know what to say or do. Had she travelled from Hull to find Simon? And why now, after five years? But of course, she wouldn't have been able to come before, she would have been too young. But how was it her parents were abroad and she hadn't gone with them? It was then that he recalled what Simon had said about his father.

He'd beaten him, he remembered. His hands had been swollen and cracked, and what else had he said? Simon *had* said something about his sister after all, that day they had first met. Yes! He'd said that his father had locked her in a cupboard!

'Have you run away from home?' he asked her. 'Is that why you're searching for your brother?'

Eleanor looked up at him and brushed away her tears. 'Why do you ask that?' she mumbled. 'You've no reason to think . . .' Fresh tears spouted and ran down her cheeks. She fished in her bag for a handkerchief. 'I can't tell you,' she said. 'I can only tell Simon.'

'Then wait here,' he said gently, 'and like I said, I'll go and fetch him. I won't be long.'

He ran back towards the hired warehouse. It wasn't a proper warehouse, more like a large shed. And it wasn't the same one they had originally worked in. They had been in several over the years, because Manners and Tully had come along on

209

occasion, usually when the building was empty of goods, and informed them that the following day they would be moving to another block.

Mikey had always had his suspicions that the company wasn't legal. The buildings they occupied were usually in out-of-the-way places and lodged between others so that they were hardly seen from any of the roadways. But they had never had any trouble and no one had ever questioned them about their authenticity. Perhaps he was wrong after all, he had thought, and in any case he had no proof.

Mikey's job was to supervise the men, tick off the number of parcels and goods that were delivered and note who had delivered them from which ship. Simon's job was to keep the consignment ledgers and payments to the men up to date. He had a head for figures and that was why he sat inside the building at a desk, whereas Mikey was usually in and out of the warehouse.

Simon Kendall, Mikey thought as he ran. I wonder why he would never give his name? Everybody calls me Quinn. I suppose he didn't want it mentioned in case his father tried to find him. Can't blame him, I suppose, if he was such a tyrant. I seem to know her face, though. Not that I would. She's not 'sort of person I would have bumped into back in Hull.

He slid to a stop outside the building. Kendall! That was 'name of the 'man who caught me with 'rabbits! And she was there! It's her! He recalled how the young girl had tossed her head when he'd grinned at her and then pulled her tongue out at him. Kendall spoke against me in court. Said I was a dangerous young criminal!

Simon was sitting outside the warehouse door munching on a piece of bread. 'Where've you been?' he asked. 'Manners has been looking for you.'

'On an errand for him. Has he forgotten? Simon.' Mikey lowered his voice. 'Somebody's waiting to see you on 'top road.'

'Who?' Simon narrowed his eyes and looked about him. 'Who wants to see me? Can't he come down here?'

Mikey was about to say that it was a she not a he, but he didn't want to give Simon any reason to ask questions.

'It's all right,' he said. 'It's not trouble.' Simon was always suspicious, always seeming to be aware of potential problems, always listening for instances of unrest or difficulties, and it was partly because of his unease that Mikey wondered if the company was authorized. Simon handled the books, so he would know.

'Come with me, then,' Simon said. 'Manners has gone off somewhere with Tully. He won't be back for ten minutes at least.'

Reluctantly Mikey turned back. He didn't really want to be at the meeting between Simon and his sister. He guessed that Simon might not be pleased to see her, and he was right.

Eleanor slipped out from her hiding place as they approached, and for a second or two it was as if Simon didn't know her. He stopped and stared, his mouth dropping.

'Good God,' he muttered. 'Is it you, Eleanor? However did you find me? Who's come with you?'

He didn't smile and made no effort to hug her or even seem glad to see her. Mikey thought him heartless, as she was so obviously relieved to see him.

'No one,' she said huskily. 'I've come alone.' She swallowed. 'I went to Nottingham to find Mama. She was – she was staying with Aunt Maud.' Too soon to tell him of their mother's disgrace, especially in front of a stranger, though the boy had stood back and turned away as if he didn't want to be part of the meeting.

'And?' He continued to stare at her. 'What then?'

'You'd written,' she said, her words quick. 'To Mama, at Aunt Maud's address. There was a slip of paper inside the letter with the name of Manners Incorporated. Mama showed it to me. She didn't know if you had put it in deliberately or not.'

He gave a slight shake of his head. 'No,' he said. 'I didn't. I don't know how it got there. I hope she didn't show it to Father!'

'Oh no! He doesn't know. Simon,' she said urgently, 'I have to speak to you. There's such a lot to tell you, but not here.' She glanced towards Mikey, who was walking about and looking anxious.

Simon shrugged. 'Where are you staying? I'll come over, only not tonight. I'm busy. When are you going back?'

It was her turn to stare at him now. 'I'm not going back,' she whispered. 'There's no one and nothing to go back to. I've come to stay with you, Simon. I need help.'

Mikey could hear only half of the conversation, but he could guess by the way the girl – Eleanor, was it? – clasped her hands together and by her agitated manner that she was in some kind of trouble, and his mind raced to think of how he could help, for he had an intuition that Simon wouldn't want to.

'You can't stay with me,' he heard Simon say. 'It isn't suitable. You'll have to go back.'

Mikey came forward. 'She could stay one night, Simon,' he said. 'Bridget is there. She'd be safe enough.'

'This is nothing to do with you.' Simon turned on Mikey with such ferocity that he was startled. 'You don't realize what kind of family we come from. She would be shocked at the way we live. Besides,' he added, and his lips were surly, 'our father might come looking for her. If Eleanor found me then it wouldn't be difficult for him and he's the last person I want to see.'

'He won't. He can't.' Eleanor's voice trembled and Mikey took a step forward. 'He's in trouble, Simon. He might even be in prison.'

'What?' Simon's face flushed with astonishment. Then he started to laugh. 'In prison! How marvellous. How absolutely marvellous. In prison, with all the people he hates. All the villains and the petty little clerks who have had their fingers in the till.'

'You're horrid!' Eleanor shrieked at him. 'Have you no pity? No compassion?'

Simon put his face close to hers. 'No. No I haven't! He made my life a misery. I can't remember him ever being kind to me.

212

Why should I think of him with anything but hatred? If you'd told me he had died I would have been pleased.'

Eleanor had gone white. 'I can't believe what you're saying. He has been strict with us, but he's our father!'

Simon lifted his shoulders in dismissal. 'You'd better go home to Mama. I feel sorry for her, of course. The shame and all that. But I expect he'll provide for her, and you. The house is safe, I suppose? You'll both be able to live there. You just won't be able to socialize with anyone.'

Mikey watched them both. Simon wasn't in the least concerned, but Eleanor looked desperate. There's something more, he thought. Something she hasn't yet told him.

'Mama isn't at home,' she said in a low voice. 'She's left Father.'

'Huh,' he said irritably, though he looked shocked. 'Good for her. I don't know how she lived with him.'

'You don't understand,' she said. 'She had already left before Father was arrested. She has gone off with a man. They're going to live in Canada.'

Simon's face turned puce; he looked like someone who had taken a vicious blow. 'What?' he said in a low voice. 'What do you mean?'

'Mama is going to live with someone else as man and wife. That's why they're going to another country, where no one knows them.'

'My mother!' His words were whispered, but there was underlying anger. 'How could she? The shame of it!' He suddenly raised his voice and there were tears in his eyes as he yelled, 'Adulterous bitch!'

CHAPTER TWENTY-SEVEN

It was nothing to do with Mikey yet he felt he had to intervene. He had seen the shocked expression on the girl's face as she took a sudden breath and staggered as if she might fall.

'Watch your language, Simon,' he said. 'You shouldn't speak like that about your mother.'

'Keep your nose out of it, Quinn,' Simon snarled. 'It's got nothing to do with you.'

'Quinn?' Eleanor turned to Mikey, an expression of puzzlement on her face.

'Yes, miss.' In spite of himself, and the situation, Mikey couldn't help but grin.

'The rabbit boy!' she breathed.

'Yes miss,' he said again.

Eleanor swallowed. The boy her father had sent to jail – or at least it was because of her father that he had gone to prison. A young criminal, he had called him, who deserved to be taught a lesson, and now her father might be languishing in the same prison cell.

'What?' Simon said. 'What's going on?'

'Nothing,' Mikey said. 'Just that I once met your sister.'

'You can't have done.' Simon was scathing. 'How could she have met the likes of you?'

Mikey stared him out. 'I'm not in 'habit of lying, so you'll have to tek my word for it.'

Simon turned away from him towards his sister. 'I can't look after you,' he muttered. 'I've hardly enough money to keep body and soul together let alone keep you as well.'

'I'll work,' Eleanor said in a quiet voice, but Simon laughed.

'Work! You! You wouldn't have any idea. What could you do? You've been sheltered all your life. You don't know anything about the real world.'

'I'm learning,' she answered. 'I've learned more in the last week than I ever knew. I thought – I thought that you'd be pleased to see me, but plainly you're not, so I'll leave and go back to the lodgings I was in before.'

Simon shrugged but Mikey said quickly, 'You could stay with us for a day or two until you think on what to do. You might be better going home,' he added softly. 'Staying with folks you know. There must be somebody.'

'My aunt in Nottingham,' she said on a whisper. 'But I don't want to go there, not whilst Mama is with—' She stopped. How much had he heard? Did he know why Simon had berated their mother in such shocking language?

'Then stay,' he persuaded her. 'You can share wi' Bridget. Have you left any of your belongings at 'other place?'

She shook her head. 'No. I didn't bring much with me, but I'd like to let them know where I am. The old lady was very kind to me when I didn't have anywhere to stay.' She looked pointedly at Simon as she emphasized that a stranger had taken her in.

'Come on then,' Mikey said decisively. 'Cover for me, Simon. I won't be long.'

Simon sullenly turned away and walked back down towards the warehouse, whilst Mikey shepherded the weeping Eleanor back towards the main road.

'I can understand Simon not wanting you to stop,' Mikey told her. 'It's a very hard life we're living and 'lodgings we're at won't be what you're used to.'

'I've been sleeping in a chair for the last two nights,' she sniffed. 'They didn't have a spare bed, but the old lady, Aunt Marie, she's called, said I was welcome to the chair. And her

215

son helped me to find out where Simon might be. Someone he knew had heard of Manners.'

'Had they?' Mikey was astounded. Perhaps he was wrong after all and the company was authorized.

She nodded. 'Yes. Someone who used to work there but left because he felt uneasy about the set-up, as he called it.'

Mikey was uneasy too. Tony Manners was too sure of himself, and Tully, who seemed to be involved in the business, was always taking him on one side and discussing things in whispers. Nor did Mikey like the way Tully had organized Bridget and Sam to work for him. He had managed to rescue William from Tully's clutches, or at least he hoped he had and that William hadn't gone to a worse fate than Sam's.

When Sam had told him about the two of them begging in that first year, Mikey had been angry. They weren't begging for themselves but for Tully, who collected money from them at intervals during the day but didn't bring them any food or drink, so that by the end of the day they were actually fainting with hunger. When the weather turned bitterly cold, Mikey saw that William was unwell; his face was pasty, his belly was swollen and he could hardly get out of bed in a morning.

Then Mikey had remembered the Reverend gentleman in Whitechapel who had organized a soup kitchen and told him he ran a school for boys, and he determined to take Sam and William there.

He'd whispered to Sam that he was taking them on a treat the next day, being Sunday, so they had to be up early, but not to tell the others or they would all want to come. At five thirty they rose and crept out, Mikey having to carry William as he was too weak to walk.

It took them all morning to get there, begging lifts when they could and walking when they couldn't, with William piggyback on Mikey, and Sam trudging determinedly beside him. They asked passers-by for directions and eventually arrived at a run-down warehouse which was filled with small boys saying prayers and singing hymns.

They sat at the back and Sam and William looked on with interest. 'Is this the treat?' Sam whispered hoarsely, and when Mikey nodded he said, 'It's great. I like singing.'

They stood up when the boys filed out and waited for the vicar and his wife to come towards them. Mikey reminded them of their last meeting and implored them to take the boys into their care.

Mrs Goodhart, the vicar's wife, gazed down on the children and gently patted William's head. 'This child is unwell,' she said softly. 'Where have you been?'

Mikey told her that the children were begging on the streets and described the conditions in which they were living.

'I remember you,' she said. 'You're from the north, are you not?'

'I'm from Hull,' Mikey told her, 'but Sam and William are from Coventry.'

'This is our position,' she told him. 'We are inundated with poor children. Our present number is over two hundred. We teach them; we have a number of volunteers who give their time, and we give the children one meal a day.' She cast a wistful glance at William and then at Sam and said, 'We also have four sick children in our own home and have room for one more. I can only take the little one.'

Sam gave a gasp and clutched William's hand. 'William'd fret wivout me, missus. We've always been together.'

'Your brother is sick,' she'd said gently. 'You would want him to be looked after, I think? Perhaps you could continue to work, Sam, and come to see him sometimes?'

Turning to Mikey, she said, 'It would be better if Sam stayed with you rather than come here and take his chances sleeping rough, as the majority of the boys do. We cannot accommodate them all; neither do we have sufficient money. And there is always the chance that they will get into trouble when they are alone at night. There are so many temptations when you have nothing of your own.'

Mikey had conferred with Sam, telling him that he would look out for him, and he could always come to him if he was bothered or distressed about anything. 'You're a strong lad, Sam,' he'd said. 'But William isn't. Shall we give him this chance?'

Of course Sam had said yes and bade a tearful goodbye to his brother and wept most of the way home.

Tully was furious with Mikey, telling him what great plans he had had for the boys' future, but Mikey didn't believe him and advised Sam to keep some of the money he earned hidden away, which was difficult as Tully searched him every evening after coming to collect him.

Now that Sam had turned twelve he was too old to beg, for he was tall and no longer looked childlike and innocent. Younger boys had taken his place and Tully gave Sam other jobs, fetching and carrying and running errands for him, for which, thanks to Mikey's intervention, the boy received a very small pittance.

'I'm sick of your interference, Quinn,' Tully had told him on many occasions and Mikey often wondered why he didn't tell him to leave, though perhaps it was because he was good at organizing the men and Tully knew that if he left, Sam and Bridget would probably leave too.

They now had rooms in a different lodging house and Bridget was there when he arrived with Eleanor. She looked very tired and was stretched out on an old sofa. She had arrived back at the house with Tully in the early hours of the morning. Mikey had heard the waggon roll up and Bridget's door slam, for she slept in her own room these days and not with Mikey, Simon and Sam.

'Who's this?' she said now.

'Simon's sister,' Mikey told her. 'She's come to stop for a bit.'

'She's not sharing my bed,' Bridget said sharply. 'She'll have to sleep on 'floor.'

Eleanor had given a start and Mikey was sure the last thing she would want was to share Bridget's bed.

'We've got a spare mattress,' he said. 'Is that all right, Miss Eleanor?'

'Coo! Hark at you. Miss Eleanor!' Bridget jeered. 'I hope I'm not expected to call you that?'

'Of course not!' Eleanor stammered. 'I don't expect anyone to call me that.' She glanced at Mikey and was reassured by his smile. 'It's very kind of you to let me stay.'

'You'll have to chip in,' Bridget told her. 'What do you do?'

'I – I have to find employment. I'll go tomorrow and find some kind of work to tide me over.'

Mikey frowned. 'I thought you were stopping until you'd decided whether or not to go home.'

'No,' Eleanor said flatly. 'I'm staying. I can't possibly go home.'

The rest of the day dragged by as she waited for Simon and Mikey to come back from work. Bridget went out but didn't ask Eleanor if she wanted to go with her. She looked round the room where they all ate and slept and wondered how her brother could live like this. There was a wooden table and four battered and wobbly chairs as well as the old sofa, and a hearth where they burned wood, but nowhere to wash except at an outside tap. The ash from the fire was heaped outside the door as it was outside every other door in the court. Much the same, she considered, as where Aunt Marie and her family lived.

She was hungry, not having eaten that day, and so she went out looking for food. How dreadful, she thought, if you haven't any money at all. She could appreciate poverty more now as she watched her own precious hoard evaporating. She found a shop selling bread and bought a currant loaf and a jug of milk. The shopkeeper charged her another threepence for the jug which he said he would give back when she returned it. She sat on a bollard and drank the milk straight down and devoured the currant loaf, returning the jug within minutes. The shopkeeper made no comment on its quick reappearance, but simply handed back her deposit.

Simon barely spoke to her when he came home from work and it was left to Mikey to ask her if she'd thought any more about what she would do if she stayed, but she felt numb and shook her head. She had been so sure that Simon, who always had ideas about most things, would help her.

What can I do, she wondered that night as she tossed on the mattress, which was only marginally more comfortable than the chair on which she had slept the two previous nights. Not a maid, for I would require references. Mama certainly wouldn't employ anyone without a recommendation. She wept then as she thought of her mother and how she had abandoned her. She could succumb to her grief as she was alone in the room, Bridget having gone out again, tossing a remark to Mikey that she might or might not be back that night; he had looked very sour at that and told her to be careful.

Eleanor was glad to be alone for she felt such heavy grief, not only about her mother and the shame of her father's disgrace but over the apparent uninterest of her brother. He was more shocked and distressed by the stain on his mother's reputation than concerned about Eleanor's having run away from home and being alone.

She wiped the tears which had trickled down her cheeks and took a hard swallow. Perhaps I could be a shop girl. I'll have to try for a high-class establishment or people will start asking me who I am and where I come from. She realized that she looked and sounded different from the working people of the docklands.

I'll ask Bridget in the morning; she seems to be the kind of girl who gets around and might know about such things.

But Bridget was late home and the next morning was sleeping heavily. Mikey, Simon and Sam had gone to work and Eleanor was again left with nothing to do. She let out a breath of exasperation. Come on, she told herself. No one is going to help you. You'll have to help yourself. She put on her coat and hat and set forth to buy more bread. She came back, cut herself two slices and ate them, then wrapped up the remains of the loaf and left it in the middle of the table. That's my contribution, she thought. Now I'm going out to catch an omnibus and go to see Aunt Marie. I'll ask her advice. She'll know what I can do.

As she put her hand on the latch a sharp rap on the door startled her. She opened it tentatively. 'Yes?' she said to the man who had put his foot in the door as if to come in. 'Wh-who are you?'

'Hello, my dear.' He had a black hat on, and now lifted it to reveal long black straggly hair. 'I was going to ask you 'same question.' He gave a sly grin, displaying gaps in his teeth, and stepped into the room. 'Friend of Bridget's, are you? Where is she? Lazy gel still in bed?'

Eleanor swallowed. 'Yes. Yes, she is.' Who is he, she thought, feeling apprehensive. He was a scarecrow of a man, with narrow face, a long nose and a long black coat.

He leaned towards her and she took a step back. 'You lookin' for work? I could fix you up, smart young lady like you!'

'No, she's not!' Bridget stood at the bedroom door. She wore just her shift and her hair was all over the place.

Tully scowled. 'Go get dressed,' he snapped. 'You ain't decent. I've been waiting for you this last half-hour. Time is money! And who did you say you were?' He turned again to Eleanor.

'She didn't say,' Bridget interrupted. 'Don't mess with her, Tully. She's Simon's sister, here on a visit.'

Tully looked thoughtful. 'Not staying, then?'

When Eleanor shook her head, he pinched his lips together. 'Pity,' he said. 'We could do with a bit o' class.'

Bridget came into the room. 'I *said* don't mess wi' her, Tully.' Her voice was spiteful. She'd obviously taken exception to the remark. 'She's a pal o' Mikey's. He's looking out for her.'

'Is he? A pal o' Quinn's, eh?' He put his hand to his chest and gave Eleanor a sweeping bow. 'In that case I'll bid you good day.'

CHAPTER TWENTY-EIGHT

It took her a long time to get back to Aunt Marie's because she became completely lost after she had stepped off the horse bus. Everything looked so different coming from the opposite end, and she was also quite flustered after her unexpected meeting with Tully. She had to ask for directions to Marble Grove several times before she eventually arrived.

Dolly was sitting in the front shop with her feet up on a wooden box, cradling the baby. When she saw Eleanor she said, 'Oh, you've turned up, 'ave you? I said we wouldn't see you again. Ma!' she yelled. 'Somebody to see you.'

Aunt Marie came trotting through and beamed when she saw Eleanor. 'I said you'd come back again to see Aunt Marie. How've you got on, m'darlin'? Did you find your brother?'

'Yes, I did, thank you.' Eleanor didn't tell her that he wasn't particularly pleased to see her. 'I wanted to come back and thank you for your kindness to me, but I also wanted to ask your advice about something.'

'Come on through, m'dear. You're just in time for a brew. Dolly, you mind the shop,' she called over her shoulder and grimaced at Eleanor as if at the laziness of her daughter-in-law.

Eleanor sat down as invited and took the cup of tea; there was no saucer to go with it, but by now she didn't expect one.

'I need to find work of some kind, Aunt Marie,' she said. 'My brother isn't earning very much and I don't want to be a burden to him. But you see,' she confided, 'I don't know what I can do. I've never had to work. I've always lived at home with my parents.'

Marie nodded wisely. 'Some people are lucky enough not to have to work, though I always say that hard work never hurt anybody and is good for body and soul. I've tried telling that to Dolly,' she added, 'but she ain't convinced.'

'Well, I'm willing,' Eleanor said, 'but I don't know who'd have me when I have no experience. Do you think I might become a shop girl?'

Marie pursed her lips, and then nodded. 'Up West, I'd think so. Them shops like somebody classy. And you're classy all right.'

Eleanor blushed. 'Do you think so?' She was embarrassed, but pleased nevertheless. Perhaps after all someone looking for employees might think the same.

'Tell you what!' Marie said. 'You're a very refined and quiet young lady. I reckon one o' them mourning shops might take you on. Usually they have men at the front of the shop and gels at the back doing the sewing, but I reckon they might look on you favourably.'

'A mourning shop?' Eleanor exclaimed. 'Oh!' The idea of such an establishment didn't really appeal to her, but perhaps Marie was right. They would want someone quiet and of a sympathetic nature to deal with bereaved clients. 'Where would I find them?' she asked.

'I'll come wiv you,' the old lady said. 'They're mostly in Oxford Street. That's where the better-off folk go, anyway. Tomorrow. Come first thing in the morning and we'll go together. Come as you are with your 'at and coat and you'll look a treat.'

Eleanor smiled as she felt hope rising. Aunt Marie was such a cheerful soul it was inspiring, and yet she always wore black.

'Are you in mourning, Aunt Marie?' she asked.

'I was,' she replied. 'My old man died twenty years ago but I couldn't afford black then, only me old black 'at. It's taken me years to get all this together.' She winked. 'But it serves me well. Folks are kinder to an old widow woman dressed in black.'

Eleanor laughed. 'You're such a tonic, Aunt Marie, and you've been a great help. I'm so glad that I met you.'

Marie patted her hand. 'You're a good gel,' she said. 'Don't you worry. We'll have you right.'

Eleanor felt quite cheerful as she travelled back towards Wapping and began to plan what she would say when applying for an occupation the next day. Should I say that my parents are dead, she wondered, and that I am in the unfortunate position of fending for myself? Or perhaps I won't say *unfortunate*; most people do have to work after all. No, I'll say that I am compassionate and understand people's sorrows and that is why I am applying for this particular type of situation. Her cheerfulness subsided as she thought of dealing with other people's grief, but then she decided that after some experience she could apply to work elsewhere, somewhere more amenable.

She hopped off the bus in Wapping and sniffed. She could smell food and her mouth began to water. She had had nothing to eat but the bread this morning and the cup of tea with Aunt Marie, and it was now well after midday. Her nose followed the aroma until she came to a pie shop where a group of people were waiting. Amongst them was Mikey.

'Hello,' she said shyly, coming up to him. 'Have you finished work?'

'For 'time being. We've another consignment coming in later so I'm grabbing summat to eat while I can.' His cheeks flushed as he spoke. 'Shall I get you something?' he asked, glancing over his shoulder at the queue forming behind them.

'Yes, please.' She opened her purse. 'What's the best thing to have?'

'Chicken pie,' he said. 'Beef's a bit stringy. And get a roasted tatie.'

'Is that what you're having?' When he nodded, she said she'd have the same.

After they'd been served, Mikey said he usually walked

down to the river and sat on the wall to eat his dinner, and she asked whether he would mind if she joined him.

'I'd like that,' he said. 'I like to look at 'shipping and think of some of them mekking their way to 'Humber docks, or coming from there as well. Freight carriers wi' grain from Holderness and fishing smacks come too, those that can carry ice.'

'Oh,' she said, 'of course. Does it remind you of home? Do you feel homesick?'

'Yeh,' he sighed. 'Sometimes I do.' He pondered. 'Well, quite a lot. I wonder about my brothers and sister and what they're doing.'

'Couldn't you write to them?' she asked. 'Simon never wrote home and I always wished that he would, but of course he didn't want our father to know where . . .' Her voice trailed away. She didn't want to air her family troubles.

Mikey glanced away. 'I should,' he murmured, 'but I never have. Simon told me about your father beating him for disobedience and that that was why he ran away.'

'Why did you?' she said as they walked. 'Run away, I mean. Were you in trouble?' Then she was embarrassed. He had left Hull after spending time in prison because of her father. 'I'm so sorry,' she murmured. 'I – I didn't mean . . .'

'It's all right,' he said, understanding her apology, or at least he thought he did. 'After I finished my time in prison there seemed to be nothing left for me in Hull. My mother had died while I was in there and my brothers and sister went into 'workhouse, and I'd nowhere to go. No home to go to.'

She turned a shocked expression towards him. 'I'm so very sorry. And it was because of my father!'

'No!' He shook his head and led her towards a small wall near the embankment, where they sat down. 'It wasn't your father's fault that I stole them rabbits. That was mine. And,' he said reassuringly, 'if I hadn't been caught I might have thought it so easy that I might have gone on to a life of crime.'

He stared across the water towards the wharves on the far

225

side, then turned to look at her. 'It was 'first time I'd ever stolen anything.' He willed her to believe him. 'I saw 'rabbits hanging there and I was tempted.'

'Were you hungry?' she asked, remembering her conversation with old Nanny.

'I expect so.' He dug into the pie with his fingers, tearing at the crust to get at the chicken and popping it into his mouth. 'We allus were. I'd no father, you see; he was drowned at sea when I was just a nipper, but still that's no excuse. I shouldn't have pinched 'em. They weren't mine.'

Eleanor smiled at him. He had gravy on his chin. '*Would* you have gone on to a life of crime?'

He grinned back at her. 'Well, no. I reckon my ma would have given me a hiding – after she'd made 'rabbit pie! And . . .' He hesitated, and then plunged on. 'If your father hadn't caught me I'd never have seen you that day. You pulled your tongue out at me!'

She laughed. 'I did, didn't I?' Then she lowered her head. 'And if you'd not been caught you wouldn't have been here to direct me to Simon.'

Mikey wiped the edges of his mouth with his fingers as he gazed at her. 'Aye,' he said. 'Life is full of ifs and buts. And what'll we do with you now? This is no place for you.'

Eleanor gave a slight toss of her head and it brought him a memory of her as a child.

'I'm going to try for a position of work,' she said. 'At a mourning shop.'

'At a mourning shop!' Bridget, stretched out on the sofa when they got back to the lodging house, was incredulous when she was told. 'You'd never get me working in one of them places. I've seen 'em in Oxford Street. 'Windows are all decked out in black and purple.' She shuddered. 'Gives me 'creeps to think about it. If I was working in a shop I'd pick one o' them that sells fancy frocks and hats wi' flowers and peacock feathers, and warm coats with a nice bit o' fox fur, though I don't like 'em with 'heads on.'

'So why don't you try for a job like that?' Mikey asked her. 'Instead of working for Tully?'

Bridget shrugged. 'It's easy money.'

'It's stealing!' Mikey snapped. 'And you know what'll happen if you get caught.'

'Shan't get caught,' she said airily. 'Cos I'm doing nothing. Tully's the one who's doing it. All I'm doing is asking for 'time of day.'

'You're setting them up for being robbed,' he argued hotly. 'It's just 'same. You're in partnership wi' Tully, who's got a string of convictions as long as my arm, and if he's caught so will you be! You'll be sent to prison or transported.'

'Well you should know,' she sneered. 'And as if you cared,' she added bitterly.

Mikey flushed. 'I do care,' he said. 'We all started together; you, me and Simon. We don't want trouble.'

Eleanor looked on, bewildered. Whatever were they talking about? What was it that Bridget did that made Mikey so worried?

'Trouble!' Bridget laughed scornfully. 'You're in it up to your neck. You're so concerned over Tully! Well, watch out for Manners. He's worse than Tully, onny he's not been caught; not yet he hasn't. And when he is, he'll drop everybody in it, including you.'

Tully picked Bridget up at six in a morning three times a week, one of the days being a Saturday, when the West End was full of sightseeing visitors. In the horse-drawn cart were two young boys who had lodgings in the same house as Tully. He drove them all into London, where the boys were stripped of their boots as Sam and William had once been and positioned strategically either outside a railway station or near some exclusive establishment, where they would give out plaintive cries of 'Spare a penny, mister' or 'Missus, we're orphans, spare a copper for a slice o' bread.'

Bridget refused to have anything to do with this operation; some small part of her found it loathsome to use children in this way, though she never voiced her objections. She waited in the cart until Tully returned and they continued into a busy part of London: Oxford Street, Covent Garden, the elegant Burlington Arcade, or the rough and tumble of one of the fairs in Shepherd Market. They chose a different area every month, thereby avoiding becoming familiar figures in any one. They had been following the same pattern over the years, Bridget bumping into a gentleman and pretending to be hurt, or occasionally 'fainting' just as Tully appeared and called for help to pick her up. In the confusion any Good Samaritan would be deprived of his wallet without even knowing it. After the incident Bridget would hobble away giving plaintive thanks. She and Tully always had a pre-arranged meeting place, often among the down-and-outs beneath an archway of a railway bridge, where no self-respecting citizen would come in search of his stolen goods. She found the experience both exhilarating and exciting and was scornful of and amused by the careless victims.

She was sure that Tully was straight with her. If they had cash from an encounter and had acquired perhaps twenty shillings in the day, Tully kept fifteen and gave her the remaining five, a fortune in Bridget's eyes. She knew that she could plead innocence if Tully was caught red-handed. The young boys never kept any of the coppers they earned. Tully took it all and gave them free board and lodging which kept them tied to him, for they had no other means of support.

Manners was a different kettle of fish altogether. Some of his business was above board and done with genuine traders, but she knew it was a front for the goods which were smuggled off the ships and into his warehouse, or on occasions into the rooms which he rented solely for his own use.

Bridget felt Manners was her way to success and the riches she craved. He wore gold rings on his fingers and a glittering chain round his neck. That first journey into London, when Tully had shown her the fine houses, had whetted her appetite for more than he could give her for thieving; but Manners was canny. Although he had invited her to stay with him on several occasions, he had given her no more than a good chop supper and not the gold she yearned for. He also kept the knuckle of his thumb on her throat as he gave her a tender kiss goodbye and said, 'Be good, Bridget, and not a word about anything you might see or hear in this house.'

She saw and heard plenty, for she was astute and quick to observe whilst feigning naivety. But one thing she couldn't fathom was Tully's connection with Manners. They seemed to be as thick as the thieves they were, and although Manners appeared to have the upper hand, she knew Tully to be a wily old fox who looked out only for himself.

Now she glanced at Eleanor and then back at Mikey. 'So you'd best keep little Miss Prim out of it,' she said peevishly. 'She'd be like butter in their hands.'

CHAPTER TWENTY-NINE

'Good day to you, madam.'

The gentleman coming towards Eleanor across the shop floor was dressed in a dark frock coat. He bowed his head and shoulders deeply. She wondered if she looked older than she was; she'd pinned back her hair into a neat and severe chignon underneath her hat. Aunt Marie was waiting discreetly on a corner further down the street; because, she had told her, anybody could tell that I'm lower down the scale than you and I don't want to spoil your chances.

'May I be of assistance?' he intoned in a sepulchral voice.

'I would like to speak to the manager, if you please,' she said.

He bowed again. 'At your service, madam. Are you recently bereaved?'

Eleanor felt a flutter of trepidation. 'Not recently,' she said quietly. 'But I find myself in the position of needing to find employment.' She hoped that he would assume from that statement that she had lost her parents and was now without financial or familial support. 'I have come to enquire whether you might have a suitable situation.'

Before he had time to do more than raise a questioning eyebrow, she went on, 'I am of a steady disposition and compassionate nature, and although I have no previous working experience I feel that I can fulfil the role.'

'I see.' He ran his hand over his long chin. 'I gather that you will not have references?'

'No,' she said. 'I have not, nor anyone to vouch for me except my brother, who has had to discontinue his studies and also find work.' Only a small lie, she considered, since Simon would perhaps have gone to university had he not run away from home.

'Most unfortunate,' he murmured. 'We none of us know what lies ahead.'

'Perhaps that's just as well,' Eleanor returned, 'for we might not be able to cope with what we knew was in front of us.'

'Indeed.' He nodded gravely, and invited her to sit down.

'At the moment we are fully staffed. I have an assistant and also a young man who is able to fill the position of mute if the occasion demands. We have sewing ladies, of course, but I deduce that this would not be a suitable position for you.'

'I can sew, of course,' she said demurely, 'but I hadn't thought of it as an occupation. I rather thought that I could be of assistance to ladies who have been bereaved.'

He nodded again and patted his mouth with long white fingers. 'I do know someone who has recently lost an assistant and has advertised for another, though I think he was looking for a young gentleman rather than a young lady.'

'Could you give me his name or company?' she asked. 'It might be worth my enquiring.'

'I will do more than that,' he said, and raising his hand gave it a little shake. 'I will take you to him myself. Just give me one moment, ah . . . and your name is?'

'Miss Eleanor Kendall, lately of Hull.'

'Very well, Miss Kendall. I will inform my assistant that I am slipping out. It isn't far,' he added. 'Just a little further along the street.'

He returned wearing a greatcoat with a black velvet collar and in his place came a younger man, also dressed in black, who bowed to Eleanor.

Aunt Marie had already informed her that the mourning

establishments were grouped together in Oxford Street, except for Peter Robinson's, a high-class establishment which was situated in Regent Street.

'May I ask your name?' Eleanor ventured as the manager directed her along the pavement.

'Ashe,' he said. 'Claude Ashe.'

Eleanor thought how well the name suited his grey countenance.

They arrived at a shop front where the window was filled with wooden adult mannequins dressed in black bombazine or crape, and neat feathered caps; around their feet was draped purple cloth, whilst smaller models depicting children were dressed in grey with white sashes. On stands at the back of the window black top hats and gloves were displayed.

Eleanor felt a sinking of her spirits. Did she really want to work in such a dismal establishment? But the shop bell was discreetly signalling their entrance and a young man was coming forward to meet them.

'Claude, my dear fellow. How do you do?' He eyed Eleanor with interest and bowed. 'Madam.'

'Miss Kendall, may I introduce Mr Christopher Henry?' Ashe said. 'Christopher, Miss Kendall finds herself in need of employment and I know you were looking for someone suitable to fill a vacancy.'

Eleanor dipped her knee. 'Good morning, Mr Henry. I would be pleased if you would honour me with an interview, though regretfully I cannot offer any references. I have recently come to London in search of my only brother who, because of his own circumstances, is not able to assist me.'

Once more she was invited to sit and Mr Ashe took his leave of them, receiving her thanks for his assistance with yet another deep bow.

Christopher Henry was a different character altogether from his colleague. Far from having a gloomy appearance he looked quite merry, and began by asking her where she was from and how she had found herself in London. She told the truth as far as possible, stretching it when need be and telling him that she was in sore need of employment to pay for accommodation so that she did not have to depend on friends to support or house her.

He sat on the counter with his legs crossed at the ankles as he listened to her and she thought that perhaps it wouldn't be too bad working for a man like this. He had a pleasant open face and she wondered how he would apply himself to someone recently bereaved. She was to find out very quickly. The doorbell pealed, but as if by instinct he had already slid down from the counter, adjusted his cravat, and was walking solemnly towards the door to greet the woman who came in. She was weeping copiously.

'My dear madam,' he said softly. In response to a lift of his eyebrows in her direction Eleanor rose from the chair, and he propelled the woman towards it and gently sat her down. 'You have had a great shock, I can tell. Let me ease the pain for you. Your father, was it? No?' The woman shook her head. 'Do not tell me it was your husband?'

The woman broke into greater spasms of weeping and he patted her hand. 'And so young for widowhood.'

Eleanor thought this was overdoing it as the woman was easily forty and must have had at least twenty years of marriage.

'Miss Kendall,' Mr Henry said. 'Would you be so kind as to offer another woman's comfort whilst I obtain a small glass of sherry? Would that help, madam? Mrs . . .'

'Green.' The woman murmured that it would, as she felt quite faint. Eleanor asked her if she wouldn't have preferred a companion to come with her.

'I have no one to ask,' Mrs Green said. 'Only my parents, and they did not care for my husband.'

Eleanor made murmurs of condolence until Mr Henry came back with a small glass on a tray. To their astonishment, Mrs Green gulped the sherry down in one swallow.

'Will you attend the funeral, madam?' Mr Henry asked. 'It is quite proper not to if you prefer.'

233

'Oh, but I will,' Mrs Green said. 'I need to show the world that I regret nothing. I wish you to make me full mourning, if you please.'

Eleanor helped Mrs Green to choose a suitable fabric of black velvet and Mr Henry called for a sewing woman from the back room to take her measurements. Eleanor saw how the client perked up considerably as the pattern was described and accessories suggested, a widow's cap, gloves and jet; and so her apprenticeship into the world of mourning and funereal rites began.

'There you are, m'dear,' Aunt Marie said when they met up again. 'I knew you were the tops for that kind of work, and now you'll be an independent woman and not 'ave to rely on your brother.'

So I will, Eleanor thought, feeling a faint glow of satisfaction. She would be able to pay for lodgings, which presented her with another dilemma. Wapping was too far to travel into London each day, and although Aunt Marie's house was nearer, and Eleanor knew the old woman would be glad of the rent, she couldn't envisage sleeping in a chair when she had to get up for work the next day.

I'll have to look for lodgings, she thought, and again asked Marie's advice.

'I know just the person,' she said. 'A pal o' mine has a lodging 'ouse just off Regent Street. Her husband is a tailor. We'll go now and see if we can get you fixed up.'

That sounds all right, Eleanor thought. I hope I can afford the rent. She had seen the fine shops in Oxford Street and Regent Street and thought it would be an excellent place to live, rather like living in the High Street at home, where they were right in the centre of things. However, doubts crept in at Aunt Marie's next words.

'Course, it won't be what you're used to, but it'll probably do you for the time being until you find your way about and get an increase in pay.'

Eleanor knew that she wouldn't be earning much to begin with until she had proved her worth, but Mr Henry had told her with a twinkle in his eye that he didn't think that would take very long.

Her heart sank as Aunt Marie led her off the main thoroughfare and into a maze of alleyways and courts. It was gloomy, even though it was not yet midday, with only a small strip of light showing above the rooftops. Some of the alleys were thick with mud and debris and there was a stink of foul air.

'Aunt Marie! I don't think I can—' she began to protest.

'We're nearly there, m'dear. Don't you look at the mess underfoot. My pal keeps a clean 'ouse, very particular she is.' She led Eleanor round one more corner to another court of a dozen houses, six on either side within touching distance of each other, with a privy and a tap at one end.

Marie knocked on the first door and waited, nodding her head confidentially at Eleanor.

I can't possibly stay in a place like this, Eleanor thought. I just can't. I'll die! It's as bad as, if not worse than, the house where Simon is living.

The door opened and Marie greeted her friend. 'Here, Liza. I want you to 'elp out this young friend o' mine. She's lookin' for some place to lay her 'ead.'

'Another waif 'n' stray, is it, Marie?' Liza was in her mid-thirties, with bright ginger hair.

'Fallen on 'ard times, she has. Needs an 'elping 'and and I knew you were just the gel to give it.'

'Come on in.' Liza opened the door wider and they stepped inside, straight into what Eleanor thought must once have been the living room but was now almost filled by a large table covered in cloth and suiting. A middle-aged man was bent over it.

'This is Bert,' Liza said, and the man glanced up and nodded and then went on plying his scissors across a piece of cloth.

It's probably clean, Eleanor considered, though it was hard to tell as practically every surface and both of the chairs were covered in sewing materials. She wondered how Bert could

235

see to sew, as the only light came from an oil lamp which threw out a dim glow.

'She needs a room,' Marie said, nodding her head towards Eleanor. 'Just got herself a nice little occupation in Oxford Street. In a mourning shop.' She raised her voice at this and Bert looked up and gave a grimace, muttering something about folks having more money than sense.

'I've only got the garret,' Liza said. 'The other room's full. You'll not want to share?'

'Oh, no!' Eleanor said, hoping this refusal would be her way out of accepting.

'Well, you can 'ave the garret to yourself,' Liza said. 'Though I'll 'ave to charge you two bob a week for it if you won't share.'

There was a sudden disturbance under the table and out crept two children, a boy and a girl; each gave Eleanor a shy grin.

'If you come,' the boy said, 'we'll be able to 'ave meat pie 'n' gravy.'

Liza swiped at him. 'That's enough from you. Get back under the table.' She apologized to Eleanor, saying that they were banished under there until Bert had finished his cutting out. 'If he spoils the cloth we can't afford to buy any more, and we don't get paid until it's finished.'

'I see!' Eleanor murmured, wondering if the rent for the garret meant the difference between their eating or not. 'Could I see the room, please?'

Liza led her up a narrow staircase to a small landing and then up an even narrower stair to the top of the house. 'It's dry,' she said, 'unless it rains.'

Eleanor gazed at her, nonplussed.

'Then it comes in at the far corner,' Liza went on, 'but we keep a bucket at the ready.'

'There's no fire,' Eleanor remarked, looking round the room. There was just a bed, a chair and a washstand; a very small window set in the cracked, sloping ceiling let in a shaft of light. 'It will be very cold.'

'I'll put an 'ot brick in the bed every night and bring you 'ot

236

water for washing every morning; and see to the chamber pot as well if you've a mind. All for the same price, as well as a bit o' supper of a night.'

Eleanor could hear the pleading in Liza's voice and she thought of the children downstairs under the table.

'All right,' she said. 'I'll take it. Will you have it ready for tomorrow?'

'Yes, miss,' Liza said. 'I've got clean sheets aired and ready to put on.'

'Thank you,' Eleanor said. 'Would you like a week's rent in advance?' And then I'll have very little money left, she thought, barely enough for the omnibus. I think I might have to walk to work. Yet the gratitude on Liza's face convinced her that she had done the right thing.

When she arrived back at Wapping later that evening, Simon was alone at the rooming house, sitting in front of a smoky fire.

'I've got work,' she told him. 'I start the day after tomorrow.'

He stared at her. 'Doing what?'

'Assistant in a mourning shop.'

He roared with laugher. 'You won't last the week out,' he scoffed. 'You have no idea about earning a living.'

'Neither had you,' she retorted, 'but you had to learn and so shall I. But I wanted to ask you a favour, Simon. Will you loan me five shillings? I'll pay you back as soon as I can, but I've paid for my lodgings and I've hardly any money left.'

'Where did you get the money from to get here?' he asked curiously. 'You had no money of your own. Or did Father grant you an allowance?'

'No, he didn't,' she said sheepishly. 'I sold some things. I needed money for the train fare to Nottingham.'

'What kind of things?'

'Things we didn't need any more.' She felt her cheeks flushing as Simon gave a sudden grin and sat up in the chair to gaze at her.

237

'You pinched something from home!' he said incredulously. 'Wow! I never thought you had it in you!'

'I'm not proud of it. But I hadn't any money of my own and Father wasn't there. I thought if I went to see Mama I'd be able to persuade her to come back. Only she wouldn't,' she said, her voice dropping.

Simon looked away. 'Well, I haven't any spare cash. I could lend you a shilling, but it'll leave me short. I haven't got five bob to my name. I'm sick of this, to be honest,' he muttered. 'I could do better than working for Manners only he won't give me a reference; I know that without even asking him.'

'But what about the other man? Tully? Would he give you one? You've known him long enough, haven't you?' But then she recalled hearing Mikey say that Tully was a thief.

Simon sneered. 'He's a criminal,' he said harshly. 'Up to no good. If I get a reference from him I'll be tarred with the same brush.'

He hadn't risen from his chair as she'd entered the house and he stretched his legs out now and folded his arms in front of him. 'So – sorry. I can't help you. You'll just have to manage the best you can.'

CHAPTER THIRTY

That night Eleanor kept to the room she shared with Bridget, and came out only once to go to the privy. Mikey was sitting across from Simon. The boy, Sam, was curled up asleep on the floor, covered over with a thin blanket. When she returned from the dark court, Mikey asked if she wanted to come and sit with them by the fire, but she refused, saying that she was going to bed. Bridget didn't come back that night and she wondered where she was.

The next morning she rose early; she had heard movement from the other room and wanted to catch Mikey before he went to work. Simon and Sam had left already, but Simon hadn't called to her before going out.

'I'm leaving,' she told Mikey. 'I've got other lodgings near Regent Street.'

'Are they all right?' he asked. 'You must be careful about where you stop.'

She was grateful for his concern. Simon hadn't even bothered to ask her where she would be staying, and she had decided that she wouldn't ask him for the shilling that he had reluctantly half offered.

She gave Mikey the address. 'I hope I'll be able to find it again.' She gave a nervous laugh. 'It's like a maze down there.'

He smiled. 'Hull's like that too,' he said. 'Though perhaps you wouldn't know that?'

She gave a woeful shake of her head. How naive she had been, how innocent, and how ignorant of how some Hull residents lived.

'I'll catch an omnibus to town,' she said, 'and take my belongings to the lodging house; then I'll explore and find my way about before tomorrow. I'll have to walk to work as I shan't have any money until I get my wages.'

Mikey frowned. 'What about food? Is that included in 'price?'

'Yes,' Eleanor said. 'And I've paid a week in advance.'

'Shouldn't have done that!' he said. 'You should've moved in first afore handing over any money.'

'Oh!' She was crestfallen. What a lot she had to learn. 'But I'm sure it will be all right. They didn't ask for it; it was my suggestion.'

His eyes crinkled as he smiled. 'They must have thought you were an angel in disguise, Ellie – Eleanor.'

Ellie, she thought. No one has ever called me that before. I rather like it.

'Simon will be coming to see if you're all right, I expect,' Mikey said. 'After you've settled in, that is. Job sounds good. You've done well.'

She felt her eyes flood with tears. Here was someone who barely knew her, offering up praise, boosting her confidence, whereas Simon had not been the least bit interested.

'Thank you,' she said. 'I don't know how I've found myself in this situation. There I was at home . . .' Her voice dropped. 'Then everything went wrong. Perhaps I acted hastily, going off to Nottingham to see my mother, but it seemed the natural thing to do. But then, but then—' She stopped short. How swiftly events had moved on.

'You suddenly found yourself in another world,' Mikey said softly. 'In a grown-up world where you had to make decisions. I do know about it.' He took hold of her hand and gently pressed it. 'I found myself in 'same situation after I came out of prison. But you'll be all right, Ellie. You're strong. Stronger than you realize. You've not had 'opportunity to show your mettle before. But you've got it now and there's nowt to stop you.'

She was so overcome by emotion at hearing his praise, and the familiar sound of home in his northern voice, that impulsively she reached up and kissed his cheek.

'Thank you so much, Mikey,' she breathed, and knew by the flush on his cheek that she had embarrassed him. 'I'm so very grateful.'

The house was easier to find than she had thought it would be. She jumped off the horse bus and walked briskly for a quarter of a mile; as her bag became heavier, she slowed down, switching it from one hand to the other. She saw across the busy street the mourning emporium where she was to start work the following day, and mentally rehearsed the route that she had taken with Marie the day before, bearing in mind the directions Liza had given her.

Once more she traversed the mean side streets, courts and alleyways, and although she didn't feel threatened – it was daylight, after all – she was conscious again of being well dressed amongst the poor. I don't know what I can do about it, she thought. The other clothes that I brought with me will stand out in just the same way. Although she didn't have a vast or lavish wardrobe, not having the need for one, all her clothes were of good cloth.

Eventually, feeling quite proud of herself, she came to the lodging house. Bert was sitting by the window but he didn't see her, so intent was he on his stitching. She knocked on the door and he looked up.

'Come in, miss.' He opened the door to let her in.

'I'm sorry, I'm afraid I don't know your surname,' Eleanor said. She didn't feel comfortable calling him Bert.

'Bertram, miss. Matthew Bertram. That's why everybody calls me Bert.'

'I see. Well, I'd rather call you Mr Bertram, Mr Bertram.'

'As you wish.' He turned back to his work by the window. 'If you'll excuse me, Miss Kendall, I have to finish this garment by this evening. Liza will be back soon, but feel free to go up to your room.'

'Yes, I will, thank you. But I wanted to ask you something, Mr Bertram. I'm starting work tomorrow, as you know, and I wondered if you would be able to make me a grey blouse? You see, I have a grey wool skirt, and because of the type of establishment I shall be working in I thought a grey or black blouse might be suitable.'

He surveyed her gravely over the top of his wire-rimmed spectacles. 'I'm a tailor, Miss Kendall. I don't make clothes for ladies.'

She bit on her lip, disappointed.

'May I offer to advise you? In my opinion grey or black will be too funereal. It's not you that's bereaved and you don't want to appear too dreary. I think you should wear a nice crisp white blouse with your grey skirt, and what if I was to make you a black bodice or waistcoat, piped with some grey ribbon to lighten it? It will look very businesslike, but very suitable for greeting sorrowing people. Sleeveless jackets for ladies are in vogue just now.'

'Oh, how kind!' she said. 'That would be perfect, as I have brought a white blouse with me. But I can't afford to have the jacket made just yet, Mr Bertram, not until I get my first week's wages.'

There was a slight twinkle in his eyes, at odds with his lugubrious expression, as he said, 'You can owe me, Miss Kendall. Liza can take your measurements and I'll make it tonight after I've finished these trousers. And if you bring down your blouse I'll crisp it up with a bit of starch and a hot iron.'

She had quite a spring in her step the following morning as she set out. Mr Bertram had produced a waistcoat made from soft wool, a piece he had left over, he said. He had made it with a basque to fit over her hips and trimmed the edges of the lapels with a grey satin ribbon, covering the tiny buttons with the same colour. He had also edged the hem with a grey silk fringe.

242

She wore her coat over the outfit as the morning was grey. There was very little light coming through her bedroom window and none at all through the one downstairs.

'Don't get lost, m'dear,' Liza said. 'It's a pea-souper this morning.'

The court was very murky and the doors and windows of the houses opposite were barely visible, but as she stepped out into the main road it was like walking into a soggy clammy wall which wet her hair and dampened her clothes. Thick grey fog swirled about her; it muffled the sound of the traffic and completely obscured any landmarks. Now and again she could hear voices calling, some of them laughing, others shouting out to ask where they were.

She groped for her handkerchief and covered her nose, and with her other hand stretched out in front of her she walked on, hoping that she would be able to find the emporium, for she had completely lost any sense of direction. Now and again the vapour lifted and she caught a glimpse of a building or a waggon, but before she could get her bearings the fog descended again and her vision was eclipsed.

It took her an hour to find her way, and that was after asking several passers-by if they knew whether she was near Henry's mourning emporium. She was very anxious about being late on her first morning, but on arriving she found that the door was locked, and although she knocked on the glass, no one came. She waited and waited, shivering with cold and feeling very damp, before she was joined by two of the seamstresses who said that they too had been lost.

'Know the way like the backs of our 'ands, don't we, Peg, but we must 'ave walked right past.'

'I'm Eleanor Kendall,' Eleanor said. 'I'm starting today as an assistant to Mr Henry.'

'That'll be young Mr Henry,' said the young woman who had introduced herself as Judy. 'Mr Josiah Henry would never have taken on a young lady, oh dear no. Mr Christopher is much more modern.'

The man himself arrived on the doorstep soon after, out

of breath and very damp. 'I've had to walk,' he grumbled as he unlocked the door. 'Didn't dare risk driving the chaise. Good morning,' he said to Eleanor. 'I'm sorry you have had to wait.'

He ushered her in and bade her be seated, and when he clasped his hands together and assumed a sorrowful expression Eleanor realized that he had forgotten who she was.

'Mr Henry,' she said, before he could speak, 'I'm Eleanor Kendall. I'm beginning employment with you today.'

His face cleared. 'Oh! So you are. Well, thank goodness for that. I can't be dealing with death right now. Come along. I'll show you where to put your coat and then perhaps you'd make us both a cup of coffee?'

I daren't tell him that this is the first time I have ever made a pot of coffee, she thought as she waited for the kettle to boil. In a room at the back of the shop was a small kitchen with a range where a fire was burning; she assumed that a caretaker had lit it. Beyond the kitchen was another room with a stove at the end of it, where the seamstresses worked at a large table. At one end of the table, set on top of a wooden packing case, was a sewing machine – something Eleanor had never seen before.

'Come and take a look, dearie,' Judy had said. 'We're one of the first mourning shops to use a sewing machine. Saves us a lot of time, especially on the ladies' dresses. I can stitch one up in a day now.'

What a lot I'm learning, she thought as she poured the water on to the coffee grounds. What a wasted life I have had. But still, she considered, I'm young; I can do so much if I want to, now that I'm no longer constrained. But as she thought of her father locked up in a prison cell she felt sad, although when she remembered her mother, probably by now on her way to Canada, she felt only anger.

At the end of the day she had attended two ladies who had been bereaved, and with Mr Christopher's help had suggested the outfits they should wear for mourning. She had never been to a funeral, let alone known what should be worn, and she was astounded at the protocol and procedure involved.

The first customer required deep black, but insisted on the latest style, because, she told Eleanor, 'I shall have to wear it for a whole year to show my sorrow.'

Eleanor didn't think her too sorrowful as she had a bright expression in her eyes, except when she pressed her handkerchief to them and proclaimed how bereft she was. When she left in her black-trimmed carriage, Mr Christopher told Eleanor that the lady in question was just twenty-three, and that her late husband, aged forty-seven, had left her very well provided for.

When Eleanor prepared to leave the shop at seven o'clock, she was very tired. The day had been interesting; she had looked in all the drawers and cupboards to check where gloves and stockings, bonnets and hatbands, umbrellas and mourning cards were kept, but the sight of so much black was, she thought, very depressing.

As she opened the door to depart, she was once more choked by thick fog. She quickly closed it again. 'Mr Christopher,' she called. 'The fog is dreadful.'

He peered out. 'So it is. I was going to look for a hansom, but there won't be any, or at least they won't take me all the way home. I'll have to stay here tonight.'

The seamstresses were still working, and would be for another hour in order to meet a customer's requirements, so once more Eleanor would have to walk alone.

'Don't get lost,' Mr Christopher said. 'Will you be all right?'

She took a breath. 'I think so,' she said. 'I'm not sure.' She opened the door again and a yellow mist swirled in. 'Good night, Mr Christopher.'

It's not far, she thought. As long as I get across the road without being run over I think I know the way. But everything looks different. She put her scarf over her mouth and struck out, once again holding her other hand in front of her to ward off anything that might be in front of her.

The fog was claustrophobic and clinging and made her

cough. She passed shop windows where dim lights were burning and gave her a rough idea of where she was. Where there were no lights she simply put one careful foot in front of the other. Pedestrians passed each other, muffled up to the eyes with scarves and shawls, and she heard the cries of men who seemed to be leading their horses rather than driving them.

I don't know where I am! Have I passed the corner? She ran her hand along the wall of a building to follow it and reached the end. Is this it? Is this where I turn? And if I turn and it isn't, how will I find my way back again? She felt like a blind woman; her throat and nose were choked with thick catarrh and she stopped to blow her nose and cough and spit.

'Is anybody there?' she called. 'Does anybody know the name of this street?'

Voices called back but they were indeterminate. She wanted to cry, she felt so lost. Some ghostly figure went past her and asked if she knew where a certain street was, but of course she didn't.

'Hello,' she shouted when she heard the rattle of wheels. 'I'm lost, can anybody help me? I'm looking for Trenton Square.'

'No idea, love,' came a voice out of the fog. 'I'm lost myself.'

She felt someone pull on her sleeve and turned, a sob in her throat. A small boy was looking up at her. He wore no coat, only the thinnest of shirts, a pair of short ragged trousers and nothing on his feet.

He pulled again at her arm. 'I'll take you, lady. I know where it is. You come wiv me.'

Should I go? He might be setting me up for someone to rob me. I have no money but they could take the coat off my back and leave me for dead. She looked down at the child, for that was all he was. His face was thin and dirty and he had a runny nose. His eyes had dark shadows beneath them.

'Are you coming, lady? I can't wait 'ere all night.'

'Yes,' she said. 'Yes, please.'

CHAPTER THIRTY-ONE

'Give me your 'and, lady,' the boy said, 'and I'll see you right. I know all of these streets.'

Eleanor gave him her gloved hand and was shocked at how thin and small his was. How was it he was out on his own in the dark and the fog? It didn't seem right.

'Do you live round here?'

'Yes, lady. All me life.' He trudged on, holding fast to her hand.

'How old are you? Aren't you young to be out on your own?'

He laughed, but then gave a hacking cough. 'No, not me. I'm ten. I know me way about.'

He led her down an alleyway. 'This is a short cut,' he said. 'Not everybody knows this way to Trenton Square, but one of me cousins lives near there and we come up here regular.'

'I'm very grateful,' Eleanor said. 'I would never have found it.'

The fog lifted slightly and she saw a house she recognized, one with boarded-up windows and a broken door. 'We're nearly there, I think.'

'We are,' he confirmed as the entrance to the court loomed in front of them. ''Ere it is. 'Ome, safe and sound. Will you be all right now, lady?'

'Thank you so much.' Eleanor took off a glove and fumbled in her purse. 'Here, I must give you something for your trouble.' She found a penny and, handing it over to him, felt how cold his hand was.

'You must be freezing,' she said. 'Do you not have a coat?'

He gave a little snigger. 'Don't know what one of them is, lady. Never had one, at any rate. But it is a bit nippy tonight, though that's a good sign, cos if the wind gets up then the fog will lift. I'll be off, then. Be seeing you.'

'Wait.' Eleanor unwound her scarf. 'Take this,' she said, wrapping it round his neck. 'You'll be warmer.'

'Ooh, thanks, lady!' His delight was evident as he grinned, his face lighting up. 'Nobody's ever give me somefink like this before.'

'You're very welcome to it,' she smiled. 'Good night.'

It was three days before the fog lifted and Eleanor dreaded each one. She developed a cold and a cough and Liza insisted on making her onion soup.

'We always have it,' she said. 'Finest thing for colds. My old gran used to make it and so did my ma.'

She poured a generous bowlful for Eleanor and did the same for Bert and the children. Then she ate what was left out of the pan.

Eleanor ate with the family. At first she had taken supper in her room, but it was cold up there and much cosier downstairs, where there was a fire. She had met the other lodger, a clerk called Simpson, who ate out and only came to his room to sleep.

'Keeps hisself to hisself,' Liza had told her. 'But that's all right by us. He's nice and quiet and pays his rent on time.'

After about three weeks Eleanor was settling into a regular routine at the emporium, and although the work wasn't arduous there were times when she would have found it depressing if it hadn't been for Mr Christopher's merry humour. She met his father, Mr Henry senior, who frowned at her when introduced and said grumpily that he didn't know what the world was coming to when young ladies wanted to earn their own living.

'You should be looking for a husband, young woman,' he scowled. 'There must be many a sensible young fellow wanting a pretty gel like you for a wife.'

She smiled and said she had not yet found one, and Mr Christopher explained to his father that Miss Kendall had found herself through no fault of her own in circumstances where she had to earn her own living.

Mr Henry humphed and asked if her father hadn't provided for her. She answered in the negative, but at his words began wondering if her father would have made provision for her to go on living at home had she stayed there.

It was getting close to Christmas; many of the shops in Oxford Street had begun to decorate their windows with colourful ribbons and gifts. Eleanor spent Sunday strolling past them and looking at the array of goods on display. She was disappointed that Simon hadn't been in touch at all, but she decided that she would buy him a small gift, for that was all she could afford after paying for her waistcoat.

On her way back she saw the young boy who had directed her to Trenton Square, and called to him.

'Hello,' she said. 'Do you remember me?'

'Yes, I do, lady.'

He looked a little sheepish and she thought he might be embarrassed by her speaking to him. Then she realized he wasn't wearing the scarf she had given him although it was a bitterly cold day.

'You're not wearing the scarf,' she said. 'Did you forget to put it on?'

He shook his head. 'No, lady. My da sold it. He got a shilling for it and that paid the rent.'

A shilling, she thought in dismay. It was lambswool. Worth far more than that. She looked at the boy, who had hung his head and didn't look back at her. They must be desperate for money.

'Does your father work?' she asked, but again he shook his head.

'He's lame, lady. Hurt 'is leg working on the docks. They

won't 'ave 'im back.' He looked up and met her eyes. 'I'm sorry about the scarf. It was lovely. Nice 'n' warm.'

'Never mind,' she said gently. 'It's more important that you paid the rent.'

He nodded, and with a wave of his hand went off up the street.

When she arrived back at Trenton Square she found she had visitors waiting on the doorstep: Mikey and young Sam.

Mikey greeted her; his cheeks were flushed as he said, 'Sam and me are going to Whitechapel next Sunday to see his brother.'

'Oh, I didn't know you had a brother, Sam.'

Eleanor didn't in fact know anything at all about Sam. She'd only met him a few times and he hadn't had much to say to her.

'He's called William,' Sam told her. 'He stays wiv some people. They look after him.'

'We wondered if you'd like to come with us,' Mikey said. 'For a day out, you know. We have to walk some of 'way but we try to hitch a lift.'

'Is it a nice place?' Eleanor asked.

Mikey pulled a face. 'No, but Sam and William go off on their own to talk about what they've been doing, and I thought that if you're not doing much . . .' His words tailed away. 'Still, I expect you'll have other things to do as it's your onny day off,' he finished lamely.

'No. No, I haven't. The truth is I'm sometimes bored on a Sunday.' She was pleased that he had asked her and flattered that he wanted her company. 'I'd like to come.'

He gave a grin. 'Good! 'Place we go to is a bit run down. I'll tell you about it and why William's there as we go.' He seemed to reconsider. 'I hope it's all right asking you.' He scraped the toe of his boot on the ground. 'I just thought that you might be interested to see what some folk do for others who have less than they have.'

Mikey puzzles me, she thought. Why has he taken it upon

himself to look after Sam and take him all that way to see his brother?'

'Yes, I would,' she said. 'Thank you for asking me. What time shall I be ready?'

'Meet us at London Bridge at about six o'clock,' he said. 'It might tek us some time to get there and we won't want to be back too late cos it's work on Monday.'

'Six in the morning, you mean?' she said, and when he grinned and nodded she thought of how she usually relished an extra hour in bed on a Sunday.

She dressed warmly the following Sunday and told Liza she would be out all day. Liza packed her a parcel of bread and cheese in case she didn't get any dinner. 'I'll keep you a chop,' she said, and Eleanor thanked her for her kindness.

Mikey and Sam were waiting for her when she arrived at just after six and Sam was pacing up and down, impatient to be off.

'We'll have to walk to begin with,' Mikey said. 'There won't be many carts on 'road just yet, with it being Sunday.'

'I expect most people will be in church,' Eleanor murmured. 'Though I haven't been since I came to London.'

Mikey glanced at her. 'I think you'll find that a lot o' folks do their chores on a Sunday,' he said. 'It's 'onny day they have off to do their washing and clean their houses. They might not have much but most folk try to keep clean.'

'Yes, of course,' she said, rather shamefaced, and thinking that she had never had to think of such things as washing or ironing and cleaning, having always had servants to do them for her.

As they walked he told her about Sam and William, and she expressed astonishment that Tully was paid to take them away by their uncle.

'But they could have been going to a terrible life,' she said. 'To be given to a total stranger who might have been cruel to them.'

Mikey nodded. 'Yes, but it might have been worse if they'd stayed. That's why I kept an eye on them and when I got

251

'opportunity I took them to these good folk who help bairns without parents or a home; but they onny had room for one and as William was sick, he stayed.' He glanced down at Sam. 'And we go to see him regular, don't we, Sam?'

'Aye, we do,' Sam said. 'And William can read and write now, which I can't.'

'I could teach you,' Eleanor said eagerly; then her voice dropped. 'Oh, but then you work, don't you, and so do I. We only have Sundays.'

'I could come over, miss,' he answered keenly. 'I know the way now that Mikey's shown me. We could meet at the bridge like we did today.'

'We could, as long as it doesn't get too cold, or' – a thought struck her – 'perhaps I could ask my landlady if I can use my room.' And maybe, just maybe, Liza would like me to teach her children too.

She felt quite buoyed up about it and vowed that the next day on the way home from work she would buy writing slates, paper and pencils.

They hitched a lift on a waggon carrying beer barrels and sat on the tail-end swinging their legs, but the horses, great big shires, plodded so slowly that after a while they decided that they could walk faster and jumped down.

Mikey knew the way directly to the warehouse school now as they had visited William often over the years he had been there, and as usual when they arrived they found the children lustily singing hymns.

They sat at the back of the hall and Sam joined in the singing; he spotted William at the front and waved to him. When the session was over, Mikey told him to go off and meet his brother and to come back in an hour, for that was all the time they had.

Mikey introduced Eleanor to the Reverend Goodhart and his wife and they gave him an account of William's progress. 'He's a harum-scarum lad,' Mrs Goodhart said, 'and I don't know how he would have fared if we hadn't taken him into our home, but he's fitted in well.' She turned to Eleanor. 'And how do you come to be in London, young lady? Not through the same circumstances as Mikey and the boys?'

'No.' Eleanor smiled wryly at her curiosity. 'My parents have had some difficulties and are no longer able to support me. I came to London to look for my brother.'

'And did you find him?' Mrs Goodhart asked solicitously.

'Simon? Yes, I did,' she nodded. 'But I don't often see him. I work and support myself.'

'Simon!' Mrs Goodhart exclaimed. 'Would that be the same Simon whom Sam describes as a toff?'

Eleanor laughed. 'Yes; and he probably thinks of himself as one too, except that he hasn't any money or fancy clothes.' She thought it odd that Sam should choose to portray Simon in that way.

'You are also from the north, I think,' Mrs Goodhart said, 'although I don't detect a strong accent like Mikey's.'

'We're from 'same town,' Mikey interjected. 'Though not from 'same background.'

'And do you have schooling for the poor in Hull?' the Reverend's wife persisted. She seemed to have an insatiable curiosity. 'As we have here, I mean.'

Eleanor confessed that she didn't know, but once again Mikey intervened. 'There are some Ragged schools,' he said. 'I went to one, but onny for twelvemonth. Hull's a fishing port and not many bairns stay on for longer than that. Sometimes their fathers tek them out of school and tek them to sea with them.' He shrugged. 'And if they're in school it means they're not working and bringing in a wage to help out. It could mean 'difference between paying 'rent or being in 'workhouse.'

'Of course,' Mrs Goodhart murmured.

When Mikey had finished speaking, it seemed to Eleanor that Mrs Goodhart looked intently at her before saying, 'But such a pity if there is no one to offer poor children shelter and a basic education such as we have here. We can't do as much as we would like to; it's a mere ripple in the pond, and we owe so much to benefactors and people who will give their time. But until the government institutes an educational system for all children, enforceable by law, we must continue.'

Eleanor was thoughtful on the way back and abashed to think that Mikey had more awareness of the world than she had, in spite of his lack of education and her good fortune in having had a private one. She asked Sam what he thought about his brother being with the Goodharts when he wasn't.

'I was a bit jealous to begin with,' he said, 'and I missed him. I'd always looked after him, you see, since our ma died. Uncle Walter used to smack him one if he cried and so I used to take him out and play wiv him until he stopped; but now, well, he's cleverer than me cos of the Goodharts and when I asked him if he'd come and work wiv me when he's old enough to leave them' – Sam took a deep breath – 'he said no, not likely. He's going to try to be an apprentice or sumfink.'

He seemed disconsolate at the thought that he would see even less of his brother in the future, and Mikey tried to jolly him along. 'You and me'll be all right though, won't we, Sam? You won't go off on your own? What'd I do without my pal?'

'No, we've got to stick together,' Sam said. 'We're the odd ones out.'

'What do you mean?' Mikey asked, puzzled. 'How are we 'odd ones out?'

Sam shrugged. 'I heard Tully and Manners talking one day. They didn't know I was there, and Tully said that somefink would be all right but for you being nosy, and Manners said, "Yes, Quinn and young Sam, they're the odd ones out."'

254

CHAPTER THIRTY-TWO

'I almost forgot,' Mikey said to Eleanor as they arrived back at London Bridge. 'Simon said to tell you that he wants to see you.'

'Oh.' She was pleased. 'When? I'm only free on a Sunday.'

'He said he would come over next Sunday morning. I suggested that here might be a place to meet. He doesn't know his way about much.'

'Doesn't he?' She was surprised. 'After five years!'

Mikey shook his head. 'He spends most Sundays in bed, unless he's got a meeting wi' Manners.'

He didn't say that Simon and Manners often spent time talking and Mikey was convinced that they were in cahoots over something which excluded even Tully. But he was curious over Sam's reporting that they were considered to be the odd ones out. There was something going on, but what?

'All right,' Eleanor said. 'Would you ask him to come at about eleven o'clock? Sam, would you like to come with him and I'll give you a reading lesson?'

Sam was delighted. 'Yes please, miss.' He grinned. 'I'll show him the way here and he can make his own way back.'

But in the event, Simon came alone. He said that Sam was wanted by Tully.

'But it's his day off,' Eleanor said. She was disappointed, as she had arranged that Liza's two children would have a lesson too.

'So what?' Simon said. 'He's at Tully's beck and call even if it is Sunday. He'll get the sack if he doesn't do as he's told.'

'It doesn't seem fair, does it?' Eleanor said glumly. 'Boys like Sam don't have much chance to make something of themselves. Mikey told me that there are hundreds of children living on the streets of London. Even little children try to earn money through street-sweeping or selling flowers.'

'Really,' Simon said in a bored voice. 'Quinn'll be an authority, I expect, considering his background.'

'Don't be unkind,' Eleanor said quickly. 'He thinks about things.'

'I haven't come here to talk about Quinn,' Simon said impatiently. 'I've come to tell you something.'

'What?' Eleanor was abrupt. Sometimes she didn't like her brother.

'Let's go and sit down somewhere,' Simon said. 'Where can we get a cup of coffee or chocolate?'

Eleanor remembered a coffee shop she had seen but never been inside. She took him down the side street and Simon walked alongside her but didn't offer her his arm.

The shop was hot and steamy and they were glad to be inside out of the cold air. The weather was changing for the worse and there had been an occasional snow shower. Simon ordered coffee and Eleanor chocolate, and as they waited Simon blurted out, 'I've heard from Mama.'

'Have you?' Eleanor was astonished. 'How did she find your address?'

Simon gazed across the room. 'I wrote to her.' He swallowed and seemed embarrassed. 'After you told me about her and this fellow Walton, I was very angry. And ashamed. I couldn't believe that she would stoop so low.'

The waitress came with their drinks and he stopped speaking. Eleanor waited.

He stirred his coffee, which was black and strong. 'And then I got to thinking that she couldn't go back to our father, not with the trouble he's in, so what else could she do? She'd have to live with Aunt Maud for ever, and who on earth could stand that? Personally I'd rather jump in the river than live with that silly old bat and her husband!'

Eleanor gasped. 'You are *so* rude!'

'It's true,' he sneered. 'Anyway, I thought I'd write to Mama and tell her that although I considered her behaviour disgraceful, I was prepared to forgive her as I realized how she had suffered.'

He took a gulp of coffee whilst Eleanor stared at him, astounded at what he was saying. 'And she wrote back to me,' he went on, 'and said that she had no regrets and their plans were going ahead. They sail from the Thames on the twenty-third of December.'

He looked at Eleanor from over the rim of his cup. 'And I'm going with them.'

She was speechless. How high-minded and shocked he had been when she had told him about their mother, and now here he was . . . She couldn't think straight. Simon going to Canada!

'To do what?' she whispered. 'What will you do when you're there?'

He shrugged. 'Don't know. But there're plenty of opportunities; that's what Mama said Mr Walton says. I'll take a chance, just like I did when I came to London. But don't tell anybody. Especially not Quinn.'

Eleanor took a sip of chocolate. It was sweet and soothing. I don't need him, she thought. He has never ever considered me even though I came all this way to find him. Not once has he asked how I'm getting on, even though he knows how sheltered a life I always had before. I could have been living on the streets of London just like the poor and the beggars for all he cares.

And her mother. Had she asked about her? Had she been worried when she had left Aunt Maud's house?

'Did you tell Mama that I was in London?' she asked.

'Well, of course,' he said. 'I told her that you had turned up here and told me about this dastardly affair. She was surprised that you'd travelled alone. Said she didn't think that you would do anything like that. She was worried when you went off so suddenly but assumed you'd gone back to Father because you were so cross with her.'

'And I suppose it was Mama's suggestion that you go with them to Canada?' Eleanor asked. 'If she told you about the opportunities there?'

'Yes,' he admitted. 'It was.'

'You were always her favourite,' she commented.

'And you were Father's,' he retaliated.

Eleanor shook her head. 'I don't think so,' she said softly. 'But it doesn't matter.'

She finished her drink and opened her purse. 'Here you are; that's for the chocolate.' She put some coins on the table and stood up. 'I have to go now. Good luck.' She put out her hand to her brother, who with an astonished look on his face pushed back his chair and stood up also.

He took her hand. 'Eleanor,' he said awkwardly, shaking her hand. 'I'm sorry if . . .' His voice tailed away.

Eleanor held back tears. 'Goodbye, Simon. I wish you well in your life.' She turned from him and walked towards the door and didn't look back.

Eleanor had given Liza extra money towards a Christmas dinner. She had gathered that money was very tight, even though Mr Bertram worked well into the night to satisfy his clients. She was gratified by her landlady's response and surprised when Liza asked her if she would like to invite her brother to join her for Christmas dinner.

'Simon is going away,' she replied, 'but might I ask a friend?'

'Course you can, dearie,' Liza said cheerfully. 'Whoever you like. There might not be much but they can share what we have and welcome.'

Eleanor wrote a note to Mikey at his lodgings, inviting him and Sam to spend Christmas Day with her and Liza's family if they had not planned anything else. She didn't hold out a lot of hope as she thought that Mikey would probably be spending the holiday with Bridget.

She received a letter back a few days later and as she read it she thought that Mikey too would benefit from some writing lessons. His spelling was atrocious, as was his punctuation, although he made himself perfectly clear when he wrote that he 'wood be very pleesed to cum'. He said that Sam would be spending the day with his brother and he would take him to Whitechapel on Christmas Eve after he had finished work, and that the Reverend Mr Goodhart would bring him back. 'I wasn't looking forward to Christmas,' he wrote. 'But now I am.'

In the week before Christmas, after leaving work, Eleanor looked again in the shop windows and the stalls in Oxford Street and thought she would like to buy one or two gifts. She saw a little doll and a train which were not too expensive and these she purchased for Liza's children. For Liza she bought a bottle of lavender water and for Mr Bertram a cigar.

She didn't know what to get for Mikey, for she didn't want to embarrass him as she was sure he wouldn't bring her a gift. But then Mr Christopher solved her problem by saying that if she wanted any gloves or scarves as gifts for anyone, then she could have them at cost price.

A black silk scarf was out of the question for Mikey, but a pair of wool gloves, she decided, would be very practical and they were within her price range.

As she was packing the gloves, for some inexplicable reason she thought of her father. Where was he? Was he in a cold prison cell? She did not want to believe what had been alleged about him in spite of knowing that he could be cold-hearted and unforgiving of others' weaknesses.

I'll write to him, she thought. It is the least I can do. I will tell him that I am alive and well and living in London, but I won't give him my address. I won't mention Mama or Simon because to do so will anger him and I will say that I hope his troubles are resolved and that he hasn't suffered too much.

*　　*　　*

Mikey had been astonished by Eleanor's invitation. He had felt very gloomy at the thought of Christmas. Since they had come to London he had spent the holiday mooching about. Bridget spent most of the day in bed, and so did Simon; Sam generally visited his brother. Mikey too could have spent the day with the Goodharts and all the children, for the Reverend and his wife always did their best to make it a joyous time, and indeed he had done so on one occasion; but Christmas Day had always been a special day when he had lived at home with his mother and siblings, and the company of the Goodharts' other homeless boys had only made him feel more lonely and unloved than ever.

It would be good to be with a real family at Christmas. I should take a gift, he thought, and wondered what he could take and how much he could afford. It was then that he remembered giving his mother a bunch of violets when he was very young and how thrilled she had been. That's what I'll do. There's sure to be a flower-seller about on Christmas Eve and we'll have been given our wages.

It was dark when they finished stacking boxes in the warehouse on Christmas Eve; Mikey went to find Manners to remind him to pay the men. Manners looked up from the desk where he was adding up figures in a ledger, a job that Simon usually did.

'Where's Simon?' Mikey asked. 'I haven't seen him all day, nor last night either, come to think.'

'That's because he's gone,' Manners said testily. 'Left. Skedaddled.'

'What do you mean? Has he gone to another job? He never said.'

Tony Manners shook his head. 'He came in yesterday morning and asked me if he could have his wages early as he owed somebody; so like a fool I gave them to him. Then when I'd handed them over he said he was off. Leaving on the evening tide. Didn't you know?' he added peevishly. 'He's gone to Canada.'

Mikey's jaw dropped. 'To Canada? He never said a word. Does Bridget know? Does his sister know?'

Manners shrugged. 'I don't know. I didn't know he had a sister. I only know that I'm checking the figures to find out if he's diddled me.'

Mikey put his hand to his jaw. If Eleanor didn't know then this news would really spoil her Christmas. He took the money for the men and asked for his own. Manners looked at him coldly as he handed it over.

'What about you?' he grunted. 'Are you going to do a runner as well?'

'Where would I go?' Mikey muttered. 'And where would I get enough money to go anywhere?'

'Well, that's why I'm checking the books,' Manners snarled. 'To find out if I'm paying for that serpent's trip.'

Mikey started to walk away, but Manners called after him. 'I've got a consignment coming in on Boxing Day. Your pal Simon was supposed to be here for it so you'll have to do it instead. It's important,' he added, 'so be here.'

'He's no pal o' mine,' Mikey called back. 'I hardly know him.'

'What do you mean? You came to London together.'

'Happen we did,' Mikey said. 'But I still don't know him. What's in 'consignment? Do we need extra men?'

'Doesn't matter what's in it; it just has to be unloaded. The two of us can manage.'

'Get Tully to help you,' Mikey muttered. He was fed up with being at everybody's beck and call.

Manners chewed on his lip. 'Tully doesn't know about it and I'd rather you didn't tell him. He's going to be somewhere else on Boxing Day anyway.'

He's up to something, Mikey thought as he walked away, and Simon and Manners were in it together, cutting out Tully; but then Simon got ideas of his own. So now what do I do? Is it risky?

He decided to put the matter out of his head for now, and after paying the men he went in search of a flower-seller to buy posies of violets; one for Eleanor, or Ellie as he liked to think of her, and one for her landlady, who had been kind enough to invite him.

When he got back to the lodging house, Bridget heard the front door and came out of her room. 'Have you seen Simon?' she asked petulantly. 'He said he'd tek me to see 'pantomime on Boxing Day and I want to know if he's got 'tickets.'

Mikey stood and stared at her. 'So you don't know!'

'What? Know what? Has summat happened?'

'He's gone away. I've just been talking to Manners.' Mikey searched Bridget's face. Would she be upset? She and Simon had been close. Mikey had seen him coming out of her room a couple of times. 'Simon's gone to Canada.'

He saw the colour drain from her cheeks and she clutched her hands to her face. 'Mother of God,' she whispered. 'Canada! That's abroad, isn't it? Near America?'

Mikey nodded. 'Manners said he sailed yesterday. So he didn't mention it to you? Not that he was thinking about it?' He must have been planning it. You don't just up sticks and get on a ship. Not to somewhere like Canada.

Bridget's face screwed up. Now it was flushed and angry, no longer pale and washed out. 'Judas!' she yelled. 'Shabby, slimy snake in 'grass.' She started to weep. 'He promised me! He said we'd go away, away from these lodgings, and have a fresh start.' She hiccuped in her weeping. 'I'd told him I was fed up wi' acting as bait for Tully, aye, and for Manners as well. He was all sweet talk, and then . . .' she sobbed, 'and then that's when he said we'd go off somewhere. Men! Vile hypocrites!' She looked at Mikey. 'I don't mean you, Mikey,' she sniffled. 'You're 'onny friend I've got. You're 'onny man I can trust.'

CHAPTER THIRTY-THREE

'Will you tek me to 'pantomime, Mikey?' Bridget wiped her eyes and blew her nose. 'Have you got any money?'

'No.' He shook his head. 'I'm doing a job wi' Manners, anyway.'

He was conscious of the violets clutched in his hand.

She suddenly noticed them. 'Who've you bought those for? Are they for me?'

'No, they're not.' No use beating about the bush, he thought. 'I've been invited somewhere for Christmas dinner and these are for—'

'They're for her, aren't they? Simon's la-di-da sister,' Bridget sneered. 'Does she know he's gone to Canada? How come she didn't tell you?'

'I don't know,' he muttered. 'Mebbe she doesn't know.'

'Pah!' she said derisively. 'Course she knows. She might have gone with him and not told you.'

Ellie wouldn't do that. Would she? She wouldn't go off suddenly, not when she had invited him for Christmas. But a doubt crept in. Perhaps Simon had surprised her with the suggestion and she had had no chance to write and tell him. He looked down at the flowers. What should he do?

He shrugged. 'I'll find out, won't I?' he said in a light-hearted manner but feeling decidedly downcast. 'But I'll have my dinner with her landlady anyway. It was her who invited me.'

Bridget's lip trembled. 'Can I come?'

He hesitated for a moment. He didn't want to be unkind, but Bridget could ruin any situation with an unthinking remark.

'I can't invite you, can I? Not up to me. Anyway,' he suddenly galvanized himself into action, 'I can't hang about now; I've got to take Sam to Whitechapel. You can come there wi' me if you like.'

'You're joking! Why would I want to walk all that way just to see a crowd o' bairns? No thanks.' She seemed to consider her options. 'Where did you say Tony Manners was?'

'I didn't,' he answered. 'But he's in 'office, doing his books.'

'Simon usually did those,' she said thoughtfully. Then she gave a snigger. 'Bet he was cooking them. He allus had plenty o' brass, anyway. I reckon he was tekking backhanders.'

'Be careful what you're saying, Bridget.'

'Oh, I will,' she said sweetly. She reached for a shawl on the back of a chair. 'I'm off out. I might not be back.' She gave him a defiant stare and then looked away. 'Happy Christmas!' she muttered.

'Thanks, and 'same to you.' Impulsively he thrust a bunch of violets towards her. 'Here. Tek these.'

She gave a triumphant grin. 'Thanks, Mikey. You're a pal.'

He went in search of Sam and found him in the warehouse repacking a crate.

'What's in there?' he asked him.

'Baccy,' Sam said. 'It's going to take me for ever! It's just come in off a ship. This crate's not going through the books, though. I heard Manners say there was no paperwork with it. It's a private arrangement for him and Tully.'

Mikey heaved a sigh. Sam generally had his ear to the ground and knew what was going on. But sooner or later Tully and Manners would be found out in their scheming, and Mikey could not dismiss the notion that those two would implicate everyone else around them, including him and Sam. The authorities would be sure to say that the workforce must have known what was happening.

'I'll help you,' he said. 'And then we'll be off. I want to see my bed some time tonight.'

It was quicker with the two of them and they'd almost finished transferring the tobacco from one crate to another when Tully appeared. He glared at Mikey. 'What 'you doing here?'

'Helping Sam to get finished,' he muttered. 'We're off to Whitechapel when we're done. It's Christmas tomorrow, in case you'd forgotten.'

'I hadn't forgotten,' Tully growled. 'But there's one more job afore you leave, my lad. I want you to—'

'No!' Mikey said. 'Lad's tired and we've to walk to Whitechapel for him to spend Christmas Day wi' his brother.'

'Too bad!' Tully snarled. 'If he leaves now then he's out of a job when he comes back.'

Mikey glanced at the weary Sam. 'What do you want to do, Sam? It's gone eight o'clock already.'

'Can't I do it on Boxing Day?' Sam asked Tully. 'I'll be back then.'

'No, it's tonight or not. You tek orders from me, not Quinn!'

Sam hesitated. Then he shook his head. 'I can't,' he said. 'I'm dead beat, Tully. I've been working since seven this morning. I don't even know if I can walk to Whitechapel.'

'Right. That's it then,' Tully snapped. 'You're out. Don't come whining to me wanting your job back.' He started to walk away.

'Wait a minute.' Sam hurried after him. 'I need my wages.'

'Come after Christmas,' Tully muttered. 'I might have 'em ready then.'

'But I need the money now.' Sam was almost weeping. 'Tully!'

'Tully!' Mikey confronted him. 'Give him his wages. He's earned them.'

'Keep your nose out of it, Quinn. It's nowt to do wi' you.'

'It is to do wi' me! Sam has to buy food and he gives towards his lodgings.'

It was no use asking Manners because he didn't give Sam his wages, Tully did. But Tully wouldn't be moved. 'Boxing Day,' he said. 'I'll pay you then. Mebbe.'

Sam wept as Tully walked off, and Mikey wished he hadn't interfered. Yet it was so unfair. 'What am I going to do, Mikey? I'll get fed tomorrow, but I've not eaten today. I was going to buy a pie.'

'I'll buy you one,' Mikey said. 'It was my fault this happened. I shouldn't have said owt.'

Sam wiped his nose on his thin shirt sleeve. 'It's not your fault,' he snuffled. 'It's not the first time Tully's kept my wages. Sometimes he's said that I haven't worked hard enough, and anyway he only gives me a pittance, barely enough to buy bread.' He swallowed away his tears. 'I'm thinking of leaving in any case, Mikey. I'm going to try to join the London Shoe-Black Brigade. They give you a uniform and you don't have to work at night. One of the men at the docks told me about 'em. And if they won't have me, I'll be a street-sweeper. You earn your own money then, straight into your hand.'

Mikey nodded. He'd seen the young boot-blacks in their red uniforms on his rare trips into London town; he'd also seen young children sweeping horse and other animal dung from the streets, so that ladies and gentlemen didn't have to walk in the mud and the muck. But those children lived on the streets. Most of them had no homes or lodgings to go to.

Sam was only slightly younger than Mikey had been when he had left Hull, and their circumstances were similar, with no family member to take care of them. Mikey had made his own decision about leaving and now Sam was doing the same.

'Let's enjoy Christmas,' Mikey said. 'Then we'll think on what to do. I'm fed up with working for Manners and Tully too. Simon's already left and mebbe it's time for a change for us as well.'

Sam didn't know about Simon, so Mikey told him what had happened. He bought him a meat pie and the lad wolfed it down as they set off on their journey. There were plenty of people about, several scurrying to buy last-minute bargains of geese or rabbit to cook the next day. The inns and hostelries were full to overflowing with men spending their wages; the sound of singing and tinny piano music could be heard as the Christmas festivities began. But there were many who were not celebrating. Whitechapel was a poor run-down area and as Mikey and Sam approached it they avoided dark street corners and alleyways when they could, for there were desperate people sleeping rough in doorways or corners of buildings. Children cried, voices shouted and dogs barked as they passed.

Carollers were singing but they too kept to the streets which had gas light; they held flickering lanterns in their mittened hands as they sang outside houses and hostelries. Mikey and Sam stopped to listen and sometimes joined in if they knew the words.

'I feel better now,' Sam admitted. 'I like Christmas. I can just remember what it was like when my ma was alive.' He gave a small smile. 'I remember stirring the Christmas pudding; and on Christmas Day we had a stocking with an orange and nuts in the toe. There wasn't much else, though there was sometimes a toy for us to share, but it didn't matter; we were just pleased that it was Christmas.' He hesitated for a moment, and then said, 'After this time, Mikey, I can come and see William on my own. There's no need for you to come wi' me. I'm nearly thirteen; old enough now to look after meself.'

'Yes,' Mikey answered, 'I know you are. But it doesn't mean that we can't do things together. If you want to ask me owt, or if you're not sure about summat, you know that I'm your pal.'

It was after midnight when Mikey turned to walk back. Mrs Goodhart had insisted that he ate a slice of spice cake and drank a glass of mulled wine; to keep out the cold, she'd said. She had asked him to stay and have Christmas dinner with them the next day, but he'd refused, saying he was going elsewhere.

'To see that young lady?' she'd asked with a twinkle. 'Eleanor? I do hope so. She was very nice.'

Embarrassed, Mikey agreed that she was and said that

Eleanor's landlady had invited him. To his delight Mrs Good-hart gave him a box of candy as a present, and he decided to give that to Mrs Bertram in place of the flowers he had given Bridget.

The church bells were pealing in Christmas Day as he went on his way, but instead of feeling joyous he was heavy-hearted. Some of the houses he passed had lit windows through which he could see families gathered, and in some of them Christmas trees were decorated with candles and coloured baubles, something his family had never had; money was too hard to come by for such frivolities.

Churchgoers were coming away from midnight mass and he heard their shouts of Christmas greeting to one another and felt lonelier than ever.

If Ellie has left and gone with Simon to Canada, as Bridget hinted, I don't know how I'll feel, he thought. I'll be devastated. But more than that I'll feel let down. Is there nobody to trust?

He hitched a ride on a waggon which took him most of the way back, and he was grateful, for his feet were sore. He had a hole in the sole of one of his boots and he knew he couldn't afford to get it repaired. I'll have to find a piece of cardboard to mend it, he thought.

There was no key to the lodging house door, for there was nothing worth stealing. He took off his boots and peeked into Bridget's room, but she wasn't there. There was no knowing where she might be. Bridget was a law unto herself and would tag on to anyone who might offer her food or entertainment. She answered only to herself and never to anyone else.

He fell asleep in the chair and awoke with a start when he heard a distant clock strike. For a minute he thought he was late for work and then he remembered it was Christmas Day.

'Happy Christmas, Mikey,' he muttered, and shivered as he washed under the pump. He wet his hair and ran his fingers over his stubble. He only shaved once a week as a rule, but today was special and he must make an effort. But the blade was blunt and he nicked his chin, making it bleed.

He gave his one and only coat a shake, and brushed down his trousers with his hands.

'Well, that's it,' he murmured as he put the coat on. 'Christmas Day or not. This is me and what I am.'

He had the address of Ellie's lodgings from the letter she had written and he found the house quite easily. Courts and alleyways he was used to, and their layout generally had a pattern to it. He came to Trenton Square and after a slight hesitation he knocked on the Bertrams' door.

He waited and then anxiously knocked again. He heard a voice inside calling for someone to get the door. Then it opened, and a smiling Eleanor stood there.

'A happy Christmas, Mikey,' she said. 'Come on in.'

CHAPTER THIRTY-FOUR

Mikey stepped inside. 'Happy Christmas, Ellie.'

Awkwardly he tucked the candy box under his arm and handed her the violets with his left hand, putting out his right to shake hers. 'Thank you for asking me.'

She gave him her hand; it was small, soft and warm. 'I'm glad you could come,' she said, a flush touching her cheeks as she took the flowers. 'Thank you. Come and meet the Bertrams.'

Mikey shook hands with Mr Bertram, who was wearing a white shirt and paisley cravat with pinstriped trousers. Very smart, Mikey thought, considering the run-down area in which they lived.

'Very kind of you to ask me, Mrs Bertram,' he said to Liza, handing her the box of candy.

'Not at all, m'dear,' she said, smiling and expressing her appreciation of the gift. 'It's nice for Miss Kendall to have her young man here for Christmas. And call me Liza; everybody else does,' she added breezily, thus covering Mikey's embarrassment and Eleanor's confusion.

Liza had put on a festive spread. A roast goose, cooked with sage, was resting on the table; the mixed aromas of goose and chestnut stuffing and apple sauce made Mikey's mouth water, and his eyes were drawn to the pan rattling on the fire where a plum pudding was boiling.

Never in his life had he eaten such a meal. Liza brought

out roast potatoes, boiled cabbage and parsnips, and he marvelled at her expertise in cooking on her cast-iron range, which belted out heat as she constantly fuelled it.

After they had eaten, Eleanor handed out the Christmas presents. Mikey was astonished and delighted with his gloves. 'I've never had a pair before,' he said. 'Never in my life!'

The children, Liza and Mr Bertram too were thrilled with the presents she had bought them. Liza dabbed her neck with the lavender water and Mr Bertram said he would light up the cigar later.

Eleanor offered to clear the table and wash the dishes but Liza would have none of it. 'I'll do them, and then me and Bert will sit with our feet up by the fire and 'ave a glass of ale.'

The small room was hot and stuffy; the fire was only just dying down to red embers. Mikey took off his jacket and sat cross-legged on the floor to examine Daniel's wooden toy train.

After a while, Liza suggested that Eleanor and Mikey might like to have a walk up Regent Street; work off your dinner, she said, and make room for tea.

Eleanor rolled her eyes; as if there could be room for tea! Mikey blew out his lips. He was absolutely stuffed.

He put his coat on again and Eleanor went upstairs to fetch hers. The day was cold but bright and sunny and in Regent Street there were crowds of people strolling along chatting with friends and carrying parcels. There was a great air of jollity and merrymaking, with everyone making the most of their day's holiday.

They walked along until they came to Oxford Street and Eleanor's place of work, and paused outside the emporium.

'Why is it called an emporium?' Mikey asked. 'Why not just a mourning shop?'

Eleanor laughed. 'I imagine that Mr Henry senior wouldn't like it to be called a shop. He's very grand,' she said. 'So he would want a grand name. It does sound rather pompous, doesn't it?'

They stood looking at the window, which was dressed in black and white, but with a seasonal atmosphere about it where the base of the window had been sprinkled with paper snowflakes. Her idea, Eleanor said shyly.

'Do you like working here?' Mikey asked. 'Don't you feel sad when people come in to buy mourning clothes?'

Eleanor considered. 'I'm sad anyway,' she confessed. 'I can't remember when I last felt happy.' She turned towards him. 'You haven't mentioned Simon, Mikey,' she said. 'You know that he's gone away?'

Mikey shuffled his feet, which were getting cold, and they drew into the shop doorway. 'I didn't know what to say about him,' he admitted. 'Not in front of the Bertrams. I onny heard yesterday that he was on his way to Canada; and . . . and well, to tell you 'truth, I was bothered that you might have left with him.' He gave a grin. 'I was so relieved when you opened 'Bertrams' door.'

'I wouldn't have gone without telling you,' she said, her eyes wide.

'But you might not have had time to get word to me, seeing as Simon went off so quick. Manners didn't find out until 'day he left either.'

'I knew,' she confessed. 'That's why he came to see me; to tell me he was leaving. With my mother,' she added. 'But he asked me not to tell anyone.' She didn't tell him about Simon's special instruction, 'especially not Quinn'.

'So why are you sad?' he asked, a frown creasing his forehead. 'Is it because you're on your own?'

'Yes. It's because I have no one,' she said softly. 'My mother and brother have left the country, and my father – my father, well; I don't know what might have happened to him.'

She pressed her lips together and Mikey saw that there were tears in her eyes.

'I understand,' he said. 'When I came out of prison, my mother had died and my brothers and sister were in 'workhouse. That's why I left and came to London.' He paused and thought of how miserable and sad he had been. 'I was looking for something to replace 'life I'd had at home.' He shook his head. 'But I never did.'

They stood silently gazing out at the passing population and the carriages and traps going by filled with jolly laughing people. It was starting to snow. Soft white flakes were drifting down, not yet settling on the ground but melting instantly. Both sighed.

'Do you know what I'd really like, Mikey?' Eleanor murmured.

He turned to her; her face was pale, and he noticed that her fair skin had a translucent lustre. He watched her moisten her lips with the tip of her tongue and he recalled the time she had put it out at him.

He smiled at the remembrance. 'No. What?'

'I'd like . . .' She heaved a breath and a vaporous mist issued from her mouth. 'I'd like to go home.'

He took hold of her hand and gently squeezed it. 'So would I.'

They talked as they walked back to Trenton Square. They had decided not to go on any further as the snow was now coming down fast, filling the darkening day with swirls of white, settling on their heads and shoulders, coating Eleanor's hat with soft flakes and speckling Mikey's dark hair.

Eleanor looked up at him. 'You're a piebald pony,' she laughed.

He tapped her gently on the nose where a snowflake had landed. 'And you're Snow White,' he teased and it seemed perfectly natural that she should put up her hand to his and that their fingers should join and stay together.

'So when shall I take you home, Ellie?' he asked softly. 'When shall we leave?'

She turned to him, her blue eyes wide. 'Do you mean it?' she said.

'If it's what you want.'

She thought for a moment. 'If I leave Mr Henry's employ now I will only have a week's wages and I'll have to pay Liza the rent due. It's only right that I do; so I won't have enough money for the train fare.' Her expression was stricken. 'When will I ever?'

Mikey gave a sudden grin. 'Train fare? I've never been on a train! When we came to London, we walked, Bridget and me; we hitched some rides and we were just outside Nottingham when we met Simon; he'd got a lift in a waggon. He used to split up from us at night, though, and find his own lodgings. But he had his money stolen and stayed with us after that. Safety in numbers.' His voice dropped. 'Then we came across Tully, who took us up in his carriage. I'd met him before . . . in prison. He offered us a lift all 'way to London and a chance of work. So we took it.

'I wouldn't expect you to walk, of course,' he said, abruptly changing the subject. 'Can you save enough if we wait till spring? And then mebbe . . .' He thought long and hard about how they could travel together but could come up with no solution. 'I don't know,' he murmured, 'mebbe get you a coach ride; public coaches are desperate for passengers, so I've heard.'

'But together?' she said. 'You said you wanted to go home too.'

'Aye, I do. But I earn hardly any money, so it'll be Shanks's pony for me again.'

'What do you mean?' she asked, puzzled. 'Who is Shanks?'

Mikey laughed. What a world apart they were. 'It means walking on your own legs. On your shanks! Haven't you heard of it?'

Eleanor shook her head. 'No, never! But I could do it, Mikey,' she said earnestly. 'I know I could.'

'Not in winter you couldn't,' he told her. 'We'll have to wait for better weather. This lot is set in for weeks.' He looked up at the sky, which now seemed to be filled with floating duck feathers. 'We left Hull in October and missed 'worst of 'weather. So let's look to spring, shall we, and mebbe we'll both have a bit of extra money?'

Reluctantly Eleanor agreed. It did make sense, of course,

but now that the idea had been voiced she was very anxious to put it into action. Home, though not always agreeable or even hospitable, seemed now to be urging her to come back. It's because it's familiar to me, she thought. I have had an adventure into the unknown by coming here to look for Simon and finding work, which is in the main very satisfying; but I could work equally well in my home town. I wouldn't consider it beneath me and wouldn't care if our acquaintances thought it was; indeed, it would be the answer to a dilemma if my father is no longer able to support me.

Mikey's hands were warm in his new gloves and every now and again he squeezed Eleanor's fingers. I could walk miles with her by my side, he thought happily. I'll gladly walk her all the way home. Then he thought of her father and how he had treated him, and realized that after he'd taken her home he'd have to say goodbye. Whether he's in prison or not, he'll still think I'm not good enough for his daughter. And I'm not.

After they had eaten a tea of muffins and spice cake, for which both found, to their surprise, that they had plenty of room after all, and indulged in a glass of hot toddy, Mikey told Eleanor he must leave. 'Better make tracks,' he said, and laughed at the puzzled look on her face. How much he would enjoy initiating her into the world of ordinary people and their phrases as they travelled the road.

'I *did* know what you meant,' she said, as she opened the door to him. 'It's just that I've never heard anyone say that before. I know nothing about real people,' she said, speaking his thoughts aloud. 'Will you teach me?' she asked softly.

'Yes,' he said, and bent to kiss her cheek.

He felt completely happy as he walked towards Wapping. He barely felt the cold, though his feet were wet and his toes numb. Ellie didn't turn away from me or seem offended when I kissed her, he thought with a tender glow. I've never wanted to kiss anybody afore, though Bridget's offered often enough, but then Bridget's like that. I've seen her kissing Simon and once I caught her giving Tully a peck on his greasy stubble.

There was no one in the lodging house when he arrived

and the place smelt cold and damp. He put a few sticks in the grate and lit a match, but it didn't catch. He went into Bridget's room and took her blanket off the bed. She's not using it, so I might as well. He took off his wet boots and rubbed his feet dry on a piece of flannel, then wrapped himself in the blanket, put on his wool gloves and sat down in the chair with a sigh. 'So that was Christmas,' he murmured. 'Best one I've had since I was just a bairn.'

The next morning he reported back at the warehouse. It was bitterly cold, the roads were wet and slushy underfoot and the sky was ominously dark. Manners wasn't there so he hung about, but after an hour he walked down towards the river. Men were working on the wharves and the ships; barges and carriers were making their way towards the docks, but there were very few workers by the warehouses. He thought it odd that Manners would expect a consignment today, the day after Christmas.

Somebody shouted his name. 'Quinn!'

He looked up and saw Tully, a black scarecrow of a figure in his flowing coat and hat.

'Where's Sam?' Tully shouted. 'I'm waiting on him.'

Mikey walked towards him. 'You told him he was finished,' he said. 'But you didn't pay him. You said for him to come today for his wages.'

'Ah!' Tully gave an exasperated grunt. 'He can come back if he's a mind to. What 'you doing down here?'

'Waiting for Manners,' Mikey said, remembering too late that Tony Manners had said that Tully wasn't involved in this job. 'He asked me to come in today.'

'What for?' Tully's eyes narrowed suspiciously. 'We're not expecting a consignment.'

Mikey shrugged. 'Don't know,' he said. 'He didn't say.'

'He told me that he wouldn't be here today and I said I wouldn't be either. Have you seen Gilby?' Tully asked abruptly.

'Gilby! No, not for weeks.' Tully's pockmarked crony rarely turned up and Mikey was at a loss to know what he did. He hardly ever spoke but only grunted when asked a question.

'So why are you here, Tully?' Mikey asked curiously.

Tully shrugged up to his ears in his greatcoat. 'I'm picking up a crate of baccy. That's why I wanted Sam. He could have hauled it on to 'cart for me.'

Tully never lifted anything if he could find someone else to do it for him.

'I'll do it,' Mikey offered. 'I'm doing nowt else.'

He walked back to the warehouse with Tully and watched as the other man unlocked the padlock with a key and opened the doors. There was a handcart inside and Mikey pushed it over towards the stacked crates. He lifted one on to the cart and knew better than to ask where it was going.

Tully picked up a crowbar which leaned against the wall. 'Open it for me, will you? Thanks,' he mumbled as Mikey forced the crate. Then he fumbled in his pocket. 'Here,' he said, giving Mikey a handful of coins. 'Share that wi' your mate Sam.' He trundled the cart out and padlocked the door again. 'Find out what Manners is up to,' he said as he turned away. 'And let me know. I'll mek it worth your while.'

'If he turns up,' Mikey said carelessly. He wouldn't do anything of the sort, of course. He knew better than to tell tales.

He watched as Tully pushed the cart to the top of the road and disappeared behind the back of a building. He was curious as to where he was going with the crate. He didn't want me to know, at any rate, or he would have asked me to push it, he thought.

He slipped down the side of a warehouse and ran along it. Like the alleyways and courts, the passages that ran between the buildings were familiar territory to him and he soon saw Tully ahead at the top of one of them.

Mikey stopped and stood to one side where he could see but not be seen, and watched as Tully looked about him. Then he saw him raise his arm and signal to someone. Mikey flattened himself against the wall and peered out. A figure appeared: a man in uniform wearing a recognizable stovepipe hat. Mikey drew in a breath. It was a constable and he was handing something to Tully. Tully put his hand in the crate, drew out what looked like a package and gave it to the policeman. Then Tully pointed towards the river as if explaining something.

'A bribe,' Mikey breathed. 'A sweetener! Now I know for sure that what we do is illegal.'

CHAPTER THIRTY-FIVE

Tully's taking a chance in broad daylight, Mikey pondered. Though mebbe the constable has an excuse ready if anybody should turn up. Still, nowt to do with me and it's best I don't get involved. He turned away and walked back towards the river and saw Manners in conversation with another man. They seemed to be arguing rather than talking.

Mikey whistled as he approached so that they would hear him. Manners looked up and glared at him.

'That mate of yours is a thief! If only I could catch him!'

'Mate? What mate? I haven't got any mates, onny Sam, and he's no thief.'

'Simon!' Manners barked. 'I paid him to settle for this consignment and he's done a runner with the money.'

Mikey shrugged. 'Nowt to do wi' me, and anyway I said before he's no pal o' mine. You trusted him wi' your books,' he said heatedly. 'Don't go blaming me.'

He'd never spoken to Manners like that before, but his blood was up. He'd just seen Tully handing goods over to a constable, and he was very sure that Simon and Manners had some kind of fishy business going on that didn't include Tully. Now Manners had lost out and didn't like it.

'Tully's about, by the way,' he said, and wondered why he was warning him, but part of him didn't want to be in the middle of a fracas between Manners and Tully. 'He's up on 'top road.'

'Listen, mate,' the other man interrupted, shaking a fist at Manners. 'Do you want these goods or not? If you do, I want my money and if you don't I'm off. I'm not hanging about round here waiting to be picked up by the damned peelers.'

'Go with him, Quinn,' Manners said abruptly and put his hand into his coat pocket. He brought out a handful of coins and counted them. Mikey drew in a breath as he caught the glint of gold and the head of the queen. Five! He watched as Manners reluctantly gave them to the other man. What could be in the consignment that was worth five gold sovereigns?

The man tossed his head to indicate that Mikey should follow him. They walked towards a building close by the wharf's edge where someone else was waiting next to a handcart. Gilby! So he was in the transaction too.

Gilby frowned when he saw Mikey. 'What 'you doing 'ere, Quinn? Simon's supposed to be here.'

'He's done a runner wiv the money,' the first man sneered.

'Who has?' Gilby snapped.

'Simon.' Mikey sighed. 'Manners gave him some money and he's gone. To Canada,' he added.

'Two-faced cur!' Gilby said venomously. 'I never did trust him. I said right from the off he was up to no good. Toffee-nosed varmint. Come on, give us an 'and.'

Mikey was staggered. It was the longest speech Gilby had ever made. Together they tried to lift the wooden crate off the handcart, but they couldn't shift it.

'We can't lift that!' Mikey protested. 'Can't we borrow 'cart? I'll bring it back after we've unloaded it.'

The stranger hesitated. 'Yeh, but just dump it; somewhere out of sight. I'll reckon on it's gone missing.'

Mikey noticed that the name on the cart denoted a company on St Katharine's dock. 'It's a weight,' he muttered. 'That's not baccy.'

'Who said it was?' Gilby blustered. 'Keep your nose out of what doesn't concern you, Quinn.'

'It concerns me if it's contraband and I'm caught with it,' Mikey said heatedly. He was getting heartily sick of being told something wasn't his concern when he would be the first in line at the magistrate's if they were caught.

Gilby glared at him and then took hold of one of the shafts whilst Mikey took the other. They heaved and the wheels started to move.

'It's onny a bit of owd marble,' Gilby muttered. 'Nowt to get het up about. Onny don't let on to Tully. This is summat I arranged wi' Manners and Simon. We could let you in on it now that Simon's gone, I suppose, if Manners agrees.'

'Mebbe.' Mikey was guarded. 'How much do I get for to-day?'

'Just the going rate,' Manners told him, when Mikey later asked him the same question. 'I'm going to have to make up for what I've lost through that toad Simon.'

'That's not my concern,' Mikey said boldly; Manners glared at him but made no further comment.

The other men had arrived for work and Mikey directed them to move some of the packing cases in the warehouse to make room for the crate. There were no more consignments due that day and, after consulting with Manners, he laid them off. They grumbled, but he shrugged and said there was nothing he could do about it. If there were no consignments then there was no work, and they wouldn't get paid.

They'd no sooner left than Manners came out of his office. 'We're moving on,' he said. 'I've found a better storage place.'

'I've just laid 'men off,' Mikey said in astonishment. Manners must surely have known before he'd told him to do so. 'We can't shift this lot on our own.'

'Yes, we can,' Manners said. 'You, me and Gilby and the waggon driver.'

'What about Tully?'

'I'll tell Tully later,' Manners said. 'It's just a precaution. And I'll recruit fresh men tomorrow. I don't trust them others and neither do I trust that cur Simon.'

There had been many changes of storage depot over the years and Manners had always said it was a precaution. Against what, Mikey had always wondered, but now he knew. It was a safeguard against the police finding them and what they were up to.

Mikey knew many of the regular dock workers and men on the wharves and they knew him; generally they were suspicious of strangers and guarded their jobs and the goods well, but as one of them had said to Mikey when he first arrived, there would always be somebody who would take advantage. Those who would, he was now convinced, were Manners, Tully and Gilby. All three were working for their own benefit as much as for each other. As for Simon, Manners was probably right about him, he thought. It would be just like him to split to the authorities, just before he sailed away.

'Where are we going?' he asked Manners.

'You'll find out,' Manners said brusquely. 'There'll be a waggon here in ten minutes and we'll get this lot loaded on to it.'

Mikey thought of the constable who had received a package from Tully. Was he still hanging about? He was in uniform so he must be on duty. Mikey's gut started to churn. If we're caught it'll be prison! I'm not a young lad any more; it'll be a longer sentence. I can't stand that – and I'd not be able to see Ellie again.

It was the thought of not seeing Eleanor above all else that decided him. 'I'll be back in a minute,' he called, and sauntered towards a building that contained latrines for the men working nearby.

'Don't be long,' Gilby shouted. 'Waggon's on its way.'

'Tough!' Mikey muttered and went inside the building. Then, checking that Manners and Gilby had their backs to him, he came straight out and rushed off in the opposite direction. He ran through one of the passageways which led to the top of the access road and came to a sudden halt. The area was swarming with police.

He turned round and ran back until he came to a cut-through running at right angles to the passageway. He slipped down it and came to some iron steps, like a ship's jack ladder, running up the side of a brick warehouse. Swiftly he climbed up and lay down on the flat roof. From there he could see the whole area. The warehouses and storage buildings covered miles and ran right down to the wharves. He could see the long snaking length of the flowing estuary, the barges, lighters, coal vessels and bigger ships bound for other lands, and he thought for a second of Simon escaping to distant shores.

Then he heard the tramp of feet and saw a platoon of constables marching towards where Manners and Gilby would be waiting, oblivious.

'That's it,' he muttered. 'I'm off.'

He shuffled on his stomach towards the place where he had climbed up; peered over, saw it was all clear and swiftly climbed down and walked, not hurriedly but as if he was out on business, towards the top road and safety.

Then he began to hurry towards the lodging house to collect his few belongings, fearful that the constables might also come knocking on that door. He was sure that Manners and Gilby, if cornered, would implicate him too. He pushed open the door and Bridget was there.

'What 'you doing back at this time?' she said, yawning. She was sitting in the chair with her feet in the hearth even though there wasn't a fire lit.

'Why does everybody question what I'm doing?' Mikey said irritably.

'Cos you're a creature of habit,' Bridget shrugged. 'You're allus so predictable. You turn up when you say you will, allus on time for work; things like that. Everybody knows you'll not do owt out of 'ordinary.'

'Really!' he said, picking up his knapsack. He crossed the room to the battered chest of drawers where he and Simon kept things like socks, and took out his other pair. Then he noticed that Simon had left a pair behind so he picked those up too and put them in his bag. He wished he still had Mrs Turner's old blanket, but that had disintegrated long ago.

'What 'you doing?' Bridget sat up. 'Are you off somewhere? Can I come?'

Mikey took a breath. Now here was a dilemma. Should he

tell her and if he did would she want to go home to Hull with him, or would she stay here and tell Manners and Tully where he'd gone? He saw that she was watching him and waiting for an answer.

'Where you going?' she repeated. 'Tell me.'

He hesitated, and then took a chance. 'What if I said I was going home? To Hull.'

She laughed, loudly and coarsely. 'Home? On your own? Not likely.' She yawned again and drew her arms above her head, lifting up her long dark hair. 'You'd never make it. Hah,' she snorted. 'You'd never have got to London but for me.' She leaned forward to catch his eye. 'Never told you, did I?'

'What?' he said sullenly, wanting to get away and yet somehow reluctant to leave her. How would she cope on her own? How would she deal with Manners and Tully?

She smiled, cunning and worldly; then she winked. 'How do you think I got 'money for 'ferry fare, or for 'journey? Who bought 'food for them first days?'

'We managed,' he said, but then remembered that Bridget's money had lasted longer than his did.

She rose from the chair and put her arms round his waist. 'Managed?' she whispered, her mouth close to his cheek. 'No, Mikey, it was me that managed. It was me who earned 'money so that we didn't starve afore we got halfway across Lincolnshire.' She ran her hands down his back. 'And who soft-soaped Manners to get us these lodgings?'

Mikey pushed her away. 'Tully got us these rooms. He said so.'

'That was because Tony Manners told him to,' she said. 'Tully's onny small fry even though he acts as if he is boss. He's not.' She turned her back on Mikey. 'Manners is.'

He took hold of her by the shoulder and turned her round to face him, and he saw her defiance crumble.

'But it didn't matter what I did for you, Mikey,' she whispered. 'It didn't matter cos you never even noticed. I was nothing to you.'

'We were friends, Bridget,' he answered, unnerved by what

she was saying. 'Are friends. I never asked you to do owt you'd be ashamed of.'

She shook her head; her eyes were bright. 'Who said I was ashamed? I'll do what I have to to get out of this pit of poverty. Not like you, Mikey.' She sneered. 'You'll never make owt of yourself. You haven't got 'backbone. Not like Simon or Manners.'

'Like Simon!' he taunted. 'Well at least I'm telling you that I'm leaving. I'm not disappearing and letting somebody else do my dirty work. *And* I'm onny tekking what's mine,' he added. 'I'm not thieving like Simon and Manners. Tek care, Bridget. There's all sorts going on wi' Tully and Manners and you shouldn't get mixed up wi' it.'

Her eyes opened wide as he put the knapsack on his back.

'You're really going?' she said. 'Sure, you're kidding me!' She caught his arm. 'Don't go, Mikey. I didn't mean what I said. Honest I didn't.'

He sighed. 'Yes, you did. And mebbe I haven't got what it takes to make summat of myself. Mebbe that's why I'm going back. I'm not like you, that's true. You've allus looked out for yourself. Nobody else. You're a bit like Simon really. Anyway,' he added, 'you wouldn't want to go back to Hull, to how you lived afore wi' your ma and da.'

She stared at him as if he was speaking a foreign language that she couldn't understand. Then, with her lips parted, she shook her head. 'No, I wouldn't,' she said softly. 'Not to my da, anyway. I'd get 'flat of his hand if I did go back.' She swallowed. 'But if you should see my ma, you could tell her – tell her that I'm doing all right. Tell her that I've got a job, and – and some friends wi' plenty o' money.'

He smiled. 'Yeh, I'll do that. When I get there.' He leaned towards her and planted a kiss on her cheek. 'Listen to what I say, Bridget. Manners and Tully could be in trouble. Especially Manners.'

Bridget nodded and touched her cheek with her fingers. 'I'm listening, Mikey,' she said. 'I'm listening to what you're saying.'

And to what you're not saying, she thought as he opened the door and took one last look back. I'm listening to you saying that you don't want me. She fought back tears. Have never wanted me.

CHAPTER THIRTY-SIX

Mikey strode purposefully out of the lodging house. He had pangs of guilt over leaving Bridget, and yet he knew in his heart she wouldn't have wanted to go home. But she wanted me to ask her, he thought. She wanted to be given the chance to refuse. Perhaps I should have granted her that. But I was scared, he pondered. Scared that she might have said yes.

But now his concern was with Sam. He hadn't come back to the lodgings last night. Perhaps he's decided to stay another day with William and the Goodharts as he had no job to come back to. But I can't leave without telling him.

He walked to the end of the street and, turning on to the main road, continued for a while and then sat down on a low wall to consider. Tate, one of the casual labourers whom he had laid off this morning, came towards him.

'Now then, Quinn,' the fellow greeted him. 'Have you been laid off as well?'

'Yeh,' Mikey lied. 'There's no work for a bit.'

'What? None tomorrow neither? I was thinking of going back tomorrow.'

Mikey shook his head. 'Nah! I'd leave it a day or two if I was you.'

The fellow grinned. 'You don't half talk funny, Quinn; has anybody ever told you?'

The man was a bit gormless, Mikey thought, but meant no

harm. 'Do I?' he said seriously. 'I was just thinking 'same thing about you. You haven't seen Sam about, have you?'

Tate shook his head. 'No. So you don't think I should apply for work yet? I need the money.'

'If I were you I'd try another company. It's a bit slow at Manners at 'minute.' He tipped a wink at Tate and hoped he'd take the hint, but the man only nodded, not understanding.

'I will then. Where do you think I should try?'

Mikey mentioned another company a fair distance away from Manners's present site, adding, 'If you should see Sam, will you tell him I was looking for him?'

Tate said he would and slouched off. Mikey gazed after him. Tate was someone who wouldn't ever better himself, he hadn't the ability to, but that was not his fault. It was what Bridget had intimated about him, though, and that hurt, for he knew it wasn't true.

He glanced down the road past the turning for the lodging house and heaved a breath of relief when he recognized the familiar figure of Sam. But his bearing was disconsolate. His head and shoulders were lowered and he was kicking desultorily at stones.

'Sam! Sam!' Mikey jumped off the wall and ran towards him, wanting to catch him before he turned the corner.

Sam looked up and stopped, but he didn't wave or grin as he normally would.

'What's up?' Mikey said. 'Didn't you have a good Christmas? Are you missing William?'

Sam shrugged. He seemed very melancholy. 'Yeh. Mrs Goodhart give me this scarf.' A bright canary-yellow muffler was round his neck. 'She give me an orange as well. She give one to all the lads.' He pulled a wry face. 'They were sour.'

'You didn't come back last night,' Mikey probed. 'Did they ask you to stop?'

Sam nodded. 'Parson Goodhart brought me back this morning. He took me into London.'

'Oh? London? What for?'

'He said he'd take me to see about joining the London

Shoe-Black Brigade. He dropped me off early cos he had to get back for a service, but when I found the office where you enrol, it was closed.' He pouted. 'They take two days off at Christmas, not like us with just Christmas Day.'

'Oh, hard luck. But you'll be able to go again.'

'I know, but I'd got all worked up about it.'

'Sam,' Mikey said. 'I want to tell you summat. I'm not working for Manners and Tully now. I've left.'

'Why?' Sam asked. 'Have you got another job?'

'No. There's trouble brewing and I decided to get out. There were loads of police about earlier, all heading down to 'warehouses.'

'I knew it!' Sam was jubilant. 'I knew they was up to somefink. Them and Simon, they've all been on the make.'

'Thing is, Sam,' Mikey said diffidently, 'I'm not stopping here. I've decided to go back to my home town.'

Sam's mouth dropped open. 'Where's that?'

'Hull. It's up north. In Yorkshire.'

'But what about me?' Sam gasped. 'You said we'd always be pals; and what about Miss Kendall? And what about Bridget?'

Odd that Sam should call Ellie Miss Kendall, Mikey thought, and Bridget by her first name. Could he tell the difference in their status, or was it because he had known Bridget right from the beginning of their life here?

Sam pressed his lips together and blinked hard. 'It's not fair!'

'But you were thinking of being a shoe-black boy,' Mikey said quietly. 'You'd have been going off to live somewhere else.'

'Yes, but,' Sam stammered and huffed out a breath, 'I'd still be in London and if you'd got another job you could've come to see me; and – and I'd even have done your boots for free.'

Mikey considered that it sounded so simple the way Sam put it, but he knew that it wouldn't have worked like that. Life was much more complicated.

'Miss Kendall – Ellie wants to go home too. She's from 'same town as me. But Bridget doesn't want to come. She wants to stay here.'

Sam nodded, but his bottom lip stuck out petulantly. 'She's thick wiv Manners, that's why. She stops over at his place sometimes.'

Mikey's spirits sank. What would Bridget do if Manners went to prison? Should I go back and warn her? He'd no sooner voiced his worries to Sam than they were disturbed by the sound of hooves and carriage wheels and a Black Maria passed them, turning in the direction of the warehouses and wharves.

Sam grabbed Mikey's arm. 'Come on,' he said urgently. 'They might have got wind of something and be going to pick up Manners and Tully, and if them two beggars see us here, they'll tell on us.'

'But what about Bridget?' Mikey suddenly panicked. 'Mebbe 'police will go to 'lodging house. I should warn her. They might be looking for goods.'

'There is none,' Sam said. 'Not at our place. But there is at Manners's lodgings. I've seen it.'

'When?' Mikey asked, amazed as always by Sam's knowledge. 'When have you been there?'

Sam grimaced and pulled Mikey off the wall. 'Come on, let's be going. Bridget'll be all right,' he said as Mikey protested. 'I followed her one night to see where she was going and she went to Manners's place. I looked through the window and it was stacked with crates and boxes. Tony Manners opened one and Bridget took out some bottles, brandy or somefink, and put them in a shopping basket. Then he opened another and brought out packets of baccy and she took some of them as well. She catches a horse bus.' He pulled on Mikey's arm. 'I've seen her, and she goes into London to sell it in the markets or somewhere.'

Mikey caught his breath. I can't believe she would do such a thing. What if she got caught? He felt sick. Still, she'll manage, he thought, hastening his steps to keep up with a fleeing Sam. Her wits are much sharper than mine.

They speeded up until they considered that they were far enough out of the area to be safe. They found another wall to sit on and Sam turned to Mikey to say, 'I'd give up the shoeblack job and come wiv you if it wasn't for William. I know I don't often see him, but he is my brother and I wouldn't like to leave him.'

'I understand, Sam,' Mikey said. 'When I came to London I left my brothers and sister behind. But I knew I couldn't earn enough money to keep us all, and they were probably better off in 'workhouse. Well,' he added disconsolately, 'not better off, but they'd get fed at least once a day.'

Sam had shuddered at the mention of the workhouse. 'That's what my uncle kept threatening us wiv. He said he'd send us there if we were any trouble.'

'We could go and see William and ask him what he thinks about you going with me to Hull,' Mikey suggested. 'Ask 'Goodharts too, see what they think.'

'Mebbe William'd come wiv us!' Sam brightened up. 'That would be good. We'd be like a proper family then.'

Mikey thought of the responsibility of looking after William as well as Sam, but he nodded. 'So we would. Will you come with me to see Ellie? She wants to come but I'm worried about her.' He took a breath. 'I don't know what we'll do for money,' he said. 'I'm practically on my beam-ends.'

It was then that he recalled that Tully had given him some money for Sam and he dug into his pocket. 'Your wages, Sam,' he said, dividing all he had with the boy. 'Tully sent them.'

'Did he?' Sam was amazed. 'Crikey. I thought I'd have to whistle for 'em.'

Mikey laughed. 'Life is full o' surprises, Sam.' He jumped off the wall. 'Come on. Let's be off and see what's round 'next corner.'

After Mikey had left, Bridget put on her boots and wrapped a shawl round her head and shoulders. She waited a couple of minutes and then went out. She stopped at the end of the street and looked up and down the main road. Mikey was talking to one of the casual labourers that Manners employed so she slipped back into a doorway, huddling into her shawl. Is he really leaving, she wondered, or will he come back?

She looked out again after a moment and saw Sam walking towards Mikey, and took the opportunity to steal out and dash towards the warehouses. I'll be stopped if anybody sees me, she thought. They don't like women being down here. I'll have to have an excuse ready. She stepped back into the shelter of a gap as a Black Maria came trundling along the road, and hoped the driver hadn't seen her.

'Summat's going on,' she breathed. 'Mikey's right about that.' She peered down the road towards the wharves. 'Is it Tully or Manners they're after?'

Furtively she crept further and further down towards the warehouse, which she already knew was about to be emptied and the goods transferred elsewhere. Manners had told her, although he hadn't said where the new warehouse was to be. He kept a lot close to his chest, did Manners, unlike Tully who would tell her most things if she was artful enough.

She saw the Black Maria stop and a sudden flurry of police appeared from all directions. Then she almost held her breath as two men with their hands shackled were pushed into the carriage by two constables. Who were they? From this safe distance she couldn't quite make out.

There was a sudden movement behind her and a clammy breath on her cheek. Bridget froze and gave a small gasp as someone put a hand on her shoulder.

'Looks like 'law caught up with 'em,' a voice rasped and she turned her head.

'Tully! How—'

Tully's black stubble creased into a grin. 'How did I know? I didn't, not till your pal Quinn gave 'game away.'

'Mikey? He wouldn't,' she protested.

'He didn't mean to.' Tully pulled her back into the gap as the police carriage rolled by. 'I saw him down here early this morning and it slipped out that he was meeting Manners. I knew nowt about any consignment arriving so I kept my eyes peeled.'

'And you tipped off 'police,' Bridget said softly. 'What a clever chap you are, Tully! But why? They'll tell on you, you know. Manners and Gilby. They'll be sure to drop you in it.'

Tully slowly shook his head. 'There's nowt wi' my name on it, darlin'. I've got all I wanted out of there. Just a few crates o' baccy and some bottles o' cognac. I didn't want to be dealing in marble and all them luxury goods like Manners and Gilby wanted. There's a bigger price to be paid for them and I've already had a trip to warmer climes. But Manners got greedy; you'll know about that,' he said, his eyes narrowing and his black eyebrows beetling. 'And he might tell on you, as well,' he added.

Bridget shrugged, but uneasily. Tully was so sharp, so astute. The chances he took were well planned, whereas Manners with his swaggering brashness was inclined to take a risk. 'I onny did what I was told,' she said.

'What about his lodgings?' Tully said quickly.

'What about 'em?'

'Was there much kept there?'

'Some,' she admitted. 'Why? Are you interested?'

He winked. 'Now there's a gel after my own heart,' he wheezed. 'Shall we just tek a peek? Bobbies won't be there yet. He won't tell 'em where he lodges. But we know, don't we, gel?'

She gave a sudden grin. 'We certainly do, Tully.' Bridget realized just where her best interests lay; he'd always looked after her, had Tully, and he had never made advances. 'Come on then,' she said. 'Let's you and me tek a look.'

CHAPTER THIRTY-SEVEN

Mikey and Sam walked all the way into London and towards Oxford Street where Mikey hoped they would be in time to catch Ellie as she was leaving work; but the emporium was closed with a notice on the door to say it would be open to attend to any needs the following day.

'My legs ache,' Sam complained. 'I've done a deal o' walking today.'

'I'd offer you a piggyback if you weren't so big,' Mikey joked. 'This time next year you'll be as big as me.'

'Our William's only small,' Sam said, 'and he's ever so skinny, even though Mrs Goodhart feeds him well. He still lives in their house, you know. He's never had to live rough.'

'He's been lucky, hasn't he?' Mikey remarked.

'Yeh,' Sam agreed. 'He's like one of her own. That's what she said, anyway.'

They continued towards Trenton Square and soon it was almost dark.

'Where'll we stop the night, Mikey?' Sam asked. 'We can't go back to the lodging house.'

'We'll have to kip down in a corner somewhere,' Mikey said.

As they'd walked from Regent Street they had seen groups of children hanging round street corners or in shop doorways. Many of the shops had closed early or not been open at all as it was Boxing Day and the youngsters had taken advantage of this, claiming their pitches earlier than usual. They looked

294

cold and hungry, Mikey thought; most of them were barefoot and dressed in thin ragged clothing that would do nothing to keep out the sharp wind.

'Spare a penny, mister.' A boy of about seven approached them. His face was blue and pinched with cold and his nose was running with thick yellow mucus. He wore boots without laces that were far too big for him.

Mikey put his hand in his pocket, drew out a penny and gave it to him. The boy touched his forehead and scooted away. Sam objected. 'You might need that penny. He's wearing boots!'

'I think he needs it more,' Mikey murmured. 'And the boots are not his. They're probably tekken it in turns to wear them. And he's not wearing socks or stockings.'

Mikey knew what it was like to wear boots on bare feet, when the leather rubbed on a heel or toe and made a weeping blister.

Sam was silenced, then said in a small voice, 'Yeh, I know. Mrs Goodhart once give me a pair o' boots. They lasted me for ages until I grew out of 'em.' He bit his lip. 'Then I cut the toecaps out.'

They arrived at Eleanor's lodgings and knocked on the door. There was an aroma of something meaty and fatty. Sam licked his lips. 'I'm hungry,' he said. 'I've not eaten since this morning.'

'I've not eaten since yesterday,' Mikey whispered in return. 'But what a blow-out! Enough to last me a week.'

The door was opened by Liza, who was wearing a white bonnet on her red curls and said in surprise, 'Back already? Or can't keep away!'

'I'm sorry to bother you, Mrs Bertram.' Mikey felt his face flushing at her innuendo. 'But I need to speak to Miss Eleanor.'

'Then you'd better come in,' she said. 'And your young friend.'

'This is Sam.' Mikey introduced him and Sam took off his cap.

'Ah! You're the young lad wiv a brother, who went out for Christmas dinner? Miss Eleanor's in her room,' Liza said. 'I'll pop up and tell her.'

Mikey and Sam stood and waited. Mr Bertram was sitting at the table, pinning a piece of cloth.

'Working today then, Mr Bertram?' Mikey said to make conversation. 'No rest for 'wicked!'

'That's right, young man, and how lucky I am to have work. There's many a tailor hard pressed to sew as much as a button on.'

'It's a nice piece o' cloth, sir,' Sam said. 'Is it for a rich gen'leman?'

'Not rich and not a gentleman,' Mr Bertram replied. 'But a man worthy of his salt; a man who's earned a good suit for his Sunday best. A tradesman; a grocer.'

Sam looked impressed. 'I should like to own a suit like that one day.'

Mr Bertram looked at Sam from over his spectacles. He observed Sam's thin shirt and ragged breeches and the bright yellow scarf, incongruous next to his worn and over-large coat. 'Then I hope you will allow me to cut your cloth.'

Eleanor came into the room, followed by Liza. Although she smiled at Mikey and Sam, she seemed anxious. 'Is there something amiss?' she asked.

Mikey nodded. 'Summat – something's come up,' he said. 'And . . .' He hesitated, unwilling to share his doubts and decision in front of the Bertrams. 'I need to talk to you.'

'Take a walk,' Liza said. 'Just to the top of the street. Young Sam can have a bowl of broth wiv us. We'll save some for you,' she said to Mikey.

Sam grinned. The last thing he wanted was to walk anywhere and the smell issuing from a pan on the fire was irresistible.

Eleanor ran upstairs for a shawl and Mikey held the door for her. They walked in silence until they reached the top of the street, and Mikey halted. 'There's no need to go any further,' he said. 'You'll want to get back for your supper. I just wanted to tell you that there's a change of plan. I've left 'firm I was working for and so has Sam.'

Eleanor turned to look at him. 'So . . . What are you saying, Mikey?'

'I'm saying that I'd like to set off for home – Hull, now.'

'But the weather,' she said in a low voice. 'There'll be more snow. And – and I was to come with you.'

'I know.' He too lowered his voice, although there was no one else to hear them. 'It's just that I don't know where else I'd get another job. I won't be able to work on 'wharves again. Manners has probably been arrested, and I'd have no reference. I mebbe could get casual labouring work but it wouldn't pay 'rent.'

'And if you go back to Hull now, what will you do for work there?' Eleanor's eyes stayed on him.

'I don't know,' he admitted. 'But I'd rather be there.'

'So would I,' she murmured. 'If I give notice to Mr Christopher tomorrow, will you wait for me, Mikey?'

He swallowed hard. 'It's just that – well, I'm really bothered about 'weather being bad! I've been thinking that if you saved up you could travel on 'train and I'd meet you in Hull.'

'It will take me weeks!' She was aghast. 'And you *promised*.' Her eyes filled with tears. 'You said you'd take me home.'

'I have to walk,' he pleaded. 'Me and Sam can do it, if he decides to come, but it's such a long way for you. I've done it. I know how difficult it is; and I came afore 'bad weather started.'

'Bridget came with you, didn't she?'

'Yeh, but, well, Bridget, she's not like you. Bridget's used to hardship, Ellie.' He put out his hand to hold hers. 'You're not,' he added softly. 'You've had a different life.'

'I agree,' she admitted. 'Even travelling alone on the train and getting work has been a big experience for me. But I can do it. I can! If you're there with me,' she added softly. 'I couldn't do it on my own.'

He felt his resistance crumbling. His anxieties had been on

297

explaining why he had to leave her behind. Now he knew that he couldn't.

They made a pact. Eleanor would give in her notice the following day and tell Mr Christopher that she had to return home immediately. She was determined to leave with Mikey, even though she had no illusions about the hardship. The weather had become increasingly cold and Mr Bertram had said there was more snow due. He could smell it on the air, he said, and she believed him.

That night Mikey and Sam slept on the Bertrams' floor. Liza said she wouldn't hear of them sleeping outside, and just as well, for the next morning when they looked out there was a fine covering of crisp snow.

Mikey walked Eleanor to Oxford Street and said he would wait on the other side of the road. If she possibly could, Eleanor would get word to him about Mr Christopher's response.

Her employer was late in arriving, it being almost nine thirty when he came breezily through the shop door. He greeted everyone very cheerfully and hoped that they had all had a merry Christmas, and then warned them that they must all prepare to wear their most compassionate expressions.

'I guarantee that within half an hour we will have our first customer. Deaths are very common at Christmas time, and once the formalities of announcements are decided, then the grieving relatives will descend upon us for their mourning weeds.'

Eleanor was already wearing a sombre face when she asked if she might speak to him before the business of the day began. He smiled at her, but then realized that her expression was an indication of real regret and not a professional one.

'My dear Miss Kendall,' he said. 'I fear some misfortune has come upon you. How can I help you?'

'I regret to inform you, Mr Christopher, that for personal reasons I must return home to my native Yorkshire at the earliest opportunity.' Eleanor didn't have to pretend anxiety, as she most certainly felt it. She did not want to be left alone in London without relative or friend. 'I realize that I must serve notice, but trust that you will understand my position and grant me leave to depart as soon as possible.'

'I am so sorry to hear it,' he said with genuine concern. 'Of course you must return. Leave at once if you feel the need. Can I help you with booking a rail ticket or other transport?'

'You are so kind,' she said tearfully, and felt conscience-stricken that she wasn't being totally honest. 'But I must return to my lodgings to collect my belongings and then depart by the quickest and cheapest route.'

Mr Christopher nodded gravely. 'We shall miss you. You have proved to be an asset. You will no doubt be able to acquire other employment when you arrive home? In fact,' he said quickly, 'allow me to write a reference immediately in case you should need one.'

Whilst Mr Christopher was writing a recommendation, Eleanor went to fetch her coat, hat and shawl from the cloak-room. By the time she returned, he was standing in the shop with the letter in his hand.

'Although it is not the normal procedure, Miss Kendall, I feel that I must at least give you a day's wages. You came in this morning when a lesser person might have left without that courtesy and I appreciate that.' He handed her a coin, which she took graciously, and dipped her knee.

'I am very grateful to you, Mr Christopher, and thank you very much, not only for your kindness but also for granting me the experience of working for you.'

He bowed his head and opened the door for her. The bell jangled and as she stepped outside a carriage drew up; the coachman wore black crape hatband and armbands; a man and a woman, both in dark clothing, descended from the carriage and came towards them. Mr Christopher bowed again to Eleanor and then turned to greet the potential clients, ushering them inside.

Eleanor saw Mikey across the street and glanced towards him but made no acknowledgement. A little further along she crossed over and slowed her step to allow him to catch up with her.

'Is it done then?' he murmured in her ear. 'Can you leave?'

'Have left,' she said. 'Mr Christopher has even given me today's wages. Wasn't that generous of him?'

'Certainly was,' he said, shortening his stride so that he walked beside her. 'Is it enough for you to pay for a train fare?'

She gave a low laugh. 'No, it is not.' She turned to face him. 'Only enough for the long walk home.'

CHAPTER THIRTY-EIGHT

Sam said that he would like to visit his brother William before making a decision about going to Hull with Mikey. 'If he wants me to stop here, then I will,' he explained, 'and I'll try again to become a shoe-black boy.'

Eleanor told Liza that she was leaving to go home, but assured her that she would pay for the week's lodgings.

Liza was visibly upset that she was leaving, and when Eleanor asked her if she would tell Marie, she wiped her eyes and said that she would.

'You catching the train then, Miss Eleanor? I ain't never been on a train. One of my relatives had her house knocked down for the railway lines. She got rehoused, though, in one of them mansion flats. Very nice it is.'

Eleanor avoided answering the question directly, but asked her if she could supply them with some food for the journey. It's so cold that I'll need to travel in all of my clothes, she thought. Coat and shawl, hat, gloves, two pairs of stockings and warm bodice and undergarments. Then she thought of Mikey and Sam. They had turned up wearing only shabby coats and trousers, and although Mikey carried a knapsack on his back it was so flat that she was sure it was empty.

'We're going to Whitechapel first to see Sam's brother,' she told Liza. 'Then we'll leave tomorrow.'

Mr Bertram was listening as he sewed at his cloth. 'So you'll have to come back into London to catch the train,' he said. 'Why don't you wait here until they come back?'

'I want to talk to Mrs Goodhart,' she said. 'I have to ask her something.'

Which was true up to a point. An idea had been niggling at her and she needed to talk it through. Mrs Goodhart was the one who could help her.

When she brought down her bag with her belongings in it, she saw the dismay on Mikey's face, though he said nothing in front of the Bertrams. He took it from her and they said their goodbyes, Eleanor promising to write as soon as she could.

'It's too heavy, isn't it?' she said, as they walked away. 'I've brought too much.'

Mikey nodded. 'Cumbersome more than heavy. When we get to 'Goodharts' we'll transfer what you need into my knapsack.'

It was late and dark when they reached Whitechapel, and extremely cold, and the Goodharts had locked up for the night. Outside their door and along the wall of the old building were shifting, murmuring heaps of clothing.

'What is it?' Eleanor whispered as Mikey knocked on the door. 'Not rats?'

'No,' he answered. 'Onny human ones. Children,' he said. 'Boys waiting for 'morning, when they'll be let inside.'

Although she had known that the Goodharts couldn't accommodate all the boys who asked for shelter, it was the first time she had seen them in such droves, sleeping rough with not so much as a blanket between them.

'I feel so guilty,' she told Mrs Goodhart. 'Coming indoors when there are so many outside.'

Mrs Goodhart shook her head. 'It is a terrible situation and we do what we can, but it is never enough. However, my dear, you may take comfort in the fact that we can only offer you a chair and not a bed, for we are quite full up.'

'It's not the first time I have spent the night sleeping on a chair,' Eleanor was able to say quite honestly and not a little proudly, feeling that she could identify with suffering even if only in a small way.

The next morning snow was thick on the ground. Many of the boys outside were so cold that they couldn't move. Mikey and Sam helped Mr Goodhart bring the worst affected inside, whilst Eleanor made soup under Mrs Goodhart's direction and then helped to feed the younger boys and those whose fingers were too cold to hold a spoon.

Eleanor felt hot tears running down her cheeks. Never again will I grumble about petty things, she vowed. I have never seen such suffering. And they are all so young! They do not deserve this.

'Why have they been abandoned?' she asked Mrs Goodhart. 'What has happened to their parents or grandparents? They surely can't all be orphans!'

'Many of them have left their homes to seek work or fend for themselves because there is not enough money to feed and clothe the whole family. Others have left because they have been beaten or ill treated.' Eleanor could see the despair in Mrs Goodhart's face. 'We are helpless! What we do isn't nearly enough,' she said in a low but angry voice. 'All over this city, children are starving and running amok. They are at the mercy of men who exploit them and then leave them to die. We need money to feed and clothe them, and educate them to expect something better from life.'

'Who can help?' Eleanor asked her. 'Surely it shouldn't be left to individuals like you and your husband and others like you?'

Mrs Goodhart gave a cynical grimace. 'We pray to God for guidance,' she said, 'and that He will send that guidance to the men in power.' She swallowed hard. 'If it were not for my husband's strong faith, enough for both of us, I would have lost mine long ago.'

There wasn't time for any more discussion then, or even for Sam to speak to his brother about the intended journey, for they were all kept busy feeding the boys and building up fires to try to get them warm. For some it was almost too late and Mikey drove Mr Goodhart's horse and trap to take three boys suffering from frostbite in their fingers and toes to the neighbouring workhouse infirmary.

When they did finally discuss their intentions, it was too late to travel, for night was almost upon them once more and snow was falling heavily.

'You can't travel in winter,' Mrs Goodhart said incredulously. She indicated Eleanor. 'This child is not fit for it. Perhaps you can,' she said to Mikey. 'But even so it will be difficult.'

'I am not a child, Mrs Goodhart,' Eleanor answered primly. 'I am – have been – a working woman.'

'That doesn't equip you for walking two hundred miles in snow and ice, or even rain and fog,' the parson said wryly. 'It would be more sensible for you to wait until spring.'

'That's what I said,' Mikey cut in. 'But I don't have a job now and Ellie doesn't want to be left behind on her own.'

'I have an idea,' Mrs Goodhart said quietly. 'If you agree, it would benefit everyone.'

They all looked at her expectantly. Mikey hoped it meant that they could stay there until the better weather. Although he thought he could survive the journey home, he was convinced that Eleanor wouldn't and it was bothering him more than he would admit.

'You have both proved yourselves useful today. You too, Sam,' she added. 'And I wondered if you would stay with us until the end of winter? We never have enough people to help and those who do have to earn a living and can't give up all of their time. If you will stay and help us with the boys, we'll feed and shelter you in return, although we can't pay you anything. Not a penny.'

A solution, Mikey thought, almost overwhelmed with relief. I shall be out of reach of Manners or Tully and Eleanor will be safe until the spring.

The answer, Eleanor thought, to the very question I was going to ask. She had listened to Mikey's stories of the children in Hull who never or hardly ever went to school. A ragged and industrial school had been opened in the town to provide education for poor boys, but as the boys who might have benefited from being there were insufficiently fed or clothed a more pressing need for their parents was to send them out to find work rather than spend the days learning their letters or numbers.

If we stay here I can learn from Mrs Goodhart, Eleanor thought, and when we return home perhaps I can put that knowledge to some good. I must do something with my life now that I can no longer rely on my parents to support me.

So it was agreed, and Sam too was pleased, as the decision of whether or not to go with Mikey and leave William behind could be put off until later.

After a week, Eleanor suggested that she could try to raise funds for the shelter, and on her own initiative she approached shops and businesses in the area begging for money. If there wasn't any money she asked for food: eggs, bread, and vegetables for making soup. She asked for blankets and bedding, clothing that was no longer needed, shirts and boots; and from young men of business who were charmed by her fragile looks she obtained promises of a regular payment as sponsor towards the education of a single boy.

'Only think,' she murmured to them. 'One day that boy might work for you, and how grateful he will be.'

December turned into January and January into a bitterly cold February when the snow lay so thick on the ground that no one ventured out and all the boys who normally slept outside were brought in and crowded in each and every corner. As March blew in, Mikey and Eleanor prepared to move on. Some of the older boys were now helping with the younger ones, and some of the people they had turned to for help came to give their time.

'I think we shall be able to leave soon,' Mikey said. 'The weather is improving, and although it might be wet it won't be so cold.'

Eleanor agreed. Over the last few weeks she had begun

to feel very homesick, even though she didn't know if there would be a home waiting for her. What would she do if her father was still in prison? What would she do if there was no longer a house she could call home? Who would help her? No one, she thought. No one at all.

'What will we do, Mikey?' she murmured. 'Where will we live?'

He shook his head and privately wondered if St Mary's archway was unoccupied. After the years he had been away would there have been any improvement in the lives of the poor? He thought of Milly, the young prostitute from Leadenhall Square. How had she fared, she and her child? I couldn't take Eleanor there, he thought. She would be very shocked. He was worried about her. I'll have to find her father, he thought, even if it means visiting him in prison. He must surely know someone who could take care of her.

They began their journey the third week in March, accompanied by Sam. Sam's brother was one of the boys to be given the chance of an education through the generosity of a sponsor. He was kitted out in nearly new clothes and was given pencils, pen and ink and several books for arithmetic, reading and writing.

'I'll come wiv you,' Sam said to Mikey. 'William doesn't need me.'

'But we do, Sam,' Mikey said reassuringly. 'I don't think we'll make it without you.'

Mikey and Sam were better equipped for the journey back than they had been when they came. They and Eleanor too had sound boots, donated by a well-wisher. They dressed in warm clothing and flat caps and Eleanor, who had sold her coat some weeks before, wore a wool cape over a flannel skirt and bodice and had made a pleated bonnet, the kind she had seen market women wear. Mikey carried a blanket in his pack as well as extra socks for the three of them.

'So, my dears, you are leaving us,' Mrs Goodhart said, and her husband stood behind her at the door. 'I am so sorry to lose you, but I know that our loss will be someone else's gain.

We wish you God speed on your journey and hope to hear of your safe arrival.'

Some of the boys stood out in the yard to see them off, including William who pressed his lips together as he hugged Sam.

'I'll make a fortune one day, Sam,' he said huskily, 'and share it wiv you.'

Sam only nodded, too full up to answer.

'Come on then,' Mikey said at last, after they had shaken hands all round. 'Let's be off.'

A great cheer went up as they waved goodbye and some of the younger boys raced up the road to accompany them. They followed them for perhaps half a mile before turning back and giving a final wave.

Mikey walked in the middle and tucked first Eleanor's arm and then Sam's into his. He didn't speak to Sam, for he could see the boy was in tears, but he squeezed his arm to let him know he understood.

He took a deep breath. What a responsibility. When he had set off for London he had wanted to travel alone, but Bridget had followed him, and on the whole he had been glad of her company. Now he had Ellie and Sam in his care, and, he thought, I couldn't be happier.

CHAPTER THIRTY-NINE

It was the beginning of June when they arrived in New Holland on the Lincolnshire shore of the Humber. 'Nearly home,' Eleanor breathed. She had never thought how pleased she would be to see these brown choppy waters. She was quite exhausted, and knew that there had been many times on the journey when but for Mikey she would have curled up in a ditch or under a hedge and died. On two occasions when she couldn't walk any further, he had physically carried her to someone's door and hammered on it to ask for refuge.

Mikey squared his shoulders. 'Not be long now.' He took a deep breath. 'By, that smells good! I can smell home. Can't you smell it, Ellie? Fish oil, glue factory and salt from estuary all mingled together.'

He grinned at her and then Sam, who was staring at the Humber in front of them. Sam didn't quite share his enthusiasm, though he was glad to be almost at journey's end. 'I thought it'd be like the Thames, but it ain't. It's different. Not so many ships.'

'Not here there aren't, there's just 'ferry and barges and fishing boats, but there's a boat builder's yard ower yonder; look.' Mikey pointed across to the northern side. 'They build big ships there, fighting ships an' all. And when we get to Hull, you'll see 'docks are crowded wi' fishing boats and steamers, Humber keels and ships from other countries.' Mikey wasn't going to let anyone think that the mighty Humber estuary

308

was in any way inferior to any other. He could hear in his head his local accent returning; he felt buoyed up with excitement.

'Have we enough money for the ferry boat?' Sam asked. 'I wouldn't fancy swimming across.'

'Nor I.' Eleanor laughed. She had been in charge of the little money they had managed to save, and the Goodharts had given them a small amount in case of emergencies which Eleanor had sewn into her skirt hem so that they were not tempted to spend it. They had all done small jobs of work to earn a slice of bread or a place on someone's floor, Mikey and Sam chopping wood or drawing water and Eleanor once tending a sick woman with a baby whilst Sam ran to fetch a doctor. On many evenings they had slept outdoors, Eleanor gathering twigs and dried leaves so that Mikey or Sam could make a fire. These had been good times, when they had sat by a flickering fire in close companionship.

They had used only sixpence of the Goodharts' money and that was during one very wet week in April, when they had had to seek shelter or die of pneumonia. Mikey had led them to the house of an old woman in Retford, who, he said, if she was still alive, would put them up for the night for six-pence.

Granny Hargreaves was still alive and surprisingly remembered him, though she confused Eleanor with Bridget. Eleanor hadn't corrected her; she was too tired and too hungry to do any more than sink to the floor in front of her fire. The old woman had given them bread and tea and Mikey drew a pail of water and chopped enough wood for a week, which Sam stacked by her hearth.

'I don't suppose you came across my grandson in London, did you?' she'd said to Mikey the next morning. 'My daughter keeps on that if ever you come back this way I should ask you.'

Mikey was amazed that she should recall her daughter's conversation from five years before. He shook his head. 'Sorry, 'fraid not,' he said. 'There's millions of people living in London. Folk coming 'n' going all 'time.' He had shrugged into his coat ready to leave. 'I expect he'll let her know when he's made his fortune.'

Granny Hargreaves had cackled derisively. 'Don't think so! He couldn't get away soon enough when he was a lad. He'll have gone to the bad I shouldn't wonder. He was always a ne'er-do-well. There was only his ma who thought the sun shone out of him.'

Mikey had smiled broadly. 'That's what mothers do,' he'd agreed.

'We've just enough money to go across, I think,' Eleanor said now.

'I hope so,' Mikey said. 'It's a long walk round.'

They consulted the notice board for the fare price and they had enough, but the last ferry of the day had gone. They would have to wait until the morning when it returned.

'Oh,' Sam groaned. 'If only there was a bridge, like in London!'

'My father used to say that there will be one some day,' Eleanor said, idly. 'He said Brunel should have been asked. But it's probably too late – he's an old man now, and what a lot of money it would cost.' She gazed out across the water. 'I didn't come this way,' she told Sam. 'I went first to Nottingham by train and then on to London.' Her eyes shone. 'I've never crossed the Humber and never imagined that I would be so thrilled to do so.'

They spent the night in a hut by the landing stage which was apparently used by the ticket collector, who had inadvertently left it unlocked. They curled up together in a corner for comfort as much as for warmth, for it was reassuring to feel another's presence close by.

Presently Sam dropped off to sleep and Eleanor pulled the blanket Mrs Goodhart had given them up to his chin. The temperature still dropped rapidly at night and it would be easy to catch a chill.

'Mikey,' she said softly. 'We're nearly home.'

He gave a slight nod. '*You're* nearly home, Ellie,' he murmured. 'I haven't a home to go to. I'm returning to my

310

home town and I don't know what's in front of me.'

Eleanor put her head on his shoulder. 'Are you anxious? I am, even though I wanted to come back. And,' she added, 'I don't know if I have a home waiting for me either.'

He shifted himself so that he could put his arm round her. 'Don't let's think on it now. There might be summat – something good waiting for us. But . . .' He hesitated. He was worried. Worried that Eleanor's father would ban him from seeing her, worried that he might send her away to live with a friend or a relative until she was of age, and he might never see her again. 'But whatever happens, Ellie, I'll never forget you and I hope you won't forget me.'

Eleanor sat up and stared at him; though it was dark in the hut, he could see how her eyes widened and her lips parted.

'Forget you!' she whispered. 'You won't go away? You won't just take me home and then leave me? Mikey!' She clutched his arm. 'I couldn't bear that! Please, say that isn't what you mean?'

'It isn't what I mean,' he assured her. 'I'm back to stay. But you're different from me, Ellie. We've not been brought up in 'same way; your father might not want me near you. Even though he has fallen on hard times, he's still a gentleman and I'm not.'

She gave a little laugh. 'I don't think he has ever been a gentleman. Not a proper one anyway. And are you forgetting, Mikey, that I too have had another life for eight months? Not long, I know, but enough for me to realize that I can have another existence. But I can't do it without you, Mikey.'

He smiled and kissed her cheek. 'I won't ever leave you,' he said softly. 'Not unless you tell me to. I love you, Ellie, and always will.'

She was comforted by his declaration. She was sure that she loved him too though she didn't say so, but snuggled up closer. Love wasn't a word she was familiar with. She hadn't heard either of her parents say it or show it, not to her or to each other. But hearing Mikey say it gave her such a feeling of warmth and contentment that she felt it must be love.

311

They watched as the ferry arrived from Hull the next morning, saw the passengers disembark, and then had to wait two hours before it set off on the return journey. It was a glorious day with an eye-watering blue sky and the sun glinting on the estuary waters.

'How long will it take us to get to the town?' Sam asked. 'Is it another long walk?'

'No.' Eleanor and Mikey spoke simultaneously. 'We land at Hull pier and there we are,' Mikey said.

They both laughed, but nervously. 'Can I suggest something?' Eleanor said hesitantly. 'If you agree, Mikey, I was going to say we could go straight to my parents' house. If there is no one there, I know how to get in through the back, and we can at least be sheltered whilst we plan what to do next.'

'Will there be food?' Sam asked. He was always hungry.

'I don't know,' Eleanor said. 'Possibly. But I don't know if Cook will still be there.'

She felt silly, shamefaced even, admitting that she had lived in a house with a cook, and she saw the expression of disbelief on Sam's face.

'Crikey.' He whistled. 'Imagine that!'

It's strange, Mikey thought as they stepped off the boat. Everything looks the same and yet somehow different. The same wooden pier, 'same ticket office with 'clock above it. There's Nelson Street and Wellington Street and 'Vittoria hotel, which was always too grand for me to go in. There's 'old hoss wash. It's me that's different, I suppose. I went away as just a lad and now I'm five years older. But not much wiser, he mused. What have I achieved? Nothing. I'm as poor as I was when I left. I might just as well have stayed here and tried to make a living.

They headed towards High Street and Eleanor's house. Mikey and Eleanor said nothing, both anxious about what was in front of them. Sam broke into their reverie.

'This is an old street, Eleanor.' He no longer called her Miss, since she had asked him not to.

'It is,' she agreed. 'It used to be the main street in Hull in

312

ancient times, but now the town is being rebuilt and people are moving out of the old area. But my father wanted to stay. His offices . . .' She faltered. 'His offices are just along there.' She waved a hand in the direction of a narrow lane. 'He preferred to stay near his work.'

Will he still be welcome there, she wondered. He was such a part of the legal community. Will they want him now?

'Here we are,' she said softly. 'This is – was, once, my home.'

She had come to a halt outside an old building with two steps up to the front door. Shutters obscured the windows and there was no light showing. Her heart sank. There was no one at home.

'Come this way,' she said quietly, and led them through a narrow iron gate at the side of the house. 'This leads to the kitchen.'

They followed her down a passage, past a side door and round to the back of the house. No one spoke and Eleanor put her hand on the door sneck. It lifted at her touch. The door was unlocked. She drew in a breath. Had someone forgotten to lock it or was there still a servant in the house?

Slowly she pushed open the door which led into a lobby. A pair of leather boots stood side by side and an umbrella leaned in the corner. She indicated that Mikey and Sam should follow her and they stepped inside. She put a finger to her lips and carefully pushed open the door which led into the kitchen.

She felt a rush of warm air and the yeasty smell of bread rising. 'Someone's here,' she breathed. 'Has the house been sold to someone else? Are we trespassing?'

A small gasp escaped her lips as she stood in the doorway looking into the kitchen. Her father sat at the kitchen table, and opposite him, with her back to the door, sat Mary.

Her father slowly lifted his head, hearing her almost inaudible exclamation. How grey and worn he looks, was her first thought, and why is he sitting in the kitchen, a place he never enters?

Mary turned and for a second they both stared at Eleanor.

Then they rose. Her father clutched the table edge as if for support.

'I told you she'd come back,' Mary murmured.

'Thank God,' her father said. His face was lined and he looked ill. He blinked rapidly and his voice was hoarse and cracked. 'Eleanor! Thank God. You're safe after all.'

CHAPTER FORTY

Mary pulled out chairs and bade them sit down. 'Oh, Miss Eleanor.' She was quite emotional. 'We've been that worried about you. Your father's had posters up all over 'country asking for information about you. Where ever have you been all this time?'

She bustled about, swinging the kettle over the fire and bringing out a large teapot, a tea caddy and a jug of milk. Then she reached for a tin and brought out a cake. Sam licked his lips.

'Yes,' her father said hoarsely. 'Where have you been, Eleanor?'

'I wrote to you, Papa,' she said. 'I wrote just before Christmas telling you that I was in London and that I was quite well.'

He shook his head and looked at Mary. 'I heard you might have been in London, but I never received a letter,' he said softly. 'Did we, Mary?'

'No sign of a letter,' she agreed. 'And practically every day I asked 'postie if he had anything for Mr Kendall.'

I don't understand, Eleanor thought. Why is Father consulting Mary and why down here in the kitchen? There would be explanations in time, she was sure, but her father was now gazing curiously at Mikey and Sam.

'Father,' she said nervously, 'these are my good friends, Mikey Quinn and Sam Hodges. We have travelled together.'

315

As she spoke she wondered if he would recognize Mikey or his name as the rabbit boy who was so cruelly sent to prison.

Mikey stood up and Sam followed suit. 'How do you do, sir?' Mikey said.

'And so you have brought my daughter safely home?' Edgar Kendall said.

Mikey felt his eyes appraising him and realized how down at heel and scruffy he must appear. He hadn't shaved since the start of their journey and his beard was unkempt and ragged. He had made an attempt to trim it with Eleanor's nail scissors but the result was uneven. Even Sam now had a downy top lip and chin. He glanced at Eleanor; she too was looking travel worn with her long tangled hair and dusty boots.

'We travelled together sir,' Mikey said. 'Ellie wanted to come home.'

His fond name for Eleanor slipped out naturally and he saw that her father had noticed, for he frowned slightly and his eyes flickered uneasily.

'Mikey brought me home, Father,' Eleanor broke in. 'But for him and Sam I would not be here yet. If at all,' she added.

'May I ask how you travelled?' Her father beckoned to Mikey and Sam to sit down. 'By train or – surely not by coach?'

'We walked, sir,' Sam butted in. 'It's a long way.'

Mr Kendall's eyebrows rose and he glanced from one to another, whilst Mary stood poised with the teapot in her hand, about to pour. 'You cannot be serious,' he said.

'Yes, Father,' Eleanor said. 'All the way. We hadn't any money to do otherwise.'

Edgar Kendall put his hand to his head. Eleanor heard him murmur so low that all she could catch was, 'What have I done?'

'Who told you I was in London, Papa?' she asked. 'If you didn't receive my letter.'

'It's such a long story, Eleanor,' he said. 'So many facets which I will tell you in time; but your aunt Maud wrote after your mother had left the country, to say that she thought I should

316

know that she had heard that you were alone in London. I believe that your brother had informed your mother and she had told Maud.'

His voice had hardened when he mentioned Simon and their mother and he went on, 'I cannot understand why I wasn't informed before. There has been so much . . .' His voice wavered, and Mary put a cup of tea in front of him and patted his shoulder.

'Don't agitate yourself, sir,' she murmured. 'It's done with now. Miss Eleanor is home safe and sound.'

'Papa, are you unwell?' Eleanor said unsteadily. Her father's face had a yellowish tinge and his hair was quite grey.

'I have been,' he said, glancing at Mary. 'But I am much better than I was. I will explain eventually.'

He's been in prison, Mikey thought. I've seen that tallow-faced pallor on prisoners' skin.

'There is much to discuss,' her father said. 'Explanations which are owed to you, and also your future to decide. Your mother will not be coming back, as I'm sure you are aware, and forgive me' – he looked at Mikey and Sam – 'but there are also some private matters to speak of.'

Eleanor was astonished that her father was so humble. The man he had been would have shown Mikey and Sam to the door without any preamble whatsoever.

'I would like my friends to stay here,' she said firmly. 'We are all very tired and hungry and they need a bed for a night or two until we decide what next to do.'

'I'll put some dinner on,' Mary said. 'You must all be famished. Your father and me have had ours; we eat early, and then Mr Kendall has a rest of an afternoon.'

So he is ill, Eleanor thought. He would never need a rest otherwise. 'May I come up with you, Papa?' she asked. 'Or would that disturb you?'

'No,' he said. 'I would like that. And I will rest much easier once I have unburdened myself.'

Eleanor followed her father to his room, leaving Mikey and Sam sitting comfortably at the kitchen table and having

317

another piece of cake whilst Mary put a hotpot in the oven to reheat.

'Where is Cook?' she asked as they entered his bedroom, which already had the bedspread turned back, although not the sheets. 'Or the other maids?'

'Gone.' He took off his slippers and his wool jacket and sat on the bed. 'Only Mary stayed. The others believed all they had heard about me and asked for their wages and references.' He sighed and lifted his legs on to the bed, shifting a pillow behind his back. 'Not that I could blame them. I would have done the same.'

'Did you go to prison, Father?' she asked quietly.

'On remand for several weeks,' he said. 'Charges were brought but not proved. I went to court and they accepted my explanation that I had been foolish enough to put my trust in someone with criminal intentions.'

Eleanor drew in a breath. 'Who?'

'My clerk. Percy Smart. I had trusted him with my clients' affairs and whilst I was . . .' he hesitated, 'whilst I was involved with other matters, he was taking advantage and using my name as surety. At first it looked as if I was siphoning off money from the clients' accounts, but he wasn't as clever as he thought; the evidence was there and he was eventually found out.'

'I remember him,' Eleanor said. 'I met him that day the police came, and he said there was some trouble, and that you would be charged with embezzlement. He also said he was to appear for the prosecution. I didn't like him,' she added. 'He was arrogant and insolent.'

'He seemed so efficient,' her father said. '"Leave it to me, sir," he used to say. "I will see to the detail." And like a fool,' he said bitterly, his eyes down, 'such a self-important fool, I did. And now, because of it, I have lost so much. At least he is now languishing in the cell meant for me.' He put his hand to his head. 'I have made many mistakes, Eleanor, and the spell in prison made me see them. I have lost my wife and son, and my good name, for even though I was proved innocent there will always be some who will choose to think otherwise.

'When I left court after being acquitted, Mary was waiting for me. The other servants had left, for you can imagine that the news was all over town, but Mary had stayed on; she kept the creditors at bay, for I had gone that day with the police and left no instructions or money. But she said that you had,' he added, 'and I was so grateful for that. And then, shortly after I returned home, I was struck by an illness of my heart. It was the shock, the doctor said, after the trauma of my arrest and the charge against me.'

'But you are all right now?' Eleanor asked anxiously. 'Or will be?'

'Perhaps,' he answered vaguely. 'But my heart is in a weakened state. I shall not be able to work again.' He gave a wry grimace. 'If in fact anyone would want me. But there is more, my dear.' Eleanor was startled. It was the first time she had ever heard a word of endearment from her father's lips. 'There is more.' He lapsed into silence, and Eleanor thought he had fallen asleep until he said, 'Your aunt Maud wrote not only to me, but to her father, your grandfather.'

'My grandfather? I haven't got a grandfather. Surely he's dead?' she exclaimed.

'He is very much alive. You won't remember him, as he saw you only once or maybe twice when you and Simon were babies. He didn't visit us because he disapproved of me. He hadn't wanted your mother to marry me, but was persuaded by his wife that it was a good match.'

'Oh,' Eleanor recalled. 'That is what Aunt Maud told me.'

'Well, your aunt took it upon herself to write and tell him of your mother's going to Canada and of my troubles also. He was shocked at your mother's conduct and has cut her out of his life, and appalled by my arrest. The disgrace,' he said quietly. 'And so there is the matter of this house.'

He shifted in the bed. 'He has said that he will try to reclaim it. He can't, of course; it is mine in law, but he said he would give it a damned good try. His very words.'

'But if he did, then we would have nothing,' Eleanor murmured. 'You would have nowhere to live.' And, she thought, you wouldn't survive.

She thought of all the people she had met who were desperately trying to keep a roof over their heads. Liza and Mr Bertram, Aunt Marie and Josh. Of the street children that the Goodharts cared for. And yet her parents, who had had so much, in their folly had carelessly thrown everything away.

'Where is my grandfather now?' she asked.

'He's still here in the town,' her father said wearily. 'Still trying to find a lawyer who will help him with the impossible.'

'I'd like to meet him,' Eleanor said. 'If he would agree.'

Her father nodded. 'He was alarmed to hear that you were alone in London. He blamed me, of course. Said I wasn't a fit parent.' He sighed. 'And he is right. For I am not. I have made many mistakes, Eleanor,' he repeated. He reached for her hand as she sat on the bed at his side. 'And I thought I had lost my daughter too, though I hope that you have now come back to me to stay.'

'I don't know yet, Father,' she said honestly. 'I'm unsure of my future. I too have had my eyes opened. I cannot waste my life by doing nothing with it. I have seen so much hardship and degradation that I didn't even know existed. I was quite ignorant of the poverty and suffering of so many, brought about by no fault of their own.'

Her father listened silently and when she had finished he said, 'So you intend to be a Good Samaritan? A philanthropist?'

His tone was ironic and so like his normal manner that she felt a jolt of disappointment. So he hadn't changed after all.

'It is not a subject for derision,' she said coldly. 'I have met good people who help others who have less than themselves. I met a poor woman who gave me food and shelter when I had nowhere else to go and asked for nothing in return. I have met a clergyman and his wife who give destitute boys an education and hot food every day. They are not rich or philanthropic; they beg from those who can afford to give even a little.'

He shook his head wearily. 'I didn't mean to mock, Eleanor,' he said, 'although I have done that so often that it is almost second nature to me. But what I meant to indicate to you is that you might not, will not, be in a position to distribute such largesse as you might wish to, for we shall be almost penniless. I have no profession, and if your grandfather should have his way, then we would have no home either.'

'But you said that he couldn't,' she exclaimed.

'He can still take me to court, and even if he loses it will cost us money. The house will have to be sold.'

Eleanor saw that he was tiring and she left him to sleep. Besides, she was hungry and desperate for something to eat.

As she passed the drawing room she peeked in. The room was shuttered and the furniture shrouded in dust sheets, and the curtains were closed.

Down in the kitchen a smell of beef hotpot greeted her. Mikey and Sam, their hands and faces freshly scrubbed, were already attacking their second helpings.

'Come along, Miss Eleanor,' Mary said. 'You're so thin I'm sure you haven't eaten since you left all those months ago.'

'It's not quite as long as that,' Eleanor said as she washed at the sink, 'though it seems twice as long. I didn't know you could cook,' she added.

'Neither did I.' Mary smiled. 'But when I saw the state of your poor father I knew I had to learn pretty quickly. He had lost so much weight with the worry and everything.'

Eleanor nodded. How much did Mary know, she wondered? Had her father confided in her?

'Mary,' she said, 'have you met my grandfather?'

'Yes, Miss Eleanor. I opened 'door to him when he came 'first time. He calls a spade a spade, I'll say that for him.' She stood pondering. 'But I reckon he's all right. He gave me his address anyway, in case I should need to get in touch with him. He saw your father's state of health and I think he was concerned, though he didn't say so.'

'So where is he staying?'

'At 'Vittoria. For another two days, and then he's travelling home.'

'I don't even know where he lives,' Eleanor murmured as she gratefully tucked in to the hotpot. 'No one has ever said.'

'Wakefield, Miss Eleanor. That's where he's from. That's where your mother was born.'

No one ever spoke of him, Eleanor thought. I assumed he was dead as I know my grandmother is, and as my father's parents are. I shall go to see him tomorrow before he leaves for home.

CHAPTER FORTY-ONE

Early the next morning, freshly bathed and in clean clothes, Eleanor set off towards the pier and the Vittoria hotel.

Mikey and Sam had slept on palliasses in the kitchen as Mary insisted she had to thoroughly air the beds upstairs before they slept in them, whereas Eleanor's had been kept constantly in readiness. They too had bathed; Mary had found Mikey a blade to shave with and they were dressed in clean shirts, Mikey in one which had been Mr Kendall's and Sam wearing one which had belonged to Simon. Now they were going in search of Mikey's sister Rose and his brothers, Ben and Tom.

'I'll have to go to 'workhouse first,' Mikey said as they walked out of High Street. 'They should know where they are, or at least where they went, and mebbe the boys are still there, though Rose will surely have left.'

But Mikey had forgotten that the workhouse, which had been in the centre of Hull for so many years, had been moved out of town into a brand new purpose-built building.

'It's onny a short walk,' he told Sam, 'a mere nothing for us.'

They walked along the Anlaby Road and came to the red-brick building and sought out the matron. The boys were still there, she told him, but at school. 'Your sister left. She got regular work and found a room she could afford.'

The matron said she thought Rose was still working in a

mill. 'But I might be wrong.' She shrugged, and Mikey got the impression that she didn't really care, for once the residents had left the workhouse what happened to them was nothing to do with her.

I'll come back and see the lads tomorrow, he decided, and they'll tell me where Rosie is. But he felt despondent. Tom and Ben will be expecting that I've made my fortune whereas things are just 'same as they were before.

Sam shuddered as they left through the workhouse gate. 'I'm glad I never had to stay in one of them places. I'd rather take a chance out on the streets.'

'Yes, me too,' Mikey agreed, 'even though 'new place is ten times better than the old one.'

They walked back into town and Mikey decided that he would go to see Mrs Turner, Bridget's mother, and give her news of Bridget.

She was still in the same house and although she didn't at first recognize Mikey, once she did she invited him and Sam inside. Mikey thought everything looked much the same except for the small boy of about three playing on the floor.

'Did Bridget run off with you?' she asked accusingly.

'She followed me, Mrs Turner,' Mikey said. 'I didn't ask her. She saw I was going on 'ferry and came after me.'

'Where did she get the money for the fare?' Mrs Turner asked. 'She had none of her own.'

'That I don't know, Mrs Turner.' At least he was being honest about that, though he had his suspicions. 'But in the end I was glad of her company. We went to London, and that's where she is now.'

'In London! Why, what ever is she doing there?' Mrs Turner seemed flabbergasted. 'Does she have work?'

'She does, she works for a – a businessman. In import and export,' he improvised. 'She's doing very well.'

Mrs Turner's face cleared. 'Well, who'd have thought it? Bridget in regular work.' She beamed. 'I'll tell her da. He's forever saying that she'll go to the bad, so he is; but now I can tell him she's doing well.'

'I'm sorry over what happened that night, Mrs Turner,' Mikey said humbly. 'Except that nothing did. And never has.'

'You're telling me the truth now, Mikey Quinn?'

'I am,' he said. 'Absolute truth.'

'Ah well!' She smiled. 'I never really believed it was your fault. I thought it was Bridget leading you astray, but now I know I was wrong over that too.' She scooped up the small boy from the floor. 'And look who we've got to take Bridget's place. A fine son to provide for his mammy and daddy in our old age.'

Eleanor's hair ruffled in the breeze as she walked in the direction of the estuary. Halfway across the choppy water the ferry boat was churning towards the Lincolnshire shore, where just yesterday she and Mikey and Sam had stood waiting for it.

I'm so glad to be home, she thought. Even if I don't know what is in front of me. And Mikey feels the same, although he says that he feels that he achieved nothing. But he must have changed, and doesn't realize it. He's self-assured and confident and won't be put upon. Quite different, I expect, from the boy sent to prison for stealing rabbits.

She went up the steps into the Vittoria and asked at the desk if Mr James Carlton was staying there. On being told that he was, she asked if someone could send up to his room and say that Miss Kendall wished to speak to him.

'I believe he's still at breakfast, miss,' the clerk said. 'I'll see if he's finished.'

He came back from the dining room a minute later to say that Mr Carlton asked if she would join him.

A distinguished-looking gentleman with white hair and sideburns rose from his table to greet her. He bowed courteously and she dipped her knee.

'I saw you come in,' he said, 'and it struck me how much you looked like my youngest daughter and now I know why. You are Eleanor. My granddaughter!'

'Yes, sir. I am.' She sat down as invited and accepted a cup of coffee. 'I didn't know you existed,' she said. 'Mama never spoke of you. I assumed you were dead.'

'And had you known otherwise, perhaps you would have come to me instead of running away to London?'

'I went first to Nottingham to see my mother and ask her to come home,' she explained. 'And when she wouldn't I decided to go to London to find my brother. Only Simon didn't want me there. He was too preoccupied with his own life to be bothered about mine.'

'You poor child,' her grandfather murmured. 'So then what did you do? You were alone, I understand. Not a desirable situation for a young lady such as you.'

'I was frightened to begin with,' she admitted. 'It was totally unlike anything I had ever known.' She then found herself telling the story of Marie who had taken pity on her and suggested that she tried for work in the mourning shop. 'The notion of looking for work was perfectly natural to her. In her life that was what everyone did. And it was the same with the Bertrams. Work was the only thing that kept them from starvation or the workhouse door.'

'So you have learned something?' her grandfather said. 'It wasn't a wasted experience?'

'Oh, not at all,' she said. 'But the greatest thing for me was that I met someone who was to become my closest friend, and eventually saw me safely home.'

'I should like to meet this saviour,' he smiled. 'How did she help? With money for the train journey or as a companion?'

'Why no,' Eleanor said. 'You don't understand. We walked. We had no money for any other transport. And it was not a female, but Mikey Quinn, my greatest friend, who was once in prison for stealing a pair of rabbits.'

She felt her grandfather's eyes searching hers. 'You travelled alone with this Michael Quinn? With no other female companion?'

She shook her head. 'Mikey,' she corrected. 'And Sam. Sam's an orphan. His brother lives with a parson and his wife. They run a school for poor boys and give them a hot meal once a day, and they also set up soup kitchens for the poor of the district.'

'Indeed! That is most commendable.'

'Grandfather,' she said. 'About the house.'

'Ah!' Mr Carlton smiled. 'I wondered when we might get round to the house. You have heard that I am going to try to get it back?' When she nodded, he murmured, 'I would never sleep easy again if I thought that your father was going to keep it for himself.'

'He said it's the law,' Eleanor said quietly.

'And so it is,' he replied brusquely, 'and it is time the law was changed! How preposterous that a woman should have to give up everything once she is married. And I suppose . . .' He lowered his voice, for it had risen rather and other people in the dining room were looking their way. 'I suppose your father has sent you here to plead on his behalf? Now that you have come home he has to give you a roof over your head, that kind of thing? Well, you don't have to worry about that, my dear. I will provide for you if your father can't.'

Eleanor swallowed hard. 'Well no,' she said. 'That wasn't what I was going to say. And besides, Father doesn't know I'm here. Mary told me where you were staying.'

He frowned. 'Mary? Who is Mary?'

'Father's servant, or I suppose she's housekeeper now.'

'So why then have you come, my dear, if it isn't about the house? Curious, were you, to meet your grandfather?'

'It is about the house,' she said. 'I want it.'

After leaving Mrs Turner, Mikey took Sam on a tour of Hull. He showed him the first dock, now renamed Queen's Dock after Victoria's visit, and explained the ring of docks which ran through the town and out into the Humber.

'Seems there might be work here,' Sam said. 'Shall we try now?'

'No time like 'present,' Mikey said. 'But I'll finish showing you 'main areas and then we'll have a plan of campaign. Thing is, though, Sam, I've been thinking that I don't want

327

to spend my life doing menial jobs. I need an education to improve myself.'

'Yeh,' Sam agreed. 'I keep thinking about William. The Goodharts have taught him to read and write and now he's getting an even better education cos of the sponsor and he's younger than me. I know nothing,' he added glumly. 'Only what I've picked up from folks I know. Eleanor promised she'd teach me to read, but then she decided to come home.'

'I'm sure she still will,' Mikey said. 'Just as soon as she's settled. But I gather there's some problem over her father.' He thought for a minute, and then said, 'I've got an idea. Come on. There's somewhere I want to go. If it's still there, that is. It was when I left Hull five years ago, onny I was too young then to tek advantage. But now I'm not.'

'What?' Sam asked. 'Where?'

'Mechanics' Institute,' he said. 'It's there to give ordinary folks a chance of education or train them for an apprenticeship.'

'Don't we have to have a job first?' Sam asked, scurrying to keep up with Mikey's urgent steps.

'That's what we've to find out,' Mikey said. 'Come on, it's not far.'

They left the dock behind them and set off along George Street, turning the corner into Grimston Street.

'It's still here,' Mikey said triumphantly. 'Let's go in and see what they can do for us.'

They came out half an hour later, Mikey much more subdued than when he went in. It seemed he had to prove his worth before he would be accepted as a scholar, although the reading room was open to him if he wanted to browse through the books there. That's no good, he thought. I'm not a good reader.

'We'll have to find work,' he said to Sam. 'So back to 'docks we go. At least we can say we have experience even if we can't provide references. And if we find work then we can pay rent for a room. We can't expect to stay with Ellie for too long.'

They went back to the dock and into the office. Mikey

introduced himself as Mikey Quinn, formerly of Hull and lately of London, with his workmate Sam Hodges. 'We work as a team,' he said. 'Experienced in handling fragile or heavy goods at Wapping wharves.'

The clerk at the desk looked at him and then at Sam. 'There might be some work for you,' he said. 'There's a shipment of goods arriving tomorrow and 'merchant requires experienced men.' He wrote the name and address on a slip of paper and pushed it towards Mikey. 'If you go now it'll show you're keen. Best I can do.'

Mikey thanked him. 'Come on, Sam,' he said as they left the office. 'I think this might be our lucky day.'

They arrived back in High Street just after midday, and walking in front of them towards Eleanor's house was Eleanor herself, her arm tucked into that of an elderly, very upright gentleman. They watched them turn into the side gate and, after a moment, followed them through and into the lobby.

Eleanor turned from the kitchen door. 'Oh, Mikey! I'm so pleased to see you. I have things to tell you.'

He grinned and took off his cap. 'We've things to tell you as well.' He was almost bursting to share the news. 'We've got jobs, both of us! There's a ship coming in from Holland tomorrow and we'll be unloading 'cargo.'

'Dutch gin then, I'll be bound?' Eleanor's companion asked.

'This is my grandfather, James Carlton,' Eleanor said. 'Grandfather, I'd like you to meet Mikey Quinn and Sam Hodges.'

'How do, sir?' Mikey said, and Sam nodded and took off his cap. 'I can't say what 'goods are, sir. It's company policy not to discuss them and we've just signed 'agreement.'

Eleanor's grandfather looked startled for a moment and then he said, 'Quite right. I beg your pardon. I shouldn't have asked.'

They all trooped into the kitchen, where Mary had cooked another huge pot of beef stew. She apologized for producing the same meal as yesterday, saying, 'I'm trying to economize as much as possible.'

'It smells delicious, Mary,' Eleanor said. 'But where's my father? Is he upstairs?'

Mary looked troubled. 'He's unwell, Miss Eleanor, and I took 'liberty of sending for 'doctor, who's with him now. Your father knocked on my door during 'night to say he wasn't well, but begged me not to tell you.'

Eleanor bit her lip. 'Should I go up, do you think?'

Her grandfather broke in. 'I think you should wait until the doctor comes down and then perhaps speak to him. He will tell you if there is anything amiss. I must say your father wasn't a good colour when I last saw him.'

'He has taken such a blow,' Eleanor murmured. 'He has lost his good name.'

Her grandfather raised his eyebrows and assumed a cynical expression but refrained from expressing an opinion. Eleanor saw it, but was unwilling to discuss or defend her father in front of Mary, or even Mikey and Sam.

'You are a remarkable young woman,' her grandfather said softly. 'Compassionate and kind.'

She looked up at him. 'He is my father,' she said simply.

Whilst Mary dished up bowls of stew for Mikey and Sam, Eleanor took her grandfather upstairs to sit in her father's study. She could tell that he was not comfortable in the kitchen and he said he did not want to eat as he had had such a late breakfast.

As they came up into the hall, the doctor was coming down the stairs. 'Miss Kendall,' he said. 'How relieved I am to see you safely home again.' He paused and looked gravely at her. 'However, I need to speak to you on the matter of your father's condition.'

She led the way into her father's study. 'First I should like to introduce you to my grandfather, James Carlton,' she said. 'Grandfather, this is Dr Robson.'

The two men shook hands, and Dr Robson declared, 'I wasn't aware that you had grandparents, Miss Kendall, but

I am very pleased to know that you have. As one so young, you are going to need the counsel and support of another member of your family.'

Eleanor opened her mouth to speak but no words came out.

'What exactly do you mean, Dr Robson?' her grandfather said. 'Is my son-in-law very ill?'

Dr Robson glanced at Eleanor. 'I have known you since you were a small child, Miss Kendall,' he said quietly. 'And you have always struck me as steadfast and resilient. You will need all your strength and fortitude now when I tell you that your father is gravely ill and unlikely to recover.'

CHAPTER FORTY-TWO

Eleanor trembled. She couldn't believe what the doctor was saying.

'Surely,' she said, 'with rest and recuperation he will—'

'No.' The doctor was grave. 'His heart is damaged and his general condition is poor. He has not looked after his health as he should. I will call again,' he said, 'but be prepared.'

I never imagined, Eleanor thought as she walked up the stairs to see her father, that my time working in the mourning emporium was preparing me for this.

Her father was sitting up in bed propped up with pillows. 'Now, Eleanor,' he said as her face crumpled. 'Don't give in to tears. You can weep later if you must, but not whilst I am still here.'

She took his hand. 'I'm so sorry.' Her voice trembled, but she did her best not to cry.

He squeezed her hand. 'That's it,' he said. 'You were always a brave girl, Eleanor. I haven't been a good father. I was brought up by strict parents, and I'm afraid I followed suit, and I'm sorry. I'm especially sorry that on one occasion I was very harsh to you.'

She nodded. 'The cupboard,' she whispered, the dark memory rushing back to her.

'Yes,' he said quietly. 'I often thought of it whilst I was locked up awaiting trial, and I realized how frightened you must have been. I deserved my punishment for what I did to you. You did not. I know now that when you spoke to Simon you did so out of tenderness, not disobedience.'

Tears trickled down her cheek. 'We won't speak of it again, Papa,' she said in a choked voice.

'But there have been other occasions,' he continued, 'when I have not behaved as a gentleman should; of those unspeakable things I will not tell, but I wanted to ask that if you should hear of them from others when I am gone, you will try to forgive me and think of me as a weak and unhappy man rather than a wicked one. Wipe your eyes,' he said gently, 'and ask your grandfather if he will come up. I don't know how much time I have left and there are arrangements to make for your welfare. I have made my will in your favour, but might I request that in any future plans you would consider Mary? She has been a great help and strength to me in these last few months and has not even asked for her salary.'

Her grandfather was waiting at the bottom of the stairs and went up immediately, whilst Eleanor stumbled down the basement steps into the kitchen. Mary was standing by the stove and pressed her lips tightly together when she saw Eleanor. She fears the worst, Eleanor thought. She was expecting this. Mikey rose from the table when he saw her tears and came towards her.

'Mikey,' she said, her resolve not to cry crumbling. 'Will you stay with me?'

He put out his arms and drew her towards him. 'Of course I will,' he said softly. 'I won't ever leave you.'

'Carlton! For God's sake, we must put our differences aside,' Edgar Kendall implored when James Carlton came into his bedroom. 'I beg you to look after Eleanor. She will have no one else in the world to look out for her.'

'She didn't know I existed until yesterday,' Carlton barked. 'How could you not have spoken of me? Although I blame Rosamund as much as you,' he added. 'I consider that you have both acted irresponsibly. I could have given Simon and Eleanor so much, in affection as much as material things.

You don't realize how lonely I have been since my wife died. Contact with my grandchildren would have eased that pain.'

'I'm sorry,' Kendall said. 'I've made many mistakes and now it is almost too late to rectify them.'

'Well, not too late for Eleanor,' the older man said. 'She is a charming, lovely young woman and it will give me much happiness to be her guardian until such time as – have you met this young fellow she travelled with?'

'Yes,' Kendall said in a tired voice. 'God knows what might have happened to her but for him. He seems a dependable sort. Looked after her, anyway. Not of good family, unfortunately, and no likely prospects—'

'He's been in prison, did you know that?' his father-in-law butted in. 'Seems he was convicted of stealing rabbits when he was just a youngster. Deplorable,' he said gruffly. 'Deplorable that a child should have to resort to stealing in order to eat.'

Eleanor's father took a breath. 'Quinn!' he gasped. 'Of course! That's who he is! How everything turns full circle. It is one more injustice I have perpetrated,' he muttered. 'You must help him, Carlton. Do what you can for him. There won't be a great deal of money, but—'

'Hah!' James Carlton was blunt. 'I think he's perfectly able to take care of himself, as is Eleanor. But yes, I will do what I can. Just one more thing, for I can see that you are tiring. I shall drop my claim to the house on condition that you leave it to Eleanor.'

'It is done,' Kendall murmured wearily. 'Already in place.'

'Because I don't know if she has told you,' the older man continued, 'but Eleanor has ideas of her own, and they include Mikey Quinn.'

'I must go home,' Eleanor's grandfather said when he came back downstairs. 'I have business to attend to, but I shall return as soon as I can and stay as long as need be.' He smiled at her. 'No need to ask if you can manage without me, as you plainly can.'

'Please don't worry about me,' Eleanor said. 'I shall spend

334

my time with Papa; and Mikey and Sam will be here, and Mary of course. But I shall be very pleased to see you back again.'

'I've aired 'beds in 'attic for Mikey and Sam,' Mary said after Eleanor's grandfather had gone. 'I sleep in Nanny's old room now, the one next to yours. It seemed pointless going all 'way up to 'top floor.'

'Oh, but you must light a fire,' Eleanor said. 'The attic room is so cold. And put extra blankets on the beds,' she added.

Sam laughed. 'You forgetting already, Miss Eleanor?' he said. 'We had only one blanket on the journey here, and only one at our lodgings.'

'I haven't forgotten,' she said. 'But you have forgotten that there is no need to call me Miss!'

He looked embarrassed. 'It don't seem right,' he said. 'Not here.'

She shrugged and smiled. 'Well, whatever you are comfortable with, Sam.'

The following morning, Mikey and Sam were off early to work. Mary brought a tray of tea and toast to Eleanor's bedroom.

'Mary,' Eleanor said, 'I know that this was expected in the old days, but it must be the last time. I need to rise early and plan my day.'

She told Mary what she had been doing in London and Mary was astonished. 'But there's no reason to do anything like that now you are home, Miss Eleanor,' she said. 'You don't need to work. We shall be able to manage.'

'But I don't want to waste my life doing nothing,' Eleanor said. 'I want to make a difference. First, though, my priority is my father. He must be made to feel loved, for I don't think he has ever felt that. And I want to make his final days as happy as I can.'

She spent the day with her father and told him all that had happened to her and how she had met up with Mikey again. 'He remembered me,' she said, 'and he has been such a good friend.'

'I realize that he has,' her father said. 'But don't rush into any relationship. You are still very young. Be advised by your grandfather; he has your welfare at heart.'

'I know that he does, but I have ideas of my own. Papa,' she said softly, 'should I write to Mama? I'm sure Aunt Maud will have a contact address.'

He sighed deeply. 'Later,' he said. 'There's no immediate hurry.' He gave a brief smile. 'She will be able to marry again if she has a mind to and if her *gentleman* asks her. And if he does not, then perhaps you might like to ask her to come back and live with you?'

'I think not, Papa,' she said firmly. 'Mama will not approve of what I want to do.'

In the evening when Mikey and Sam came back from work they were both bursting with enthusiasm.

'It's been grand to be working,' Mikey said. 'And for a legitimate company. I was always on tenterhooks with Tully and Manners as to what they were up to.' He grinned, and said, 'And 'next thing is to get an education. I'm going to join 'Mechanics' Institute now that I've got a job and try to improve myself.' He didn't add 'to be more worthy of you, Ellie', but that's what he meant.

'I've seen my brothers,' he told her. 'I went back to 'workhouse after we'd finished work. I've left a message with them for Rosie, to tell her that she can get in touch with me here and that you'll know where I am. But they said they haven't seen her in weeks. They don't know where she is.'

He pondered for a moment and then said, 'Sam and me have been talking and when we get our wages we'll look for a room to share. We'll be able to afford it,' he added.

Eleanor was startled. 'But there's no need,' she began. 'There's room enough here. And you said you would stay with me,' she pleaded.

'I did,' Mikey replied. 'And I will. We'll stay until your grandfather gets back, of course we will, and whilst your father is – is so ill; but it's not right for us to tek advantage.' He tried not to

look at the consternation in her eyes. 'You have a life to plan.'
And, he thought, it might not include me.

Something woke Eleanor during the night. Some sound,
though she couldn't be sure what it was. She got out of bed and
put on her dressing robe and went to her bedroom door to
listen. There was something. She quietly crept to her father's
bedroom. The door was ajar and she pushed it open. Mary
was standing at the side of the bed.

'I was just coming to fetch you, Miss Eleanor,' she whispered.
'I heard something and got up.'

'So did I,' Eleanor whispered back. 'Is he worse?'

'Yes, I think so. Should I fetch 'doctor?'

'Yes. Shall I ask Mikey or Sam to go with you?'

Mary nodded. 'Please. It's very dark.'

Eleanor hurried up to the top floor whilst Mary went to get
her shawl. She tapped on the attic door.

'Mikey,' she said softly. 'Can you come?'

He was bare-chested and his hair was tousled when he came
to the door, but he quickly went back inside to put on a shirt
and waken Sam.

'Sam will go wi' Mary,' he said, 'and I'll stop wi' you.' He put
his hand on her shoulder. 'Try not to be afraid, though it will
be hard for you.' He remembered his feeling of helplessness
when he was told that his mother had died.

'You'll stay with me?' she asked.

'I told you that I will,' he answered quietly. 'For as long as
you want me to.'

He took her hand and they went back down to her father's
room. He pulled a chair up to the side of the bed; then, taking
a folded blanket from the bottom of the bed, he wrapped it
round her shoulders and sat her down. He took hold of her
hand and, standing by her side in vigil, felt that he was at last
honouring his mother's last moments.

The end came before Mary returned with the doctor, who told
Eleanor that even if he had arrived sooner there was nothing
he could have done to stop the inevitable.

337

There was little to organize, for Edgar Kendall had already put arrangements in place. John Thomas, the senior partner in his former practice, came to the house as soon as he heard the news of his death, to express his sympathy and tell Eleanor that she could rely on him to assist with any of her needs.

'Your father was unjustly accused,' he said, 'and we would like to make amends. He had served this practice for many years. His will is straightforward and all he had comes to you. There is not a great deal of money but enough for you to live on, providing you are not extravagant, and of course the house is yours.'

On the evening following the funeral, Eleanor's grandfather said he wished to speak to both Eleanor and Mikey. This is it, Mikey thought as he washed his hands and face and brushed his hair before going downstairs. He felt sick with anxiety. He wants me gone. He's Eleanor's guardian. He'll have plans for her future.

Eleanor smiled nervously at her grandfather. He knows what I want to do, but he could overrule me now that he is my guardian. I am not old enough in the eyes of the law to do as I wish.

'Come and sit down.' At Eleanor's suggestion, James Carlton had taken over the study since his return and made it his domain. Eleanor had rarely entered it when her father used it and had considered it a forbidding place. Now it was cluttered with books and newspapers, and even her grandfather's slippers in the hearth, which gave it a more comfortable and welcoming appearance.

'It is early days since your father's death, Eleanor,' he said, 'but I wish you to think very hard about your future. And as for you – er – Mikey . . .' James Carlton had some difficulty in using Mikey's first name; he didn't wish to address him as Quinn in case it seemed belittling, yet he would always address his peers by their surname, 'I would like to hear about your plans if you would permit me. So shall we start with you?'

Mikey pondered. Eleanor might not like what he had to say.

338

She wanted him to help her with her project, and he would. But he also had to prove himself. He had to know what he was really made of.

'I want to earn a living,' he said. 'That's 'first thing. And then I want to improve myself. I've enrolled at 'Mechanics' Institute, but I'm having some difficulty because I'm not a good reader, and not much of a hand at writing either. But I'm good with numbers and at organizing people. And 'first step is done.' He grinned. 'My boss is pleased with me and I think he'll keep me on when this shipment is finished with.'

'Good.' James Carlton nodded amiably.

He's pleased, I bet, that I didn't mention Ellie, Mikey thought. Well, I don't have to tell him everything.

'And you, Eleanor.' Her grandfather turned to her. 'Are you still set on your original idea?'

'Yes,' she said and her voice was quiet. 'I am. I've discussed it already with you and with Mikey. I want to turn this house into a shelter and school for poor children. Girls as well as boys. We can use the downstairs rooms for a schoolroom and two dormitories. It will take money to convert it, but I think there will be enough.' She looked at Mikey and swallowed. 'But I don't know if I can do it without you, Mikey,' she said softly.

He stood up and came over to her. 'I'll work day and night for you, Ellie,' he said softly. 'Don't doubt me, please. But I have to earn a living. I have to prove myself,' and he added so softly that her grandfather didn't quite catch what he was saying, 'and I have to show that I'm worthy of you.'

Her face lit up and she smiled, but surreptitiously put her finger to her lips.

'Well then; if you agree, this is what I propose,' Carlton said. 'I can see very well that you young people are fond of each other and I have no judgement to make on that, except to say that Quinn' – he reverted to the norm – 'is quite right in that he has to make a living; but what I would like to do, if you will allow me, is arrange a tutor for you to catch up with your basic education. It won't take long, I'm sure. You are obviously an intelligent fellow. And then whatever you should decide to do in the future you will be well equipped to achieve.

'And for you, Eleanor,' he went on, 'I think it might be wise if I came to live here whilst you are making the necessary arrangements to alter the house. It won't do for workmen to come here knowing that you are alone. I promise that I won't interfere, but everyone will be aware of my presence and I can perhaps advise on monetary matters and make sure that you don't overspend your allowance.'

'Oh, Grandfather!' Eleanor beamed, whilst Mikey seemed overwhelmed. 'That would be wonderful—'

She was interrupted by an urgent knocking on the door. 'So sorry,' Mary said. 'But there's a young woman, well a girl really, at 'back door. She's almost dead with exhaustion and she's asking for you, Mikey. She says her name's Rosie.'

CHAPTER FORTY-THREE

Hull 1860

'Rosie! Rosie! Can you come?' Eleanor called. 'The young Brooke boy is not well. Will you bring him up a hot drink, please?'

Rose, her fair hair neatly pushed under her cap, came upstairs five minutes later carrying a jug of cocoa. She was round-faced and pretty, a different girl entirely from the one who had fallen at Mary's feet two years before.

When they had coaxed the story out of her that evening, it seemed that she had been wandering the streets for several weeks after the cotton mill had closed down. She had had various jobs of work, pan-scrubbing in hostelry kitchens, washing at the washhouse, and other such menial tasks, but none had paid enough for her to rent a room, so she had slept out in the streets before finally walking to the workhouse to ask for admittance.

Ben and Tom had told her that Mikey had come back to Hull and in desperation she had decided to come and find him.

Mary made up a bed for her and gave her nourishing soup, whilst Eleanor's grandfather sent for the doctor who said, gravely, that he doubted she would recover as she was on the brink of starvation. But she did. Buoyed up by seeing Mikey again and being fed and comfortable in a warm bed, she recovered very quickly.

Eleanor had taken to her instantly and asked her to stay. She was now Mary's right hand, and had proved invaluable to Eleanor in bridging the gap between her and the street children who, when the house was up and running, had started to drift in as soon as the word got round that there was food and shelter for the asking. Not all wanted the schooling, but that was the proviso. If they wanted to be fed and have a bed to sleep in, then they must at least have some lessons in reading and writing. 'To better yourself,' Eleanor said to each and every one of them. Some of them drifted away, willing to take a chance on their own again after one good meal, but there were others brought by desperate parents who begged that their children might be given an opportunity which they couldn't provide. One such young mother brought her small son Walter, who, she said, was doomed to penury just like her if he wasn't given a chance.

Eleanor took the child in. Mikey had seen the woman walking away from the house; he told Eleanor that he knew her and that she and others like her had been kind to him when he was destitute and lonely.

There were Ragged schools in the town, but Eleanor hated the name. 'It's so offensive,' she said to Mikey, who in two years had risen to be foreman of the import and export company, but along with Sam still came regularly to help with physical jobs in the house and to deal with some of the unruly boys. 'Why should some children be considered only fit for the Ragged schools and not for the normal schools better-off children attend?'

In order to fund the house in the first six months she had written to local businessmen asking for their charitable assistance; Mr Thomas, the lawyer, had advised her on whom to approach, and in some instances she had appealed to them in person, rather as she had for the Goodharts. The money came in slowly at first, but she had a winning way and a charming smile which persuaded them that they might indulge her. Two altruistic female teachers who came knocking at her door, both in meagre circumstances, were offered food and accommodation and a small salary for teaching the rudiments of reading and writing.

James Carlton hovered in the background, never interfering, never giving advice unless it was asked for, and never offering to finance her project, for he knew how much she wanted to do this on her own initiative.

Mikey had applied for his brother Ben to work in the company office as a junior clerk. He was a very steady character and from his workhouse schooling had a good head for figures and a neat hand. Tom, on the other hand, was a boy always on the lookout for adventure; Mikey was sure that one day he would go to sea, just as their father had. They had both come to live with Mikey and Sam in a lodging house with a warm-hearted hard-working woman as their landlady, who was not unlike how their own mother had been.

It was summer now and there were only a few children in the house. Most preferred to be outside whilst the weather was so sunny and warm and Eleanor was quite glad of the respite. She thought too that she should give some time to her much loved grandfather, who had begun to seem rather unwell, often taking an afternoon nap.

She had told him how much difference he had made to her life. 'I feel so comfortable with you, Grandfather,' she said one day. 'I only wish that we had known each other when I was a child. I could never confide in my parents as I can in you, not without fear of saying the wrong thing or annoying them in some way.'

Her father's old study was now her grandfather's room and out of bounds to the children. Eleanor had placed a sofa in there so that he might rest undisturbed and yet be near to the hub of activity if he should feel like being involved.

She sat next to him now and he took her hand. 'You have brought me such happiness, my dear,' he said softly. 'And yes, I too regret the wasted years. But then, no sense in looking back and wishing for what cannot be.' He patted her hand.

'I'm very proud of you, you know. You have made a great success of this children's house, and in such a short time. I have known that sometimes you've scraped around for money and I could have helped you, but didn't as I thought that was how you wanted it to be.'

'Oh, and it was,' she said. 'I wanted to make a difference myself.'

'Which you have,' he declared. 'But I must warn you now . . .'

She gazed at him in some trepidation. What was he going to say?

'I must warn you that although you only have your father's allowance at present, there will come a time when you will be a very rich young woman.' He looked earnestly at her. 'Your mother and your aunt will receive only a small inheritance when I shuffle off this mortal coil. Now that your mother has married her Mr Walton, I feel that he can take care of her expenses; and of course your aunt's husband has money of his own. As for your brother' – he harrumphed gruffly – 'I heard from your aunt Maud that he is to marry a rich farmer's daughter, so he will have money; but in any case, I don't know him and he doesn't know me so I will not include him. So, Eleanor, whether you like it or not, and whatever you choose to do with it is up to you, one day you will have a nice little nest egg.' He smiled at her. 'So what do you say to that, m'dear?'

She took a deep breath. 'Well, first of all, thank you, Grandfather. Thank you so very much. But second, please don't let Mikey know anything about it, for I don't want to lose him, and I rather fear that the knowledge that I will be a rich heiress just might frighten him away for good.'

Mikey was jubilant. Ecstatic. The opportunity he had been waiting for, the possibility which had been murmured to him several weeks before, had actually come to fruition. His manager was having to give up work because of ill health and had told him in confidence that he was going to put Mikey's name forward as his preferred candidate to replace him.

'You're still young for such responsibility,' he had said, 'but I believe that you can cope with it. And,' he had added, 'this company needs young blood if it's going to expand.'

Mikey had thanked him and told him that he wasn't all that young. He was going to be twenty-one very shortly and officially a grown man.

This morning, the owner of the company had called him into his office and offered him the position.

'You're looking pleased with yourself,' Sam commented as they walked towards their lodgings. 'Lost a tanner and found a bob?'

'Yes,' Mikey grinned. 'Something like that. But I can't tell you yet, cos it's not official.'

Which was not strictly true. It was to be announced on Monday morning, but Mikey wanted Eleanor to be the first to know, and there was a reason for that also.

'I'm going to call in at High Street,' he said to Sam as they reached the turning for their lodgings, which were in a street off the Market Place. 'I'll catch you up later. Tell Mrs Dawson I won't be in for supper.'

'More for me then,' Sam said cheerfully.

They parted company and Mikey continued on towards the Children's House, as they had named it. What will Ellie say, he wondered, and what will her grandfather think? Eleanor was still under his guardianship until she came of age. He rehearsed in his head how he would answer what Mr Carlton would surely say: that he was of a lower class than Eleanor, and even worse had been in prison.

Yes, sir, he thought he would reply. I realize that, and I did once make a mistake and was punished, but since then my standards have been high.

He felt queasy with nerves and was relieved when he opened the kitchen door and found Eleanor alone.

'Mikey!' Eleanor greeted him cheerfully. She wore a white apron over her plain grey dress and was mixing something with a wooden spoon in a baking bowl. They all used the back door for coming and going, except for the children who used the front after ringing the bell, which Mikey knew was the complete reversal of what was normal.

'We're planning a party!' she said.

'Are you? Is it somebody's bothday?'

Eleanor smiled. She had flour on her cheeks and his heart flipped over. 'Yes,' she said. 'Somebody very special is having a birthday tomorrow and I rather think he was going to let it slip by unnoticed.'

He raised his eyebrows. 'I don't usually bother with both-days,' he murmured. 'At least I never did. But perhaps this one is quite special.'

'It is!' she agreed. 'Your coming of age.' She wiped her hands on a towel and went to put the kettle on the range.

'You're very domesticated these days,' he laughed. 'Baking. Mekking tea!'

'Yes.' Her eyes were merry. 'I can't imagine what my mother would think if she saw me; but I love it. Do you think I would make somebody a good wife, Mikey?'

He was completely thrown by her remark. She was joking, of course. 'Yes,' he parried hoarsely. 'I think mebbe you would.'

'Well, I've had to learn to be economical,' she said, 'because there's been very little money.' Her cheeks flushed as she spoke. 'All of my allowance goes on the house and the children's needs.'

'So you'd have to marry a man of substance, Ellie, if you wanted luxuries.'

She considered. 'I suppose so. But then,' she said light-heartedly, 'I've never had those anyway. My father was never lavish or extravagant with material things, though perhaps my mother might have liked him to be, so I wouldn't miss what I've never had.'

'Ellie,' he said slowly. 'Erm, where is everybody?' He didn't want to be disturbed.

'Mary and Rosie are giving the children their supper and Grandfather is in his room having his. Why?'

'I, erm, I wanted to tell you what happened at work today.'

'Oh!' She made the tea and put the teapot on the table and

346

brought out a cake tin. 'Come and sit down and have a slice of currant loaf. I didn't make it,' she confessed. 'Mary did.'

'Will you listen to me, Ellie?' he said, putting his hand over hers. 'Leave that for a minute. I've summat to tell you. Something,' he said, when he saw the tilt of her eyebrows. 'Something really important.'

She gazed at him earnestly. 'Tell me?' she asked, and moistened her lips with her tongue. 'Or ask me?'

'Tell you,' he said. 'I've been made manager of 'company. Bert Straw is leaving and I'm to have his job! It's been offered and I've accepted and it'll be announced on Monday. It'll mean an increase in salary and I'm to have my own office with my name on 'door.' His eyes gleamed. 'Bert told me weeks ago that he was recommending me and I've been keeping it under my hat in case it didn't happen. But it has,' he crowed jubilantly. 'It has!'

'Oh, Mikey!' Her voice was husky. 'I'm so proud of you. I knew you would do well, and so did Grandfather. He said you were very resourceful and bound to succeed in whatever you did.'

'Did he?' Mikey was astonished.

'Yes,' she answered softly. 'He has a great regard for you.'

Mikey considered. The one stumbling block that he thought was in front of him; was it crumbling away? 'Really?'

'Yes.' She smiled. 'Really! Ever since you took up his offer of education, and studied at the Mechanics' Institute.'

Mikey nodded. 'I couldn't have done it without his help in providing me with a tutor to get me started. I'll be forever grateful to him.' He gazed at her. 'You must tek after him, Ellie, and not your mother or father at all.'

'I hope so,' she said softly. 'He's a good person.'

'Ellie,' he said. '*Now* I want to ask you something. I'm in a position to ask you a question now. I'll be earning good money as manager. Enough to support a wife and family.'

'Yes?' she breathed. 'So what are you saying, Mikey? Or asking, I mean?'

He stood up and came round to where she was sitting at the

other side of the table. He reached for her hands and pulled her to her feet.

'I'm asking you, Miss Kendall, if you will do me 'great honour of being my wife? Subject to your grandfather's approval, o' course!' he added anxiously.

'Oh, but he does approve, Mikey,' she whispered. 'I've already asked him if he does.'

'You've asked him?' His heart beat faster as he drew her close. 'Why did you ask him that?'

'Because I had decided that as it was your coming of age tomorrow, I was going to throw away convention and ask *you* to marry *me*! That's why I'm baking! I'm making a celebration cake for a birthday or an engagement or both. I asked Grandfather's opinion and he said that although it was unheard of in his day, times were changing. And he also said' – she laughed softly and put her arms round him – 'he said that I should do it now because as you were such a good catch you were sure to be snatched up very soon.'

Mikey bent to kiss the tip of her nose, then each cheek, and finally, something he had wanted to do for a long time, her lips.

'I don't believe a word you are saying, Miss Kendall,' he murmured. 'I think you're mekking it up! But I don't care. I love you.'

'And I love you, Mikey – my rabbit boy.' She looked deeply into his eyes and remembered how she had looked into them all those years ago when they were only children. He had reassured her then, as he'd looked back at her, that all was well. And now she knew that it was.

ral Sense School

n moral sense was first used by the 3rd Earl of
ury, whose writings reflect the optimistic tone both
hool of thought he founded and of so much of the
hy of the 18th-century Enlightenment. Shaftesbury
that Hobbes had erred by presenting a one-sided
f human nature. Selfishness is not the only natural
There are also natural feelings such as benevolence,
y, sympathy, gratitude, and so on. These feelings give
affection for virtue" – what Shaftesbury called a moral
which creates a natural harmony between virtue and
est. Shaftesbury was, of course, realistic enough to
edge that there are also contrary desires and that not
e are virtuous all of the time. Virtue could, however,
mended because – and here Shaftesbury drew upon a
Greek ethics – the pleasures of virtue are superior to
sures of vice.

Butler, a bishop of the Church of England, developed
ury's position in two ways. He strengthened the case
rmony between morality and enlightened self-interest
ing that happiness occurs as a by-product of the
ion of desires for things other than happiness itself.
ho aim directly at happiness do not find it; those
oals lie elsewhere are more likely to achieve happiness
Butler was not doubting the reasonableness of pursu-
s own happiness as an ultimate aim. He held, however,
ect and simple egoism is a self-defeating strategy.
will do better for themselves by adopting immediate
her than their own interests and living their everyday
accordance with these more immediate goals.

's second addition to Shaftesbury's account was the
onscience. This he conceived as a second natural guide

only that organisms must be thought of "as if" they were the
product of design – and that is by no means the same as saying
that they are deliberately produced.

Problems of Ethical Philosophy

It was Thomas Hobbes who brought ethics into the modern
era. He developed an ethical position based only on the facts of
human nature and the circumstances in which humans live.
The philosophical edifice he constructed stands on its own
foundations; God merely crowns the apex.

Hobbes started with a severe view of human nature: all
voluntary acts of human beings are aimed at pleasure or self-
preservation. His definition of good is equally devoid of
religious or metaphysical assumptions. A thing is good, according to him, if it is "the object of any man's appetite or
desire". He insisted that the term must be used in relation to a
person – nothing is simply good in itself, independently of any
person who may desire it.

This unpromising picture of self-interested individuals who
have no notion of good apart from their own desires served as
the foundation of Hobbes' account of justice and morality in
his masterpiece, *Leviathan; or, The Matter, Form, and Power
of a Commonwealth, Ecclesiastical and Civil* (1651). Starting
with the premise that humans are self-interested and that the
world does not provide for all their needs, Hobbes argued that
in the hypothetical state of nature, before the existence of civil
society, there was competition between individuals for wealth,
security, and glory. What would ensue in such a state is
Hobbes' famous "war of all against all", in which there could
be no industry, commerce, or civilization, and in which human
life would be "solitary, poor, nasty, brutish, and short". The

struggle would occur because each individual would rationally pursue his own interests, but the outcome would be in no one's interests.

How can this disastrous situation be avoided? Not by an appeal to morality or justice; in the state of nature these ideas have no meaning. Yet, everyone wishes to survive, and everyone can reason. Reason leads people to seek peace if it is attainable, but to continue to use all the means of war if it is not. Peace may be obtained only by means of a social contract, in which each person agrees to give up his right to attack others in return for the same concession from everyone else. And such a contract must be enforced. To do this everyone must hand over his powers to some other person or group of persons who will punish anyone who breaches the contract: the "sovereign" or Leviathan – who might be a monarch, an elected legislature, or almost any other form of political authority.

There was, of course, immediate opposition to Hobbes' views. The English theologian Ralph Cudworth believed that the distinction between good and evil does not lie in human desires but is something objective that can be known by reason, just like the truths of mathematics. Henry More, another leading member of the Cambridge Platonists, attempted to give effect to the comparison between mathematics and morality by formulating moral axioms that could be recognized as self-evidently true. In marked contrast to Hobbes, More included an "axiom of benevolence": "If it be good that one man should be supplied with the means of living well and happily, it is mathematically certain that it is doubly good that two should be so supplied, and so on." Here, More was attempting to build on something that Hobbes himself accepted – namely, the desire of each individual to be supplied with the means of living well. More, however, wanted to enlist reason to show how one

could move beyond this narrow benevolence.

Samuel Clarke, a theologian and for his role as Newton's acolyte in a v Leibniz, the next major intuitionist, a benevolence in slightly different wor sible for a "principle of equity", wh the Golden Rule so widespread in a lated with a new precision: "Whate unreasonable for another to do fo judgement I declare reasonable or u like case should do for him." As for moral truths are known, Clarke a More's analogy with truths of mathe that what human reason discerns unfitness" about the relationship be actions. The right action in a given s fitting one; the wrong action is unf known intuitively and is self-eviden

Such intuitionism faces a serious been a barrier to its acceptance: hov moral truth provide one with a mo the desire for profit? Some used the powerful God. Other thinkers, howe it is reasonable to do what is good in of any external power, human or div the development of the major alter 17th- and 18th-century British mora theory. The debate between the in sense theorists aired for the first tin central issues in moral philosophy: is or on feelings?

The M

The te Shaftes of the philoso believe picture passion generos one an sense – self-inte acknov all peo be reco theme the ple

Josep Shaftes for a h by cla satisfac Those whose as well ing one that di Egoists goals o lives in

Butle idea of

to conduct, alongside enlightened self-interest. Butler believed that there is no inconsistency between the two; he admitted, however, that sceptics may doubt "the happy tendency of virtue", and for them conscience can serve as an authoritative guide.

Butler also argued for a broader empiricism, which for him centred on the significance of humans as moral agents and on a reasonableness that need not always conform to a mathematical paradigm. In a matter of great consequence, a person's action can be reasonable even though there may be little supporting evidence for his decision and though, indeed, the evidence may be very much against it. It may, thus, often be a moral duty to act in such problematical circumstances. This led to Butler's famous doctrine of probability – "probability is the very guide of life."

The moral sense school reached its fullest development in the works of the Scottish philosopher Francis Hutcheson and his countryman David Hume. Hutcheson was concerned with showing, against the intuitionists, that moral judgement cannot be based on reason and therefore must be a matter of whether an action is "amiable or disagreeable" to one's moral sense. Like Butler's notion of conscience, Hutcheson's moral sense does not find pleasing only, or even predominantly, those actions that are in one's own interest. On the contrary, Hutcheson conceived moral sense as based on a disinterested benevolence. This led him to state, as the ultimate criterion of the goodness of an action, a principle that was to serve as the basis for the utilitarian reformers: "That action is best which procures the greatest happiness for the greatest numbers."

Hume, like Hutcheson, held that reason cannot be the basis of morality. His chief ground for this conclusion was that morality is essentially practical: there is no point in judging something good if the judgement does not incline one to act accordingly. Reason alone, however, Hume regarded as "the slave of the passions". Reason can show people how best to achieve their ends, but it cannot determine what those ends should be; it is incapable of moving one to action except in accordance with some prior want or desire. Hence, reason cannot give rise to moral judgements. "'Tis not contrary to reason to choose my total ruin, to prevent the least uneasiness of an Indian or person wholly unknown to me," Hume stated. His point was simply that to have these preferences is to have certain desires or feelings; they are not matters of reason at all.

Hume's forceful presentation of this argument against a rational basis for morality would have been enough to earn him a place in the history of ethics, but it is by no means his only achievement in this field. In the *Treatise* he points, almost as an afterthought, to the fact that writers on morality regularly start by making various observations about human nature or about the existence of a God – all statements of fact about what is the case – and then suddenly switch to statements about what ought or ought not to be done. Hume says that he cannot conceive how this new relationship of "ought" can be deduced from the preceding statements that were related by "is", and he suggests that these authors should explain how this deduction is to be achieved. The point has since been called Hume's Law and taken as proof of the existence of a gulf between facts and values, or between "is" and "ought".

Hume's positive account of morality is in keeping with the moral sense school: "The hypothesis which we embrace is plain. It maintains that morality is determined by sentiment. It defines virtue to be whatever mental action or quality gives to a spectator the pleasing sentiment of approbation; and vice the contrary." In other words, Hume takes moral judgements to be based on a feeling. They do not reflect any objective state of the world.

Normative Ethics and Utilitarianism

After the moral sense school, the focus shifted to which actions are right and which are wrong, the province of normative ethics. The impetus to the discussion of normative ethics was provided by the challenge of utilitarianism. The essential principle of utilitarianism was, as mentioned earlier, put forth by Hutcheson. Curiously, it was further developed by the English theologian William Paley. He held that right and wrong are determined by the will of God, yet because he believed that God wills the happiness of his creatures, his normative ethics were utilitarian: whatever increases happiness is right; whatever diminishes it is wrong.

Notwithstanding these predecessors, Jeremy Bentham is properly considered the father of modern utilitarianism. It was he who made the utilitarian principle serve as the basis for a unified and comprehensive ethical system that applies, in theory at least, to every area of life. Never before had a complete, detailed system of ethics been so consistently constructed from a single fundamental ethical principle.

Bentham's ethics began with the proposition that nature has placed human beings under two masters: pleasure and pain. Anything that seems good must be either directly pleasurable or thought to be a means to pleasure or to the avoidance of pain. Conversely, anything that seems bad must be either directly painful or thought to be a means to pain or to the deprivation of pleasure. From this Bentham argued that the words right and wrong can be meaningful only if they are used in accordance with the utilitarian principle, so that whatever increases the net surplus of pleasure over pain is right and whatever decreases it is wrong.

Bentham then considered how one is to weigh the consequences of an action and thereby decide whether it is right or wrong. One must, he says, take account of the pleasures and pains of everyone affected by the action, and this is to be done on an equal basis: "Each to count for one, and none for more than one." One must also consider how certain or uncertain the pleasures and pains are, their intensity, how long they last, and whether they tend to give rise to further feelings of the same or of the opposite kind. Bentham did not allow for distinctions in the quality of pleasure or pain as such; he affirmed that "quantity of pleasure being equal, pushpin is as good as poetry." This led his opponents to characterize his philosophy as one fit for pigs. Yet Bentham never thought that the aim of utilitarianism was to explain or to justify ordinary moral views; it was, rather, to reform them.

Philosophy and Religion

Although philosophers of the modern period are usually thought to be purely secular thinkers, in fact nothing could be further from the truth. From the early 17th century until the middle of the 18th century, all the great philosophers incorporated substantial religious elements into their work. Blaise Pascal in the 17th century had propagated a religious doctrine, in his 18 *Lettres écrites par Louis de Montalte à un provincial*, better known as *Lettres Provinciales* (1657; *Provincial Letters*), and *Pensées* (1670; *Thoughts*), that taught the experience of God through the heart rather than through reason. In his *Meditations*, Descartes offered two distinct proofs of the existence of God and asserted that no one who does not have a rationally well-founded belief in God can have knowledge in the proper sense of the term. Spinoza began his *Ethics* with a proof of God's existence and then discussed at length its implications for understanding all reality. And Berkeley explained the apparent stability of the sensible world by appealing to God's constant thought of it.

Among the reasons modern philosophers are mistakenly thought to be primarily secular thinkers is that many of their epistemological principles, including some that were designed to defend religion, were later interpreted as subverting the rationality of religious belief. Hobbes, for instance, argued that the proposition that faith is rational belonged not to the intellect but to the will. The significance of religious propositions, in other words, lies not in what they say but in how they are used. To profess a religious proposition is not to assert a factual claim about the world, which may then be supported or refuted with reasons, but merely to give praise and honour to God and to obey the commands of lawful religious authorities.

In *An Essay Concerning Human Understanding*, Locke further eroded the intellectual status of religious propositions by making them subordinate to reason in several respects. First, reason can restrict the possible content of propositions allegedly revealed by God; in particular, no proposition of faith can be a contradiction. Furthermore, because no revelation can contain an idea not derived from sense experience, we should not believe St Paul when he speaks of experiencing things as "eye hath not seen, nor ear heard, nor hath it entered into the heart of man to conceive . . .".

Another respect in which reason takes precedence over faith is that knowledge based on immediate sense experience is always more certain than any alleged revelation. Rational proofs in mathematics and science also cannot be controverted by divine revelation. "Nothing that is contrary to, and inconsistent with, the clear and self-evident dictates of reason", says Locke, "has a right to be urged or assented to as a matter of faith."

According to Locke, faith shares a room with probable truths, which are propositions of which reason cannot be certain. There are two types of probable truth: that which concerns observable matters of fact, and that which goes "beyond the discovery of our sense". Religious propositions can belong to either category. Thus the propositions "Caesar crossed the Rubicon" and "Jesus walked on water" belong to the first category, because they make claims about events that would be observable if they occurred; while propositions like "Angels exist" belong to the second category, because they concern entities that by definition cannot be objects of sense experience. Although it might seem that Locke's mixing of religious and scientific claims helped to secure a place for the former, in fact it did not. For Locke also held that "reason must judge" whether or not something is a revelation, and more generally that "Reason must be our last judge and guide in everything."

For Descartes, both the rise of modern science and the rediscovery of ancient scepticism were important influences. The challenge of scepticism, as Descartes saw it, is vividly described in his *Meditations*. Descartes distinguished two sources of knowledge: intuition and deduction. Intuition is an unmediated mental "seeing", or direct apprehension. Descartes' intuition of his own thinking guarantees that his belief that he is thinking is true. Thus, Descartes attempted to prove to his own satisfaction that God, the primary cause of his material universe and the laws of nature, exists; that the standard for knowing something is having a "clear and distinct" idea of it; that mind is more easily known than body; that the essence of matter is extension; and, finally, that most of his former beliefs are true. Unfortunately for Descartes, few people were convinced by these arguments.

Many of Descartes' successors can be best understood by reference to him. Nicolas Malebranche, a French Cartesian philosopher, and the occasionalist philosophers were more radical than Descartes; they dispensed with any unity whatever in human beings and linked together mind and body by means of the constant correlation effected by God himself, claiming that mental events were merely "occasions" for God effecting material change. For Spinoza, the whole universe had not only Descartes' two attributes of mentality and materiality but an infinite number of attributes, and it could be alternatively named God or Nature. Each existent in the world could be pictured as a particular whirlpool in an infinitely deep sea made up of endless layers of particular fluids of which man knows only two – mentality and materiality. Leibniz viewed Descartes' minds as the only ultimate existents, so that even material things were colonies of souls. God was viewed as the supreme monad (the ultimate substance) that establishes coherence and harmony among all other monads. What appears to human beings as the external world is, so to speak, the result of blurred vision on the part of those groups of monads that are human beings.

Berkeley, in his major work, *A Treatise Concerning the Principles of Human Knowledge* (1710), retained Locke's beliefs in the existence of mind, substance, and causation as an unseen force or power in objects. As we have seen, for Berkeley, nothing existed except ideas and spirits (minds or souls). Ostensibly physical objects like tables and chairs were really nothing more than collections of sensible ideas. This philosophy later inspired the clichéd question of whether a tree falling in an uninhabited forest makes a sound, though Berkeley would never considered it in these terms. He sometimes says that a table in an unperceived room would be perceived if someone were there. But does it exist when it is not perceived?

Berkeley's answer is that, when no human is perceiving a table or other such object, God is; and it is God's thinking that keeps the otherwise unperceived object in existence. Berkeley's doctrine that things unperceived by human beings continue to exist in the thought of God was not novel. It was part of the traditional belief of Christian philosophers from Augustine through Aquinas and at least to Descartes that God not only creates all things but also keeps them in existence by thinking of them.

According to Kant, because human beings can experience the world only as a system that is bounded by space and time and completely determined by causal laws, it follows that they can have no theoretical (i.e., scientific) knowledge of anything that is inconsistent with such a realm or that by definition exists independently of it – this includes God, human freedom, and the immortality of the soul. Nevertheless, belief in these ideas is justified, because each is a necessary condition of our conceiving of ourselves as moral agents. Kant held that all human beings, in their awareness of and reverence for the categorical imperative, share in one religion; the pre-eminence of Christianity lies in the conspicuous way in which Jesus enshrined this moral ideal.

Deism and "Natural Religion"

Inevitably, during the Enlightenment the method of reason was applied to religion itself. The product of a search for a natural – rational – religion was Deism, which, although never an organized movement, conflicted with Christianity for two centuries, especially in England and France. The English Deists – who included Charles Blount, the 3rd Earl of Shaftesbury, Anthony Collins, Thomas Woolston, Matthew Tindal, Thomas Morgan, Thomas Chubb, and John Toland –

espoused what they termed "natural religion", a certain body of religious knowledge that is inborn in every person or that can be acquired through the rational examination of nature, as opposed to the religious knowledge acquired through either revelation or the teaching of any church.

For the Deist a very few religious truths sufficed, and they were truths felt to be manifest to all rational beings: the existence of one God, often conceived of as architect or builder, the existence of a system of rewards and punishments administered by that God, and the obligation of human beings to virtue and piety. The Deists who presented purely rationalist proofs for the existence of God, usually variations on the argument from the apparent design or order of the universe, were able to derive support from the vision of the lawful physical world that Newton had delineated. Although the Deists differed among themselves, they joined in attacking both the existing religious establishment and the wild manifestations of the dissenters. The Deist ideal was sober natural religion without the trappings of Catholicism and the High Church in England, and free from the passionate excesses of Protestant fanatics.

For many religious Deists the teachings of Christ were not essentially novel but were, in reality, as old as creation, a republication of primitive monotheism. Religious leaders had arisen among many peoples – Socrates, Buddha, Muhammad – and their mission had been to effect a restoration of the simple religious faith of early people. Some writers, while admitting the similarity of Christ's message to that of other religious teachers, tended to preserve the unique position of Christianity as a divine revelation. It was possible to believe even in prophetic revelation and still remain a Deist, for revelation could be considered as a natural historical occurrence consonant with the definition of the goodness of God. The more extreme Deists, of course, could not countenance this degree of divine intervention in human affairs.

Natural religion was sufficient and certain; the tenets of all positive religions contained extraneous, even impure elements. Deists accepted the moral teachings of the Bible without any commitment to the historical reality of the reports of miracles. Most Deist argumentation attacking the literal interpretation of Scripture as divine revelation leaned upon the findings of 17th-century biblical criticism. Woolston, who resorted to an allegorical interpretation of the whole of the New Testament, was an extremist even among the more audacious Deists. He formally joined the Deists with his book *The Moderator Between an Infidel and an Apostate* (1725).

In addition to questioning prophecies and the resurrection of Christ, Woolston insisted on an allegorical interpretation of biblical miracles. He applied his principles in particular in *A Discourse on Our Saviour's Miraculous Power of Healing* (1730). Tindal was perhaps the most moderate of the group. Toland was violent; his denial of all mystery in religion was supported by analogies among Christian, Judaic, and pagan esoteric religious practices, equally condemned as the machinations of priests. In 1696 he published his celebrated *Christianity Not Mysterious*, in which he tried to show that not all biblical doctrines require faith in order to be understood but are, rather, perfectly intelligible to human reason unaided by divine revelation. The book caused a public uproar, and proceedings were brought against him.

The Deists were particularly vehement against any manifestation of religious fanaticism and enthusiasm. In this respect Shaftesbury's *Letter Concerning Enthusiasm* (1708) was probably the crucial document in propagating their ideas. Revolted by the Puritan fanatics of the previous century and by the wild hysteria of a group of French exiles prophesying in London in

1707, Shaftesbury denounced all forms of religious extravagance as perversions of true religion. Any description of God that depicted his impending vengeance, vindictiveness, jealousy, and destructive cruelty was blasphemous. Because sound religion could find expression only among healthy men, the argument was common in Deist literature that the preaching of extreme asceticism, the practice of self-torture, and the violence of religious persecutions were all evidence of psychological illness and had nothing to do with authentic religious sentiment and conduct. The Deist God, ever gentle, loving, and benevolent, intended men to behave toward one another in the same kindly and tolerant fashion.

Ideas of this general character were voiced on the Continent at about the same period by such men as Pierre Bayle, even though he would have rejected the Deist identification. During the heyday of the French philosophes, the more daring thinkers – Voltaire among them – gloried in the name Deist and declared the kinship of their ideas with those of rationalist English ecclesiastics, who would have repudiated the relationship. The dividing line between Deism and atheism among the philosophes was often rather blurred, as is evidenced by *Le Rêve de d'Alembert* (written in 1769; *The Dream of d'Alembert*), which describes a discussion between the two "fathers" of the *Encyclopédie*: the Deist d'Alembert and the atheist Diderot. Diderot had drawn his inspiration from Shaftesbury, and thus in his early career he was committed to a more emotional Deism. Later in life, however, he shifted to the atheist materialist circle of the Baron d'Holbach.

English Deism was transmitted to Germany primarily through translations of Shaftesbury. In a commentary on Shaftesbury published in 1720, Leibniz accepted the Deist conception of God as an intelligent creator but refused the contention that a God who metes out punishments is evil.

H.S. Reimarus, author of many philosophical works, maintained in his *Apologie oder Schutzschrift für die vernünftigen Verehrer Gottes* (*Defence for the Rational Adorers of God*) that the human mind by itself without revelation was capable of reaching a perfect religion. Reimarus did not dare to publish the book during his lifetime, but it was published in 1774–8 by Gotthold Ephraim Lessing, one of the great seminal minds in German literature. According to Lessing, the common person, uninstructed and unreflecting, will not reach a perfect knowledge of natural religion; he will forget or ignore it. Thus, the several positive religions can help people achieve more complete awareness of the perfect religion than could ever be attained by any individual mind.

William Paley and the Argument from Design

Although the argument for a divine designer of the universe had been propounded by medieval thinkers, it was developed in great detail in 17th- and 18th-century Europe by writers such as Robert Boyle, John Ray, Samuel Clarke, and William Derham and at the beginning of the 19th century by William Paley. They asked: is not the eye as manifestly designed for seeing, and the ear for hearing, as a pen for writing or a clock for telling the time; and does not such design imply a designer? The belief that the universe is a coherent and efficiently functioning system likewise, in this view, indicates a divine intelligence behind it.

Robert Boyle strove to demonstrate ways in which science and religion were mutually supportive. For Boyle, studying nature as a product of God's handiwork was an inherently religious duty. He argued that this method of study would, in return, illuminate God's omnipresence and goodness, thereby enhancing a scientist's understanding of the divine. *The Chris-*

tian Virtuoso (1690) summarized these views and may be seen as a manifesto of Boyle's own life as the model of a Christian scientist. In 1691 Ray published *The Wisdom of God Manifested in the Works of the Creation*, which argued that the correlation of form and function in organic nature demonstrates the necessity of an omniscient creator. In 1704–5 Samuel Clarke, who became chaplain to the bishop of Norwich and to Queen Anne, gave two sets of lectures, published as *A Demonstration of the Being and Attributes of God* (1705) and *A Discourse Concerning the Unchangeable Obligations of Natural Religion* (1706). In the first he attempted to prove the existence of God by a method "as near to Mathematical, as the nature of such a Discourse would allow". In the second he argued that the principles of morality are as certain as the propositions of mathematics and thus can be known by reason unassisted by faith.

It was an English Anglican priest, the utilitarian philosopher William Paley, the author of influential works on Christianity, ethics, and science, who wrote the standard exposition in English theology of the teleological argument for the existence of God, also known as the argument from design. His book *Natural Theology* (1802) is a sustained argument explaining the apparent design of humans and their parts, as well as the design of all sorts of organisms, in themselves and in their relations to one another and to their environment. Paley's fundamental claim is that "there cannot be design without a designer; contrivance, without a contriver; order, without choice means suitable to an end, and executing their office in accomplishing that end, without the end ever having been contemplated."

Natural Theology conveys extensive and accurate biological knowledge in such detail and precision as was available at the time of its publication. After each meticulous description of a biological object or process, Paley drew again and again the same conclusion – only an omniscient and omnipotent deity could account for these marvels and for the enormous diversity of inventions that they entail. The strength of the argument against chance derived, according to Paley, from a notion that he named relation: "wherever this is observed in the works of nature or of man, it appears to me to carry along with it decisive evidence of understanding, intention, art . . . all depending upon the motions within, all upon the system of intermediate actions."

The argument of design had been criticized by Hume in his *Dialogues Concerning Natural Religion* (posthumously published in 1779). While Hume conceded that the world constitutes a more or less smoothly functioning system he suggested that this may have come about as a result of the chance permutations of particles falling into a temporary or permanent self-sustaining order, which thus has the appearance of design. A century later Charles Darwin's discovery that the adaptations displayed by living organisms are the result of natural selection within a changing environment made the idea of order without design much more plausible.

8

KEY FIGURES: THINKERS, WRITERS, AND REVOLUTIONARIES

The people who formulated the ideas of the Enlightenment fall into three groups. There were the scientists and philosophers, men like Isaac Newton and René Descartes, who began to develop the key ideas that propelled the huge changes of the period. There were the writers, those like David Hume and Jean-Jacques Rousseau, who created the philosophies that shaped the modern world. Finally, there were the political leaders, those like Thomas Paine and Edmund Burke, who would turn their world upside down.

They inherited a Renaissance world, in which there had been a rebirth of the ideas of classicism. People had begun to think about the kind of world they wanted – its economics, its politics, its culture, its science, its religion. In the Enlightenment they recast that world with ideas that would turn it into something recognizably modern, ideas that still frame how we live today.

Francis Bacon (1561–1626)

Bacon was born in London, the younger son of the Lord Keeper of the Great Seal, Sir Nicholas Bacon, by his second marriage. From 1573 to 1575 Bacon was educated at Trinity College, Cambridge, but his weak constitution caused him to suffer ill health there. He then went to France as a member of the English ambassador's suite. He was recalled abruptly after the sudden death of his father, who left him relatively little money. Bacon remained financially embarrassed virtually until his death.

In 1576 Bacon had been admitted as an "ancient" (senior governor) of Gray's Inn. In 1579 he took up residence there and after becoming a barrister in 1582 progressed in time through the posts of reader (lecturer at the Inn), bencher (senior member of the Inn) and queen's (from 1603 king's) counsel extraordinary, to those of solicitor general and attorney general. However, this did not satisfy his political and philosophical ambitions.

Bacon occupied himself with the tract "Temporis Partus Maximus" ("The Greatest Part of Time") in 1582; it has not survived. In 1584 he sat as member of Parliament for Melcombe Regis in Dorset and subsequently represented Taunton, Liverpool, the County of Middlesex, Southampton, Ipswich, and the University of Cambridge. In 1589 a "Letter of Advice" to the queen and *An Advertisement Touching the Controversies of the Church of England* indicated his political interests. In 1593 he took a stand objecting to the government's intensified demand for subsidies to help meet the expenses of the war against Spain. Elizabeth I took offence, and Bacon was in disgrace during several critical years when there were chances for legal advancement.

Some time before July 1591, Bacon had become acquainted with the Earl of Essex, a favourite of the queen, but although he recommended Bacon for several offices, Bacon failed to obtain them. By 1598 Essex's failure in an expedition against Spanish treasure ships made him harder to control and he returned against orders. In June 1600 Bacon found himself as the queen's learned counsel taking part in the informal trial of his patron. He was freed, but after Essex's abortive attempt of 1601 to seize the queen and force her dismissal of his rivals, Bacon viewed Essex as a traitor and drew up the official report on the affair. After Essex's execution Bacon, in 1604, published the *Apologie in Certaine Imputations Concerning the Late Earle of Essex* in defence of his own actions.

Bacon was one of the 300 new knights dubbed in 1603. The following year he was confirmed as learned counsel and sat in the first Parliament of the new reign under James I. In the autumn of 1605 he published his *Advancement of Learning*, dedicated to the king, and in the following summer he married Alice Barnham, the daughter of a London alderman. It was not until June 1607 that his petitions and his vigorous though vain efforts to persuade the Commons to accept the king's proposals for union with Scotland were at length rewarded with the post of solicitor general.

In 1609 his *De Sapientia Veterum (The Wisdom of the Ancients)*, in which he expounded what he took to be the hidden practical meaning embodied in ancient myths, came out. It proved to be, next to the *Essays* (1601), his most popular book in his own lifetime. In 1614 he seems to have written *The New Atlantis*, his far-seeing scientific utopian work, not printed until 1626.

After the death of James' chief minister, Robert Cecil, Earl of Salisbury in 1612, Bacon renewed his efforts to gain influence with the king, writing a number of remarkable papers of advice upon affairs of state and, in particular, upon the relations between crown and Parliament. Bacon was made attorney general in 1613. He came increasingly into conflict with Coke, the champion of the common law and of the independence of the judges. Eventually Coke was dismissed for defying an order. Bacon was appointed lord keeper of the great seal in March 1617. The following year he was made lord chancellor and Baron Verulam, and in 1620–21 he was created Viscount St Albans.

Between 1608 and 1620 he prepared at least 12 draftings of his most celebrated work, the *Novum Organum*, and wrote several minor philosophical works. He won the attention of scholars abroad as the author of the *Novum Organum*, published in 1620, and the developer of the *Instauratio Magna* (*Great Instauration*), a comprehensive plan to reorganize the sciences and to restore man to that mastery over nature that he was conceived to have lost by the fall of Adam.

In 1618 Bacon fell foul of George Villiers when he tried to interfere in the marriage of the daughter of his old enemy, Coke, and the younger brother of Villiers. Then, in 1621, two charges of bribery were raised against him. Bacon admitted the receipt of gifts but denied that they had ever affected his judgement. Unable to defend himself by discriminating between the various charges or cross-examining witnesses, he settled for a penitent submission and resigned the seal of his office. The sentence was harsh, and included a fine of £40,000, imprisonment in the Tower of London, disablement from holding any state office, and exclusion from Parliament and the verge of court (an area of 12 miles' radius centred on where the sovereign is resident).

Bacon did not have to stay long in the Tower, but the ban from access to the library of Charles Cotton and from consultation with his physician he found more galling. He offered his literary powers to provide the king with a digest of the laws, a history of Great Britain, and biographies of Tudor monarchs. He prepared memorandums on usury and on the prospects of a war with Spain; he expressed views on educational reforms; he even returned, as if by habit, to draft papers of advice to the king or to Buckingham and composed speeches he was never to deliver.

Two out of a plan of six separate natural histories were composed – *Historia Ventorum* (*History of the Winds*) appeared in 1622 and *Historia Vitae et Mortis* (*History of Life and Death*) in the following year. Also in 1623 he published the *De Dignitate et Augmentis Scientiarum*, a Latin translation, with many additions, of the *Advancement of Learning*. He also corresponded with Italian thinkers and urged his works upon them. In 1625 a third and enlarged edition of his *Essayes* was published. It was not until January 20 1623, however, that he was admitted to kiss the king's hand; a full pardon never came. He died at the Earl of Arundel's house on April 9 1626.

René Descartes (1596–1650)

René Descartes was born in La Haye (now Descartes), France. In 1606 he was sent to the Jesuit college at La Flèche, where young men were trained for careers in military engineering, the judiciary, and government administration. In 1614 he went to Poitiers, where he took a law degree in 1616. In 1618 he went to Breda in the Netherlands, where he spent 15 months as an informal student of mathematics and military architecture in the peacetime army of the Protestant stadholder, Prince Maurice. In Breda, Descartes was encouraged in his studies of science and mathematics by the physicist Isaac Beeckman, for whom he wrote the *Compendium Musicae* (*Compendium of Music*; written 1618, published 1650), his first surviving work.

Descartes spent the period between 1619 and 1628 travelling in northern and southern Europe. While in Bohemia, he invented analytic geometry. He also devised a universal method of deductive reasoning, based on mathematics, that is applicable to all the sciences, which he later formulated in *Discours de la méthode* (1637; *Discourse on Method*) and *Regulae ad Directionem Ingenii* (*Rules for the Direction of the Mind*; written by 1628 but not published until 1701). Descartes also investigated reports of esoteric knowledge.

Descartes shared a number of Rosicrucian goals and habits. He lived alone and in seclusion, changed his residence often, practised medicine without charge, attempted to increase human longevity, and took an optimistic view of the capacity of science to improve the human condition. Despite these affinities, Descartes rejected the Rosicrucians' magical and mystical beliefs.

In 1622 Descartes moved to Paris. There he gambled, rode, fenced, and went to the court, concerts, and the theatre. Among his friends were the poets Jean-Louis Guez de Balzac and Théophile de Viau, the mathematician Claude Mydorge, and Father Marin Mersenne, a man of universal learning who became Descartes' main contact with the larger intellectual world. At a talk in 1628, Descartes denied the alchemist Chandoux's claim that probabilities are as good as certainties in science and demonstrated his own method for attaining certainty. Within weeks Descartes left for the Protestant Netherlands, where he felt he could enjoy greater liberty; he did not return to France for 16 years.

In 1629 Descartes wrote the first draft of his *Meditationes de Prima Philosophia* (*Meditations on First Philosophy*). The physician Henri Regius, who taught Descartes' views at the

University of Utrecht in 1639, involved Descartes in a fierce controversy with the Calvinist theologian Gisbertus Voetius that continued for the rest of Descartes' life. In his *Letter to Voetius* of 1648, Descartes made a plea for religious tolerance and the rights of human beings. In 1635 Descartes' daughter Francine was born to Helena Jans but she died of scarlet fever at the age of five.

Just as he was about to publish *Le monde* (1664; *The World*), in 1633, Descartes learned that the Italian astronomer Galileo had been condemned for publishing the view that the Earth revolves around the Sun. Because of this, Descartes suppressed *The World*, hoping that eventually the church would retract its condemnation. In 1637 he published *Discourse on Method*, one of the first important modern philosophical works not written in Latin. In 1641 he published the *Meditations on First Philosophy*. The inclusion of critical responses by several eminent thinkers as well as Descartes' replies constituted a landmark of cooperative discussion in philosophy and science at a time when dogmatism was the rule.

Descartes' general goal was to help human beings master and possess nature. He provided understanding of the trunk of the tree of knowledge in *The World* and in works on dioptrics, meteorology and geometry, and he established its metaphysical roots in the *Meditations*. He then spent the rest of his life working on the branches of mechanics, medicine, and morals. Descartes' *L'Homme, et un traité de la formation du foetus* (*Man, and a Treatise on the Formation of the Foetus*) was published in 1664. In 1644 Descartes published *Principia Philosophiae* (*Principles of Philosophy*), a compilation of his physics and metaphysics. In 1644, 1647, and 1648, Descartes returned to France for brief visits on financial business and to oversee the translation into French of the *Principles*, the

Meditations, and the *Objections and Replies*. In 1647 he also suggested to Blaise Pascal the famous experiment of taking a barometer up Mount Puy-de-Dôme to determine the influence of the weight of the air.

The translator Claude Clerselier's brother-in-law, Hector Pierre Chanut, who was a French resident in Sweden and later ambassador, helped to procure a pension for Descartes from Louis XIV, though it was never paid. Later, Chanut engineered an invitation for Descartes to the court of Queen Christina, one of the most important and powerful monarchs in Europe. Descartes went reluctantly, arriving early in October 1649. While delivering statutes for a Swedish Academy of Arts and Sciences to the queen on February 1 1650, he caught a chill, and soon developed pneumonia. He died on February 11.

Robert Boyle (1627–91)

Robert Boyle was born into one of the wealthiest families in Britain, the fourteenth child and seventh son of Richard Boyle, the 1st Earl of Cork, secretary of state for Ireland. After education at Eton College and a grand tour with his brother, Boyle returned to England in 1644, where he took up residence at his hereditary estate of Stalbridge in Dorset. Here he embarked upon a literary career and in 1649 he began investigating nature via scientific experimentation. From 1647 until the mid-1650s, Boyle remained in close contact with a group of natural philosophers and social reformers gathered around the intelligencer Samuel Hartlib, most notably George Starkey, who heightened Boyle's interest in experimental chemistry.

In 1654 Boyle was invited to Oxford, where he was exposed to the latest developments in natural philosophy and became associated with a group of notable natural philosophers and physicians, including John Wilkins, Christopher Wren, and John Locke, who formed the "Experimental Philosophy Club". Much of Boyle's best-known work dates from this period, including the construction of the air pump with Robert Hooke. Their resultant discoveries were published in Boyle's first scientific publication, *New Experiments Physico-Mechanicall, Touching the Spring of the Air and its Effects* (1660). One of their findings, published in 1662, later became known as "Boyle's law".

Boyle's work emphasized experiment and observation, and he advocated a mechanistic view of the universe. Among his influential publications were *The Sceptical Chymist* (1661), and the *Origine of Formes and Qualities* (1666). Boyle also maintained a lifelong pursuit of transmutational alchemy. He was a devout and pious Anglican who keenly championed his faith, and his conception of his own life and the role of a Christian scientist was summarized in *The Christian Virtuoso* (1690).

In 1668 Boyle left Oxford and took up residence with his sister Katherine Jones, Vicountess Ranelagh, in her house on Pall Mall in London. There he set up an active laboratory, and published at least one book nearly every year. Living in London also provided him the opportunity to participate actively in the Royal Society. He was offered the presidency of the Royal Society (in 1680) and the episcopacy but declined both. He died at age 64 after a short illness exacerbated by his grief over Katherine's death a week earlier. He left his papers to the Royal Society and a bequest for establishing a series of lectures in defence of Christianity. These lectures, now known as the Boyle Lectures, continue to this day.

Benedict de Spinoza (1632–77)

Spinoza's grandfather and father were Portuguese Jews who had found refuge in Amsterdam after Holland's successful revolt against Spain and the granting of religious freedom. Spinoza's mother died when Benedict was a child. and in 1654 Benedict's father died. His studies were mainly Jewish, but he was an independent thinker and soon incurred the disapproval of the synagogue authorities for his interpretations of Scripture. The Jewish authorities, after trying vainly to silence Spinoza with bribes and threats, excommunicated him in July 1656, and he was banished from Amsterdam for a short period by the civil authorities. He stayed with Franciscus van den Enden, a former Jesuit and ardent classical scholar, who had opened a school in Amsterdam. At the same time, Spinoza was becoming expert at making lenses, supporting himself partly by grinding and polishing lenses for spectacles, telescopes, and microscopes; he also worked as a tutor.

Spinoza was a scientific humanist who justified power solely by its usefulness. He desired toleration and intellectual liberty, believing state power had no intrinsic divine or metaphysical authority. A kind of reading and discussion circle for the study of religious and philosophical problems came into being under the guidance of Spinoza. In order to collect his thoughts, however, and reduce them to a system, he withdrew in 1660 to Rijnsburg, near Leiden. There he wrote *Korte Verhandeling van God, de Mensch en deszelfs Welstand* (written *c.* 1662; English translation *Spinoza's Short Treatise on God, Man, and His Well-Being,* 1910) and *Tractatus de Intellectus Emendatione* (*Treatise on the Correction of the Understanding*), both of which were ready by April 1662. He also completed the greater part of his geometrical version of Descartes' *Principia Philosophiae* and the first book of his *Ethics*. The former was published under the title *Renati des Cartes Principiorum Philosophiae Pars I et II, More Geometrico Demonstratae, per Benedictum de Spinoza* (1663), with an introduction explaining that Spinoza did not share the views expressed in the book. This was the only book published in Spinoza's lifetime with his name on the title page.

Spinoza became dissatisfied with the informal method of exposition that he had adopted previously and turned instead to the geometrical method in the manner of Euclid's *Elements*. His masterpiece, the *Ethica Ordine Geometrico Demonstrata* (*Ethics*), was set out in this manner. Spinoza, like his contemporaries, held that definitions are not arbitrary but that there is a sense in which they may be correct or incorrect. In his unfinished *Tractatus de Intellectus Emendatione* (1670; *On the Improvement of the Understanding*), he held that a sound definition should make clear the possibility or the necessity of the existence of the object defined.

In May 1670 Spinoza moved to The Hague, where he remained until his death. When the *Ethics* was completed in 1675, Spinoza had to abandon the idea of publishing it, though manuscript copies were circulated among his close friends. Spinoza concentrated his attention on political problems and began his *Tractatus Politicus* (*Political Treatise*), which he did not live to finish. He died in 1677.

John Locke (1632–1704)

John Locke was reared in Pensford, six miles south of Bristol. In 1652 he entered Christ Church, Oxford. He interested himself in studies outside the traditional programme, particularly experimental science and medicine. He graduated in 1656, gaining an MA two years later, around which time he was elected a student (the equivalent of fellow) of Christ Church. In 1660, he was appointed tutor in his college.

In 1661 Locke inherited a portion of his father's estate, which ensured a modest annual income. His studentship would eventually be subject to termination unless he took holy orders, which he declined to do. Not wishing to make teaching his permanent vocation, he taught undergraduates for four years only. He served as secretary to a diplomatic mission to Brandenburg in 1665, and on his return was immediately offered, but refused, another diplomatic post. His chief interests at the time were natural science and the study of the underlying principles of moral, social, and political life. To remedy the narrowness of his education, he read contemporary philosophy. He also collaborated with Robert Boyle, who was a close friend, and Thomas Sydenham, an eminent medical scientist.

It was as a physician that Locke first came to the notice of the statesman Lord Ashley (later to become the 1st Earl of Shaftesbury). Introduced in 1666, the following year he joined Ashley's household in London as family physician and adviser on his general affairs. Ashley stood firmly for a constitutional monarchy, for a Protestant succession, for civil liberty, for toleration in religion, for the rule of Parliament, and for the economic expansion of Britain. Since these were already aims to which Locke had dedicated himself, there existed from the first a perfect understanding between them. Ashley entrusted Locke with negotiating his son's marriage with the daughter of the Earl of Rutland; he also made him secretary of the group that he had formed to increase trade with America. Locke helped to draft a constitution for the new colony of Carolina, a document that extended freedom of worship to all colonists, denying admission only to atheists.

During the following decades, Locke continued to pursue philosophical and scientific problems. In 1668 he became a fellow of the newly formed (1663) Royal Society. Groups of friends met in his rooms, and it was at one such meeting that Locke set out his view of human knowledge in two drafts (1671), the beginnings of the thinking that 19 years later would blossom into his famous *Essay*. In these London years, too, Locke encountered representatives of Cambridge Platonism, a school of Christian humanists. Their tolerance, emphasis on practical conduct, and rejection of materialism were features that he found most attractive. This school was closely related in spirit to another school that influenced Locke at this time, that of latitudinarianism.

In 1672 Ashley was raised to the peerage as the 1st Earl of Shaftesbury and at the end of that year was appointed lord high chancellor of England. Though he soon lost favour and was dismissed, while in office he established the Council of Trade and Plantations, of which Locke was secretary for two years. Locke, who suffered greatly from asthma, found the London air and his heavy duties unhealthy, and in 1675 returned to Oxford. Six months later he departed for France, where he stayed for four years (1675–9), spending most of his time in Paris and Montpellier. In France during the 1670s, Locke made contacts that deeply influenced his view of metaphysics and epistemology, particularly with the Gassendist school and its leader, François Bernier.

Upon Locke's return to England, he found the country torn by dissension. For a year Shaftesbury, one of the many who wished to bar James the Duke of York (later James II) as a Roman Catholic from the succession, had been imprisoned in the Tower, but, by the time Locke returned, he was back in favour once more as lord president of the Privy Council. When he failed, however, to reconcile the interests of the king and Parliament, he was dismissed; in 1681 he was arrested, tried, and finally acquitted by a London jury. A year later he fled to

Holland, where in 1683 he died. Locke, who was now being closely watched, crossed to Holland in September 1683.

While his sojourn in Holland was happier than he had expected it to be, at home, Locke was deprived of his studentship at Christ Church and named on a list sent to the Hague as one of 84 traitors wanted by the English government. He remained abroad for more than five years, until James II was overthrown, and William of Orange was invited by Protestants to seize the throne. Locke, in February 1689, crossed in the party that accompanied the Princess of Orange, now to be crowned Queen Mary II of England. He refused ambassadorial posts but accepted a membership in the Commission of Appeals. But the London air again bothered him, and in 1691 he retired to Oates, the house of his friends Sir Francis and Lady Masham in Essex, and subsequently made only occasional visits to London.

In these last years of his life, he was the intellectual leader of the Whigs and the younger generation turned to him constantly for guidance. In "the glorious, bloodless revolution", the main aims for which Shaftesbury and Locke had fought were achieved: England became a constitutional monarchy; advances were made in securing the liberty of subjects in the law courts; and in achieving greater religious toleration and freedom of thought and expression. Locke himself drafted the arguments that saw the restrictive Act for the Regulation of Printing abolished in 1695 and the freedom of the press secured.

The main task of this last period of his life, however, was the publication of his works: The *Epistola de Tolerantia* (1689; *A Letter Concerning Toleration*), *Two Treatises of Government* (1690), and *An Essay Concerning Human Understanding*, which was not published until December 1689. Locke's last years were spent in the peaceful retreat of Oates. Locke's letters to Edward Clarke from Holland, advising him on the best upbringing for his son formed the basis of his influential *Some Thoughts Concerning Education* (1693). In 1695 he published a dignified plea for a less dogmatic Christianity in *The Reasonableness of Christianity*. John Locke was buried in the parish church of High Laver.

Sir Isaac Newton (1642–1727)

Isaac Newton was born in Woolsthorpe, the only son of a local yeoman, who had died three months before, and of Hannah Ayscough. Within two years his mother married a second time and her husband left young Isaac with his grandmother. For nine years Isaac was effectively separated from his mother, and his pronounced psychotic tendencies have been ascribed to this traumatic event. After his mother was widowed a second time, she determined that her first-born son should manage her now considerable property. Newton could not bring himself to concentrate on rural affairs, however, and he was sent back to the grammar school in Grantham to prepare for the university. By June 1661, he was ready to matriculate at Trinity College, Cambridge. Some time during his undergraduate career, he discovered the works of the French philosopher René Descartes and the other mechanical philosophers.

Beginning in 1664 Newton wrote the *Quaestiones* in his notebook, revealing that he had by then discovered the new conception of nature that provided the framework of the scientific revolution. He had also read Henry More, the Cambridge Platonist, and was thereby introduced to another intellectual world, the magical hermetic tradition, which sought to explain natural phenomena in terms of alchemical and magical concepts. Newton had also begun his mathematical studies. He discovered the binomial theorem, and he developed the calculus, a more powerful form of analysis that employs infinitesimal considerations in finding the slopes of curves and areas under curves. By 1669 Newton was ready to write a tract summarizing his progress, *De Analysi per Aequationes Numeri Terminorum Infinitas* (*On Analysis by Infinite Series*), which circulated in manuscript through a limited circle and made his name known. During the next two years he revised it as *De Methodis Serierum et Fluxionum* (*On the Methods of Series and Fluxions*). The word fluxions, Newton's private rubric, indicates that the calculus had been born. He had become the leading mathematician in Europe.

Newton received his bachelor's degree in April 1665, but that year the plague closed the university, and for most of the following two years he was forced to stay at his home. He was elected to a fellowship in Trinity College in 1667, after the university reopened. Two years later he was recommended for the chair of mathematics. For this he had to deliver an annual course of lectures. He chose the work he had done in optics.

His theory of colours, like his later work, was first transmitted to the world through a paper to the Royal Society of London. This first led him into disagreement with Robert Hooke, one of the leaders of the Royal Society, a dispute that would continue on and off for the rest of his life. Newton was unable rationally to confront criticism, and less than a year after submitting the paper, he was so unsettled by the discussion that he withdrew into virtual isolation. In 1675, during a visit to London, however, Newton thought he heard Hooke accept his theory and was emboldened to bring forth a second paper, identical to most of Book II as it later appeared in the *Opticks*. This demonstrated for the first time the existence of periodic optical phenomena.

In 1704 Newton combined a revision of his optical lectures with the paper of 1675 and a small amount of additional material in his *Opticks*. A second piece which Newton had sent with the paper of 1675 provoked new controversy. Entitled *An Hypothesis Explaining the Properties of Light*, it was in fact a general system of nature. Hooke apparently claimed that Newton had stolen its content from him, and Newton boiled over again, though the issue was quickly controlled by an exchange of formal, excessively polite letters. Newton was also engaged in another exchange on his theory of colours with a circle of English Jesuits in Liège, and their contention that his experiments were mistaken lashed him into a fury. In 1678, the correspondence provoked a complete nervous breakdown and for six years he withdrew from intellectual commerce except when others initiated a correspondence, which he always broke off as quickly as possible.

During his time of isolation, Newton immersed himself in alchemy and his conception of nature underwent a decisive change. His *Hypothesis of Light* of 1675, with its universal ether, had been a standard mechanical system of nature. In about 1679, Newton abandoned this thesis and began to ascribe the phenomena to attractions and repulsions between particles of matter. Late in 1679 another application for the idea was suggested in a letter from Hooke, who mentioned his analysis of planetary motion. From Newton's work on this, the crucial propositions on which the law of universal gravitation would ultimately rest would eventually emerge.

In 1684, Newton sent a short tract entitled *De Motu* (*On Motion*) to the astronomer Edmond Halley, who had visited him. In two and a half years, this grew into *Philosophiae Naturalis Principia Mathematica* (*Mathematical Principles of Natural Philosophy*), containing the laws of motion of visible bodies. When the Royal Society received the completed manuscript of Book I in 1686, Hooke again raised the cry of plagiarism, a charge that cannot be sustained in any meaningful sense. Hooke would have been satisfied with a generous acknowledgement; Newton, instead, went through his manuscript and eliminated nearly every reference to Hooke.

The *Principia* immediately raised Newton to international prominence. Newton found satisfaction in the role of patron to young scientists. His friendship with Fatio de Duillier, a Swiss-born mathematician resident in London who shared Newton's interests, was the most profound experience of his adult life. He broadened his circle and tasted London life. When Newton, a fervent if unorthodox Protestant, helped to lead the resistance of Cambridge to James II's attempt to Catholicize it, he made the acquaintance of a broader group, including John Locke. Fatio suggested that he find a position in London, and in 1696, he was appointed warden of the mint. Although he did not resign his Cambridge appointments until 1701, he moved to London and henceforth centred his life there.

In 1693, the termination of his relationship with Fatio precipitated a crisis. Samuel Pepys and John Locke, both personal friends of Newton, received wild, accusatory letters. Both men were alarmed for Newton's sanity; and, in fact, Newton had suffered at least his second nervous breakdown. The crisis passed, and Newton recovered his stability. Only briefly did he ever return to sustained scientific work, however. In his later years, he devoted much time to religion and theology. In 1703 he was elected president of the Royal Society. In 1705 Queen Anne knighted him, the first occasion on which a scientist was so honoured.

Newton's rule of the Royal Society brought him into confrontations with John Flamsteed, the Astronomer Royal, and Gottfried Wilhelm Leibniz, the German philosopher and mathematician. In the 1690s, as he worked on the lunar theory, Newton tried to force the publication of Flamsteed's catalogue of stars. Flamsteed's observations, the fruit of a lifetime of work, were, in effect, seized despite his protests and prepared for the press by his mortal enemy, Edmond Halley. Flamsteed by court order had the printed catalogue returned to him before it was generally distributed. Newton sought his revenge by systematically eliminating references to Flamsteed's help in later editions of the *Principia*.

Newton's conflict with Leibniz had them both making charges of plagiarism over the origination of calculus. While it is established that Newton developed the calculus before Leibniz seriously pursued mathematics, it is also agreed that Leibniz later arrived at the calculus independently. However, because Newton had only hinted in the *Principia* at his method, not publishing it until he appended two papers to the *Opticks* in 1704, Leibniz's paper of 1684 first made the calculus a matter of public knowledge. Newton appointed an "impartial" committee to investigate the issue, secretly wrote the report officially published by the society, and reviewed it anonymously in the *Philosophical Transactions*. The battle with Leibniz dominated the final 25 years of Newton's life.

Until nearly the end, Newton presided at the Royal Society and supervised the mint. During his last years, his niece, Catherine Barton Conduitt, and her husband lived with him.

Charles-Louis de Secondat, Baron de La Brède et de Montesquieu (1689–1755)

Baron de Montesquieu was educated at the Collège de Juilly, which provided a sound education on enlightened and modern lines. Charles-Louis left Juilly in 1705, continued his studies at the faculty of law at the University of Bordeaux, graduated and became an advocate in 1708. In 1715 he married Jeanne de

Lartigue, a wealthy Protestant, who brought him a respectable dowry of 100,000 livres and in due course presented him with two daughters and a son, Jean-Baptiste. In 1716 his uncle, Jean-Baptiste, Baron de Montesquieu, died and left to his nephew his estates, with the barony of Montesquieu, near Agen, and the office of deputy president in the Parlement of Bordeaux. The young Montesquieu, at 27, was now socially and financially secure.

In 1721 he published his *Lettres persanes* (English translation *Persian Letters*, 1722), in which he gave a brilliant satirical portrait of French and particularly Parisian civilization, supposedly seen through the eyes of two Persian travellers. The work's anonymity was soon penetrated, and Montesquieu became famous. Montesquieu now sought to reinforce his literary achievement with social success. Going to Paris in 1722, he was assisted in entering court circles by the Duke of Berwick, and made the acquaintance of the English politician Viscount Bolingbroke, whose political views were later to be reflected in Montesquieu's analysis of the English constitution. In Paris his interest in the routine activities of the Parlement in Bordeaux, however, had dwindled. His office was marketable, and in 1726 he sold it, a move that served both to re-establish his fortunes, and enabled him to enter the French Academy.

He embarked on a grand tour, ending it in the company of the statesman and wit Lord Chesterfield in England, where he remained until the spring of 1731. Here he was presented at court and received by the Prince of Wales, at whose request he later made an anthology of French songs. He was elected a Fellow of the Royal Society, attended parliamentary debates, read the political journals of the day, became a Freemason and bought extensively for his library. His stay in England was one of the most formative periods of his life.

On his return to France he decided to devote himself to literature. Apart from a tiny but controversial treatise on *La monarchie universelle* (*The Universal Monarchy*), printed in 1734 but at once withdrawn (so that only his own copy is extant), he was occupied with an essay on the English constitution and with his *Considérations sur les causes de la grandeur des Romains et de leur décadence* (1734; *Considerations on the Causes of the Grandeur and Decadence of the Romans*). After the publication of the *Considerations*, he embarked on a major work on law and politics, which appeared in November 1748 under the title *De l'esprit des lois, ou du rapport que les lois doivent avoir avec la constitution de chaque gouvernement, les moeurs, le climat, la religion, le commerce, etc.* (*The Spirit of the Laws*, 1750).

After the book was published, praise came to Montesquieu. The philosophers of the Enlightenment accepted him as one of their own, as indeed he was. The work was controversial, however, and a variety of denunciatory articles and pamphlets appeared. Notwithstanding the favourable disposition of the pope, the work was placed on the Index of Forbidden Books in 1751. This, though it dismayed Montesquieu, was but a momentary setback. He had already published his *Défense de l'esprit des lois* (1750; *Defence of the Spirit of the Laws*).

It was to be expected that the editors of the *Encyclopédie* should wish to have his collaboration, and d'Alembert asked him to write on democracy and despotism. Montesquieu declined, saying that he had already had his say on those themes but would like to write on taste. The resultant *Essai sur le goût* (*Essay on Taste*), first drafted about 25 years earlier, was his last work.

Thomas Hobbes (1588–1679)

Hobbes' father, a vicar, abandoned his three children to the care of his brother, a well-to-do glover in Malmesbury. At 15, Hobbes went to Magdalen Hall in Oxford, where he devoted most of his time to books of travel and the study of maps. Upon his graduation in 1608, he became a private tutor to William Cavendish, afterward 2nd Earl of Devonshire. In 1610 Hobbes visited France and Italy with his pupil. On returning home he decided to make himself a classical scholar. The chief fruit of Hobbes' classical studies was his translation of Thucydides, published in 1629. The same year Hobbes went abroad again, as travelling companion to the son of Sir Gervase Clifton.

The turning point in his intellectual history occurred at about this time, when, in Euclid's *Elements*, he traced the proofs back through proposition after proposition and was thus demonstratively convinced of their truth. In 1630 Hobbes was recalled from Paris to teach the young Earl of Devonshire, William Cavendish, son of his late patron. He began to investigate the diversity of motion, laying out his ideas in his first known philosophical work, *A Short Tract on First Principles*.

During a third trip abroad, this time with the younger Cavendish, Hobbes' interest in science and philosophy was stimulated by his contact with the leaders of the new thought in Europe. He was able to discuss his ideas in Paris with the circle of Marin Mersenne and, in 1636, with Galileo. He then planned a philosophical trilogy: *De Corpore* (1655; *Concerning the Body*) was to show that physical phenomena are explicable in terms of motion; *De Homine* (1658; *Concerning Man*) was to show what specific bodily motions are involved in human cognition and appetition; and *De Cive* (1642;

Concerning Citizenship) was to deduce from what had already been established the proper organization of men in society.

In 1637 Hobbes returned to England to find the country in the political ferment that preceded the Civil War, and he decided because of this threat to publish the last part of his planned philosophy first. *The Elements of Law, Natural and Politic* – Part I on man and Part II on citizenship – was circulated in manuscript in 1640. It contained most of the political and psychological doctrines for which Hobbes is famous and which reappeared in *De Cive* and *Leviathan*.

When strife became acute in 1640, Hobbes feared for his safety and retired to Paris. He was soon in contact with later fugitives from England. He rejoined the Mersenne circle, wrote "objections" to the *Meditationes* and the *Dioptrique* of René Descartes, and in 1642 published *De Cive*. Hobbes spent the next four years working on optics and on *De Corpore*. In 1646 the young Prince of Wales, later to become Charles II, sought refuge in Paris, and Hobbes accepted an invitation to instruct him in mathematics.

He turned once more to political theory. In 1647 he published a second, augmented edition of *De Cive* and in 1651 an English version. In 1650 the manuscript of *The Elements of Law* was published in two parts, as *Human Nature* and *De Corpore Politico* (*Of the Body Politic*). Hobbes' masterpiece *Leviathan; or, The Matter, Form, and Power of a Commonwealth, Ecclesiastical and Civil* was published in 1651.

Though Hobbes was now 63 years of age, he was to retain his vigour for another quarter of a century. Hobbes had made enemies at Oxford by the publication of *Leviathan*, and he now came under attack for the philosophies published in *De Corpore*, which was published at last in 1655. Hobbes had been so impressed by Galileo's achievements in mechanics that he sought to explain all phenomena and, indeed, sense itself in terms of the motion of bodies. Further disagreements raged over his onslaught on the newfangled methods of mathematical analysis in *Dialogus Physicus, sive de Natura Aeris* (1661; *Dialogue on Physics, or on the Nature of Air*) and his *De Principiis et Ratiocinatione Geometrarum* (1666), which was designed to humble the professors of geometry by showing that their works contained much uncertainty and error. *Quadratura Circuli, Cubatio Sphaerae, Duplicatio Cubi* (1669; *The Squaring of the Circle, The Cubing of the Sphere, The Doubling of the Cube*) gave Hobbes' solutions to these famous problems – solutions promptly refuted by the mathematician John Wallis. In 1678 appeared his last piece of all, *Decameron Physiologicum* (*Ten Questions of Physiology*), a new set of dialogues on physiological questions.

After the Restoration in 1660, Hobbes enjoyed a new prominence. Though his presence at court scandalized the bishops and the chancellor, the king relished his wit. He even granted Hobbes a pension of £100 a year and had his portrait hung in the royal closet. It was not until 1666, when the House of Commons prepared a bill against atheism and profaneness, that Hobbes felt seriously endangered, for the committee to which the bill was referred was instructed to investigate *Leviathan*. Hobbes, then verging upon 80, burned such of his papers as he thought might compromise him and set himself to inquire into the state of the law of heresy.

The results of his investigations appeared in three short dialogues and in a tract entitled *An Historical Narration Concerning Heresy and the Punishment Thereof* (1680), in which he maintained that since the abolition of the high court of commission there was no court of heresy to which he was amenable and that, in any case, nothing was to be declared heresy but what was at variance with the Nicene Creed.

Although Parliament dropped the bill on atheism, Hobbes could never afterward get permission to print anything on subjects relating to human conduct, the king apparently having made it the price of his protection that no fresh provocation should be offered to popular sentiment.

In his last years Hobbes amused himself by returning to the classical studies of his youth. His autobiography in Latin verse with its playful humour, occasional pathos, and sublime self-complacency was brought forth at the age of 84. In 1675 he produced a translation of the *Odyssey* in rugged English rhymes, and as late as four months before his death, he was promising his publisher "somewhat to print in English".

Anthony Ashley Cooper, 3rd Earl of Shaftesbury (1671–1713)

Shaftesbury's early education was directed by John Locke, and he attended Winchester College. He entered Parliament in 1695 and, succeeding as 3rd Earl of Shaftesbury in 1699, attended Parliament regularly in the House of Lords for the remainder of William III's reign. He pursued an independent policy in the House of Lords as well as in the House of Commons. In July 1702 he retired from public life.

Shaftesbury's philosophy owed something to the Cambridge Platonists, who had stressed the existence in man of a natural moral sense. Shaftesbury advanced this concept against both the orthodox Christian doctrine of the fall and against the premise that the state of nature was a state of unavoidable warfare. Shaftesbury's neoplatonism, his contention that what man sees of beauty or truth is only a shadow of absolute beauty or truth, dominated his attitude to religion and to the arts.

During his lifetime his fame as a writer was comparatively slight, for he published little before 1711; in that year appeared his *Characteristicks of Men, Manners, Opinions, Times,* in which his chief works were assembled. The effect of this book was immediate and was felt on the European continent as well as in England; indeed, English Deism was transmitted to Germany almost entirely through translations of his writings.

Voltaire (François-Marie Arouet) (1694–1778)

Voltaire attended the Jesuit college of Louis-le-Grand in Paris, where he learned to love literature, the theatre, and social life. After leaving, he was employed as secretary at the French embassy in The Hague, where he became infatuated with the daughter of an adventurer. Fearing scandal, the French ambassador sent him back to Paris. Despite his father's wishes, he wanted to devote himself wholly to literature, and he frequented the Temple, then the centre of free-thinking society. After the death of Louis XIV, under the morally relaxed Regency, Voltaire became the wit of Parisian society. But when he dared to mock the dissolute regent, the Duc d'Orléans, he was banished from Paris and then imprisoned in the Bastille for nearly a year (1717).

Behind his cheerful facade, he was fundamentally serious and set himself to learn the accepted literary forms. In 1718, after the success of *Oedipe*, the first of his tragedies, he was acclaimed as the successor of the great classical dramatist Jean Racine and thenceforward adopted the name of Voltaire. He worked at an epic poem whose hero was Henry IV, in which his contemporaries saw the ideal of tolerance that inspired the poem. These literary triumphs earned him a pension from the regent and the warm approval of the young queen, Marie. He thus began his career of court poet.

In the Salons he professed an aggressive Deism, which scandalized the devout. As the result of a quarrel with the

Chevalier de Rohan, he was beaten, taken to the Bastille, and then conducted to Calais on May 5 1726, from where he set out for London. In England he met such English men of letters as Pope, Swift, and Congreve. He admired the liberalism of English institutions, and was convinced that it was because of their personal liberty that the English, notably Sir Isaac Newton and John Locke, were in the forefront of scientific thought. He returned to France at the end of 1728 or the beginning of 1729 and decided to present England as a model to his compatriots in the *Lettres philosophiques* or *Lettres sur les Anglais* (1734; *Philosophical Letters* or *Letters on England*).

Scandal followed publication of this work and a warrant of arrest was issued in May of 1734. Voltaire took refuge in the château of Mme du Châtelet at Cirey in Champagne. She was passionately drawn to the sciences and metaphysics and a laboratory of the physical sciences was installed. After *Adélaïde du Guesclin* (1734), a play about a national tragedy, Voltaire brought *Alzire* to the stage in 1736 with great success. In his *Éléments de la philosophie de Newton* (1738; *Elements of the Philosophy of Newton*), he popularized those discoveries of English science.

Because of a lawsuit, he followed Mme du Châtelet to Brussels in May 1739, and thereafter they were constantly on the move between Belgium, Cirey, and Paris. Voltaire corresponded with the Crown Prince of Prussia, and when the prince acceded to the throne as Frederick II (the Great), he visited him. When the War of the Austrian Succession broke out, Voltaire was sent to Berlin (1742–3) on a secret mission to rally the King of Prussia – who was proving himself a faithless ally – to the assistance of the French army. Such services brought him into favour again at Versailles and he was appointed historiographer, gentleman of the king's chamber, and academician. He amassed a vast fortune through the manipulations of Joseph Pâris Duverney, the financier in charge of military supplies.

At this time he wrote his first *contes* (stories). *Micromégas* (1752) measures the littleness of man in the cosmic scale; *Vision de Babouc* (1748) and *Memnon* (1749) dispute the philosophic optimism of Gottfried Wilhelm Leibniz and Alexander Pope. In 1748 at Commercy, where he had joined the court of Stanislaw (the former king of Poland), he detected the love affair of Mme du Châtelet and the poet Saint-Lambert. The next year she died in childbirth. The failure of some of his later plays aggravated his sense of defeat. He yielded to the invitation of Frederick II and set out for Berlin on June 28 1750. At first he was enchanted by his sojourn but he became involved in a lawsuit with a moneylender and quarrels with prominent noblemen, and left Prussia in 1753. At length he found asylum at Geneva, where he purchased a house called Les Délices, at the same time securing winter quarters at Lausanne. He now completed his two major historical studies, *Le Siècle de Louis XIV* (1751; *The Age of Louis XIV*), a book on the century of Louis XIV, and *Essai sur les moeurs* (first complete edition, 1756), which traced the course of world history since the end of the Roman Empire.

At Geneva, he had at first been welcomed and honoured as the champion of tolerance. But soon he made those around him feel uneasy. His presentation of plays was stopped, and his improper mock-heroic poem "La Pucelle" (1755) was printed by booksellers in spite of his protests. In 1758 he wrote what was to be his most famous work, *Candide*.

In 1758 Voltaire bought Ferney together with Tourney in France, on the Swiss border. By crossing the frontier he could thus safeguard himself against police incursion from either country. At Ferney, Voltaire developed a modern estate, renovated the church and meddled in Genevan politics, taking the side of the workers (or *natifs*, those without civil rights), and installing a stocking factory and watchworks on his estate in order to help them. In 1777 he received a popular acclamation from the people of Ferney. In 1815 the Congress of Vienna halted the annexation of Ferney to Switzerland in his honour.

His main interest at this time was his opposition to *l'infâme*, a word he used to designate the church, especially when it was identified with intolerance. He multiplied his personal attacks, directing *Le sentiment des citoyens* (1764) against Rousseau. He constructed a personal *Encyclopédie*, the *Dictionnaire philosophique* (1764), enlarged after 1770 by *Questions sur l'Encyclopédie*. Among the mass of writings of this period are *Le blanc et le noir* (*The White and the Black*), *Princesse de Babylone*, a panorama of European philosophies in the fairyland style of *The Thousand and One Nights*; and *Le taureau blanc*. Again and again Voltaire returned to his chosen themes: the establishment of religious tolerance; the growth of material prosperity; respect for the rights of man by the abolition of torture and useless punishments.

Tancrède proved to be Voltaire's last triumph. It was the theatre that brought him back to Paris in 1778, to direct the rehearsals of *Irène*. On March 30 he went to the French Academy amid acclamations, and, when *Irène* was played before a delirious audience, he was crowned in his box. His health was profoundly impaired by all this excitement and on May 30 he died. His remains were transferred to the Panthéon during the Revolution in July 1791.

David Hume (1711–76)

Hume was the younger son of Joseph Hume, the modestly circumstanced laird, or lord, of Ninewells, a small estate about nine miles distant from Berwick-upon-Tweed. He entered Edinburgh University when he was about 12 years old and left it at 14 or 15, as was then usual. Pressed a little later to study law (in the family tradition on both sides), he found it distasteful and instead read voraciously in the wider sphere of letters. Because of the intensity and excitement of his intellectual discovery, he had a nervous breakdown in 1729, from which it took him a few years to recover.

In 1734, after trying his hand in a merchant's office in Bristol, he came to the turning point of his life and retired to France for three years. Most of this time Hume spent at La Flèche on the Loire, studying and writing *A Treatise of Human Nature*, his attempt to formulate a full-fledged philosophical system. Returning to England in 1737, he set about publishing the *Treatise*. The poor reception of this, his first and very ambitious work, depressed him; but his next venture, *Essays, Moral and Political* (1741–2), won some success. Perhaps encouraged by this, he became a candidate for the chair of moral philosophy at Edinburgh in 1744. Objectors alleged heresy and even atheism, pointing to the *Treatise* as evidence. Unsuccessful, Hume left the city, where he had been living since 1740, and began a period of wandering on the Continent.

During his years of wandering some fruits of his studies appeared: a further *Three Essays, Moral and Political* (1748) and *Philosophical Essays Concerning Human Understanding* (1748), better known as *An Enquiry Concerning Human Understanding*, the title Hume gave to it in a revision of 1758. The *Enquiry Concerning the Principles of Morals* (1751) was a rewriting of Book III of the *Treatise*. It was in these works that Hume expressed his mature thought.

Following the publication of these works, Hume spent several years (1751–63) in Edinburgh, with two breaks in

London. In 1752 Hume was made keeper of the Advocates' Library at Edinburgh and turned to historical writing. His *History of England*, extending from Caesar's invasion to 1688, came out between 1754 and 1762, preceded by *Political Discourses* (1752). These brought him fame, abroad as well as at home. He also wrote *Four Dissertations* (1757), which he regarded as a trifle, although it included a rewriting of Book II of the *Treatise* (completing his purged restatement of this work) and a brilliant study of "the natural history of religion".

The most colourful episode of his life ensued: in 1763 he left England to become secretary to the British embassy in Paris under the Earl of Hertford. For four months in 1765 he acted as chargé d'affaires at the embassy. When he returned to London at the beginning of 1766 (to become, a year later, under-secretary of state), he brought Jean-Jacques Rousseau, the Swiss philosopher connected with the *Encyclopédie* of Diderot and d'Alembert, with him and found him a refuge from persecution in a country house at Wootton in Staffordshire.

In 1769, somewhat tired of public life and of England too, he again established a residence in his beloved Edinburgh. He issued five further editions of his *History of England* between 1762 and 1773 as well as eight editions of his collected writings (omitting the *Treatise*, *History*, and ephemera) under the title *Essays and Treatises* between 1753 and 1772, besides preparing the final edition of this collection, which appeared posthumously (1777), and *Dialogues Concerning Natural Religion*, held back under pressure from friends and not published until 1779. His curiously detached autobiography, *The Life of David Hume, Esquire, Written by Himself* (1777; the title is his own), is dated April 18 1776. He died in his Edinburgh house after a long illness and was buried on Calton Hill.

Jean-Jacques Rousseau (1712–78)

Rousseau's mother died in childbirth and he was brought up by his father. His father got into trouble with the civil authorities and had to leave Geneva to avoid imprisonment. Thus Rousseau lived for six years as a poor relation in his mother's family, until he, too, at the age of 16, fled from Geneva to live the life of an adventurer and a Roman Catholic convert in the kingdoms of Sardinia and France.

Rousseau was fortunate in finding in the province of Savoy a benefactress named the Baronne de Warens, who provided him with a refuge in her home and employed him as her steward. She also furthered his education to such a degree that the boy who had arrived on her doorstep as a stammering apprentice who had never been to school developed into a philosopher, a man of letters, and a musician.

Rousseau reached Paris when he was 30 and met Denis Diderot. The two soon became immensely successful as the centre of a group of intellectuals who gathered round the great French *Encyclopédie*. At this time Rousseau wrote music as well as prose, and one of his operas, *Le devin du village* (1752; *The Cunning-Man*), attracted so much admiration from the king and the court that he might have enjoyed an easy life as a fashionable composer. Then, at the age of 37 Rousseau had what he called an "illumination" while walking to Vincennes to visit Diderot, when it came to him in a "terrible flash" that modern progress had corrupted instead of improved men. He went on to write his first important work, a prize essay for the Academy of Dijon entitled *Discours sur les sciences et les arts* (1750; *A Discourse on the Sciences and the Arts*), in which he argues that the history of man's life on earth has been a history of decay. Throughout his life he kept returning to the thought that man is good by nature but has been corrupted by society and civilization.

In 1752 Rousseau became involved in a dispute over the performance of *opera buffa*, the new Italian opera – which he was against in contrast to many of the Encyclopédists – and decided to devote his energies henceforth to literature and philosophy. He began to look back at some of the austere principles that he had learned as a child. He had by then acquired a mistress, an illiterate laundry maid named Thérèse Levasseur. To the surprise of his friends, he took her with him to Geneva, presenting her as a nurse. Although her presence caused some murmurings, Rousseau was readmitted easily to the Calvinist communion of his youth, his literary fame having made him very welcome to a city that prided itself as much on its culture as on its morals.

Rousseau had by this time completed a second *Discourse* in response to a question set by the Academy of Dijon: "What is the origin of the inequality among men and is it justified by natural law?" In response to this challenge he produced a masterpiece of speculative anthropology, his *Discours sur l'origine et les fondements de l'inégalité parmi les hommes* (1755; *Discourse on the Origin and Basis of Inequality Among Men*). The argument follows on from that of his first *Discourse* by developing the proposition that natural man is good and then tracing the successive stages by which man has descended from primitive innocence to corrupt sophistication. Having written the *Discourse* to explain how men had lost their liberty in the past, he went on to write another book, *Du contrat social ou princpes du droit politique* (1762; *The Social Contract; or Principles of Political Right*), to suggest how they might recover their liberty in the future.

In 1754 Rousseau had returned to Paris and the company of his friends around the *Encyclopédie*. But he became increasingly ill at ease in such worldly society and began to quarrel with his fellow philosophes. By the time his *Lettre à d'Alem-*

bert sur les spectacles (1758; *Letter to Monsieur d'Alembert on the Theatre*) appeared in print, defending the Calvinist orthodoxy of Geneva, which had been criticized in d'Alembert's article on the city for the *Encyclopédie*, Rousseau had already left Paris to pursue a life closer to nature on the country estate of his friend Mme d'Épinay near Montmorency. When the hospitality of Mme d'Épinay proved to entail much the same social round as that of Paris, Rousseau retreated to a nearby cottage, under the protection of the Maréchal de Luxembourg. But even this highly placed friend could not save him in 1762 when his treatise on education, *Émile*, was published and scandalized the pious Jansenists of the French Parlements. Described by the author as a treatise on education, *Émile* is not about schooling but about the upbringing of a rich man's son by a tutor who is given unlimited authority over him. At the same time the book sets out to explore the possibilities of an education for republican citizenship. In Paris, as in Geneva, they ordered the book to be burned and the author arrested; all the Maréchal de Luxembourg could do was to provide a carriage for Rousseau to escape from France. Rousseau spent the rest of his life as a fugitive.

The years at Montmorency had been the most productive of his literary career; besides *The Social Contract* and *Émile*, *Julie; ou la nouvelle Héloïse* (1761; *Julie; or The New Eloise*) came out within 12 months, all three works of seminal importance. *The New Eloise* was clearly inspired by Rousseau's own curious relationship – at once passionate and platonic – with Sophie d'Houdetot, a noblewoman who lived near him at Montmorency. In *La profession de foi du vicaire savoyard* (1765; *The Profession of Faith of a Savoyard Vicar*) Rousseau sets out what may fairly be regarded as his own religious views. Rousseau could never entertain doubts about God's existence or about the immortality of the soul. He also attached great importance to conscience, opposing this both to the bloodless categories of rationalistic ethics and to the cold tablets of biblical authority.

This minimal creed put Rousseau at odds with the orthodox adherents of the churches and with the openly atheistic philosophes of Paris, so that he felt himself increasingly isolated, tormented, and pursued. He reacted to the suppression of *The Social Contract* in Geneva by indicting the regime of that city-state in a pamphlet entitled *Lettres écrites de la montagne* (1764; *Letters Written from the Mountain*) in which Geneva was depicted as a republic that had been taken over by "25 despots". After that Rousseau temporarily found refuge in England, after the Scottish philosopher David Hume took him there and secured the offer of a pension from King George III; but once in England, various symptoms of paranoia began to manifest themselves in Rousseau, and he returned to France incognito. Believing that Thérèse was the only person he could rely on, he finally married her in 1768, when he was 56 years old.

In the remaining 10 years of his life Rousseau produced primarily autobiographical writings, mostly intended to justify himself against the accusations of his adversaries. The most important was his *Confessions*. He also wrote *Rousseau juge de Jean-Jacques* (1780; *Rousseau, Judge of Jean-Jacques*) to reply to specific charges by his enemies and *Les rêveries du promeneur solitaire* (1782; *Reveries of the Solitary Walker*). In his last years, he was once again afforded refuge on the estates of great French noblemen, first the Prince de Conti and then the Marquis de Girardin, in whose park at Ermenonville he died.

Denis Diderot (1713–84)

Diderot was the son of a widely respected master cutler. He was tonsured in 1726, though he did not in fact enter the

church. Awarded the degree of master of arts in the University
of Paris in 1732, he then studied law as an articled clerk in the
office of Clément de Ris. He dropped an early ambition to
enter the theatre and, instead, taught for a living, led a
penurious existence as a publisher's hack, and wrote sermons
for missionaries. He frequented the coffee houses, particularly
the Régence and the Procope, where he met the philosopher
Jean-Jacques Rousseau in 1741 and established a friendship
with him that was to last for 15 years, until it was broken by a
quarrel.

In 1741 he met Antoinette Champion, daughter of a linen
draper, and in 1743 he married her – secretly, because of his
father's disapproval. In order to earn a living, Diderot undertook translation work and in 1745 published a free translation
of the *Inquiry Concerning Virtue* by the 3rd Earl of Shaftesbury, whose fame and influence he spread in France. Diderot's
own *Pensées philosophiques* (1746; *Philosophic Thoughts*), an
original work with new and explosive anti-Christian ideas,
contains many passages directly translated from or inspired by
Shaftesbury. The proceeds of this publication, as of his allegedly indecent novel *Les bijoux indiscrets* (1748; *The Indiscreet
Jewels*), were used to meet the demands of his mistress,
Madeleine de Puisieux, with whom he broke a few years later.
In 1755 he met Sophie Volland, with whom he formed an
attachment that was to last more than 20 years.

In 1745 the publisher André Le Breton approached Diderot
with a view to bringing out a French translation of Ephraim
Chambers' *Cyclopaedia*. Diderot undertook the task with the
distinguished mathematician Jean le Rond d'Alembert as co-
editor but soon profoundly changed the nature of the publication, broadening its scope and turning it into an important
organ of radical and revolutionary opinion.

In 1749 Diderot published the *Lettre sur les aveugles* (*An*

Essay on Blindness), remarkable for its proposal to teach the blind to read through the sense of touch. This daring exposition of the doctrine of materialist atheism, with its emphasis on human dependence on sense impression, led to Diderot's arrest and incarceration in the prison of Vincennes for three months. Diderot's work on the *Encyclopédie*, however, was not interrupted for long, and in 1750 he outlined his programme for it in a *Prospectus*, which d'Alembert expanded into the momentous *Discours préliminaire* (1751). The history of the *Encyclopédie*, from the publication of the first volume in 1751 to the distribution of the final volumes of plates in 1772, was checkered with delays, criticisms and problems with censorship.

While editing the *Encyclopédie*, Diderot managed to compose most of his own important works as well. In 1751 he published his *Lettre sur les sourds et muets* (*Letter on the Deaf and Dumb*), which studies the function of language and deals with points of aesthetics, and in 1754 he published the *Pensées sur l'interprétation de la nature* (*Thoughts on the Interpretation of Nature*), an influential short treatise on the new experimental methods in science. Among his philosophical works, special mention may be made of *L'Entretien entre d'Alembert et Diderot* (written 1769, published 1830; *Conversation Between d'Alembert and Diderot*), *Le rêve de d'Alembert* (written 1769, published 1830; *D'Alembert's Dream*), and the *Eléments de physiologie* (1774–80; *Elements of Physiology*). In these works Diderot developed his materialist philosophy and arrived at startling intuitive insights into biology and chemistry. He also wrote four works of prose fiction. Diderot's plays make tedious reading today, but his theories on drama, expounded in *Entretiens sur le fils naturel* (1757; *Discussion on the Illegitimate Son*) and *Discours sur la poésie dramatique* (*Discourse on Dramatic Poetry*), were to exercise a determining influence on the German dramatist

Gotthold Lessing. His analysis of art, artists, and the technique of painting, and his *Essai sur la peinture* (written 1765, published 1796; *Essay on Painting*) have won him posthumous fame.

The completion of the *Encyclopédie* in 1772 left Diderot without a source of income. To relieve him of financial worry, Catherine the Great first bought his library through an agent in Paris, requesting him to retain the books until she required them, and then appointed him librarian on an annual salary for the duration of his life. He wrote for her the *Plan d'une université pour le gouvernement de Russie* (*Plan of a University for the Government of Russia*). He stayed five months, long enough to become disillusioned with enlightened despotism as a solution to social ills.

In 1774 Diderot, now old and ill, worked on a refutation of Helvétius' work *De l'homme* (1772; *On Man*), which was an amplification of the destroyed *De l'esprit* (*On the Spirit*). He wrote *Entretien d'un philosophe avec la Maréchale* (*Conversation with the Maréchale*) and published in 1778 *Essai sur les règnes de Claude et de Néron* (*Essay on the Reigns of Claudius and Nero*). Usually known as *Essai sur la vie de Sénèque* (*Essay on the Life of Seneca*), the work may be regarded as an apologia for that Roman satirist and philosopher. The death of Sophie Volland in February 1784 was a great grief to him; he survived her by a few months, dying of coronary thrombosis in the house in the rue de Richelieu that Catherine the Great had put at his disposal.

Adam Smith (1723–90)

Adam Smith was the son by second marriage of Adam Smith, comptroller of customs at Kirkcaldy, and Margaret Douglas, daughter of a substantial landowner. At the age of 14, in 1737,

Smith entered the University of Glasgow, already remarkable as a centre of the Scottish Enlightenment. There he was deeply influenced by Francis Hutcheson, professor of moral philosophy, from whose economic and philosophical views he was later to diverge but whose magnetic character seems to have been a main shaping force in Smith's development. Graduating in 1740, Smith won a scholarship and travelled on horseback to Oxford, where he stayed at Balliol College. His years there were spent largely in self-education, from which Smith obtained a firm grasp of both classical and contemporary philosophy.

Returning to his home after an absence of six years, Smith cast about for suitable employment. The connections of his mother's family, together with the support of Lord Henry Kames, resulted in an opportunity to give a series of public lectures in Edinburgh. In 1751, at the age of 27, he was appointed professor of logic at Glasgow, from which post he transferred in 1752 to the more remunerative professorship of moral philosophy.

Smith then entered upon a period of extraordinary creativity, combined with a social and intellectual life that he afterward described as "by far the happiest, and most honourable period of my life". He was made dean of faculty in 1758. Among his wide circle of acquaintances were not only members of the aristocracy, many connected with the government, but also a range of intellectual and scientific figures that included Joseph Black, a pioneer in the field of chemistry; James Watt, later of steam-engine fame; Robert Foulis, a distinguished printer and publisher and subsequent founder of the first British Academy of Design; and, not least, the philosopher David Hume, a lifelong friend whom Smith had met in Edinburgh. Smith was also introduced during these years to the company of the great merchants who were carrying on the colonial trade that had opened to Scotland following its union with England in 1707. One of them, Andrew Cochrane, had been a provost of Glasgow and had founded the famous Political Economy Club. From Cochrane and his fellow merchants Smith undoubtedly acquired the detailed information concerning trade and business that was to give such a sense of the real world to *The Wealth of Nations*.

In 1759 Smith published his first work, *The Theory of Moral Sentiments*. Didactic, exhortative, and analytic by turns, it lays the psychological foundation on which *An Inquiry Into the Nature and Causes of the Wealth of Nations* was later to be built. The *Theory* quickly brought Smith wide esteem and in particular attracted the attention of Charles Townshend, later chancellor of the Exchequer responsible for the measures of taxation that ultimately provoked the American Revolution, who was searching for a tutor for his stepson and ward, the young Duke of Buccleuch. Smith resigned his Glasgow post in 1763 and set off for France the next year as the tutor of the young duke.

They stayed mainly in Toulouse, where Smith began working on a book (eventually to be *The Wealth of Nations*), but had a two-month sojourn in Geneva, where he met Voltaire, for whom he had the profoundest respect. They then went to Paris, where Hume, then secretary to the British embassy, introduced Smith to the great literary Salons of the French Enlightenment. The stay in Paris was cut short when the younger brother of the Duke of Buccleuch, who had joined them in Toulouse, took ill and perished.

Smith worked in London until the spring of 1767 with Lord Townshend, a period during which he was elected a fellow of the Royal Society. Late that year he returned to Kirkcaldy, where the next six years were spent dictating and reworking *The Wealth of Nations*, followed by another stay of three years in London, where the work was finally completed and published in 1776.

The Wealth of Nations was received with admiration by Smith's wide circle of friends and admirers, although it was by no means an immediate popular success. The work finished, Smith went into semi-retirement. The final years of his life passed quietly, with several revisions of both major books but with no further publications. He died at the age of 67.

Immanuel Kant (1724–1804)

Kant lived in the remote province where he was born for his entire life. At the age of eight he entered a Pietist school and in 1740 he enrolled in the University of Königsberg as a theological student. Here Kant began reading the work of Newton and, in 1744, started his first book, dealing with a problem concerning kinetic forces. After the death of his father in 1746, he left the university and found employment as a family tutor. In 1755, aided by the kindness of a friend, he was able to complete his degree at the university and take up the position of *Privatdozent*, or lecturer, a position he held for 15 years.

He taught mathematics and physics initially, and soon also moral philosophy and logic, but he was never to lose his interest in scientific developments. That it was more than an amateur interest is shown by his publication within the next few years of several scientific works. The three dissertations he wrote exemplify his interests: *De Igne* (*On Fire*), in which he argued that bodies operate on one another through the medium of a uniformly diffused elastic and subtle matter that is the underlying substance of both heat and light; *Monodologia Physica* (1756), which contrasted the Newtonian methods of thinking with those employed in the philosophy then prevailing in German universities; and

Principiorum Primorum Cognitionis Metaphysicae Nova Dilucidato (1755), on the first principles of metaphysics.

During the 1760s he became increasingly critical of Leibnizianism. According to one of his students, Kant was then attacking Leibniz, Wolff, and Baumgarten, was a declared follower of Newton, and expressed great admiration for the moral philosophy of the Romanticist Jean-Jacques Rousseau. His principal work of this period was *Untersuchung über die Deutlichkeit der Grundsätze der natürlichen Theologie und der Moral* (1764; *An Inquiry into the Distinctness of the Fundamental Principles of Natural Theology and Morals*). In this work he attacked the claim of Leibnizian philosophy that philosophy should model itself on mathematics and aim at constructing a chain of demonstrated truths based on self-evident premises. Besides attacking the methods of the Leibnizians, he also began criticizing their leading ideas. Some indication of Kant's own possible alternative to the Leibnizian position can be gathered from his curious *Träume eines Geistersehers erläutert durch Träume der Metaphysik* (1766; *Dreams of a Spirit-Seer, Illustrated by Dreams of Metaphysics*). This work is an examination of the whole notion of a world of spirits, in the context of an inquiry into the spiritualist claims of Emanuel Swedenborg, a scientist and biblical scholar.

Finally, in 1770 Kant was appointed to the chair of logic and metaphysics, a position in which he remained active until a few years before his death. The *Inaugural Dissertation* of 1770 that he delivered on assuming his new position already contained many of the important elements of his mature philosophy. After the *Dissertation*, Kant published virtually nothing for 11 years. Then in the next next nine years he wrote the great *Critiques* which brought a revolution in philosophical thought and established the new direction in which it was to go in the years to come. In 1781 came the *Kritik der reinen Vernunft* (*Critique of Pure Reason*), in 1788 the *Kritik der praktischen Vernunft* (*Critique of Practical Reason*) and in 1790 the *Kritik der Urteilskraft* (*Critique of Judgement*).

The critical philosophy was soon being taught in every important German-speaking university, and young men flocked to Königsberg as a shrine of philosophy. From 1790 his health began to decline seriously. The writings that he then completed consist partly of an elaboration of subjects not previously treated in any detail, and partly of replies to criticisms and the clarification of misunderstandings. With the publication in 1793 of his work *Die Religion innerhalb der Grenzen der blossen Vernunft* (*Religion within the Boundary of Pure Reason*), Kant became involved in a dispute with Prussian authorities on the right to express religious opinions. He returned to the forbidden subject in his last major essay, *Der Streit der Fakultäten* (1798; *The Conflict of the Faculties*). After a gradual decline Kant died in Königsberg on February 12 1804.

Edward Gibbon (1737–94)

Gibbon's grandfather, Edward, had made a considerable fortune and his father, also Edward, was able to live an easy-going life in society and Parliament. This allowed Edward, too, to have independent means throughout his life. It was on visits to country houses with his father where he had the run of libraries filled with old folios that he early discovered his "proper food", history. By his fourteenth year he had already covered the main fields of his subsequent masterpiece, applying his mind as well to difficult problems of chronology.

He was entered at Magdalen College, Oxford, on April 3

1752, about three weeks before his fifteenth birthday. The authorities there failed to look after him or to note his absences from the college. Left to himself, Gibbon turned to theology and read himself into the Roman Catholic faith, into which he was received on June 8 1753. His father, outraged because under the existing laws his son had disqualified himself for all public service and office, acted swiftly, and Edward was dispatched to Lausanne and lodged with a Calvinist minister, the Rev. Daniel Pavillard. There, he mastered the bulk of classical Latin literature and studied mathematics and logic. He also became perfectly conversant with the language and literature of France, which exercised a permanent influence on him. These studies made him not only a man of considerable learning but a stylist for life. He was publicly readmitted to the Protestant communion at Christmas 1754.

He began his first work, written in French, *Essai sur l'étude de la littérature* (1761; English translation *An Essay on the Study of Literature*, 1764). In the latter part of his exile Gibbon entered more freely into Lausanne society. He attended Voltaire's parties. He formed an enduring friendship with a young Swiss, Georges Deyverdun, and also fell in love with and rashly plighted himself to Suzanne Curchod, a pastor's daughter of great charm and intelligence. In 1758 his father called Gibbon home shortly before his twenty-first birthday and settled an annuity of £300 on him. However, he found that his father and his stepmother were implacably opposed to his engagement, and he was compelled to break it off. He never again thought seriously of marriage.

From 1760 until the end of 1762, his studies were seriously interrupted by his service on home defence duties with the Hampshire militia. In January 1763, Gibbon left England and spent some time in Paris, making the acquaintance of several philosophes, Denis Diderot and Jean le Rond d'Alembert among others. In 1764 he went to Rome, where he made an exhaustive study of the antiquities and, on October 15 1764, while musing amid the ruins of the Capitol, was inspired to write of the decline and fall of the city.

At home, the next five years were the least satisfactory in Gibbon's life. He was dependent on his father and although aged nearly 30 had achieved little in life. He and Deyverdun published two volumes of *Mémoires littéraires de la Grande Bretagne* (1768–9). In 1770 he sought to attract some attention by publishing *Critical Observations on the Sixth Book of the Aeneid*. In 1770 his father died, and in 1772 Gibbon established himself in Bentinck Street, London, and concentrated on his Roman history. At the same time he entered fully into social life. In 1775 he was elected to the Club, the brilliant circle that the painter Sir Joshua Reynolds had formed round the writer and lexicographer Dr Samuel Johnson. In the previous year he had entered Parliament and was an assiduous, though silent, supporter of Lord North.

The first quarto volume of *The History of the Decline and Fall of the Roman Empire* was published in February 1776, immediately scoring a success that was resounding, if somewhat scandalous because of the last two chapters in which he dealt with great irony with the rise of Christianity. He was assailed by many pamphleteers and subjected to much ridicule. For the most part he ignored his critics. Only to those who had accused him of falsifying his evidence did he make a devastating reply in *A Vindication of Some Passages in the Fifteenth and Sixteenth Chapters of the Decline and Fall of the Roman Empire* (1779).

In the same year he obtained a valuable sinecure as a commissioner of trade and plantations. Shortly after that he composed *Mémoire justificatif* (1779; a French and English version, 1780), a masterly state paper in reply to continental criticism of the British government's policy in America. In 1781 he published the second and third volumes of his history, bringing the narrative down to the end of the empire in the West. In 1782, however, Lord North's government fell, and soon Gibbon's commission was abolished. To economize he left England and joined Deyverdun in a house at Lausanne. There he quietly completed his history in three more volumes, writing the last lines of it on June 27 1787. He soon returned to England with the manuscript, and these volumes were published on his fifty-first birthday, May 8 1788. The completion of this great work was acclaimed on all sides.

Returning to Lausanne, Gibbon turned mainly to writing his memoirs. His happiness was broken first by Deyverdun's death in 1789, quickly followed by the outbreak of the French Revolution and the subsequent apprehension of an invasion of Switzerland. He had now become very fat and his health was declining. In 1793 he suddenly returned to England on hearing of the death of Lady Sheffield, the wife of his long-standing friend Lord Sheffield whom he had met at Lausanne. The journey aggravated his ailments, and he died in a house in St James' Street, London.

John Wilkes (1725–97)

Wilkes was the second son of Israel Wilkes, a successful malt distiller. He was educated at an academy at Hertford and afterward privately tutored. His marriage on May 23 1747 to Mary Meade, heiress of the manor of Aylesbury, brought him a comfortable fortune and an assured status among the gentry of Buckinghamshire. Profligate by nature, Wilkes became a member of the "Medmenham Monks", members of the so-called Hell-Fire Club.

In 1754, at the suggestion of Earl Temple, Wilkes stood unsuccessfully for election to Parliament for Berwick-upon-Tweed. In 1757, after an election campaign said to have cost him £7,000, much of it in bribes to voters, he was returned to Parliament for Aylesbury. Recklessly overspending, and ever deeper in debt, he hoped to retrieve his fortunes by political advancement.

In 1762, as author of a political newspaper, the *North Briton*, Wilkes began to give support to Earl Temple's campaign against the ministry of Lord Bute, partly provoking Bute's decision to retire. Wilkes was now encouraged to publish "No. 45" of the *North Briton*, attacking ministerial statements in the King's Speech, which Wilkes described as false. Wilkes was arrested but later released on the grounds that the arrest had been a breach of parliamentary privilege. However, when the government secured from Wilkes' private press the proof sheets of "Essay on Woman", an obscene parody on Alexander Pope's "Essay on Man", which Wilkes had commenced, but not completed, printing, it was declared a libel and a breach of privilege. At the same time the Commons, on a government motion, declared "No. 45" a seditious libel.

During the Christmas vacation Wilkes, recovering from a wound sustained in a duel provoked by exchanges in the House, stole off to Paris to visit his daughter and decided not to return to face prosecution. On January 20 1764, the ministers carried the motion for his expulsion from the Commons. In February he was tried in absentia and found guilty of publishing a seditious libel ("No. 45") and an obscene and impious libel (the "Essay"). Sentence was deferred pending his return, and in due course he was pronounced an outlaw for impeding royal justice.

For the next four years Wilkes pursued a profligate career on the Continent, chiefly in Paris, vainly hoping that a change of ministry would bring in friends who would secure him relief and advancement. Early in 1768 he returned to London, determined to stand as an opponent of the government in the name of public liberty. The ministers, perhaps unwisely, failed to arrange his immediate arrest. Though defeated in London, he was elected for Middlesex. At the end of April he gave himself up to the authorities, and early in June his outlawry was reversed on a technical point. Then, waiving his privilege as a member of Parliament, he submitted to sentences totalling two years in jail and fines of £1,000 on the two charges on which he had been convicted in 1764.

Having made this gesture he wanted a pardon and restitution. In the following months he attempted to reopen the whole question of his conviction by a petition to the Commons complaining of illegality in the proceedings against him. The ministers once more secured his expulsion from the Commons on February 3 1769. The popularity in the metropolis of his stand against the government ensured his re-election for Middlesex on three subsequent occasions, until the House declared his defeated opponent, Henry Luttrell, the duly elected member and Wilkes was finally expelled.

In 1769 the Society for the Defence of the Bill of Rights was set up by supporters of Wilkes, to further his cause and to settle his debts. Though excluded from Parliament he determined to follow his ambitions and his vendetta with the ministers in the City of London, becoming an alderman in 1769, sheriff in 1771, and lord mayor in 1774. Re-elected for Middlesex in 1774, after pledging himself to the radical programme, he spoke on a number of occasions against the American Revolutionary War and once (1776) in support of parliamentary reform. In 1780, during the Gordon Riots against Roman

Catholics, he took firm action to put down the rioters, from whom a few years before he had been glad to receive support. In Middlesex he remained popular, being re-elected on his radical platform in 1780 and in 1784. In 1782 the expunging from the Commons journals of the resolution of 1769 against him vindicated his defence of the rights of parliamentary electors. After 1784 the issues that had made him popular were cold, and his fire was spent. He died in London in 1797.

Edmund Burke (1729–97)

Burke, the son of a solicitor, entered Trinity College, Dublin, in 1744 and moved to London in 1750 to begin his studies at the Middle Temple. There follows an obscure period in which Burke lost interest in his legal studies, was estranged from his father, and spent some time wandering about England and France. In 1756 he published anonymously *A Vindication of Natural Society: A View of the Miseries and Evils Arising to Mankind*, a satirical imitation of the style of Viscount Bolingbroke that was aimed at both the destructive criticism of revealed religion and the contemporary vogue for a "return to Nature".

A contribution to aesthetic theory, *A Philosophical Enquiry into the Origin of Our Ideas of the Sublime and Beautiful,* which appeared in 1757, gave him some reputation in England. In agreement with the publisher Robert Dodsley, Burke initiated *The Annual Register* as a yearly survey of world affairs; the first volume appeared in 1758 under his (unacknowledged) editorship, and he retained this connection for about 30 years. In 1757 Burke married Jane Nugent. From this period also date his numerous literary and artistic friendships, including those with Dr Samuel Johnson, Oliver Goldsmith, Sir Joshua Reynolds, and David Garrick.

After an unsuccessful first venture into politics, Burke was appointed secretary in 1765 to the Marquess of Rockingham, leader of one of the Whig groups, and he entered the House of Commons that year. Burke remained Rockingham's secretary until the latter's death in 1782. Burke took an active part in the domestic constitutional controversy of George III's reign when the king was seeking to reassert a more active role for the crown without infringing on the limitations of the royal prerogative set by the revolution settlement of 1689. Burke's chief comment on this issue is his pamphlet *Thoughts on the Cause of the Present Discontents* (1770).

In 1774 Burke was elected a member of Parliament for Bristol. He held this seat for six years. For the rest of his parliamentary career he was member for Malton, a pocket borough of Lord Rockingham's. It was at Bristol that Burke made the well-known statement on the role of the member of Parliament: the elected member should be a representative, not a mere delegate pledged to obey undeviatingly the wishes of his constituents.

Burke gave only qualified support to movements for parliamentary reform; his main concern was the curtailment of the crown's powers. He made a practical attempt to reduce this influence as one of the leaders of the movement that pressed for parliamentary control of royal patronage and expenditure. He was also connected with an act regulating the civil list.

A second great issue that confronted Burke in 1765 was the quarrel with the American colonies. Burke's best-known statements on this issue are two parliamentary speeches, "On American Taxation" (1774) and "On Moving his Resolutions for Conciliation with the Colonies" (1775), as well as "A Letter to . . . the Sheriffs of Bristol, on the Affairs of America" (1777). Authority, he argued, must be exercised with respect for the temper of those subject to it, if there was not to be collision of power and opinion. Burke made a wide historical survey of the growth of the colonies and of their present economic problems. In the place of narrow legalism he called for a more pragmatic policy on Britain's part that would admit the claims of circumstance, utility, and moral principle in addition to those of precedent.

Burke was also concerned with other imperial issues. On Ireland, he consistently advocated relaxation of the economic and penal regulations, and steps toward legislative independence. He also devoted many years to the problems of India. Burke in the 1760s and 1770s opposed interference by the English government in the East India Company's affairs as a violation of chartered rights. As the most active member of a select committee appointed in 1781 to investigate the administration of justice in India, Burke drafted the East India Bill of 1783, which proposed that India be governed by a board of independent commissioners in London. After the defeat of the bill, Burke's indignation came to centre on Warren Hastings, governor-general of Bengal from 1772 to 1785. It was at Burke's instigation that Hastings was impeached in 1787.

After the outbreak of the French Revolution in 1789, Burke, after a brief suspension of judgement, was both hostile to it and alarmed by favourable English reaction. He was provoked into writing his *Reflections on the Revolution in France* (1790). Burke's deeply-felt antagonism to the new movement propelled him to the plane of general political thought; it provoked a host of English replies, of which the best known is Thomas Paine's *Rights of Man* (1791–2).

In 1794, at the conclusion of Hastings' impeachment, Burke retired from Parliament. His last years were clouded by the death of his only son, on whom his political ambitions had come to centre. He continued to write, defending himself from his critics, deploring the condition of Ireland, and opposing any recognition of the French government (notably in "Three Letters Addressed to a Member of the Present Parliament on the Proposals for Peace, with the Regicide Directory of France" [1796–7]).

Thomas Paine (1737–1809)

Paine was born of a Quaker father and an Anglican mother. His formal education was meagre, and at 13 he began work with his father as a corset maker and then tried various other occupations unsuccessfully, finally becoming an officer of the excise. Paine's life in England was marked by repeated failures. He had two brief marriages. He was dismissed from the excise office after he published a strong argument in 1772 for a raise in pay as the only way to end corruption in the service. Just when his situation appeared hopeless, he met Benjamin Franklin in London, who advised him to seek his fortune in America and gave him letters of introduction.

Paine arrived in Philadelphia on November 30 1774. His first regular employment was helping to edit the *Pennsylvania Magazine*. In addition Paine published numerous articles and some poetry, anonymously or under pseudonyms. One such article was "African Slavery in America", a scathing denunciation of the African slave trade, which he signed "Justice and Humanity".

Paine had arrived in America when the conflict between the colonists and England was reaching its height. After blood was spilled at the Battle of Lexington and Concord on April 19 1775, Paine argued that the cause of America should not be just a revolt against taxation but a demand for independence. He put this idea into *Common Sense*, which came off the press on January 10 1776. The 50-page pamphlet sold more than 500,000 copies within a few months. More than any other single publication, *Common Sense* paved the way for the Declaration of Independence, unanimously ratified July 4 1776.

During the war that followed, Paine served as volunteer aide-de-camp to General Nathanael Greene. His great contribution to the patriot cause was the 16 "Crisis" papers issued between 1776 and 1783, each one signed "Common Sense". "The American Crisis. Number I", published on December 19 1776, opened with the inflammatory words: "These are the times that try men's souls," and Washington ordered it read to all the troops at Valley Forge.

In 1777 Congress appointed Paine secretary to the Committee for Foreign Affairs. He held the post until early in 1779, when he became involved in a controversy with Silas Deane, a member of the Continental Congress, whom Paine accused of seeking to profit personally from French aid to the United States. But in revealing Deane's machinations, Paine was forced to quote from secret documents to which he had access as secretary of the Committee for Foreign Affairs. As a result he was forced to resign his post.

Paine's desperate need of employment was relieved when he was appointed clerk of the General Assembly of Pennsylvania on November 2 1779. In this capacity he had frequent opportunity to observe that American troops were at the end of their patience because of lack of pay and scarcity of supplies. Paine took $500 from his salary and started a subscription for the relief of the soldiers. In 1781, pursuing the same goal, he accompanied John Laurens to France. The money, clothing, and ammunition they brought back with them were important to the final success of the Revolution. Paine also appealed to the separate states to cooperate for the well-being of the entire nation. In "Public Good" (1780) he included a call for a national convention to establish a strong central government under "a continental constitution".

At the end of the American Revolution, Paine again found himself poverty-stricken. His patriotic writings had sold by the hundreds of thousands, but he had refused to accept any profits in order that cheap editions might be widely circulated. In a petition to Congress endorsed by Washington, he pleaded for financial assistance. It was buried by Paine's opponents in Congress, but Pennsylvania gave him £500 and New York a farm in New Rochelle. Here Paine devoted his time to inventions, concentrating on an iron bridge without piers and a smokeless candle.

In April 1787 Paine left for Europe to promote his plan to build a single-arch bridge across the wide Schuylkill River near Philadelphia. But he was soon diverted and in December 1789 he published anonymously a warning against the attempt of Prime Minister William Pitt to involve England in a war with France over Holland, reminding the British people that war had "but one thing certain and that is increase of taxes". But it was the French Revolution that now filled Paine's thoughts. Enraged by Edmund Burke's attack on the uprising of the French people in his *Reflections on the Revolution in France*, he rushed into print with his celebrated answer, *Rights of Man* (1791). The book immediately created a sensation. At least eight editions were published in 1791, and the work was quickly reprinted in America, where it was widely distributed by the Jeffersonian societies. When Burke replied, Paine came back with *Rights of Man, Part II,* published in February 1792.

To the ruling class Paine's proposals spelled "bloody revolution", and the government ordered the book banned and the publisher jailed. Paine himself was indicted for treason, and an order went out for his arrest. But he was en route to France, having been elected to a seat in the National Convention, before the order for his arrest could be delivered. Paine was tried in absentia, found guilty of seditious libel, and declared an outlaw, and Rights of Man was ordered permanently suppressed.

In France Paine hailed the abolition of the monarchy but deplored the terror against the royalists and fought unsuccessfully to save the life of King Louis XVI, favouring banishment rather than execution. He was to pay for his efforts to save the king's life when the radicals under Robespierre took power. Paine was imprisoned from December 28 1793, to November 4 1794, when, with the fall of Robespierre, he was released and, though seriously ill, readmitted to the National Convention.

While in prison, the first part of Paine's Age of Reason was published (1794), and it was followed by Part II after his release (1796). The publication of his last great pamphlet, "Agrarian Justice" (1797), with its attack on inequalities in property ownership, added to his many enemies in establishment circles. Paine remained in France until September 1 1802, when he sailed for the United States. He quickly discovered that his services to the country had been all but forgotten and that he was widely regarded only as the world's greatest infidel. Despite his poverty and his physical condition, worsened by occasional drunkenness, Paine continued his attacks on privilege and religious superstitions. He died in New York City in 1809 and was buried in New Rochelle.

Thomas Jefferson (1743–1826)

Jefferson's father, Peter Jefferson, was a self-educated surveyor, while his mother, Jane Randolph Jefferson, was descended from one of the most prominent families in Virginia. In 1760, Jefferson entered the College of William and Mary in Williamsburg. He read law with Wythe, the leading legal scholar in Virginia, from 1762 to 1767, then left Williamsburg to practice.

In 1768 he made two important decisions: first, to build his own home, eventually named Monticello and, second, to stand as a candidate for the House of Burgesses. He entered the Virginia legislature just as opposition to the taxation policies of the British Parliament was coalescing and his support for resolutions opposing Parliament's authority over the colonies was resolute.

In 1772 he married Martha Wayles Skelton, an attractive and delicate young widow whose dowry more than doubled his holdings in land and slaves. In 1774 he wrote *A Summary View of the Rights of British America*, which was quickly published, and catapulted him into visibility as an early advocate of American independence. His reputation thus enhanced, the Virginia legislature appointed him a delegate to the Second Continental Congress in the spring of 1775.

Jefferson's inveterate shyness prevented him from playing a significant role in the debates within the Congress. His chief role was as a draftsman of resolutions. In that capacity, on June 11 1776, he was appointed to a five-person committee, to draft a formal statement of the reasons why a break with Great Britain was justified; this became the Declaration of Independence. Jefferson returned to Virginia in October 1776 and immediately launched an extensive project for the reform of the state's legal code to bring it in line with the principles of the American Revolution. He sought and secured the abolition of primogeniture, entail, and remnants of feudalism that discouraged a broad distribution of property; he proposed a comprehensive plan of educational reform designed to assure access at the lowest level for all citizens and state support at the higher levels for the most talented; and he advocated a law prohibiting any religious establishment and requiring complete separation of church and state. The last two proposals were bitterly contested. Taken together, these legal reforms capture the essence of Jefferson's political philosophy.

At the end of what was probably the most creative phase of his public career, personal misfortune struck. Elected governor of Virginia in 1779, he was caught off-guard by a surprise British invasion in 1780 against which the state was defenceless. His flight from approaching British troops was described in the local press, somewhat unfairly, as a cowardly act of abdication. Then, in September 1782, his wife died after a difficult delivery in May of their third daughter. These two disasters caused him to vow that he would never again desert his family for his country.

Jefferson agreed, albeit reluctantly, to serve as a delegate to the Continental Congress in December 1782, where his major contribution was to set forth the principle that territories in the West should not be treated as colonies but rather should enter the Union with status equal to the original states once certain conditions were met. Then, in 1784, he agreed to replace Franklin as American minister to France. During his five-year sojourn in Paris, his only significant achievement was the negotiation of a $400,000 loan from Dutch bankers that allowed the American government to consolidate its European debts. It was also during this period that he became briefly infatuated with Maria Cosway, who was married to a prominent English miniaturist. Then, in 1788, he initiated a sexual liaison with his attractive young mulatto slave Sally Hemings. He departed France late in 1789, just at the onset of mob violence.

Even before his departure from France, Jefferson had overseen the publication of *Notes on the State of Virginia*. *Notes* contained an extensive discussion of slavery, a strong assertion that it violated the principles on which the American Revolution was based, and the most explicit assessment that Jefferson ever wrote of what he believed were the biological differences between blacks and whites. Despite this, Jefferson owned, on average, about 200 slaves at any point in time. To protect himself from facing the reality of his problematic status as plantation master, he constructed a paternalistic self-image as a benevolent father caring for what he called "my family".

Jefferson returned to the United States in 1789 to serve as the first secretary of state under President George Washington. His major concern about the new Constitution was the absence of any bill of rights. During his tenure as secretary of state (1790–93), foreign policy was his chief responsibility. While all parties embraced some version of the neutrality doctrine, the specific choices posed by the ongoing competition for supremacy in Europe between England and France produced a bitter conflict. Jefferson favoured a pro-French version of neutrality, arguing that the Franco-American treaty of 1778 obliged the United States to honour past French support during the war for independence, and that the French Revolution embodied the "spirit of '76" on European soil. This remained his unwavering position throughout the decade.

Jefferson's position on domestic policy during the 1790s was a variation on the same ideological dichotomy. Jefferson came to regard the consolidation of power at the federal level as a diabolical plot to subvert the true meaning of the American Revolution. As Jefferson saw it, the entire Federalist commitment to an energetic central government with broad powers over the domestic economy replicated the arbitrary policies of Parliament and George III, which the American Revolution had supposedly repudiated as monarchical and aristocratic practices, incompatible with the principles of republicanism. By the middle years of the decade two distinctive political camps had emerged, calling themselves Federalists and Republicans (later Democratic-Republicans). An embryonic version of the party structure was congealing, and Jefferson, assisted and advised by Madison, established the rudiments of the first opposition party in American politics under the Republican banner.

In 1796 he ran for the presidency against Adams. The highly combustible political culture of the early republic reached a crescendo in the election of 1800; Jefferson was elected on the thirty-sixth ballot. The major message of Jefferson's inaugural address was conciliatory. Its most famous line ("We are all republicans – we are all federalists") suggested that the scatological party battles of the previous decade must cease. He described his election as a recovery of the original intentions of the American Revolution. In Jefferson's truly distinctive and original formulation, the coherence of the American republic did not require the mechanisms of a powerful state to survive or flourish.

In 1804 Jefferson was easily re-elected. Initially, at least, his policies as president reflected his desire for decentralization. The major achievement of his first term defied his own principles. In 1803 Napoleon decided to consolidate his resources for a new round of the conflict with England by selling the vast Louisiana region, and although it violated Jefferson's constitutional scruples, he reasoned that the opportunity to double the national domain was too good to miss. His major disappointment also had its origins in Europe with the resumption of the Napoleonic Wars, which resulted in naval blockades in the Atlantic and Caribbean that severely curtailed American trade and pressured the US government to take sides in the conflict. Jefferson's response was the Embargo Act (1807), which essentially closed American ports to all foreign imports and American exports. By the time he left office in March 1809, Jefferson was a tired and beaten man.

During the last 17 years of his life Jefferson maintained a crowded and active schedule. Monticello became a veritable hotel during these years, on occasion housing 50 guests. The lack of privacy caused Jefferson to build a separate house on his Bedford estate about 90 miles (140 km) from Monticello, where he periodically fled for seclusion. He died on July 4 1826.

Maximilien de Robespierre (1758–94)

Robespierre was the son of a lawyer in Arras. In 1769 he was awarded a scholarship to the famous college of Louis-le-Grand in Paris, where he distinguished himself in philosophy and law. He received a law degree in 1781 and became a lawyer at Arras, where he set up house with his sister Charlotte. He was appointed a judge at the Salle Épiscopale, a court with jurisdiction over the provostship of the diocese. His private practice provided him with a comfortable income.

He was admitted to the Arras Academy in 1783 and soon became its chancellor and later its president. By 1788 Robespierre was already well known for his altruism. As a lawyer representing poor people, he had alarmed the privileged classes by his protests in his *Mémoire pour le Sieur Dupond* (*Report for Lord Dupond*) against royal absolutism and arbitrary justice. When the summoning of the Estates-General was announced, he issued an appeal entitled *À la nation artésienne sur la nécessité de réformer les Etats d'Artois* (*To the People of Artois on the Necessity of Reforming the Estates of Artois*). In March 1789 the citizens of Arras chose him as one of their representatives, and the Third Estate (the commons) of the bailiwick elected him fifth of the eight deputies from Artois. Thus he began his political career at the age of 30.

Robespierre was kept out of the committees and from the presidency of the National Assembly; only once, in June 1790, was he elected secretary of the National Assembly. In April he had presided over the Jacobins, a political club promoting the ideas of the French Revolution. In October he was appointed a judge of the Versailles tribunal.

Robespierre nevertheless decided to devote himself fully to his work in the National Assembly, where the constitution was being drawn up. Grounded in ancient history and the works of the French philosophers of the Enlightenment, he welcomed the Declaration of the Rights of Man and of the Citizen, which formed the preamble of the French constitution of September 3 1791, and he insisted that all laws should conform to it. He fought for universal suffrage, for unrestricted admission to the national guard, to public offices, and to the commissioned ranks of the army, and for the right to petition. He opposed the royal veto, the abuses of ministerial power, and religious and racial discrimination. He defended actors, Jews, and black slaves and supported the reunion of Avignon, formerly a papal possession, with France in September 1791. In May he had successfully proposed that all new deputies be elected to the next legislature so that, as a new body, it would better express the people's will.

His passionate fight for liberty won him more enemies, who called him a dangerous individual – and worse. After the flight of Louis XVI (June 20–21 1791), for which Robespierre vainly demanded his trial, the slanders against the Revolutionary deputy became twice as violent. He hastened the vote on the constitution so as to attract "as many of the democratic party as possible". Martial law was proclaimed, and at the Champ-de-Mars the national guard opened fire on a group demanding the abdication of the king. Robespierre, his life threatened, went to live with the family of the cabinetmaker Maurice Duplay. He managed to keep the Jacobin Club alive after all of its moderate members had joined a rival club. When the

National Assembly dissolved itself, the people of Paris organized a triumphal procession for Robespierre.

Although he had excluded himself and his colleagues from the new Legislative Assembly, Robespierre continued to be politically active, giving up the lucrative post of public prosecutor of Paris, to which he had been elected in June 1791. Henceforth, he spoke only at the Jacobin Club, until August 1792. When Brissot's supporters stirred up opinion against him, Robespierre founded a newspaper, *Le défenseur de la constitution* (*Defence of the Constitution*), which strengthened his hand, and attacked Lafayette.

The reverses suffered by the French army after France had declared war on Austria and Prussia had been foreseen by Robespierre, and, when invasion threatened, the people rallied to him. When the insurrection broke out on August 10 1792, Robespierre took no part in the attack on the Tuileries Palace, but his *section* Les Piques nominated him to the insurrectional Commune. He exonerated the mob, and on September 5 the people of Paris elected him to head the delegation to the National Convention.

The Girondins – who favoured political but not social democracy and who controlled the government and the civil service – accused Robespierre of dictatorship from the first sessions of the National Convention. At the king's trial, which began in December 1792, Robespierre called for death. His new journal, *Les lettres à ses commettants* (*Letters to his Constituents*), kept the provinces informed. The king's execution did not, however, resolve the struggle between the Girondins and the Montagnards, the deputies of the extreme left. A kind of "popular front" was formed between the Parisian sansculottes, the poor, ultraleft republicans, and the Montagnards. On May 26 1793, Robespierre called on the people "to rise in insurrection". Five days later he supported a decree of the National Convention indicting the Girondin leaders and Dumouriez's accomplices. On June 2 the decree was passed against 29 of them.

After the fall of the Girondins, the Montagnards were left to deal with the country's desperate position. In his diary, Robespierre noted that what was needed was "une volonté une" ("one single will"), and this dictatorial power was to characterize the Revolutionary government. Its essential organs had been created, and he set himself to make them work. On July 27 1793, Robespierre took his place on the Committee of Public Safety, which had first been set up in April. He strove to prevent division among the revolutionaries by relying on the Jacobin societies and the vigilance committees. Henceforward his actions were to be inseparable from those of the government as a whole. As president of the Jacobin Club and then of the National Convention, he denounced the schemes of the Parisian radicals known as the Enragés, who were using the food shortage to stir up the Paris *sections*. Robespierre answered the demonstrators on September 5 by promising maximum prices for all foodstuffs and a Revolutionary militia for use in the interior against counter-revolutionaries and grain hoarders.

In order to bring about a mass conscription, economic dictatorship, and total war, he asked to intensify the Reign of Terror. But he objected to pointless executions, protecting those deputies who had protested the arrest of the Girondins and of the king's sister. Those who wanted to halt the Reign of Terror and the war attacked the policies of the Committee of Public Safety with increasing violence.

A Deist in the style of Rousseau, Robespierre disapproved of the anti-Christian movement and the "masquerades" of the cult of reason. In a report to the National Convention in May, he affirmed the existence of God and the immortality of the soul and strove to rally the revolutionaries around a civic religion and the cult of the Supreme Being. The National Convention elected him president, on 16 Prairial (June 4), by a vote of 216 out of 220. In this capacity he led the festival of the Supreme Being ("Etre suprême") in the Tuileries Gardens on 20 Prairial (June 8), which was to provide his enemies with another weapon against him.

After the law of 22 Prairial (June 10) reorganizing the Revolutionary Tribunal, which had been formed in March 1793 to condemn all enemies of the regime, opposition to Robespierre grew; it was led by those *représentants en mission* whom he had threatened. His influence was challenged in the Committee of Public Safety itself, and the Committee of General Security – which felt slighted by the General Police Bureau directed by Robespierre, Georges Couthon, and Louis de Saint-Just – became even more hostile. In the cafes he was accused of being a moderate.

Unremitting work and frequent speeches had undermined Robespierre's health, and he became irritable and distant. Embittered by the slanders and by the accusations of dictatorship being spread both by the royalists and by his colleagues, the Montagnards, he stayed away from the National Convention and then, after 10 Messidor (June 28), from the Committee of Public Safety, confining his denunciations of counterrevolutionary intrigues to the Jacobin Club. At the same time, he began to lose the support of the people. From his partial retirement Robespierre followed the unleashing of the Great Terror in the summer of 1794 and the progress of opposition.

Attempting to regain his hold on public opinion, Robespierre reappeared at the Committee of Public Safety on 5 Thermidor (July 23) and then, on 8 Thermidor (July 26), at the National Convention, to which he turned as his judge. His last speech was at first received with applause, then with disquiet, and finally the parliamentary majority turned against him. Despite his successful reception that evening at the Jacobin Club, Robespierre's adversaries succeeded the next day in preventing him from speaking before the Convention, which indicted him together with his brother, Augustin, and three of his associates. Robespierre was taken to the Luxembourg prison, but the warden refused to jail him. Declared an outlaw by the National Convention, Robespierre severely wounded himself by a pistol shot in the jaw at the Hôtel de Ville, throwing his friends into confusion. The soldiers of the National Convention attacked the Hôtel de Ville and easily seized Robespierre and his followers. In the evening of 10 Thermidor (July 28), the first 22 of those condemned, including Robespierre, were guillotined before a cheering mob on the Place de la Révolution (now the Place de la Concorde).

The Jacobin Club (1789–94)

The Jacobins originated as the Club Breton at Versailles, where the deputies from Brittany to the Estates-General (later the National Assembly) of 1789 met with deputies from other parts of France to concert their action. The group was reconstituted, probably in December 1789, after the National Assembly moved to Paris, under the name of Society of the Friends of the Constitution, but it was commonly called the Jacobin Club. Its purpose was to protect the gains of the Revolution against a possible aristocratic reaction. The club soon admitted non-deputies – usually prosperous bourgeois and men of letters – and acquired affiliates throughout France. By July 1790 there were about 1,200 members in the Parisian club and 152 affiliate clubs.

In July 1791 the Jacobin Club split over a petition calling for the removal of Louis XVI after his unsuccessful attempt to flee

France; many of the moderate deputies left to join the rival club of the Feuillants. Maximilien Robespierre was one of the few deputies who remained, and he assumed a position of prominence in the club.

After the overthrow of the monarchy, in August 1792 (in which the Jacobin Club, still reluctant to declare itself republican, did not have a direct role), the club entered a new phase as one of the major groups directing the Revolution. With the proclamation of the republic in September, the club changed its name to Society of the Jacobins, Friends of Liberty and Equality. It acquired a democratic character with the admission of the leftist Montagnard deputies in the National Convention (the new legislature) and also a more popular one as it responded to the demands of the Parisian working and artisan class. Through the early phase of the Convention, the club was a meeting place for the Montagnards, and it agitated for the execution of the king (January 1793) and for the overthrow of the moderate Girondins (June 1793).

With the establishment of the Revolutionary dictatorship, beginning in the summer of 1793, the local Jacobin clubs became instruments of the Reign of Terror. (In 1793 there were probably 5,000 to 8,000 clubs throughout France, with a nominal membership of 500,000.) The clubs, as part of the administrative machinery of government, had certain duties: they raised supplies for the army and policed local markets. As centres of public virtue, the clubs watched over people whose opinions were suspect, led the dechristianizing movement, and organized Revolutionary festivals.

The Parisian club was increasingly associated with Robespierre, who dominated the Revolutionary government through his position on the Committee of Public Safety. It supported Robespierre in his attacks on the enemies of the Revolution and helped him resist the growing demands of the discontented

workers for a controlled economy. After the fall of Robespierre on 9 Thermidor, year II (July 27 1794), the Parisian
club, now a symbol of dictatorship and terror, was temporarily closed. It reopened as a centre of opposition to the
Thermidorian government, but it was permanently closed
on 21 Brumaire, year III (November 11 1794). The Club
du Panthéon in 1795 and Club du Manège of 1799 briefly
revived the Jacobin spirit, while some local clubs lasted until
the year VIII (1799–1800) despite their having been officially
banned.

Mary Wollstonecraft (1759–97)

The daughter of a farmer, Wollstonecraft taught school and
worked as a governess, experiences that inspired her views in
Thoughts on the Education of Daughters (1787). In 1788 she
began working as a translator for the London publisher James
Johnson, who published several of her works, including the
novel *Mary: A Fiction* (1788). Her mature work on woman's
place in society is *A Vindication of the Rights of Woman*
(1792), which calls for women and men to be educated
equally.

   In 1792 Wollstonecraft left England to observe the French
Revolution in Paris, where she lived with an American, Captain Gilbert Imlay. In the spring of 1794 she gave birth to a
daughter, Fanny. The following year, distraught over the
breakdown of her relationship with Imlay, she attempted
suicide. Wollstonecraft returned to London to work again
for Johnson and joined the influential radical group that
gathered at his home and that included William Godwin,
Thomas Paine, Thomas Holcroft, William Blake, and, after
1793, William Wordsworth. In 1796 she began a liaison with
Godwin, and on March 29 1797, Mary being pregnant, they

were married. The marriage was happy but brief; Mary Wollstonecraft Godwin died 11 days after the birth of her second daughter, Mary.

The publication of *Vindication* caused considerable controversy but failed to bring about any immediate reforms. From the 1840s, however, members of the incipient American and European women's movements resurrected some of the book's principles.

9

KEY TEXTS: EXTRACTS AND FURTHER READING

Extracts

René Descartes, *Discourse on Method* (1637)

from Part II

Among the branches of philosophy, I had, at an earlier period, given some attention to logic, and among those of the mathematics to geometrical analysis and algebra, – three arts or sciences which ought, as I conceived, to contribute something to my design. But, on examination, I found that, as for logic, its syllogisms and the majority of its other precepts are of avail – rather in the communication of what we already know, or even as the art of Lully, in speaking without judgement of things of which we are ignorant, than in the investigation of the unknown; and although this science contains indeed a number of correct and very excellent precepts, there are, nevertheless, so many others, and these either injurious or superfluous, mingled with the former, that it is almost quite as difficult to effect a severance of the true from the false as it is to extract a Diana or a Minerva from a rough block of marble.

Then as to the analysis of the ancients and the algebra of the moderns, besides that they embrace only matters highly abstract, and, to appearance, of no use, the former is so exclusively restricted to the consideration of figures, that it can exercise the understanding only on condition of greatly fatiguing the imagination; and, in the latter, there is so complete a subjection to certain rules and formulas, that there results an art full of confusion and obscurity calculated to embarrass, instead of a science fitted to cultivate the mind.

By these considerations I was induced to seek some other method which would comprise the advantages of the three and be exempt from their defects. And as a multitude of laws often only hampers justice, so that a state is best governed when, with few laws, these are rigidly administered; in like manner, instead of the great number of precepts of which logic is composed, I believed that the four following would prove perfectly sufficient for me, provided I took the firm and unwavering resolution never in a single instance to fail in observing them.

The first was never to accept anything for true which I did not clearly know to be such; that is to say, carefully to avoid precipitancy and prejudice, and to comprise nothing more in my judgement than what was presented to my mind so clearly and distinctly as to exclude all ground of doubt.

The second, to divide each of the difficulties under examination into as many parts as possible, and as might be necessary for its adequate solution.

The third, to conduct my thoughts in such order that, by commencing with objects the simplest and easiest to know, I might ascend by little and little, and, as it were, step by step, to the knowledge of the more complex; assigning in thought a certain order even to those objects which in their own nature do not stand in a relation of antecedence and sequence.

And the last, in every case to make enumerations so complete, and reviews so general, that I might be assured that nothing was omitted.

John Locke, *Two Treatises on Government* (1690)

from Second Treatise, Chapter XVIII, "Of Tyranny"
Sec. 199 . . . Tyranny is the exercise of power beyond right, which no body can have a right to. And this is making use of the power any one has in his hands, not for the good of those who are under it, but for his own private separate advantage. When the governor, however entitled, makes not the law, but his will, the rule; and his commands and actions are not directed to the preservation of the properties of his people, but the satisfaction of his own ambition, revenge, covetousness, or any other irregular passion . . .

Sec. 202. Wherever law ends, tyranny begins, if the law be transgressed to another's harm; and whosoever in authority exceeds the power given him by the law, and makes use of the force he has under his command, to compass that upon the subject, which the law allows not, ceases in that to be a magistrate; and, acting without authority, may be opposed, as any other man, who by force invades the right of another.

This is acknowledged in subordinate magistrates. He that hath authority to seize my person in the street, may be opposed as a thief and a robber, if he endeavours to break into my house to execute a writ, notwithstanding that I know he has such a warrant, and such a legal authority, as will empower him to arrest me abroad. And why this should not hold in the highest, as well as in the most inferior magistrate, I would gladly be informed. Is it reasonable, that the eldest brother, because he has the greatest part of his father's estate, should thereby have a right to take away any of his younger brother's portions? Or that a rich man, who possessed a whole country, should from thence have a right to seize, when he pleased, the cottage and garden of his poor neighbour?

The being rightfully possessed of great power and riches, exceedingly beyond the greatest part of the sons of Adam, is so far from being an excuse, much less a reason, for rapine and oppression, which the endamaging another without authority is, that it is a great aggravation of it: for the exceeding the bounds of authority is no more a right in a great, than in a petty officer; no more justifiable in a king than a constable; but is so much the worse in him, in that he has more trust put in him, has already a much greater share than the rest of his brethren, and is supposed, from the advantages of his education, employment, and counsellors, to be more knowing in the measures of right and wrong.

Sec. 203. May the commands then of a prince be opposed? May he be resisted as often as any one shall find himself aggrieved, and but imagine he has not right done him? This will unhinge and overturn all polities, and, instead of government and order, leave nothing but anarchy and confusion.

Sec. 204. To this I answer, that force is to be opposed to nothing, but to unjust and unlawful force; whoever makes any opposition in any other case, draws on himself a just condemnation both from God and man.

Joseph Addison, "Pleasures of Imagination", *Spectator* No. 411, June 21 1712

Our sight is the most perfect and most delightful of all our senses. It fills the mind with the largest variety of ideas, converses with its objects at the greatest distance, and continues the longest in action without being tired or satiated with its proper enjoyments. The sense of feeling can indeed give us a notion of extension, shape, and all other ideas that enter at the eye, except colours; but at the same time it is very much straitened and confined in its operations, to the number, bulk, and distance of its particular objects. Our sight seems designed to supply all these defects, and may be considered as a more delicate and diffusive kind of touch, that spreads itself over an infinite multitude of bodies, comprehends the largest figures, and brings into our reach some of the most remote parts of the universe.

It is this sense which furnishes the imagination with its ideas; so that by the pleasures of the imagination, or fancy (which I shall use promiscuously), I here mean such as arise from visible objects, either when we have them actually in our view, or when we call up their ideas into our minds by paintings, statues, descriptions, or any the like occasion. We cannot, indeed, have a single image in the fancy that did not make its first entrance through the sight; but we have the power of retaining, altering, and compounding those images, which we have once received, into all the varieties of picture and vision that are most agreeable to the imagination; for by this faculty a man in a dungeon is capable of entertaining himself with scenes and landscapes more beautiful than any that can be found in the whole compass of nature.

There are few words in the English language which are employed in a more loose and uncircumscribed sense than those of the fancy and the imagination. I therefore thought it necessary to fix and determine the notion of these two words, as I intend to make use of them in the thread of my following speculations, that the reader may conceive rightly what is the subject which I proceed upon. I must therefore desire him to remember, that by the pleasures of the imagination, I mean only such pleasures as arise originally from sight, and that I divide these pleasures into two kinds my design being first of all to discourse of those primary pleasures of the imagination, which entirely proceed from such objects as are before our eyes; and in the next place to speak of those secondary pleasures of the imagination which flow from the ideas of visible objects, when the objects are not actually before the eye, but are called up into our memories, or formed into agreeable visions of things that are either absent or fictitious.

The pleasures of the imagination, taken in their full extent, are not so gross as those of sense, nor so refined as those of the understanding. The last are, indeed, more preferable, because they are founded on some new knowledge or improvement in the mind of man; yet it must be confessed, that those of the imagination are as great and as transporting as the other. A beautiful prospect delights the soul, as much as a demonstration; and a description in Homer has charmed more readers than a chapter in Aristotle. Besides, the pleasures of the imagination have this advantage above those of the understanding, that they are more obvious, and more easy to be acquired. It is but opening the eye, and the scene enters. The colours paint themselves on the fancy, with very little attention of thought or application of mind in the beholder. We are struck, we know not how, with the symmetry of anything we see, and immediately assent to the beauty of an object, without inquiring into the particular causes and occasions of it.

A man of polite imagination is let into a great many pleasures, that the vulgar are not capable of receiving. He can converse with a picture, and find an agreeable companion in a statue. He meets with a secret refreshment in a description, and often feels a greater satisfaction in the prospect of fields and meadows, than another does in the possession. It gives him, indeed, a kind of property in everything he sees, and makes the most rude, uncultivated parts of nature administer to his pleasures: so that he looks upon the world, as it were in another light, and discovers in it a multitude of charms, that conceal themselves from the generality of mankind.

There are, indeed, but very few who know how to be idle and innocent, or have a relish of any pleasures that are not criminal: every diversion they take is at the expense of some one virtue or another, and their very first step out of business is into vice or folly. A man should endeavour, therefore, to make the sphere of his innocent pleasures as wide as possible, that he may retire into them with safety, and find in them such a satisfaction as a wise man would not blush to take. Of this nature are those of the imagination, which do not require such a bent of thought as is necessary to our more serious employments, nor, at the same time, suffer the mind to sink into that negligence and remissness, which are apt to accompany our more sensual delights, but, like a gentle exercise to the faculties, awaken them from sloth and idleness, without putting them upon any labour or difficulty.

We might here add, that the pleasures of the fancy are more conducive to health, than those of the understanding, which are worked out by dint of thinking, and attended with too violent a labour of the brain. Delightful scenes, whether in nature, painting, or poetry, have a kindly influence on the body, as well as the mind, and not only serve to clear and brighten the imagination, but are able to disperse grief and melancholy, and to set the animal spirits in pleasing and agreeable motions. For this reason Sir Francis Bacon, in his

Essay upon Health, has not thought it improper to prescribe to his reader a poem or a prospect, where he particularly dissuades him from knotty and subtle disquisitions, and advises him to pursue studies that fill the mind with splendid and illustrious objects, as histories, fables, and contemplations of nature.

Voltaire, *Letters on England* (1734)

Chapter VIII, "On Mr Locke"

Perhaps no man ever had a more judicious or more methodical genius, or was a more acute logician than Mr Locke, and yet he was not deeply skilled in the mathematics. This great man could never subject himself to the tedious fatigue of calculations, nor to the dry pursuit of mathematical truths, which do not at first present any sensible objects to the mind; and no one has given better proofs than he, that it is possible for a man to have a geometrical head without the assistance of geometry. Before his time, several great philosophers had declared, in the most positive terms, what the soul of man is; but as these absolutely knew nothing about it, they might very well be allowed to differ entirely in opinion from one another . . .

Such a multitude of reasoners having written the romance of the soul, a sage at last arose, who gave, with an air of the greatest modesty, the history of it. Mr Locke has displayed the human soul in the same manner as an excellent anatomist explains the springs of the human body. He everywhere takes the light of physics for his guide. He sometimes presumes to speak affirmatively, but then he presumes also to doubt.

Instead of concluding at once what we know not, he examines gradually what we would know. He takes an infant at the instant of his birth; he traces, step by step, the progress of his understanding; examines what things he has in common with beasts, and what he possesses above them. Above all, he consults himself: the being conscious that he himself thinks.

"I shall leave," says he, "to those who know more of this matter than myself, the examining whether the soul exists before or after the organisation of our bodies. But I confess that it is my lot to be animated with one of those heavy souls which do not think always; and I am even so unhappy as not to conceive that it is more necessary the soul should think perpetually than that bodies should be for ever in motion."

With regard to myself, I shall boast that I have the honour to be as stupid in this particular as Mr Locke. No one shall ever make me believe that I think always: and I am as little inclined as he could be to fancy that some weeks after I was conceived I was a very learned soul; knowing at that time a thousand things which I forgot at my birth; and possessing when in the womb (though to no manner of purpose) knowledge which I lost the instant I had occasion for it; and which I have never since been able to recover perfectly.

Mr Locke, after having destroyed innate ideas; after having fully renounced the vanity of believing that we think always; after having laid down, from the most solid principles, that ideas enter the mind through the senses; having examined our simple and complex ideas; having traced the human mind through its several operations; having shown that all the languages in the world are imperfect, and the great abuse that is made of words every moment, he at last comes to consider the extent or rather the narrow limits of human knowledge.

It was in this chapter he presumed to advance, but very modestly, the following words: "We shall, perhaps, never be capable of knowing whether a being, purely material, thinks or not." This sage assertion was, by more divines than one, looked upon as a scandalous declaration that the soul is material and mortal. Some Englishmen, devout after their way, sounded an alarm. The superstitious are the same in society as cowards in an army; they themselves are seized with a panic fear, and communicate it to others.

It was loudly exclaimed that Mr Locke intended to destroy religion; nevertheless, religion had nothing to do in the affair, it being a question purely philosophical, altogether independent of faith and revelation. Mr Locke's opponents needed but to examine, calmly and impartially, whether the declaring that matter can think, implies a contradiction; and whether God is able to communicate thought to matter. But divines are too apt to begin their declarations with saying that God is offended when people differ from them in opinion; in which they too much resemble the bad poets, who used to declare publicly that Boileau spake irreverently of Louis XIV, because he ridiculed their stupid productions . . .

If I might presume to give my opinion on so delicate a subject after Mr Locke, I would say, that men have long disputed on the nature and the immortality of the soul. With regard to its immortality, it is impossible to give a demonstration of it, since its nature is still the subject of controversy; which, however, must be thoroughly understood before a person can be able to determine whether it be immortal or not. Human reason is so little able, merely by its own strength, to demonstrate the immortality of the soul, that it was absolutely necessary religion should reveal it to us.

It is of advantage to society in general, that mankind should believe the soul to be immortal; faith commands us to do this; nothing more is required, and the matter is cleared up at once. But it is otherwise with respect to its nature; it is of little importance to religion, which only requires the soul to be virtuous, whatever substance it may be made of. It is a clock which is given us to regulate, but the artist has not told us of what materials the spring of this clock is composed.

I am a body, and, I think, that's all I know of the matter. Shall I ascribe to an unknown cause, what I can so easily impute to the only second cause I am acquainted with? Here all the school philosophers interrupt me with their arguments, and declare that there is only extension and solidity in bodies, and that there they can have nothing but motion and figure. Now motion, figure, extension and solidity cannot form a thought, and consequently the soul cannot be matter. All this so often repeated mighty series of reasoning, amounts to no more than this: I am absolutely ignorant what matter is; I guess, but imperfectly, some properties of it; now I absolutely cannot tell whether these properties may be joined to thought. As I therefore know nothing, I maintain positively that matter cannot think. In this manner do the schools reason.

Mr Locke addressed these gentlemen in the candid, sincere manner following: At least confess yourselves to be as ignorant as I. Neither your imaginations nor mine are able to comprehend in what manner a body is susceptible of ideas; and do you conceive better in what manner a substance, of what kind soever, is susceptible of them? As you cannot comprehend either matter or spirit, why will you presume to assert anything?

Jean-Jacques Rousseau, *The Social Contract; or Principles of Political Right* (1762)

Book I, Chapter I

Man is born free; and everywhere he is in chains. One thinks himself the master of others, and still remains a greater slave than they. How did this change come about? I do not know. What can make it legitimate? That question I think I can answer.

If I took into account only force, and the effects derived from it, I should say: "As long as a people is compelled to obey, and obeys, it does well; as soon as it can shake off the yoke, and shakes it off, it does still better; for, regaining its liberty by the same right as took it away, either it is justified in resuming it, or there was no justification for those who took it away." But the social order is a sacred right which is the basis of all other rights. Nevertheless, this right does not come from nature, and must therefore be founded on conventions . . .

I suppose men to have reached the point at which the obstacles in the way of their preservation in the state of nature show their power of resistance to be greater than the resources at the disposal of each individual for his maintenance in that state. That primitive condition can then subsist no longer; and the human race would perish unless it changed its manner of existence.

But, as men cannot engender new forces, but only unite and direct existing ones, they have no other means of preserving themselves than the formation, by aggregation, of a sum of forces great enough to overcome the resistance. These they have to bring into play by means of a single motive power, and cause to act in concert.

This sum of forces can arise only where several persons come together: but, as the force and liberty of each man are the chief instruments of his self-preservation, how can he pledge them without harming his own interests, and neglecting the care he owes to himself? This difficulty, in its bearing on my present subject, may be stated in the following terms:

"The problem is to find a form of association which will defend and protect with the whole common force the person and goods of each associate, and in which each, while uniting himself with all, may still obey himself alone, and remain as free as before."

This is the fundamental problem of which the Social Contract provides the solution.

The clauses of this contract are so determined by the nature

of the act that the slightest modification would make them vain
and ineffective; so that, although they have perhaps never been
formally set forth, they are everywhere the same and everywhere tacitly admitted and recognized, until, on the violation
of the social compact, each regains his original rights and
resumes his natural liberty, while losing the conventional
liberty in favour of which he renounced it.

These clauses, properly understood, may be reduced to one –
the total alienation of each associate, together with all his
rights, to the whole community; for, in the first place, as each
gives himself absolutely, the conditions are the same for all;
and, this being so, no one has any interest in making them
burdensome to others.

The Instructions of Catherine II to the Legislative Commission of 1767

**The Instructions to the Commissioners for Composing a New
Code of Laws**
Chapter XIX
439. Of the Composition of the Laws.

447. Every subject, according to the order and Place to which
he belongs, is to be inserted separately in the Code of Laws –
for instance, under judicial, military, commercial, civil, or the
police, city or country affairs, etc. etc.

448. Each law ought to be written in so clear a style as to be
perfectly intelligible to everyone, and, at the same time, with
great conciseness. For this reason explanations or interpretations are undoubtedly to be added (as occasion shall require)
to enable judges to perceive more readily the force as well as
use of the law . . .

449. But the utmost care and caution is to be observed in adding these explanations and interpretations, because they may sometimes rather darken than clear up the case; of which there are many instances [in the existing laws].

450. When exceptions, limitations, and modifications are not absolutely necessary in a law, in that case it is better not to insert them; for such particular details generally produce still more details.

451. If the Legislator desires to give his reason for making any particular law, that reason ought to be good and worthy of the law . . .

452. Laws ought not to be filled with subtle distinctions, to demonstrate the brilliance of the Legislator; they are made for people of moderate capacities as well as for those of genius. They are not a logical art, but the simple and plain reasoning of a father who takes care of his children and family.

453. Real candour and sincerity ought to be displayed in every part of the laws; and as they are made for the punishment of crimes, they ought consequently to include in themselves the greatest virtue and benevolence.

454. The style of the laws ought to be simple and concise: a plain direct expression will always be better understood than a studied one.

455. When the style of laws is tumid and inflated, they are looked upon only as a work of vanity and ostentation . . .

511. A Monarchy is destroyed when a Sovereign imagines that he displays his power more by changing the order of things than by adhering to it, and when he is more fond of his own imaginations than of his will, from which the laws proceed and have proceeded.

512. It is true there are cases where Power ought and can exert its full influence without any danger to the State. But there are cases also where it ought to act according to the limits prescribed by itself.

513. The supreme art of governing a State consists in the precise knowledge of that degree of power, whether great or small, which ought to be exerted according to the different exigencies of affairs. For in a Monarchy the prosperity of the State depends, in part, on a mild and condescending government.

514. In the best constructed machines, Art employs the least moment, force, and fewest wheels possible. This rule holds equally good in the administration of government; the most simple expedients are often the very best, and the most intricate the very worst.

515. There is a certain facility in this method of governing: It is better for the Sovereign to encourage, and for the Laws to threaten . . .

519. It is certain that a high opinion of the glory and power of the Sovereign would increase the strength of his administration; but a good opinion of his love of justice will increase it at least as much.

520. All this will never please those flatterers who are daily instilling this pernicious maxim into all the sovereigns on Earth, that Their people are created for them only. But We think, and esteem it Our glory to declare, that "We are created for Our people." And for this reason, We are obliged to speak of things just as they ought to be. For God forbid that after this legislation is finished any nation on Earth should be more just and, consequently, should flourish more than Russia. Otherwise, the intention of Our laws would be totally frustrated; an unhappiness which I do not wish to survive.

521. All the examples and customs of different nations which are introduced in this work [the Instructions] ought to produce no other effect than to cooperate in the choice of those means which may render the people of Russia, humanly speaking, the most happy in themselves of any people upon the Earth.

Adam Smith, *An Inquiry into the Nature and Causes of the Wealth of Nations* (1776)

Chapter 1, "Of the Division of Labour"

The greatest improvements in the productive powers of labour, and the greater part of the skill, dexterity, and judgement, with which it is anywhere directed, or applied, seem to have been the effects of the division of labour. The effects of the division of labour, in the general business of society, will be more easily understood, by considering in what manner it operates in some particular manufactures. It is commonly supposed to be carried furthest in some very trifling ones; not perhaps that it really is carried further in them than in others of more importance: but in those trifling manufactures which are destined to supply the small wants of but a small number of people, the whole number of workmen must necessarily be small; and those employed in every different branch of the work can often be collected into the same workhouse, and placed at once under the view of the spectator.

In those great manufactures, on the contrary, which are destined to supply the great wants of the great body of the people, every different branch of the work employs so great a number of workmen, that it is impossible to collect them all into the same workhouse. We can seldom see more, at one time, than those employed in one single branch. Though in such manufactures, therefore, the work may really be divided into a much greater number of parts, than in those of a more trifling nature, the division is not near so obvious, and has accordingly been much less observed.

To take an example, therefore, from a very trifling manufacture, but one in which the division of labour has been very often taken notice of, the trade of a pin-maker: a workman not educated to this business (which the division of labour has rendered a distinct trade), nor acquainted with the use of the machinery employed in it (to the invention of which the same division of labour has probably given occasion), could scarce, perhaps, with his utmost industry, make one pin in a day, and certainly could not make twenty. But in the way in which this business is now carried on, not only the whole work is a peculiar trade, but it is divided into a number of branches, of which the greater part are likewise peculiar trades. One man draws out the wire; another straights it; a third cuts it; a fourth points it; a fifth grinds it at the top for receiving the head; to make the head requires two or three distinct operations; to put it on is a peculiar business; to whiten the pins is another; it is even a trade by itself to put them into the paper; and the important business of making a pin is, in this manner, divided into about eighteen distinct operations, which, in some manufactories, are all performed by distinct hands, though in others the same man will sometimes perform two or three of them.

I have seen a small manufactory of this kind, where ten men only were employed, and where some of them consequently performed two or three distinct operations. But though they were very poor, and therefore but indifferently accommodated with the necessary machinery, they could, when they exerted themselves, make among them about twelve pounds of pins in a day. There are in a pound upwards of four thousand pins of a middling size. Those ten persons, therefore, could make among them upwards of forty-eight thousand pins in a day. Each person, therefore, making a tenth part of forty-eight thousand pins, might be considered as making four thousand eight hundred pins in a day. But if they had all wrought separately and independently, and without any of them having been educated to this peculiar business, they certainly could not each of them have made twenty, perhaps not one pin in a day; that is, certainly, not the two hundred and fortieth, perhaps not the four thousand eight hundredth, part of what they are at present capable of performing, in consequence of a proper division and combination of their different operations.

In every other art and manufacture, the effects of the division of labour are similar to what they are in this very trifling one, though, in many of them, the labour can neither be so much subdivided, nor reduced to so great a simplicity of operation. The division of labour, however, so far as it can be introduced, occasions, in every art, a proportionable increase of the productive powers of labour. The separation of different trades and employments from one another, seems to have taken place in consequence of this advantage.

Declaration of Independence (1776)

In Congress, July 4 1776

When in the Course of human events, it becomes necessary for one people to dissolve the political bands which have connected them with another, and to assume among the powers of the earth, the separate and equal station to which the Laws of Nature and of Nature's God entitle them, a decent respect to the opinions of mankind requires that they should declare the causes which impel them to the separation. We hold these truths to be self-evident, that all men are created equal, that they are endowed by their Creator with certain unalienable Rights, that among these are Life, Liberty and the pursuit of Happiness. That to secure these rights, Governments are instituted among Men, deriving their just powers from the consent of the governed, That whenever any Form of Government becomes destructive of these ends, it is the Right of the People to alter or to abolish it, and to institute new Government, laying its foundation on such principles and organizing its powers in such form, as to them shall seem most likely to effect their Safety and Happiness.

Prudence, indeed, will dictate that Governments long established should not be changed for light and transient causes; and accordingly all experience hath shown, that mankind are more disposed to suffer, while evils are sufferable, than to right themselves by abolishing the forms to which they are accustomed. But when a long train of abuses and usurpations, pursuing invariably the same Object evinces a design to reduce them under absolute Despotism, it is their right, it is their duty, to throw off such Government, and to provide new Guards for their future security. Such has been the patient sufferance of these Colonies; and such is now the necessity which constrains them to alter their former Systems of Government. The history of the present King of Great Britain is a history of repeated injuries and usurpations, all having in direct object the establishment of an absolute Tyranny over these States.

To prove this, let Facts be submitted to a candid world. He has refused his Assent to Laws, the most wholesome and necessary for the public good. He has forbidden his Governors to pass Laws of immediate and pressing importance, unless suspended in their operation till his Assent should be obtained; and when so suspended, he has utterly neglected to attend to them. He has refused to pass other Laws for the accommodation of large districts of people, unless those people would relinquish the right of Representation in the Legislature, a right inestimable to them and formidable to tyrants only. He has called together legislative bodies at places unusual, uncomfortable, and distant from the depository of their public Records, for the sole purpose of fatiguing them into compliance with his measures. He has dissolved Representative Houses repeatedly, for opposing with manly firmness his invasions on the rights of the people. He has refused for a long time, after such dissolutions, to cause others to be elected; whereby the Legislative powers, incapable of Annihilation, have returned to the People at large for their exercise; the State remaining in the mean time exposed to all the dangers of invasion from without, and convulsions within. He has endeavoured to prevent the population of these States; for that purpose obstructing the Laws for Naturalization of Foreigners; refusing to pass others to encourage their migration hither, and raising the conditions of new Appropriations of Lands. He has obstructed the Administration of Justice, by refusing his Assent to Laws for establishing Judiciary powers. He has made judges dependent on his Will alone, for the tenure of their offices, and the amount and payment of their salaries. He has erected a multitude of New Offices, and sent hither swarms of Officers to harrass our people, and eat out their substance. He has kept among us, in times of peace, Standing Armies, without the Consent of our legislatures. He has affected to render the Military independent of and superior to the Civil power. He has combined with others to subject us to a jurisdiction foreign to our constitution, and unacknowledged by our laws; giving his Assent to their Acts of pretended Legislation: For quartering large bodies of armed troops among us: For protecting them, by a mock Trial, from punishment for any Murders which they should commit on the Inhabitants of these States: For cutting off our Trade with all parts of the world: For imposing Taxes on us without our Consent: For depriving us in many cases, of the benefits of Trial by Jury: For transporting us beyond Seas to be tried for pretended offences: For abolishing the free System of English Laws in a neighbouring Province, establishing therein an Arbitrary government, and enlarging its Boundaries so as to render it at once an example and fit instrument for introducing the same absolute rule into these Colonies: For taking away our Charters, abolishing our most valuable Laws, and altering fundamentally the Forms of our Governments: For suspending our own Legislatures, and declaring themselves invested with power to legislate for us in all cases whatsoever. He has abdicated Government here, by declaring us out of his Protection and waging War against us. He has plundered our seas, ravaged our Coasts, burnt our towns, and destroyed the lives of our people. He is at this time transporting large Armies of foreign Mercenaries to compleat the works of death, desolation and tyranny, already begun with circumstances of Cruelty & perfidy scarcely paralleled in the most barbarous ages, and totally unworthy the Head of a civilized nation. He has constrained our fellow Citizens taken Captive on the high Seas to bear Arms against their Country, to become the executioners of their friends and Brethren, or to fall themselves by their Hands. He has excited domestic insurrections amongst us, and has endeavoured to bring on the inhabitants of our frontiers, the merciless Indian Savages, whose known rule of warfare, is an undistinguished destruction of all ages, sexes and conditions. In every stage of these Oppressions We have Petitioned for Redress in the most humble terms: Our repeated Petitions have been answered only by repeated injury. A Prince, whose character is thus marked by every act which may define a Tyrant, is unfit to be the ruler of a free people. Nor have we been wanting in attentions to our British brethren. We have warned them from time to time of attempts by their legislature to extend an unwarrantable jurisdiction over us. We have reminded them of the circumstances of our emigration and settlement here. We have appealed to their native justice and magnanimity, and we have conjured them by the ties of our common kindred to disavow these usurpations, which, would inevitably interrupt our connections and correspondence. They too have been deaf to the voice of justice and of consanguinity. We must, therefore, acquiesce in the necessity, which denounces our Separation, and hold them, as we hold the rest of mankind. Enemies in War, in Peace Friends.

We, therefore, the Representatives of the United States of America, in General Congress, Assembled, appealing to the Supreme Judge of the world for the rectitude of our intentions, do, in the Name, and by Authority of the good People of these Colonies, solemnly publish and declare, That these United Colonies are, and of Right ought to be Free and Independent States; that they are Absolved from all Allegiance to the British Crown, and that all political connection between them and the State of Great Britain, is and ought to be totally dissolved; and that as Free and Independent States, they have full Power to levy War, conclude Peace, contract Alliances, establish Commerce, and to do all other Acts and Things which Independent

States may of right do. And for the support of this Declaration, with a firm reliance on the protection of Divine Providence, we mutually pledge to each other our Lives, our Fortunes and our sacred Honor.

Thomas Paine, *The American Crisis*, December 23 1776

These are the times that try men's souls. The summer soldier and the sunshine patriot will, in this crisis, shrink from the service of their country; but he that stands it now, deserves the love and thanks of man and woman. Tyranny, like hell, is not easily conquered; yet we have this consolation with us, that the harder the conflict, the more glorious the triumph. What we obtain too cheap, we esteem too lightly: it is dearness only that gives every thing its value. Heaven knows how to put a proper price upon its goods; and it would be strange indeed if so celestial an article as FREEDOM should not be highly rated. Britain, with an army to enforce her tyranny, has declared that she has a right (not only to TAX) but "to BIND us in ALL CASES WHATSOEVER," and if being bound in that manner, is not slavery, then is there not such a thing as slavery upon earth. Even the expression is impious; for so unlimited a power can belong only to God.

Immanuel Kant, *Critique of Pure Reason* (1781)

Preface to the First Edition

[Our age is the age of criticism, to which everything must be subjected. The sacredness of religion, and the authority of legislation, are by many regarded as grounds of exemption from the examination of this tribunal. But, if they on they are exempted, they become the subjects of just suspicion, and cannot lay claim to sincere respect, which reason accords only to that which has stood the test of a free and public examination.] . . .

This path – the only one now remaining – has been entered upon by me; and I flatter myself that I have, in this way, discovered the cause of – and consequently the mode of removing – all the errors which have hitherto set reason at variance with itself, in the sphere of non-empirical thought. I have not returned an evasive answer to the questions of reason, by alleging the inability and limitation of the faculties of the mind; I have, on the contrary, examined them completely in the light of principles, and, after having discovered the cause of the doubts and contradictions into which reason fell, have solved them to its perfect satisfaction.

It is true, these questions have not been solved as dogmatism, in its vain fancies and desires, had expected; for it can only be satisfied by the exercise of magical arts, and of these I have no knowledge. But neither do these come within the compass of our mental powers; and it was the duty of philosophy to destroy the illusions which had their origin in misconceptions, whatever darling hopes and valued expectations may be ruined by its explanations.

My chief aim in this work has been thoroughness; and I make bold to say that there is not a single metaphysical problem that does not find its solution, or at least the key to its solution, here. Pure reason is a perfect unity; and therefore, if the principle presented by it prove to be insufficient for the solution of even a single one of those questions to which the very nature of reason gives birth, we must reject it, as we could not be perfectly certain of its sufficiency in the case of the others.

Declaration of the Rights of Man and of the Citizen (1789)

(Adopted by the National Assembly during the French Revolution on August 26 1789, and reaffirmed by the Constitution of 1958.)

Preamble

The representatives of the French people, formed into a National Assembly, considering ignorance, forgetfulness or contempt of the rights of man to be the only causes of public misfortunes and the corruption of Governments, have resolved to set forth, in a solemn Declaration, the natural, unalienable and sacred rights of man, to the end that this Declaration, constantly present to all members of the body politic, may remind them unceasingly of their rights and their duties; to the end that the acts of the legislative power and those of the executive power, since they may be continually compared with the aim of every political institution, may thereby be the more respected; to the end that the demands of the citizens, founded henceforth on simple and uncontestable principles, may always be directed toward the maintenance of the Constitution and the happiness of all.

In consequence whereof, the National Assembly recognizes and declares, in the presence and under the auspices of the Supreme Being, the following Rights of Man and of the Citizen.

Article first – Men are born and remain free and equal in rights. Social distinctions may be based only on considerations of the common good.

Article 2 – The aim of every political association is the preservation of the natural and imprescriptible rights of man. These rights are Liberty, Property, Safety and Resistance to Oppression.

Article 3 – The source of all sovereignty lies essentially in the Nation. No corporate body, no individual may exercise any authority that does not expressly emanate from it.

Article 4 – Liberty consists in being able to do anything that does not harm others: thus, the exercise of the natural rights of every man has no bounds other than those that ensure to the other members of society the enjoyment of these same rights. These bounds may be determined only by Law.

Article 5 – The Law has the right to forbid only those actions that are injurious to society. Nothing that is not forbidden by Law may be hindered, and no one may be compelled to do what the Law does not ordain.

Article 6 – The Law is the expression of the general will. All citizens have the right to take part, personally or through their representatives, in its making. It must be the same for all, whether it protects or punishes. All citizens, being equal in its eyes, shall be equally eligible to all high offices, public positions and employments, according to their ability, and without other distinction than that of their virtues and talents.

Article 7 – No man may be accused, arrested or detained except in the cases determined by the Law, and following the procedure that it has prescribed. Those who solicit, expedite, carry out, or cause to be carried out arbitrary orders must be punished; but any citizen summoned or apprehended by virtue of the Law, must give instant obedience; resistance makes him guilty.

Article 8 – The Law must prescribe only the punishments that are strictly and evidently necessary; and no one may be punished except by virtue of a Law drawn up and promulgated before the offence is committed, and legally applied.

Article 9 – As every man is presumed innocent until he has been declared guilty, if it should be considered necessary to arrest him, any undue harshness that is not required to secure his person must be severely curbed by Law.

Article 10 – No one may be disturbed on account of his opinions, even religious ones, as long as the manifestation of such opinions does not interfere with the established Law and Order.

Article 11 – The free communication of ideas and of opinions is one of the most precious rights of man. Any citizen may therefore speak, write and publish freely, except what is tantamount to the abuse of this liberty in the cases determined by Law.

Article 12 – To guarantee the Rights of Man and of the Citizen a public force is necessary; this force is therefore established for the benefit of all, and not for the particular use of those to whom it is entrusted.

Article 13 – For the maintenance of the public force, and for administrative expenses, a general tax is indispensable; it must be equally distributed among all citizens, in proportion to their ability to pay.

Article 14 – All citizens have the right to ascertain, by themselves, or through their representatives, the need for a public tax, to consent to it freely, to watch over its use, and to determine its proportion, basis, collection and duration.

Article 15 – Society has the right to ask a public official for an accounting of his administration.

Article 16 – Any society in which no provision is made for guaranteeing rights or for the separation of powers, has no Constitution.

Article 17 – Since the right to Property is inviolable and sacred, no one may be deprived thereof, unless public necessity, legally ascertained, obviously requires it, and just and prior indemnity has been paid.

Edmund Burke, *Reflections on the French Revolution* (1790)

You had all these advantages in your ancient states; but you chose to act as if you had never been moulded into civil society, and had everything to begin anew. You began ill, because you began by despising everything that belonged to you. You set up your trade without a capital. If the last generations of your country appeared without much lustre in your eyes, you might have passed them by, and derived your claims from a more early race of ancestors.

Under a pious predilection for those ancestors your imaginations would have realized in them a standard of virtue and wisdom, beyond the vulgar practice of the hour: and you would have risen with the example to whose imitation you aspired. Respecting your forefathers, you would have been taught to respect yourselves. You would not have chosen to consider the French as a people of yesterday, as a nation of lowborn servile wretches until the emancipating year of 1789. In order to furnish, at the expense of your honour, an excuse to your apologists here for several enormities of yours, you would not have been content to be represented as a gang of Maroon slaves, suddenly broke loose from the house of bondage, and therefore to be pardoned for your abuse of the liberty to which you were not accustomed, and ill fitted. Would it not, my worthy friend, have been wiser to have you thought, what I, for one, always thought you, a generous and gallant nation, long misled to your disadvantage by your high and romantic sentiments of fidelity, honour, and loyalty; that events had been unfavourable to you, but that you were not enslaved through any illiberal or servile disposition; in your most devoted submission, you were actuated by a principle of public spirit, and that it was your Country you worshipped, in the person of your king?

Had you made it to be understood, that in the delusion of this amiable error you had gone further than your wise ancestors; that you were resolved to resume your ancient privileges, whilst you preserved the spirit of your ancient and your recent loyalty and honour; or if, diffident of yourselves, and not clearly discerning the almost obliterated constitution of your ancestors, you had looked to your neighbours in this land, who had kept alive the ancient principles and models of the old common law of Europe meliorated and adapted to its present state – by following wise examples you would have given new examples of wisdom to the world.

You would have rendered the cause of liberty venerable in the eyes of every worthy mind in every nation. You would have shamed despotism from the earth, by showing that freedom was not only reconcilable, but, as when well disciplined it is, auxiliary to law. You would have an unoppressive but a productive revenue. You would have had a flourishing commerce to feed it. You would have had a free constitution; a potent monarchy; a disciplined army; a reformed and venerated clergy; a mitigated but spirited nobility, to lead your virtue, not to overlay it; you would have had a liberal order of commons, to emulate and to recruit that nobility; you would have had a protected, satisfied, laborious, and obedient people, taught to seek and to recognize the happiness that is to be found by virtue in all conditions; in which consists the true moral equality of mankind, and not in that monstrous fiction, which, by inspiring false ideas and vain expectations into men destined to travel in the obscure walk of laborious life, serves only to aggravate and embitter that real inequality, which it never can remove; and which the order of civil life establishes as much for the benefit of those whom it must leave in an humble state, as those whom it is able to exalt to a condition more splendid, but not more happy. You had a smooth and easy career of felicity and glory laid open to you beyond anything recorded in the history of the world; but you have shown that difficulty is good for men.

Compute your gains: see what is got by those extravagant and presumptuous speculations which have taught your leaders to despise all their predecessors, and all their contemporaries, and even to despise themselves, until the moment in which they became truly despicable. By following those false lights, France has bought undisguised calamities at a higher price than any nation has purchased the most unequivocal blessings! France has bought poverty by crime! France has not sacrificed her virtue to her interest, but she has abandoned her interest, that she might prostitute her virtue. All other nations have begun the fabric of a new government, or the reformation of an old, by establishing originally, or by enforcing with greater exactness some rites or other of religion.

All other people have laid the foundations of civil freedom in severer manners, and a system of a more austere and masculine morality. France, when she let loose the reins of regal authority, doubled the license of a ferocious dissoluteness in manners, and of an insolent irreligion in opinions and practices; and has extended through all ranks of life, as if she were communicating some privilege, or laying open some secluded benefit, all the unhappy corruptions that usually were the disease of wealth and power. This is one of the new principles of equality in France.

France, by the perfidy of her leaders has utterly disgraced the tone of lenient council in the cabinets of princes, and disarmed it of its most potent topics. She has sanctified the dark, suspicious maxims of tyrannous distrust; and taught kings to tremble at (what will hereafter be called) the delusive plausibilities of moral politicians. Sovereigns will consider those, who advise them to place an unlimited confidence in their people, as subverters of their throne; as traitors who aim at their destruction, by leading their easy good nature, under specious pretences, to admit combinations of bold and faithless men into a participation of their power. This alone (if there were nothing else) is an irreparable calamity to you and to mankind.

Remember that your parliament of Paris told your king, that, in calling the states together, he had nothing to fear but the prodigal excess of their zeal in providing for the support of the throne. It is right that these men should hide their heads. It is right that they should bear their part in the ruin which their counsel has brought on their sovereign and their country. Such sanguine declarations tend to lull authority asleep; to encourage it rashly to engage in perilous adventures of untried policy; to neglect those provisions, preparations, and precautions, which distinguish benevolence from imbecility; and without which no man can answer for the salutary effect of any abstract plan of government or of freedom. For want of these, they have seen the medicine of the state corrupted into its poison. They have seen the French rebel against a mild and lawful monarch, with more fury, outrage, and insult, than ever any people has been known to rise against the most illegal usurper, or the most sanguinary tyrant. Their resistance was made to concession; their revolt was from protection; their blow was aimed at a hand holding out graces, favours, and immunities.

Mary Wollstonecraft *A Vindication of the Rights of Woman, with Strictures on Political and Moral Subjects* (1792)

An extract from Chapter 5, "Animadversions on Some of the Writers Who Have Rendered Women Objects of Pity, Bordering on Contempt"

I now appeal from the reveries of fancy and refined licentiousness to the good sense of mankind, whether, if the object of education be to prepare women to become chaste wives and sensible mothers, the method so plausibly recommended in the foregoing sketch, be the one best calculated to produce those ends? Will it be allowed that the surest way to make a wife chaste, is to teach her to practise the wanton arts of a mistress, termed virtuous coquetry by the sensualist who can no longer relish the artless charms of sincerity, or taste the pleasure arising from a tender intimacy, when confidence is unchecked by suspicion, and rendered interesting by sense?

The man who can be contented to live with a pretty useful companion without a mind, has lost in voluptuous gratifications a taste for more refined enjoyments; he has never felt the

calm satisfaction that refreshes the parched heart, like the
silent dew of heaven – of being beloved by one who could
understand him. In the society of his wife he is still alone,
unless when the man is sunk in the brute. "The charm of life",
says a grave philosophical reasoner, is "sympathy; nothing
pleases us more than to observe in other men a fellow-feeling
with all the emotions of our own breast."

But, according to the tenor of reasoning by which women
are kept from the tree of knowledge, the important years of
youth, the usefulness of age, and the rational hopes of futurity,
are all to be sacrificed, to render woman an object of desire for
a short time. Besides, how could Rousseau expect them to be
virtuous and constant when reason is neither allowed to be the
foundation of their virtue, nor truth the object of their in-
quiries?

But all Rousseau's errors in reasoning arose from sensibility,
and sensibility to their charms women are very ready to
forgive! When he should have reasoned he became impas-
sioned, and reflection inflamed his imagination, instead of
enlightening his understanding. Even his virtues also led him
farther astray; for, born with a warm constitution and lively
fancy, nature carried him toward the other sex with such eager
fondness, that he soon became lascivious. Had he given way to
these desires, the fire would have extinguished itself in a
natural manner, but virtue, and a romantic kind of delicacy,
made him practise self-denial; yet, when fear, delicacy, or
virtue restrained him, he debauched his imagination; and
reflecting on the sensations to which fancy gave force, he
traced them in the most glowing colours, and sunk them deep
into his soul.

He then sought for solitude, not to sleep with the man of
nature; or calmly investigate the causes of things under the
shade where Sir Isaac Newton indulged contemplation, but

merely to indulge his feelings. And so warmly has he painted what he forcibly felt, that, interesting the heart and inflaming the imagination of his readers; in proportion to the strength of their fancy, they imagine that their understanding is convinced, when they only sympathize with a poetic writer, who skilfully exhibits the objects of sense, most voluptuously shadowed, or gracefully veiled; and thus making us feel, whilst dreaming that we reason, erroneous conclusions are left in the mind.

Why was Rousseau's life divided between ecstasy and misery? Can any other answer be given than this, that the effervescence of his imagination produced both; but, had his fancy been allowed to cool, it is possible that he might have acquired more strength of mind. Still, if the purpose of life be to educate the intellectual part of man, all with respect to him was right; yet, had not death led to a nobler scene of action, it is probable that he would have enjoyed more equal happiness on earth, and have felt the calm sensations of the man of nature, instead of being prepared for another stage of existence by nourishing the passions which agitate the civilized man.

But peace to his manes! I war not with his ashes, but his opinions. I war only with the sensibility that led him to degrade woman by making her the slave of love.

> . . . "Curs'd vassalage,
> First idoliz'd till love's hot fire be o'er,
> Then slaves to those who courted us before."
>   Dryden.

The pernicious tendency of those books, in which the writers insidiously degrade the sex, whilst they are prostrate before their personal charms, cannot be too often or too severely exposed.

Let us, my dear contemporaries, arise above such narrow prejudices! If wisdom is desirable on its own account, if virtue, to deserve the name, must be founded on knowledge; let us endeavour to strengthen our minds by reflection, till our heads become a balance for our hearts; let us not confine all our thoughts to the petty occurrences of the day, nor our knowledge to an acquaintance with our lovers' or husbands' hearts; but let the practice of every duty be subordinate to the grand one of improving our minds, and preparing our affections for a more exalted state!

Beware then, my friends, of suffering the heart to be moved by every trivial incident: the reed is shaken by a breeze, and annually dies, but the oak stands firm, and for ages braves the storm.

Were we, indeed, only created to flutter our hour out and die – why let us then indulge sensibility, and laugh at the severity of reason. Yet, alas! even then we should want strength of body and mind, and life would be lost in feverish pleasures or wearisome languor.

But the system of education, which I earnestly wish to see exploded, seems to presuppose, what ought never to be taken for granted, that virtue shields us from the casualties of life; and that fortune, slipping off her bandage, will smile on a well-educated female, and bring in her hand an Emilius or a Telemachus. Whilst, on the contrary, the reward which virtue promises to her votaries is confined, it is clear, to their own bosoms; and often must they contend with the most vexatious worldly cares, and bear with the vices and humours of relations for whom they can never feel a friendship.

There have been many women in the world who, instead of being supported by the reason and virtue of their fathers and brothers, have strengthened their own minds by struggling with their vices and follies; yet have never met with a hero, in the shape of a husband; who, paying the debt that mankind owed them, might chance to bring back their reason to its natural dependent state, and restore the usurped prerogative, of rising above opinion, to man.

FURTHER READING

Isaiah Berlin, *The Age of Enlightenment: The 18th Century Philosophers Selected, with Introduction and Interpretive Commentary*, New American Library, New York, 1956.

Alexander Broadie, *The Cambridge Companion to the Scottish Enlightenment*, Cambridge University Press, Cambridge, 2003.

Peter Gay, *The Enlightenment Vol 1: The Rise of Modern Paganism*, W.W. Norton & Co, New York, 1995.

Peter Gay, *The Enlightenment Vol 2: Science of Freedom*, W.W. Norton & Co, New York, 1995.

A.C. Grayling, *Toward the Light of Liberty: The Struggles for Freedom and Rights That Made the Modern Western World*, Walker & Co, New York, 2007.

A.C. Grayling, *Descartes: The Life and Times of a Genius*, Walker & Co, New York, 2006.

Arthur Herman, *The Scottish Enlightenment: The Scots' Invention of the Modern World*, Fourth Estate, London, 2003.

Jonathan Hill, *Faith in the Age of Reason: The Enlightenment from Galileo to Kant*, Intervarsity Press, Illinois 2004.

Paul Hyland, Olga Gomez and Francesca Greensides (eds), *The Enlightenment: A Sourcebook and Reader*, Routledge, London, 2003.

Jonathan I. Israel, *Radical Enlightenment: Philosophy and the Making of Modernity, 1650–1750*, Oxford University Press, Oxford, 2002.

Isaac Kramnick (ed.), *The Portable Enlightenment Reader*, Viking Portable Library, Penguin, New York, 1996.

Roy Porter, *Enlightenment: Britain and the Creation of the Modern World*, Penguin, London, 2001.

John W. Yolton, Roy Porter, Pat Rogers and Barbara Maria Stafford (eds), *The Blackwell Companion to the Enlightenment*, Blackwell, Oxford, 1991.

INDEX

Notes: Where more than one page number is listed against a heading, page numbers in bold refer to significant treatment of a subject

Britannica®

Since its birth in the Scottish Enlightenment Britannica's commitment to educated, reasoned, current, humane, and popular scholarship has never wavered. In 2008, Britannica celebrated its 240th anniversary.

Throughout its history, owners and users of *Encyclopædia Britannica* have drawn upon it for knowledge, understanding, answers, and inspiration. In the Internet age, Britannica, the first online encyclopædia, continues to deliver that fundamental requirement of reference, information, and educational publishing – confidence in the material we read in it.

Readers of Britannica Guides are invited to take a FREE trial of Britannica's huge online database. Visit

<u>https://ideas.britannicaguides.com</u>

to find out more about this title and others in the series.